S. S. BAZINET

Traces
of
ANGELS

book two
OPEN WIDE MY HEART

Renata Press
Albuquerque, New Mexico

This book is a work of fiction. Names, characters, places, businesses, organizations and events are either the product of the author's imagination or are used fictitiously. Any resemblance to actual persons, living or dead, events or locales is entirely coincidental.

Published by Renata Press
Albuquerque, New Mexico
www.renatapress.com

Visit the author's website:
www.ssbazinet.com

ISBN: 978-1-937279-30-1

For all those who enjoy an uplifting story about the bonds of friendship, family and the healing power of the heart!

One

CHICAGO SURGEON, MATTHEW Howell, nervously shifted his six-foot-three frame in the SUV's passenger seat. He was focused on the vehicle's windshield wipers. The two rigid, metal arms were designed to keep the glass free of rain or snow, but they were having trouble doing their job. A freak snow storm was quickly blanketing the Appalachian Mountains, and the struggling wipers were no match for the ferocious winds driving the snowfall in their direction.

Matthew wasn't one who made heavenly requests very often, but he made an exception in this case. He could only pray that the SUV's driver, Doctor Eric Lloyd, would keep their vehicle on the road. He also forced himself to take a breath. He'd been holding it ever since they left Blacksburg, Virginia. No, that wasn't true. They'd been driving a good hour before he stopped breathing. An hour into the trip, they ran into the storm. According to the weather forecast, it was supposed to be a rain storm, but the mountains had a different idea. They didn't respect weather forecasts. They didn't respect anyone crazy enough to travel the winding, roller coaster roads. Even in good weather, they could be treacherous.

Matthew withdrew his hand from the dashboard long enough to massage his fingers. They were stiff and white-knuckled after clutching the padded panel for so long. He glanced at Eric. The man was a good three inches shorter than Matthew, had a slender build and had grown up in the area. Matthew was depending on Eric to deliver some good news. "I guess you've experienced your share of snowstorms like this, right? Driving in crazy weather is probably routine."

Eric shot him an anxious look and went back to staring at the white, snowy surface ahead of him. He gripped the steering wheel as doggedly as Matthew had held on to the dash. "You never get used to driving in these conditions."

Matthew noted the breathless way Eric responded. The guy was clearly frightened by their circumstances. It triggered the anger Matthew had been trying to hold in. "We should have turned back when we saw that first snowflake, Eric."

Eric returned an irritated look. "As I remember, Doctor Howell, you announced it was going to rain."

"The calendar says it's spring. How was I supposed to know how insane these mountains can be at this time of year? You're the expert. You should have corrected my naïve comment."

Eric huffed out a laugh. "Correct you? And face the wrath you like to spew out whenever someone challenges your opinion?"

"What do you mean? I'm as open-minded as anyone I know."

"Oh please, don't talk like that, or we'll be hit by lightning next."

Matthew grabbed the dash again, bracing himself for whatever was coming. "All I know is that I've had it with these trips to that forsaken place called Elkville. If I make it out of these mountains alive, I'm never coming back."

"Right, and what about Lea? She loves Elkville. Now that the new medical facility is up and running, she's become part of the team. She and my mom are always talking and planning. They want to start an outreach program for the surrounding areas."

Matthew felt his jaw tighten even more. Lea meant everything to him, but he wondered how much their marriage meant to her. Before he could respond to Eric's question. The big SUV started sliding, zig-zagging its way forward on the narrow road. "Holy hell, Eric!" Matthew yelled. "Stop the car!"

"I'm trying!" Eric shouted back. "It's a steep grade, and it's icy!"

As the car spun out of control, Matthew knew the grim reaper was laughing, getting ready to collect a couple of souls. But it was not a good day to die. He was too young. He was at the height of his career as a surgeon. "And Lea thinks she might be pregnant," he gasped.

The possibility of impending fatherhood was the reason he was making the trip to Elkville. But he might not have to worry about such matters. Given the circumstances they were facing, even if Lea were pregnant, his child might have to grow up without a dad. It was a cruel thought, and the last one he had before the SUV slammed into something, bounced off and went over the edge of the mountain.

Lea stood at the window of her home. The cozy structure had been a present from her father, Raymond Ferguson. He'd built it for her and Matthew to use when they stayed in Elkville. The modern residence looked out of place on a street populated by ill-kept houses crippled by age and poverty. Most of the homes dated back to a time when people had very little money to spend on shelter.

Lea and Matthew's home was located next to Margaret Lloyd's old dwelling. The lot next to Margaret's house had been vacant for a long time. For Lea, it was the ideal location. She couldn't be happier having Margaret as her neighbor.

She wasn't happy about the weather. Her brow was narrowed with concern as she watched the inches of snow piling up on the street. Matthew and Eric were out in the storm, and she didn't know if they were in trouble. There was no cell phone coverage in the mountains or in Elkville, and hours had passed since she'd last spoken to Matthew.

"Lea, come and have a cup of tea," Margaret called from the kitchen. "And these oatmeal cookies I brought over are fresh."

Margaret was like a second mother to Lea. Shortly after the snow started to fall, Margaret came over to check on her. Now the kind, nurturing woman was trying to distract her from her worries.

"No thanks, Mom," Lea called back. "My stomach's too queasy."

Margaret came striding into the room, cup in hand. "Lea, please sip a little of this peppermint tea. It'll help if you're feeling poorly."

Lea held her stomach. "I just wish I knew what's going on with me. Do I have a flu bug, or am I pregnant?"

Margaret handed her the cup. "Wouldn't that be something if you were pregnant?"

Lea forced herself to take a taste of the tea. "Matthew is supposed to be bringing me a test kit."

Margaret paused. "So much is happening. You might be expecting and—"

"And Elkville finally has a medical facility," Lea said with a smile.

"You seem to enjoy being part of the business end of things."

Lea held the tea close and stared out the window again. "Yes, I guess I am. But for the moment the only thing I can think about is Matthew and Eric."

Margaret joined Lea, putting her hands on the window seal and leaning in. "Fretting about it isn't going to bring them home any sooner. I should know. I can't tell you how many times I stood waiting and worrying about Eric's dad."

"But at least both of you wanted to be here. Matthew is the opposite. He hates it here. He's always saying stuff like, 'It's going to be the death of me'." Lea's body trembled, and she hugged herself. "Oh Mom, I'm scared that he's going to prove himself right," she cried as tears filled her eyes.

Two

MATTHEW MOANED OUT the first thoughts that came to him. "After all my efforts to be a good husband, after all the lives I've saved as a surgeon, what's my reward? I've ended up in hell." His eyes were shut tight, and he was afraid to open them. When the car went off the road and started sliding down the mountain, he'd been so terrified that he hadn't wanted to see what was happening. All movement stopped abruptly. But that didn't mean anything good. They could be resting on a cliff for all he knew.

His mind began playing out a dozen scenarios, and every one of them was horrifying. The car sliding again and picking up speed. Maybe hitting a boulder. Or the car flipping, then rolling over and over until it exploded in flames. Being trapped and burned to death. His body charred beyond recognition. Lea crying at his funeral. That last thought lingered and almost made him smile. "It serves her right for making me come here," he mumbled through gritted teeth.

"Matthew?"

Matthew's mind stalled for a moment when he heard Eric calling out to him. Eric Lloyd had become a friend, a close friend, the man Matthew had asked to be his best man at his wedding. "Yes?"

"Are you alright?"

Matthew slowly opened his eyes. The wipers were still valiantly trying to clear the snow off the windshield. Other than that, all he saw was more snow. Matthew sucked in a breath "Define the word, alright, Eric."

"Are you hurt?"

Matthew realized he was out of touch with his body. He did a quick appraisal. "I think I slammed my head against a side window." He reached up and fingered a spot near his temple. "Ouch."

Eric patted Matthew's shoulder. "Sorry, I lost control."

It took all of Matthew's willpower not to comment. Eric was one of those people who used every critical word to punish himself. Still, Matthew couldn't forget Eric's track record with vehicles. In the past, the cardiologist had gone through a very tough period. He'd been trying to come to grips with his childhood. While driving in the mountains, raging at his fate, his car had gone off the road in a heavy downpour. Eric survived, but the car was totaled.

Matthew kept his voice as neutral as possible. "This mountain sucks."

Eric tried to start the engine. When nothing happened, he turned off the wipers. "We better think about what to do next. And let's make sure to pick our best options. Otherwise things could get a lot worse."

Matthew gave him a smoldering look, still trying to contain his anger. "Thanks, Eric, that's just what I needed to hear."

"The good news is—"

"Good news? There's no good news. We're out in a blizzard, stranded on the side of a mountain. And who knows how far we are from any kind of shelter."

"That's true."

Matthew clenched his fists. Eric's quiet attitude was having an opposite effect on his nerves. It was prompting an emotional storm he'd been trying to hold back. During the past few months, he and Lea had had frequent arguments about her involvement in Elkville's business. But no matter what Matthew said, she seemed determined to spend more and more time in the remote community. It was the last place on Earth that Matthew wanted to think about, much less visit. But he wasn't only heading to Elkville, it looked like he could die trying to get there. He turned on Eric hoping to restrain himself and failing.

"This is your fault, Eric! You just had to fill Lea's mind with all those sob stories about Elkville when you should have known what a patsy she is. Now, she can't stop her crusading. She has to try to save every sick person on this mountain, despite the fact they choose to live on the outskirts of Hades!"

Eric's stared back with questioning eyes. "You're blaming me for your wife being compassionate?"

"I'm totally onboard with her compassion. But instead of helping out in her own back yard, she's gone for weeks at a time, traveling to a place you introduced to her."

Eric pulled back, looking straight ahead, but he didn't respond. Finally, he released his seatbelt. "I'm going to get out and see how far we are from the road."

Matthew grabbed Eric's arm. "Before you do anything rash, let's be sure we're on solid ground."

"At least we're not on too much of an incline. That's a plus."

"Right." Matthew let out a heavy breath. After verbally expressing feelings that had been eating at him for months, he felt suddenly worn. "I'll check my side," he said as he pushed open his door. He put a tentative foot on the snowy ground and got out just enough to look around. Once back in the car, he felt a little better. "You're right. We're on a fairly level patch."

"I'll find out how close we are to the road," Eric said. He exited the car and quickly closed his door. Matthew tried to follow the man's movements, but the snow on the windows rendered it impossible to see anything. His worry genes, something he'd never exercised until he'd met Lea, kicked in. "Oh hell, Eric can be a bit of a klutz," he whispered. "I hope he doesn't slip and keep going."

Matthew wasn't the sentimental type, but the thought of Eric falling to his death was a sobering one. It would be like losing an innocent, a person who always gave all he had and more.

Eric had grown up with a father who dominated his life with an iron fist. He was still trying to recover his self-worth. Matthew knew Eric had a fragile ego, but he'd just unloaded all his crap on the guy. It was a disturbing thought. He had no desire to take over the role of Eric's father. He had another thought that was more worrying. If Lea was pregnant, maybe their child would be better off without Matthew as his parent.

The miserable thoughts were still plaguing Matthew when Eric got back in the car. His white-blond hair was covered in snow, and he was shivering as he rubbed his hands together. He gave Matthew a quick glance. "You're right about the car being safe where it is, but if we'd gone a few feet further—"

"Spare me the details," Matthew ordered. Hearing himself, he frowned, remembering his own father scolding him. "I mean—"

Eric's probing blue eyes came to rest on Matthew's face. "I'm sorry about everything, Matthew."

Matthew slammed the top of the dash with a fist. "Dammit, Eric, stop giving into my crap."

"I don't understand."

"Of course you don't. We both grew up with ego-centered, control freaks as fathers. I learned to ignore my upbringing. But you're still incapable of having faith in yourself or telling people they're full of it when they unload on you."

Eric averted his eyes. "One time when I was ten or eleven, my dad took me out on a call. It was snowy coming back. All I remember is sitting in the passenger seat, so scared I couldn't catch my breath. Part of it was the car sliding around on the icy roads, but more than that it was hearing my dad. He was so angry and loud that I started to cry and—"

"What? Go on," Matthew urged.

Eric shook his head. "Forget it. Like you said, I have to ignore all that and be the man he wanted me to be."

Matthew sat back, not forcing the issue. He didn't think he'd be much help anyway. "With this mess we're in, what do you think we should do?"

"We're probably ten miles from Elkville. We better stay put for now. When the weather let's up, we can try walking the rest of the way."

"What about Lea and your mom. They'll be worried as hell."

"Mom's been through this kind of thing lots of times," Eric said in a wistful voice. "Hopefully, she can help Lea to remain as calm as possible. But I'm worried about Teresa too."

Matthew thought about Eric's beautiful wife. Slender and tall, Teresa had gorgeous red hair and eyes that reminded him of sparkling emeralds. "Listen Eric, it's my turn to say I'm sorry. I don't know how I could forget about Teresa."

"She's been so patient with all my moods and insecurities. How she puts up with me is a mystery."

"There you go again, Eric, putting yourself down. Aren't you ever going to give yourself a break?"

Eric shrugged. "Maybe my dad was right about me. I'm not the strong person he wanted as his son. I'm not like you, Matthew."

Matthew pounded the dash again. "That does it! I've tried to be patient, but I'm sick and tired of you always playing the victim card, always using it as an excuse to whine and complain."

Eric glared back. "Maybe, but if I'm a victim, so are you. Constantly fuming about how Lea's done you wrong by caring about

14

others. You missed your calling. You should be writing country songs about how bad you have it."

Matthew could have continued the argument, but he managed enough self-control to still his tongue. He'd already allowed his emotions too much expression. Such behavior would do nothing but erode his self-respect.

Eric spoke as the minutes of silence ticked on. "That was unfair of me, Matthew, to say those things—"

"Don't start groveling. If I have to be trapped in this car with you, just shut up."

Eric pulled his shoulders back. "I will not shut up. I'm going to take your advice, Doctor Howell, and I'm going to give myself a break."

"What's that mean?"

"Since we have nothing better to do, I'm going to stop putting myself down and start reciting my merits."

"Just be quiet, Eric!"

"Or what? You'll pound me into the ground like you're pounding that dashboard? I don't think so. You care too much about your precious hands. If you bruised them beating on me it might affect your ability to be the awesome surgeon you're always going on about."

"What? When do I ever talk about what I do?"

"We weren't on the road fifteen minutes before I had to hear about your last 'extremely challenging' case. If that's what you discuss with Lea, no wonder she goes off to Elkville."

The remark almost unleashed Matthew's need to do exactly what Eric said. He was ready to give Eric's jaw a good pounding. Instead, he sucked up his anger and closed his eyes. "I'm taking a nap, Eric. So if you have to recite your merits, do it quietly."

Three

DOCTOR TERESA WILLIS now happily called herself Doctor Teresa Lloyd. She sat on the living room sofa, remembering the day she married Eric. It was her best day ever. Standing at the altar, she'd been so excited, so happy to be Eric's bride. She remembered their vows and how eagerly she'd repeated them. "To have and to hold, from this day forward, for better, for worse, for richer, for poorer, in sickness and in health, until death do us part."

The last five words repeated in her mind. She'd just talked to Eric's mother, Margaret, and found out that Eric was missing. She tried not to react and forced herself to silently listen to Margaret explain that she shouldn't worry. Eric was probably taking shelter somewhere.

Teresa knew it was a lame excuse, offered by a mother who was trying to cope with the situation. Neither of them wanted to talk about what they were really thinking. Where in the world could Eric take shelter on a mountain? Still, Teresa tried to remain as calm as possible. She was a cardiologist. She'd spent a lot of time in the ER. Life-threatening circumstances were common.

However, one very important fact overrode all her experiences as a doctor. Eric wasn't a patient. Eric was her everything. She enjoyed her role as a healer, but her private life was centered on the man she loved with all her heart. And that man was traveling the scary roads to Elkville in a raging blizzard.

It was a horrible thought. She was slightly terrified when she made the trip to the remote settlement. Narrow roads, poorly maintained pavement, steep grades that made her stomach nauseous, it was a very frightening journey. She couldn't imagine making that trip in a snow storm.

She clutched the pendant she was wearing. A couple of weeks before Eric left for Elkville, he'd given her the beautiful heart-shaped ruby. He must have secretly squirreled away the money to buy it since she usually handled the finances. She covered her mouth when clarity hit. "I bet he used that money that was supposed to go for car repairs and new tires. Oh lord, he needed those tires."

What if a tire blew out when he was going seventy miles per hour on the beltway? She cringed, but that was Eric, her beautiful husband. Sometimes his heart overrode his practicality. The thought made her squeeze the pendant more fervently. "Thank goodness, he's driving to Elkville in a rented SUV."

As for the car repairs, she made a mental note to make sure Eric attended to the tire issue when he returned home. Another thought followed. What if the mountain took her sweet man's life, and he came home in a casket?

She stood up and shook off the thought. She wouldn't go there. Life couldn't be that cruel. She'd already had enough misery growing up without parents. Eric was like the prize she got for surviving all that unhappiness. She refused to think he could be snatched away.

She slumped back down on the sofa when she realized how tired she was. She'd put in a long day. She wasn't only taking care of her own patients, she was tending to Eric's as well. She needed to close her eyes for a bit. If an emergency came up, she had to be rested enough to take care of it properly. With that thought in mind, she didn't mean to, but she fell asleep almost immediately.

Four

PAUL GLASS CARRIED a mug of tea into the living room and surveyed the space. Cans of paint, tarps and other painting accessories filled a corner, but other than that, the room looked quite orderly. It was a strange thought, but he felt at home in Elkville, and he liked the house he'd purchased there.

He still marveled at himself and how he could enjoy a simple life. Elkville had a "sit in your rocking chair and rock" pace of living. It was the opposite of Chicago where he'd lived most of his life. The city suited his needs. He'd relished Chicago's many cultural opportunities, its high-rise malls, fine dining and unique architecture. It had been a perfect location for his psychiatric practice.

As that practice thrived and his reputation grew, he often flew to other areas of the country and Europe. He gave lectures and attended cases that were deemed difficult, and sometimes hopeless. All in all, he'd been very proud of the results he got. Thoughts of retirement barely came to mind in spite of the fact that he was old enough to step away from his job.

His life changed drastically when he met Margaret Lloyd. After being a life-long bachelor, he fell in love. Unfortunately, Margaret wasn't ready for that kind of relationship. Rejection hurt so much that he began to fail at his job. He began to make mistakes. Things got so bad that he'd even suffered a heart attack. When all the drama and dust settled, he had to make peace with himself. Margaret never became his partner, but she did become a friend. That friendship deepened after he moved to Elkville.

Paul walked over to the front window and stared out at the beautiful scene in front of him. Everything had been transformed by the snow. Even the old picket fence, with some of its slats missing, looked picturesque. For a moment, Paul wondered if he should fix the

18

fence. It was on his to-do list, but with the snow adorning the eyesore, it reminded him of something out of a Norman Rockwell painting.

Margaret told him he was crazy for buying the old, dilapidated house and its falling-down fence. But he'd liked the two-story structure as soon as he saw it. He'd grown up in a similar house. Besides it was only a couple of doors away from Margaret's home.

But she'd been right about the condition of the house. It was in a very poor state. He'd had to replace the roof, repair the shingle exterior, put in new plumbing and electrical, update the bath and kitchen and install central heating and cooling. The remodeling job had taken a lot of time and a good bit of money. Fortunately, he didn't need to worry about the expense.

Between monies he had accumulated from investments and selling his high rise condo in Chicago, he could afford to live very comfortably. He'd even been prepared to help with the cost of building a medical facility for Elkville, but Raymond Ferguson told him it wasn't necessary. Raymond wanted to foot the bill. It was a generous gesture on Raymond's part, even if he was very wealthy and could afford to be charitable.

The facility had ended up being called The Lloyd-Howell Clinic. Its name honored Margaret's deceased husband, Eric Lloyd Senior, a doctor who dedicated his life to bringing medical care to the area, and it also honored Raymond's daughter, Lea, and her husband, Matthew Howell.

Recently the clinic had been completed and was staffed by a young doctor named Ned Finney. He was a talented man whom Raymond had recruited. Even though Ned graduated from UCLA, a top ranking medical school, the man didn't put on airs. He was a friendly sort, at least on the surface. With Paul spending time at the new clinic, he was getting to know the young doctor. Ned had a very professional, very straight forward attitude. Their conversations usually involved the clinic and its role in the area.

Margaret had taken a liking to the young doctor. She often invited Paul to dinner and since Ned's arrival, she'd asked him to join them on a number of occasions. Paul figured Ned reminded Margaret of her son, Eric, a son she missed more than she admitted. However, except for both of them having blue eyes, they differed totally in appearance. Ned had jet black hair whereas Eric's was white blond. Eric was fit enough, but he didn't have Ned's well-muscled physique.

With Eric coming to Elkville for a visit, Paul wondered how he'd get along with Ned Finney once they got to know one another. A paw, scratching at his trousers, brought Paul out of his musings. He smiled and looked down at his canine friend, Duke. When Paul first recused him, he guessed the dog was probably getting up there in age. However, with care and a proper diet, Duke looked a lot better since his rescue. His muzzle wasn't quite as gray as it had been, and his ribs no longer showed. Paul stroked Duke's head. "Do you have to go out again? I just walked you a half hour ago."

Duke was quick to respond to Paul's question. He swiveled round and trotted back to his red-plaid, dog bed. It was clear that he'd had enough of the cold and blowing snow. Paul couldn't blame him. No matter how beautiful the snow was, being out in it was a different matter. Just walking down to Margaret's house and back earlier had chilled Paul to the bone. Part of the problem was the light weight jacket he'd worn. After a warming spell that lasted a week, Paul had put his heavy winter jacket in a trunk in the attic. If he wanted to brave the weather again, he'd have to retrieve it.

Reflecting on the cold that had seized hold of the area, he worried about Eric and Matthew. Margaret told him that the two men were hours overdue. They had to be stuck on the mountain or worse. They might have had an accident.

Paul had offered to take his truck and look for them, but Margaret didn't think he'd find them in the blizzard conditions. She was also worried about him driving on the dangerous mountain roads and having an accident himself. Paul agreed with her. Chicago's city streets were more his style. In the meantime, there was nothing he could do but sit and wait for the storm to pass.

Five

MATTHEW WOKE UP in the dark. Rubbing the sleep from his eyes, it took a moment to fully recall where he was. He was in an SUV, stuck on the side of a mountain, but he hadn't frozen to death. He was even fairly warm. Eric had advised that they bring along their winter coats. They both put the outer garments over a couple layers of sweaters. Everything felt too tight, but they were somewhat protected from the cold. With his gloved hands tucked under his arms, they were warm too. He felt almost calm until he focused on the howling wind and the way the car was being buffeted about.

He reached out to Eric, felt for his arm and nudged it. "Eric! Eric?"

When Eric remained unresponsive, Matthew had a moment of concern. He was warm enough, but what about Eric? The interior of the car was very cold, and Eric was quite lean with no extra body fat. He shook Eric's arm again. "Eric, wake up!"

Eric moved a little and finally came awake with a start. "Teresa? What is it? Is it the hospital?"

"Eric, it's Matthew. We both fell asleep, remember?"

"Matthew?" Eric straightened in his seat. "Why is it so dark?" he asked in a sleepy voice.

Matthew looked around. "The snow has covered all the windows."

Eric fished around in an inner pocket. A moment later the interior was dimly lit with the light from Eric's phone. He smiled. "At least it's good for something."

"That's great, but I wish we could contact someone to rescue our butts."

Eric ignored his remark and checked his phone. "I think we've been asleep for a few hours. It's six o'clock."

Matthew yawned. "That late? I must have been more tired than I thought, but I feel better. So what's our next move?"

"Maybe the storm has let up. I'll get out and check on the weather."

"Make it quick. You don't want to stay out there any longer than necessary."

"Yes, Mom," Eric said as he pushed open his door and got out. A couple of minutes later, he was back in the car. "It's not snowing. But it's very slippery, and the temperature is dropping."

"Fantastic," Matthew grumbled.

"There's probably six to eight inches of snow on the ground but the drifts are deeper."

"I've read about situations like this. Maybe we could put some kind of marker on the road in case someone passes by. In the morning, we could start walking to Elkville."

"What do you suggest we use as a road marker?"

Matthew smiled. "I have just the thing. Lea gave me a red flannel robe for Christmas and insisted I bring it. If we could find something to tie the belt to, it could do the trick."

"There's tall brush just off the shoulder of the road. Give me the robe, and I'll take it topside."

Matthew stretched and did a couple of shoulder rolls. "That's okay. It's my turn. Besides, I need to get out and stretch my legs"

"Are you sure? You'd have to scale an incline getting back to the road."

Matthew shrugged him off. The car felt claustrophobic, and he needed some fresh air. "I'll be fine. I not only have a warm coat, I'm wearing the proper footwear. Something I've learned to bring whenever I visit this forsaken part of the country."

"Really?" Eric crossed his arms. "You call what you're wearing proper footgear? You're sporting a very nice pair of running shoes. They're not going to cut it in this snow."

"They're as good as what you're wearing."

"You're not used to this kind of terrain. I am."

"We get plenty of snow in Chicago. I think I know what I'm doing."

Eric threw up his hands. "Whatever you say."

"What, Eric? You don't think I can handle putting a road marker out? You don't have much faith in me, do you?"

Again, Eric remained silent and started fiddling with his phone.

Matthew found himself getting angry again. Eric might be self-effacing, but he could be extremely irritating too. He always thought he was tougher when it came to his old stomping grounds. Matthew would show him a little Chicago grit.

After he found his robe in his luggage and let himself out of the car, he regretted his boasting almost immediately. He'd only gone a few yards, plodding through the drifts, facing cruel, icy winds, when he decided he was going to have to use all his strength and that Chicago grit to accomplish his task.

Getting up to the road was a challenge, a big challenge. The wind became his first opponent. Its gusts were fierce and almost tore the robe from his grasp. A brilliant idea helped to correct the problem. The oversized robe had sleeves big enough to go over his coat. That was a plus. He put on the garment, cinched the belt and continued with his mission, trying to get up the incline that separated him from where he stood. Not only snow, but brush and heavy undergrowth blocked his path. After a few unsuccessful attempts to breach the thicket, he finally found an area of rockier ground. It definitely looked like it afforded better access to the road.

Clawing his way upwards, slipping on snowy, hard surfaces and having to regain traction, the relatively short distance would probably remain in his memory as a task equal to scaling one of the seven summits. It was a ridiculous comparison, but it helped him to keep going. His cheeks were pelted by countless, wind-driven bits of snow. The brambles were worse. Thorny plants had managed to grow and flourish between the rocky sections. They kept snaring his robe. Every time he tried to free the garment, he usually slipped in the process. As he was trying to regain his feet, he was repeatedly assaulted by the wild, wind-driven, sticker-laden branches. When he lost his footing and went down on his knees, Matthew's face got the worst of the punishment, making him feel like he was in a fight with a batch of alley cats having a go at him. Instead of giving up the battle, he became even more determined to accomplish his goal. It became a man against the mountain saga, and he wouldn't let himself surrender to a mountain he despised.

By the time he returned to the SUV, he was heaving out his breaths, but he was happy with himself. On the other hand, Eric seemed alarmed when he aimed his phone's light at Matthew. He let out a gasp. "Oh, dear lord, Matthew! What happened?"

"I took care of the road marker problem. I think it'll grab the attention of anyone passing."

"No, I mean your face. It's all cut up and bleeding."

"Damn bramble bushes! I'm grateful that my face lost all feeling while was up top, trying to tie the robe to a bush."

"I'll get my medical bag and get you cleaned up."

Matthew frowned. "Better do it fast before the feeling comes back."

"I will, but first I want to thank you. I'm impressed with what you did. You're tougher than I thought."

"Thanks," Matthew said, but when he smiled, he felt the first twinge of pain returning.

Six

NED FINNEY ARRIVED at Margaret Lloyd's house, looking forward to dinner. He hadn't known Margaret, Lea Howell and Paul Glass for that long, but they already treated him like a friend. He couldn't have had a better start in his new job as Elkville's doctor.

Margaret's son, Eric, and Matthew Howell, Lea's husband were supposed to be at the dinner. He'd met both men briefly, but he didn't get to know them very well. Eric had grown up in Elkville and might be a valuable resource in helping him learn more about the area and its inhabitants. Margaret had been forthright in that regard, but Eric could give Ned a different perspective. Margaret said Eric accompanied his father, the area's previous doctor, on many of his house calls.

As for Matthew Howell, Ned would have to wait and see to form any opinion. The Chicago surgeon definitely had an edge and hadn't seemed overly friendly. However, Lea, Matthew's wife, was his opposite. The beautiful, petite woman made frequent trips to Elkville to help the clinic get established. She took care of administrative duties while visiting, but she also stayed in touch when she returned to Chicago. She helped with overseeing the financial end of things, a position that she seemed to enjoy.

Ned knocked on Margaret's door, stomping his feet to get the snow off. After a day that had seen blizzard conditions, the snow had finally let up. He'd shoveled out the walks around the clinic before he came over. Noticing Margaret's snow-covered driveway and side walk, he'd see if he could clear the snow for her too.

When the door opened, Ned was surprised to see Margaret looking so upset. He reached out at once. "What's wrong, Margaret?"

Margaret stepped back and gestured him in with teary eyes. "Eric and Matthew never arrived. I'm afraid something's happened to them."

Paul and Lea joined them in the small foyer. Both of them looked upset too. It was obvious from Lea's red eyes that she'd been crying. She stepped forward and spoke in a hesitant voice. "They should have arrived hours ago. They must have had an accident." She paused and let out a little sob. "What if Matthew is dead?"

Margaret quickly put an arm around Lea's slender shoulders. "Don't say that or think it, please, Lea. Like I told you before, Eric and Matthew probably had the sense to pull over and wait out the storm."

Paul patted Lea's hand. "Margaret's right. They're both smart and careful."

"Careful?" Lea cried. "I love Eric dearly, but his car went off the mountain during that heavy rain. He's lucky to have survived."

Ned knew he had to intervene before emotions intensified even more. "I'll go look for them. Like Margaret said, they're probably stranded on the mountain."

His announcement got an immediate response from Lea. "Margaret told Paul it was too dangerous, but if you think there's a chance you could find them, I'd be forever grateful."

Margaret looked at Lea and then at Ned. "That was before the snow stopped. If you can help without endangering your life, Ned, I'd be grateful too."

Ned smiled. "I've done a bit of driving in the mountains. I'll use chains on my truck."

Paul quickly dug a hand in his pocket. "Your truck is older. Take mine," he said as he handed Ned the keys. "It's a four door extended cab with plenty of room. I have chains, too."

Margaret glanced at Paul. "Thank you. That's a wonderful idea."

Paul smiled. "The truck has an exterior spotlight that'll work well in the dark. If I go too, Ned can drive, and I can keep a lookout for a stranded vehicle."

Ned nodded. "Good plan."

Paul grabbed his coat off the rack where it was hanging. "Let's go to my house, and we'll get those chains on."

Before Paul could say anything more, Duke came running over from the living room. Paul smiled and shook his head. "You stay here, boy, and take care of Lea and Margaret."

Lea approached the dog and stroked his head. "It's too cold out there for you, Duke."

Paul gave Duke a gesture that told the dog to stay put. Duke seemed doubtful at first, but he finally obeyed his master. Turning, he went over to the throw rug in the living room where he'd been sleeping.

Ned signaled to Paul. "We better keep moving."

* * *

Once they were on the road, Paul glanced over at Ned. "I was impressed with the way you put those chains on. You made it look almost easy."

"My dad is a forest ranger. We lived in places where we had to use chains quite a bit in the winter."

"And you remembered to bring blankets, rope and other emergency supplies. That was smart. Did living in those areas give you the experience you need in times like this?"

"Yes, it did," Ned stated flatly. "But maybe we shouldn't talk about that now. We don't know where Eric and Matthew got into trouble. Let's both keep a sharp lookout while we're driving."

Paul felt his cheeks redden. He'd been chatting away, forgetting to stay attentive to their mission. Ned was much younger, but the man clearly knew how to maintain his focus on whatever needed his attention. It was a valuable asset for a rural doctor who would pretty much be on his own in a lot of tough circumstances.

They moved very slowly down the highway, and Paul made sure to do as Ned had instructed. He checked for any sign of something out of place. He wasn't sure how far they'd gone when he noticed a movement on the side of the road. It was different than the blowing limbs or bushes he'd been seeing. Ned must have seen it too. He slowed the truck to a crawl and pointed. "Look there. That red patch."

They pulled over and stopped in front of what looked like some material being blown about in the wind. Ned grabbed a pistol grip spotlight and opened his door. "Better stay in the truck, Paul. I'll check it out."

Paul waited anxiously as Ned examined whatever it was that they'd found. He was impressed with the light Ned was using. It was one of the items the young doctor had picked up at his living quarters at the clinic before they left. Its beam's illumination was perfect for checking the drop-off area of the road. Paul felt a chill when he thought about Eric and Matthew's vehicle plummeting down the side. If it had, he could only hope neither of the men was seriously injured.

Ned returned to the truck and gave Paul an encouraging look. "I think we found them. I'm not sure because of the snow covering it, but I think I spotted a white vehicle."

"What are you going to do?" Paul asked.

Ned opened the rear door on the extended cab and took out what looked like climbing rope and some fancy gloves. His black hair was being blown about in a frenzy of windy gusts. "It'll be slippery getting back and forth on the incline, and there's a lot of brush," he explained. "I'll attach some rope to the truck and use it to make the going easier."

"Is there anything I can do?" Paul asked.

Ned put up the hood on his snorkel jacket and fastened the flap over his lower face. He handed Paul a two-way radio and slipped a second one into his jacket pocket. "I'll let you know what's going on once I get to the vehicle."

"Have you done this kind of thing before?"

"Yes, I have. So try not to worry."

Most of Ned's face was covered, but his blue eyes caught a bit of light. In that moment, Paul saw deep concern reflected back to him. In that moment, he also saw Ned's unyielding commitment to duty. Paul knew with certainty that Eric, Matthew and Elkville were in the hands of the right man.

Seven

THE CAR WAS getting colder, and few words had been spoken since Matthew's return. His valiant effort to put out a road marker had succeeded, but his face bore witness to what he'd gone through. Eric hoped his fellow passenger wasn't hurting too much. "How are you doing?"

Matthew looked at his side window. Like Eric's, it was cracked enough to let some air circulate. The remainder of the window was covered in snow. "I'm fine," he said in a listless voice. "I just hate sitting here and doing nothing. How about you?"

"I feel the same way, but I still think staying put might be best."

"After what it took to get that road marker in place, I have to agree."

Eric grabbed hold of the steering wheel and scowled. "I've been thinking about what you said."

"About what?"

"About acting like a victim. You have a point, but I don't know how to change. I make progress, then I fall back into the same, old pattern."

"Don't forget that you told me I act like a victim too. That hurt," Matthew said.

"Maybe we both should have kept our mouths shut."

"Maybe."

Eric tightened his grip on the steering wheel. "Tell me, Matthew, is this the way life is supposed to be? I have a gorgeous wife, and I help people in my job, but I don't know how to enjoy any of it. It's like this voice in my head never stops saying I'm not doing enough."

Matthew sat back and stared at the snow-covered windshield. "The voice in my head says Lea's not doing enough."

"What are you talking about?"

29

"Bottom line, she thinks she loves me, but she hardly has time for us. Between her studies and taking care of the clinic, she hardly knows I exist."

"She won't always be studying or taking care of the clinic."

"No, but she'll always be more passionate about something other than me."

"That's hard to believe."

"Why? Like you said, old patterns have a way of resurrecting themselves."

"But you were so crazy about each other when you got married."

Matthew's voice became low and mocking. "Yes, I let myself believe we were finally getting a break. It was a fool's dream."

Eric's brows narrowed with confusion. "I don't understand how you can talk that way when Lea thinks she might be pregnant. Surely the two of you have—"

"Have what?" Matthew let out a scoffing laugh. "The way things have been in the bedroom, I don't even know if a pregnancy is possible."

Eric sighed. "I had no idea it's been so rough."

Matthew snorted out his reply. "I was stupid to think that there's a thing called love. In the end, it's all an illusion."

Eric sat back, not understanding how to process Matthew's obvious pain or his own unresolved problems. "Maybe that's life. Once the crap starts happening, it keeps repeating until we feel too beat up to go on."

"That's true, but when we wake up and another day is waiting for us, we don't have a choice, do we?"

"I guess not." Before Eric could say any more, he heard a tapping on his window and someone calling to him.

"Eric, Matthew, thank goodness, we found you!"

The voice was a cheerful one. It was the happy voice of someone rescuing them. The sound contrasted sharply with the way Eric felt. After letting his fears surface, he wasn't ready to be found. He wasn't ready to face Elkville. He might have grown up there, but it seemed to hold nothing but bad memories. Those memories felt like the obstacles that kept him from moving forward in his life. Even the idea of seeing his mother again was difficult. He loved her without question, but she too was a reminder of painful experiences that branded his mind, holding him in some stagnant prison he couldn't escape.

Matthew seemed less than happy too. When Eric glanced at him, the surgeon looked like he was still falling off a mountain.

* * *

Matthew sat huddled in Paul's truck with a blanket around him. He occupied the front passenger seat, and Paul sat behind him next to Eric. Since Matthew was the bigger person, Paul insisted on giving him the seat with more leg room.

Matthew wasn't grateful. He didn't want to be sitting in Paul's truck. He didn't want to be rescued after his conversation with Eric. He'd said things that he hadn't wanted to hear. Rescue meant he'd have to face Lea, the person who was his wife, the person who proved that Matthew had been a fool to believe in the "happily ever after" fairytale.

But when he'd been at the altar, he'd suspended all logic. He'd wanted so much to believe in such nonsense. When he said, "I do," he'd been entranced by the idea of true and lasting love and commitment.

Things had changed drastically. Lea's life centered on her new interests and had little to do with Matthew. If she was pregnant, the commitment would still be there. Matthew would never abandon their child or stop supporting Lea.

He simply understood that his wants and desires were part of the dream he'd fallen into. He didn't want to wake up from the dream and have to face facts. But to go on believing such drivel would mean giving up his integrity.

Integrity was a core value in Matthew's life. Its meaning was something he'd often contemplated. It involved being truthful to who he was, not letting himself be fooled when facts were hard to accept. It meant being honest no matter what. Paul Glass once referred to integrity as self-awareness.

Eric would probably find it hard to believe, but Matthew was very self-aware. He knew he was ego-centered and harsh. He knew he could dominate others and be fine with that. He hadn't thought himself a victim until Eric mentioned it, but if it were true, then he'd throw that facet of his personality in with his other faults. He'd accept them all because that was part of having integrity. And at this point, integrity was about the only thing he could hold on to for sure.

31

He stared out the truck window, trying to prepare himself to live with that integrity when he heard his rescuer, Ned Finney, talking to him. He looked over with a scowl. "What did you say?"

Ned kept his eyes on the road. "I was wondering how you're doing. You've been very quiet."

Matthew stiffened. Why did Ned Finney need to question him? Was it because the guy was a doctor and wanted to assess Matthew's physical condition? Or was he simply being annoying? "I'm one hundred percent fine," he growled through gritted teeth.

"Good," Ned replied as he glanced at his rear view mirror. "And how about you, Eric?"

Eric hesitated then spoke up. "I'm one hundred percent fine, too."

Matthew could hear the acute irritation in Eric's voice. Neither of them wanted Ned Finney asking questions. Somehow Matthew found Eric's attitude comforting. In that moment, as they rode to Elkville on a snowy road, they shared a bond. It was a bond that cut deep. They had both admitted to living lives they didn't want, lives that were miserable, but at least they were both honest with themselves.

Paul spoke up. "Are you sure, Eric. You look pretty stressed to me."

Matthew turned around and glared at Paul. "Leave the man alone, Paul. He says he's okay."

"I'm trying to be helpful," Paul said.

"No, instead of listening to what you're being told, you're grilling people," Matthew insisted.

Eric smiled. "Thanks, Matthew, at least you're listening."

Matthew turned to face the front, threw off the blanket, and sat up straighter. "And I'm going to keep listening, Eric. So don't be shy when you want to speak up for yourself."

Paul cleared his throat. "Sorry if I was out of line, Eric."

Eric didn't hesitate this time. "You were out of line. So stop looking for trouble."

Matthew smiled when he heard Eric's tone. It was clear and direct. It gave him hope for the guy. Maybe Eric wasn't going to stay a victim forever. Maybe with a little support, he'd start feeling good about himself, and hopefully take charge of what he wanted and get it. But what about his own life? Was there any chance things would change with Lea? He wouldn't get his hopes up, not again.

Eight

MARGARET SAT IN her living room with Lea. They were waiting anxiously while Ned Finney and Paul were out searching for Eric and Matthew. For Lea's sake, Margaret tried to put on a brave face. She even tried to fool herself in to believing the men were okay. But she understood how easy it would be for them to be injured or worse.

A sense of dread was a familiar feeling. It had plagued her life ever since she moved to the Appalachians so many years ago with her husband, Ricky. He'd been caught in many a storm while traveling the dangerous mountain roads. He'd been extremely lucky to have always come home in one piece.

Ricky was a gentle name she called her husband when he was alive. But Doctor Eric Richard Lloyd Senior wasn't always gentle, especially with their son, Eric. Neither was the place where Eric grew up. Elkville was poverty-ridden and located in a harsh and primitive area. It hadn't been a good place to raise her son. But when Eric was growing up, she wouldn't let herself think about how difficult his life was. Her focus was on his father and believing that he was a good man, a dedicated man, a man who gave his everything to his patients. Contemplating the hardships Eric had endured because of her negligence was overwhelming. She had to retrieve a tissue from her pocket and dab her eyes.

"Mom, what is it?" Lea asked.

When she heard Lea refer to her in a motherly way, Margaret had a brief moment of respite from her misery. Even if she wasn't actually Lea's mother, she loved their relationship. It was very much like that of a parent and child. But Margaret hadn't given Eric the same care and attention that she'd given Lea. She swiped at her eyes again. "It's my fault that Eric and Matthew are out there."

"What do you mean?"

33

"You talked about Matthew hating this place, but Eric feels the same way. If it weren't for me living here, he'd try to forget it ever existed. Instead, it's become a place that's impossible for either of them to forget. With Paul and your father building the clinic and both of us getting so involved, Eric and Matthew have been forced to share a life they never wanted."

Lea bit her lip as tears welled up and streamed down her face. "Matthew and I seem to be fighting constantly."

"Oh Lea, that's terrible."

"At this point, if I'm not pregnant, I think he's going to want a divorce."

"What do you mean? Matthew loves you."

Lea looked away. "When we were on our honeymoon, I promised him that he'd never have to go through hell again, but I think I broke that promise." She sniffled back her tears. "I guess I'm like you, Mom. I like Elkville, and it's been so exciting seeing the clinic being built. Now that it's up and running, I love being part of that too."

"And Matthew?"

"I love him, but—"

"Lea, goodness knows I'm not an expert on marriage, but I always thought it was important to support your husband."

"And what did that get you, Mom? You forfeited your needs and desires the minute you married Eric's dad."

"Maybe, but it's Eric I'm worried about. He was miserable and tormented as a child, and from the way he acts, he's never recovered."

Lea clutched her stomach. "If I'm pregnant, I don't want that for my child."

"Not only your child, Lea. You're forgetting that it would also be Matthew's child."

"So I should go back to Chicago, be some perfect mother and wife and forget about Elkville."

"Maybe you should. But just because you'd be a wife and mother, you could also have a career there."

"But I like it here."

"Why?"

"I don't know. Maybe it's because you're here, and it feels like home."

"Don't you feel that way when you're with Matthew?"

"Matthew's working most of the time. You know, the life of a doctor and all that. But when I'm here, I have a life I enjoy."

"Don't you miss Matthew?"

"Sure, sometimes, but I'm usually so busy with my studies and the clinic. By the time I go to sleep, I'm too exhausted to think about him."

"Well, if he and Eric went off that mountain, I guess you won't have to think about him at all."

"Mom, what a horrible thing to say!"

Margaret shook her head and began to sob. "That's how I feel, like a horrible person!"

Lea got up, went over to Margaret and sat down next to her. "It's not true," she said. She put her arms around Margaret's shoulders. "You're the kindest person I know."

Margaret hugged her back, and soon they were both crying.

Before either of them could dry their tears, the front door opened. "We're here," Eric called out.

When Margaret heard Eric's voice, the only thing she wanted was to jump up, run over to her son and hug him with all her strength. But she couldn't move. Her guilt and Lea's confession of woes were so disturbing that she sat where she was, crying and holding on to Lea.

Eric came striding into the living room with Matthew right behind him. "Mom, what's wrong?" Eric asked.

Before Margaret could answer, Matthew crouched down in front of Lea. "Is it the baby? Did you lose our baby, Lea? If you did, I'm here for you. I'll always be here for you!"

Margaret heard the love and concern in Matthew's voice. He could be hard-nosed type, but that wasn't who he was when it came to the woman he loved. His voice was open and full of the devotion he'd had for Lea. But Margaret knew the truth. Lea wasn't ready to return that devotion.

The thought was sad and tragic. But the pain didn't stop there. Her son's innocence and endless struggle to find himself was heartbreaking. But hadn't she contributed to the plight of both Matthew and Eric? It was a devastating thought.

Since her return to Elkville, everyone saw her as this sweet older woman who walked through the small community like some savior.

"There's Margaret Lloyd! She came back to us! She found a way to bring us the medical care we needed."

But Margaret knew the truth. She came back to Elkville to save herself. She didn't know how to make a life in Baltimore so she ran back to what she knew. Paul followed her. It was Paul who got Lea's father interested in a clinic.

Margaret had been thrilled. Her husband's dream could finally become a reality. But what did she have to do with it? Nothing.

Lea was so spot on when she talked about Margaret's past and abandoning her dreams. She'd started off as an artist, but she never returned to the beautiful canvases she'd once painted. No, she was still clinging to Ricky and what he wanted even though he was dead and buried.

Her life felt all wrong, a travesty she didn't want to face. But her failure didn't matter now. The die was cast, and people were paying for her inability to live her truth. The resulting pain took hold so powerfully that she couldn't catch her breath. Eric tried to help as her body started shaking violently. But what could he do? Could he stop her life from crumbling? She didn't think so.

Nine

TERESA HELD THE phone close to her ear. When she woke up from her nap, her only thought was Eric's welfare and finding out if he was okay. She quickly called Margaret's home number. After a half dozen rings, she didn't understand why Margaret or Lea didn't pick up? She was about to end the call when someone answered. She thought she recognized the voice.

"Paul? Is that you?"

When she got an affirmative answer, she continued. "It's Teresa, Eric's wife."

Paul's tone changed immediately. "Teresa, so nice to hear from you."

"I'm calling about Eric. Is there any news? Did he ever get to Elkville?"

Paul hesitated. "Yes, he got here safely."

Teresa held the phone a little tighter. "I wish he would have called me."

"I'm sorry, but things have been a bit hectic. Margaret isn't well. We don't know what's wrong with her."

Teresa hesitated. Eric was very close to his mother. "Oh Paul, you don't think it's anything serious, do you?"

"I don't know."

Teresa could hear Paul's distress. He didn't seem to be handling Margaret's condition very well. Perhaps he was still in love with her. "Paul, try not to worry too much. You have to take care of yourself if you're going to be there for Margaret and her family."

"You're right. Thank you."

"Would you tell Eric I called and ask him to call me back when he gets a chance?"

"Yes, of course," Paul said.

There was silence after that. Paul had ended the call without a goodbye.

Teresa put her phone on the side table. She was grateful that Eric was safe, but Margaret sounded like she was in trouble. Ever since Eric's mother moved back to Elkville, they had shared numerous conversations, mostly on the phone. Teresa felt she'd gotten to know Margaret a little. Still the chats never went far enough. Margaret changed the subject whenever Margaret's life became part of the conversation.

The more Teresa pondered Margaret's attitude, the more she felt the woman was suffering from some inner demons. Now, those inner demons might be surfacing. Teresa decided to think about it over dinner. With Eric away, she'd settle for a frozen meal. She put a chicken curry and rice dinner in the microwave.

While her meal was warming, her thoughts returned to Eric. He was a little like Margaret. He didn't like to discuss his problems. But she only had to look into his distracted, blue eyes to know he wasn't at peace. He had inner demons, too.

She took some silverware out of a drawer, placed it on the table and paused. If only she could help out with whatever was happening in Elkville. She wanted to feel that she was a part of the family when a crisis arose. Ever since marrying Eric, she'd tried her best to do just that, but she never got very far. It was frustrating to remain the outsider.

When she tried to discuss the matter with Eric, he'd give her that regretful smile and tell her she was better off not being involved. But how long was she supposed to be the one kept in the dark? Eric might say it was for her best, but she didn't agree.

She took out her meal, sat down at the kitchen table and made a decision. She was going to visit Elkville. With the weekend coming up, neither she nor Eric had any patient appointments scheduled. She'd also cancel appointments for the coming week. Anything that involved any urgency could be handled by colleagues. She had a couple of good friends who were excellent doctors. She'd helped both of them out in the past. Now, they could return the favor.

As her plans came together, she had a moment of doubt. Would the mountain roads be passable? She checked her weather app and smiled. A warming spell was following in the wake of the storm. That was promising. Another idea came to mind. She'd rent a four-wheel vehicle and drive to Elkville. But she wouldn't tell Eric she was coming. She'd surprise him.

The more she considered such an adventure, the more enthusiastic she felt. Since becoming a doctor, she'd adopted a conservative, play-it-safe attitude. But she hadn't always been like that. During her teenage years, she'd worn her thick, red-hair half-way down her back and sported a rebellious outlook. A teacher once called her a "wild child."

That same teacher eventually convinced her to make something of her life. That's when she buckled down and studied. Getting good marks became her new goal. She found out how smart she was. With little effort, she rose to the top of her class. She also learned how to fit in and become an articulate person who could make the grade and get into medical school.

Later, when she met Eric, she hardly remembered being anything but a dedicated doctor who wasn't interested in any form of "wildness." But maybe she needed to resurrect a little of that part of her personality. A tingle of anticipation took hold of her body when she thought about sharing a bit of her wild side with Eric.

Ten

MARGARET WAS IRRITATED with herself and embarrassed by her behavior. She'd let her feelings get the best of her. Now, she was suffering the consequences. She sat in her bed, propped up by heavy, down pillows. Eric stood over her, very concerned and questioning her. She listened to the stern tone of his voice and felt like a child whose parent was letting her know she couldn't take care of herself.

"Mom, you have to tell me what's going on. Are you overdoing it with the clinic? Are you looking after yourself? Or are you still being the person who thinks the world rests on her shoulders?"

"Eric, I already told you I'm fine. I simply got worried when I didn't hear from you."

Eric shook his head. "No, it has to be more than that. You were shaking. You were dizzy. You're hiding something."

Margaret looked away and stiffened. She had no intention of discussing her feelings with her son. "Eric, you can project whatever you want, but I'm going to repeat for the umpteenth time, I just had a bad scare."

"A scare? You scared the heck out of me and the rest of us. I arrived here and saw you sobbing and on the verge of collapse. Now you're holding in whatever it is that's really going on. You know that's not good for your health. I've already lost one parent who wouldn't talk to me. Now, you're doing the same thing."

There was a knock on the bedroom door, and Paul peeked in a moment later. "Eric, Teresa called a little while ago. She's been very worried about you. I told her you were fine, but that you were with your mother and would call her back later."

Eric gave Margaret a final, censuring look and headed for the door. "That's just great. I've been so concerned about Mom that I

40

forgot to call Teresa," he said as he eased past Paul and headed out into the hall.

Paul took a step into the bedroom. "How are you doing, Margaret?"

Margaret scowled. "My goodness, Paul, don't you start."

Paul edged a little closer and stood at the bottom of the bed. "I don't understand. You're the third person in the last couple of hours to indicate that I've offended them in some way."

Margaret noticed Paul's dejected face. "I'm sorry. I didn't mean it that way."

"I'm simply concerned about you. You seemed so upset when we arrived. Then you—"

"Why are you saying things that make me feel worse?" Margaret demanded.

"My concern is making you feel worse? I guess you and Eric have a lot in common." Paul took a step back. "Perhaps I should leave."

Margaret avoided Paul's eyes and smoothed out her covers instead. "Maybe that would be best. I don't feel like having anyone else standing over me."

* * *

Paul retreated from the bedroom with a pinched look and a quickened heartbeat. Earlier, after he and Ned rescued Matthew and Eric, he'd been severely reprimanded by both men. The look Matthew gave him wasn't only harsh, it made him feel like he was facing some grizzly that was readying for a fight. Eric's scornful face wasn't much different. Between the two, he'd been on the receiving end of a lot of antagonism.

He'd thought Margaret would be the person who soothed his injured pride. And he didn't think a little pride in himself was too much to ask. When he was a practicing psychiatrist, he had a reputation for being exceptional. His work with difficult patients was sometimes the subject of articles in respected mental health journals.

After talking to Margaret, that pride had suffered a severe blow. He cared about her. If he was honest, he'd admit that he still had deep feelings of love and concern for the woman. But what was his reward for those feelings. He barely asked about her health, and she let him have the full brunt of her anger. Instead of making him feel a little better, she practically threw him out of her bedroom.

He took the stairs to the lower level of the house, trying to contain his anger. He hadn't felt so unwanted in a long time. Without a word to anyone, he grabbed his coat from the rack in the hall. Duke came running over, nosing his leg as he slipped his jacket on. "Come on boy, let's go home."

Before Paul could get out the door, Ned, who'd been sitting in the living room, joined him. "What's going on, Paul? If Duke needs to be walked, I'll be happy to take him out."

Paul took a leash out of his pocket and attached it to Duke's collar. He had to force himself to take a breath. Ned Finney was trying to be helpful, and Paul didn't want to take his resentment out on the wrong person. "Thanks, Ned, but Duke's fine. It's simply time for me to go home."

"Lea and Matthew are in the kitchen. Lea insisted on fixing something for dinner. Aren't you going to stay?"

"No, thank her for me, but I think the family needs some space right now. As for dinner, I have a leftover turkey breast in the refrigerator."

Ned smiled. "I've heard you're an excellent cook."

"I appreciate it." Paul's hand relaxed a little when he realized he'd been holding on too tightly to Duke's leash. Ned's friendly manner was just the thing he needed to calm himself. "Do you think you'd like to join me for dinner? I've also got mashed potatoes, gravy and green beans. There's plenty for two."

Ned glanced towards the kitchen. Raised voices could be heard along with pans clanging and drawers being slammed shut. "You know, that's a great idea. Like you said, the family probably needs some time to process everything that's happened."

"Yes, absolutely," Paul said as he opened the door. "I'll go home and start heating up those leftovers while you tell Lea about eating at my house. See you in a bit."

* * *

Lea threw a dish cloth into the sink and turned on the water. "I'm sorry I can't be the wife you want me to be, Matthew."

Matthew stood a few feet away, leaning against a counter. "Wife? I hardly know I have a wife. I spend more time with magazine salesmen than I do with you. In fact, I'd love if one dropped by the apartment, at least I could talk to someone once in a while."

Lea shut off the water and turned to face him. "Maybe you could adopt a better bedside manner and talk to your patients for a change. But no, you're one of those arrogant doctors who think they're too good to talk to a sick person."

"I do my job and make sure those sick people have a chance to get better. If they want chit-chat, they can talk to someone who has time for idle chatter."

"Idle chatter can be nice. When you get home, all I get is your complaints about something that didn't go right, or you rattle on about some nurse who didn't do her job. You have no idea about how to communicate properly."

Ned walked into the kitchen before Matthew could respond. He nodded at Matthew and smiled at Lea. "Thank you for thinking of me, Lea, but Paul's invited me to have dinner at his place."

Lea wiped her hands and went over to where he stood. "Oh Ned, I'm sorry for not properly thanking you." She reached out and took his hand. "You went out after this horrible storm. Risking your own life, you managed to find Eric and Matthew. Do you know how wonderful you are?"

Ned's face turned a bright red. "I'm happy I could help," he said as he carefully pulled his hand away. "Anyway, if you need anything, you know where I am."

After Ned left the room, Matthew pushed off the counter. His brown eyes were bright and sharply focused when he came over to where Lea stood. He turned her around to face him. "Really? Ned Finney?"

Lea stared up at him. "What are you talking about?"

Matthew crossed his arms. "Just give it to me straight. Is Ned Finney the reason you spend so much time in this dump?"

"What? That's ridiculous!"

"Ridiculous? No, I don't think so." He reached in his pocket and pulled out a small box. "Here's that pregnancy test you wanted. If you're pregnant, the next step will be finding out if it's mine."

"That is the most insane thing I've heard yet."

"No, the insanity was you running away when we got engaged the first time. Insanity was me going nuts worrying about you. Insanity was finding you in Baltimore, living with the Lloyds, and in love with Eric. Now, you've run off to Elkville and fallen for the handsome Ned Finney. Well, I've had it. I'm done. Do whatever you want. Clearly, I have no place in your life."

Before Lea could stop him, Matthew stormed out of the kitchen. He was shouting to Ned. "Finney, wait up!"

Lea hurried out of the kitchen and followed him to the hall. Ned was zipping up his coat. "Matthew Howell, don't you go hitting people like you hit Eric," she yelled.

Matthew turned so fast, Lea nearly bumped into him. "I'm not going to hurt anyone. I'm leaving."

"And then what?"

"I'm going to that new clinic your rich daddy built. I'm staying there long enough to get some sleep. In the morning, I'm going to find a way to get back to Chicago. After that, who knows? But some day, I can only pray that this whole nightmare about loving you will fade away. Maybe then I'll have some peace in my life."

Eric walked into the hall from the old office addition. "What's all the shouting? What's happening out here?"

Matthew took a breath and steadied himself. "Something that should have never happened, Eric. I let myself fall in love. Now, I'm correcting that mistake, and I don't want to talk about it. I'm going to spend the night at the clinic."

"The clinic? That's a good idea," Eric said. "Mom's made it clear that she doesn't want me around here. If you don't mind, I'll join you."

"Suit yourself," Matthew said as he grabbed his coat. He turned to Ned. "I could use a ride to the clinic, Finney."

Ned looked confused and shrugged. "No problem."

All three men were gone a moment later.

* * *

Lea stared at Margaret's front door in a kind of daze. Everything between her and Matthew had escalated so quickly. When she came back to the moment, she looked at what she was clutching to her chest. It was the pregnancy kit. When she and Matthew were first married, they decided that having a family would be wonderful too. Now, it was almost as if she was remembering two different people.

She walked to the sofa and collapsed on its soft cushions. Her marriage was in serious trouble. According to Matthew, it was over. She should have felt devastated by that fact, but she didn't. She felt confused and slightly numb. If she did a bit of back tracking, she knew she'd once been a happy bride. She loved Matthew, and he loved her. When they were married, they both took their vows with eagerness and joy. Afterwards, when they were together, it felt so right. She was where she wanted to be, with a man she adored. There was a lightness to their interactions, a playful feeling that buoyed up their time together and their love making.

As the days and months passed, the playfulness slipped away. Matthew had a busy life, and so did she. She got very absorbed in learning about her father's corporate world. Her father shared what excited him about running a thriving business. The more she learned, the more she wanted to educate herself about that world. She took courses that included business management, economics and financial management. As the clinic began to take shape, she found a place to apply what she was learning. Everything fit together so well.

All the while, her life with Matthew continued to drift into the shadows. When Matthew started working longer hours, she hardly noticed. Her excitement revolved around her own life, a life apart from the man she'd vowed to love. She told Margaret that it was because she wanted to be more than a wife, but was that an excuse? Was there something else going on?

Sitting in Margaret's living room, with the house so quiet and nothing to distract her, she needed answers. Searching for any kind of clues, she remembered a little book. "My old diary," she whispered breathlessly.

The diary didn't explain what was currently going on, but it did provide a lot of answers to her past. It was a personal record of a time she couldn't remember. It described her life and the person she'd once been before an accident claimed her memories. That person wasn't nice. That "old" Lea was high-strung, argumentative, and could even be abusive to her parents and Matthew. After reading her diary, Lea decided that her amnesia was a gift.

Having no memories was an opportunity to leave a frightening existence behind. It enabled her to start over, and she'd had lots of help on her journey to self-discovery. The Lloyds, Margaret and Eric, took her into their home and hearts. They helped her to gradually adopt a new identity. She became a gentler, kinder person, a person who was balanced and happy. Whereas the "original" Lea could be cold, defensive and even heartless, the "new" Lea was someone who was helpful, giving and understanding.

In recent days, those qualities were still there when she interacted with Margaret and Eric. They were there when she interacted with Ned Finney and the inhabitants of Elkville. But they were sadly lacking in her relationship with Matthew. Instead of appreciating his good qualities, she was always looking for ways to point out his deficiencies and faults. She'd begun to act like the "old" Lea she'd read about in her diary.

Her breath caught at her next, terrifying thought. It was so shocking and unexpected she had to cover her mouth to keep from vomiting out the churning sickness in her stomach. Her next thought was an acute awareness of what was happening to her. It was so clear and revealing that it had the power to take her world, all her ideas about educating herself and being on her own and sweeping all those ideas off the table. Once they were gone, what remained on the table was the truth.

She was being possessed by a demon of sorts. A punishing personality was back in her life. And day by day it was gaining ground. It started out by distancing her from Matthew, the person who'd been on his knees earlier, the person who was her champion. Over the past months, the old personality had made him the enemy.

She rubbed at her temples as the sharp pain of a headache and the sickening pain of what she was facing took hold. Her future was set. Matthew was only the first who would fall away. Soon that personality that didn't trust, that lashed out at everyone, would take over all her relationships. No one would be safe from her caustic tongue and abusive nature.

Living that kind of life wasn't a life worth living. But she didn't know how to stop what was happening to her. It was like her fate was sealed. She got up from the sofa, slowly walked to the hall and opened the front door. There was no need to put on her coat. A coat didn't matter. A coat couldn't protect her from the cold, frigid person who lived inside her.

TRACES OF ANGELS

She stepped out the door and started walking. The snow that lay all around her was beautiful. It pushed back the darkness of night. It was a soothing blanket that covered all the flaws that plagued that thing called life. It was a transforming agent. It changed the harsh, ugly, run-down houses into softer, gentler versions of themselves. If only the snow could do the same for her. If only she could lose herself in the snow, maybe it could drive out the darkness inside of her.

Eleven

MATTHEW WALKED THROUGH the newly completed clinic with Eric following him. He did his best not to notice much about the facility. He didn't care if it was well-equipped or not. It was simply a place for him to sleep. His earlier nap had helped, but he felt exhausted again.

Ned Finney showed them down the hall to a room that had several beds. "Thanks," Matthew muttered as he went over to the one furthest from the door. He'd been told that animals sometimes sought out shelter in a cave when wounded. He felt like one of those animals, but he didn't have a cave. A bed at the clinic would have to do.

Ned pointed to a door. "There's a kitchen down that hall. If you're hungry, help yourself to whatever I have. And that other door leads to an adjoining bathroom."

Eric walked over to a second bed. "You live here, right Ned?"

"Yes, I have quarters on the other side of the hall. Mr. Ferguson was kind enough to make sure I felt comfortable here."

Eric sat down on his bed. "I'm told he spent a small fortune on the place. Of course, what else does he have to do with his excess funds?"

"He's been very cordial whenever we've met," Ned replied.

Matthew checked his pillow and tossed it back on the bed. "He was cordial to me too. He even warned me not to marry his daughter. Unfortunately, I didn't listen. So take heed if he hands out any more warnings."

Ned returned an uneasy smile. "Well, I better get going. Paul invited me to dinner."

Eric's eyes narrowed. "How nice, you're dining with Paul Glass, the big shot shrink. I bet he never thought he'd end up in Elkville."

"You don't like Doctor Glass?" Ned asked.

"I met the good doctor after Lea's father asked him to help Lea. While he was showing off his skills, a number of disastrous incidents occurred. Right, Matthew?"

Matthew replied in a curt tone. "As I remember, Paul told me to buckle up. He said it was going to be a bumpy ride. I didn't want a bumpy ride, but Paul got his wish."

"That's right," Eric said, glancing at Ned.

Matthew continued. "His ride included Lea's mother wanting a divorce from Raymond. Raymond was hospitalized when he almost suffered a heart attack. Eric's mother stopped speaking to him after Paul divulged a secret Margaret had been keeping for most of her married life. Then Eric was overcome with personal trauma and decided to give up medicine and nearly killed himself falling down the Ferguson's grand, marble staircase."

Eric sucked in a breath. "Yes, we all had quite a time with Paul at the helm. Of course, you left out one detail. Paul Glass started hitting on my mother five minutes after they met."

"How very professional of him," Matthew added.

Ned looked back, speechless. "I had no idea."

Matthew grabbed his toiletry bag. "I guess you're another innocent, Doctor Finney. I just hope you survive the monumental task you've taken on."

"So far, there hasn't been much happening," Ned said in nearly a whisper.

Eric lay back on the bed, folded his hands and sighed. "Enjoy it while you can. It's the best advice I can give you. Oh, and one more thing. Paul has a habit of choking on stuff he puts in his mouth. My mom had to give him CPR after he had a bad run-in with an olive."

Matthew walked towards the bathroom. "He's right, Ned. Paul could be your first big emergency. He had a heart attack after he choked."

Ned ran a hand through his thick, black hair. "You've given me a lot to think about, guys, but I better get going."

Matthew waved as he shut the bathroom door. Ned Finney seemed like a nice enough person. Thinking the younger man a possible threat to his marriage was probably absurd on his part. But he'd spoken in anger. Not a good thing. What he needed to do was turn off his brain, brush his teeth and go to sleep.

He was ready for step three after he climbed into bed. Ned had gone, and the room was quiet. He might just get an uneventful night of rest. He'd barely closed his eyes when Eric spoke up.

"I've been thinking about what we told Ned. We gave him the facts, but we left out something important," Eric said. "Lea came out of that fiasco better than ever. Maybe Paul did something right."

"What's this Paul crap?" Matthew asked. "You were the miracle worker, Eric. You were the one who helped Lea and me. I don't know what magic you have, but you should at least give yourself credit where it counts."

"Thanks, I appreciate the thought."

Matthew paused. "By the way, how's Teresa? Did you talk to her?"

"We had a short conversation, but she said she was tired and going to bed early. I hope she's okay. She didn't quite sound herself."

"Stop worrying and get some shut eye," Matthew grumbled. "We'll both need it if we're going to face tomorrow in Elkville."

* * *

By the time Ned left the clinic and returned to Paul's house, his mind was spinning with new ideas about his dinner host. Ned had only known Paul as a helpful friend. He'd felt solace in having Paul close when he had questions concerning the clinic or Elkville.

With Paul's experience as a well-known psychiatrist, he could be an ally if Ned needed more than advice in an emergency. Paul did have a medical degree. Matthew and Eric's recital of the man's failings put a different slant on Paul's capabilities. They repeated in Ned's mind as he parked his truck in front of Paul's house. After he turned off the engine, he sat in the cab with narrowed brows. Were Matthew and Eric right?

Ned went over some earlier events in the day. What he found was a number of disturbing indicators in Paul's behavior. When Paul was leaving Margaret's house, it was clear that he was upset, and he wasn't handling whatever was bothering him very well. His face was flushed, and his breathing was noticeably faster. Even his interaction with his dog was telling. His hand was shaky when he put on Duke's leash. These plainly displayed signs of insecurity were enough to give Ned pause. He had to ask himself why he hadn't picked up on Paul's unstable nature sooner. Perhaps he hadn't wanted to see it. Perhaps he wanted to believe that he was surrounded by a few people he could trust if a crisis arose.

He'd taken on a job that not many doctors would want. He'd agreed to move to an isolated area, away from many of the aspects of modern society that people took for granted. If a medical emergency arose, everyone was depending on him to take care of it.

But what if he couldn't handle what was thrown at him. Back in his ER days, when a car crash victim came in, he could shout out orders and a flock of assistants were there to help him. In Elkville, it would be very different. He wouldn't have anyone there to take orders. He was completely on his own. He hadn't wanted to contemplate that dose of reality. He'd used the thought of Paul Glass being close as a way of bolstering his confidence. But according to Matthew and Eric, he was deluding himself.

He climbed out of his truck and headed for Paul's front door. One bright spot showed up to boost his attitude. He did have help, at least for one night. If Paul choked on a piece of turkey and had a heart attack, a cardiologist and surgeon were close, sleeping back at the clinic.

* * *

Margaret strained to listen for any sounds coming from the lower level of the house. It was dead quiet. A little earlier, she'd heard an argument. She figured Lea and Matthew were having one of those quarrels that Lea mentioned. Margaret's response was to pull up the covers and try to ignore the whole affair.

She wasn't going to stick her nose in someone else's business ever again. She was going to change her ways and let Lea, Matthew and Eric work things out on their own. What choice did she have? At this point, Lea and Eric made it clear that they didn't want to listen to her anyway. Still, she'd go downstairs and check to see if everyone had gone. Lea hadn't been feeling well all day. Perhaps she went home with Matthew. Eric might have gone with them if he was sulking. As a child, he could get very moody when they argued, and he'd never changed his response to their disagreements since. He'd probably return home after he cooled off.

51

She got out of bed and quickly grabbed for her robe. There was an unusual draft of cold air in the room. That wasn't normal. Eric had insisted on having a new heating system installed. It usually kept her room toasty warm. She hunched her shoulders, disappointed that the furnace was broken while people were visiting. Oh well, she'd do what she'd always done. She'd light the old wood stove in the living room.

She opened the door to the hall and felt the chill air turn colder. That didn't seem right. Even if the furnace wasn't working, the house shouldn't have cooled off so fast. Slipping down the stairs, she immediately saw the source of the problem. The front door was wide open. A freezing wind was blowing in, replacing the warmth in the old structure with its icy chill. She hurried over and forced the door shut. She glanced around and called out. "Lea? Eric? Matthew?"

When she didn't get an answer, she pursed her lips with exasperation. "Who could have been so careless to leave a door open like that?"

She walked into her living room, snatched up her phone and called Lea's house. Again, there was no answer. She felt her anxiety rising as her frustration turned to concern. Where could everyone be? She called Paul next and finally heard his voice on the other end of the line. "Paul, where is everyone?"

Paul explained that Ned Finney was with him, and that Eric and Matthew were spending the night at the clinic. Margaret clutched the phone. "But where's Lea?" she asked. "I called her house, and she didn't answer."

Paul came up with an explanation. "Maybe she took the phone off the hook and went to bed."

Margaret nodded. "Maybe you're right. If she doesn't want to talk to Matthew, that would make sense."

"Do you want me to check on her?"

Margaret hesitated. Paul sounded like he wanted, maybe even needed, to help. She decided to let him do as he'd suggested. "Yes, Paul, please check on her, and tell her I'm here if she needs anything."

While Paul was doing what he'd promised, Margaret went back upstairs. For the heck of it, she checked her spare bedrooms. There was a chance that Lea had fallen asleep in one of them.

"She's not here, so where can she be?" she asked aloud. Hopefully Paul would return with good news. In the meantime, she decided to change into slacks and a sweater. If any trouble should arise, she wanted to be dressed and ready for it.

* * *

After talking to Margaret about Lea, Paul returned to the dining room and looked at his guest. "Ned, while I'm checking on Lea, finish your dinner."

Ned put his fork down, wiped his mouth with a napkin and stood up. "Is there something wrong?"

"Probably not, but Margaret isn't sure about Lea's whereabouts. When Margaret tried to reach her, Lea didn't answer her phone."

"I'd be happy to jog down to her house if you want."

Paul headed to his front door. "No, I'll go. It'll make me feel better if I check on Lea in person. It won't take but five minutes, and I should be back. So finish your meal, and I'll serve coffee and some cookies Margaret gave me when I return."

Duke ran over to Paul and stared up at him. Paul shook his head as he zipped up his jacket and slipped his feet into some boots. "No, you can't come. You have to stay here, fella, and keep Ned company."

"Remember, I'm not far away if you need anything," Ned said.

Paul nodded and let himself out the door. The night air was brisk, but refreshing. He took in a bracing lungful and was enjoying the moment until a hardy gust of wind threatened to steal his next breath. It was going to be a long, cold night if the wind didn't die down. Moving as quickly as he could through the snow, it didn't take him long to get to Lea's house. There were no lights on inside the dwelling, but maybe that was because Lea was sleeping. Glancing at the driveway and sidewalk, he began to feel the first twinges of fear. There were no signs of foot traffic between Margaret's house and Lea's. If Lea had gone home, surely there would be tracks in the snow.

Just in case he was wrong, he went up to the front door and rang the bell. After ringing it a couple of more times, he began to pound the door with a fist. "Come on, Lea, wake up if you're in there."

When he didn't get an answer, he tried the knob. Lea had a habit of never locking her door. When the door opened, he almost felt a sense of relief. It quickly vanished after he called out Lea's name a number of times and there was no response. He turned on the foyer light and made his way through the rooms. After he checked the upstairs, he returned to the foyer. Lea wasn't home. The house was empty.

He let himself out and slammed the door behind him. The wind was picking up. Fighting more gusts, he was grateful to be wearing his winter jacket as he ran across the yard to Margaret's property. He took the porch stairs more slowly, trying to catch his breath. He let himself into Margaret's house without ringing or knocking. As they became close friends, they'd dropped those formalities. "Margaret? Where are you?"

Margaret came down the steps almost immediately. "Paul, did you find her?"

Paul shook his head. "No, she's not at home. Maybe we better call Matthew. I'm sure he'll want to know his wife is missing."

Margaret reached out for Paul's arm. "Maybe that's where she is. Maybe she wanted to make up with Matthew."

"Maybe, but her SUV is still in the garage."

Margaret turned and hurried to a desk in the living room. Grabbing the phone, she tried to connect with the clinic. It kept ringing, but no one answered.

Paul was already headed out the door. "I'll get Ned, and we'll drive over there."

"I should come too," Margaret called after him.

"No, stay here in case Lea contacts you."

"I don't think that's going to happen," Margaret said in a teary voice.

Paul gave her a final glance. "Please, Margaret, I have to get back to Ned and go to the clinic. I'll let you know what's happening the minute I know."

Twelve

MATTHEW KNEW HE must be dreaming, and it was a wonderful dream. He was on a beach, basking in the sun. Everything was peaceful until a persistent ringing joined the sound of waves and seagulls overhead.

"Matthew, is that a phone?" Eric called out in a drowsy voice.

Matthew rubbed his eyes and forced himself awake. "A phone? Maybe."

Eric switched on a light mounted over his bed and propped himself up on an elbow. "It must be located in another part of the clinic. Someone could be in trouble."

Matthew felt too tired to move. "The ringing's stopped. I guess they'll have to call back." He looked at the little clock on the side table. "Great, we just got to sleep."

Eric got up and headed for the door. "I'll check Ned's room. I'm sure he has a phone in there. Someone might have left a message."

Matthew rubbed his eyes again, remembering his dream. It reminded him of the honeymoon that he and Lea had spent in Kauai. They'd never been happier. Lea found ways to make him laugh, and he found ways to show her how special she was. They were inseparable, sharing everything with a freedom neither knew existed. Reflecting on those two weeks, Matthew couldn't understand how things had changed so drastically. Before he had time to think about how much he missed Lea, Eric returned to the room.

"Matthew, my mom's number was on the caller ID. I phoned her back and—"

"Yes, spit it out," Matthew demanded in a brusque tone. He didn't want to discuss phone conversations. He wanted to go back to sleep and dream about the beach and Lea.

Eric approached Matthew's bed. "I'm sorry, but I have some upsetting news. No one can find Lea. She's missing."

Matthew sat up and glared back. "Missing? Elkville isn't big enough for someone to go missing. Is her car gone?"

"I don't know. Mom said that Paul and Ned are on their way over. We can talk to them when they get here." Eric averted his eyes. "There's one more thing. Mom found Lea's coat hanging in the hall."

"What are you talking about?" Matthew was trying his best to think clearly, but Eric's statement didn't compute.

Eric continued. "Mom is afraid that Lea is out in this weather—"

"And she's not wearing a coat? That's nuts. A person would have to be crazy to be outside without some protection."

As soon as he spat out the words, Matthew had a sinking feeling in the pit of his stomach. Lea's behavior had been steadily getting more and more erratic. He'd made the assumption that she'd fallen out of love with him. He'd never considered another possibility that she was relapsing into a state of emotional turmoil. He got out of bed and grabbed his clothes off a chair. "Oh hell, maybe that's it. Maybe Lea's gone haywire again."

Eric was getting dressed too. "That makes sense. At times, she hasn't been quite the same sweet person she used to be. When we talk on the phone, she's been distant, even curt and aloof at times."

Matthew fumbled with the buttons on his shirt. "I've been an idiot not to see what was happening. Like you said, instead of paying attention, I played the injured party. All the while, Lea was losing touch with the person she really is, the person I married."

* * *

Margaret had been assigned a duty. She was to take care of Duke. Before Paul drove back to the clinic with Ned, he explained that the dog might have to go out while he was away. Since Paul couldn't take the time to walk him, Margaret agreed to take over the job. But caring for a dog was a first for her. Perhaps it was because of her upbringing. Pets weren't a part of her childhood. After she married Ricky, neither of them saw a reason to have a dog or cat.

As a young boy, Eric had once begged his parents to take in a stray puppy he'd found, but his father flatly refused. Ricky's excuse was that they didn't have money to waste on a pet. Eric was heartbroken, but Margaret put aside his grief just like she put most unpleasantries aside.

Pain was part of life. But at least she could be proud of her husband's efforts to alleviate some of it. He did his part to ease its grip on people's lives, and she put any extra energy she had in to helping him.

After all those years of no pets, Margaret found it strange that she was babysitting one. Duke was lying on the special, throw rug that she'd put down for him. She couldn't abide dog hair getting scattered everywhere. She'd made sure that Paul knew he'd have rules to follow when he brought the dog to her house. Afterwards, when Paul took the dog home, Margaret made sure to take the rug outside and give it a good shaking. When she saw all the hair flying off in the breeze, she'd think about how foolish it was for Paul to have an animal that simply added more work to a person's day.

Margaret looked at her canine house guest and felt a little resentful. She was busy worrying about a lost daughter. She didn't have time to take care of Duke. But that wasn't fair to the animal. He was depending on her for a chance to use the outdoor facilities. She forced herself out of her seat and went to get his leash.

She was about to reach for it when she saw Lea's coat on an adjoining hanger. She removed the jacket from its hook and held it close. She could smell Lea's perfume on the collar and inhaled deeply. She prayed that the men would quickly find Lea and bring her home.

She wasn't the only one attentive to Lea's coat. Duke had come over and was nosing the garment like he often nosed Paul's jacket.

Margaret stared down at him. "You like her too, don't you, Duke?"

Duke became more animated and let out a little whine. Seeing his enthusiastic response, Margaret put out her hand and carefully stroked his head. When their eyes connected, Margaret knew she'd never seen a more open, friendly expression than the one Duke was wearing. It was almost as if he was smiling at her. In that moment, her feelings towards the dog softened a little. He couldn't help that he depended on her. If she thought about what the dog had gone through before Paul found him, she felt even more impressed by the dog's forgiving nature. "After someone starved you and shot you, you're still so ready to give people another chance."

Duke reacted by nosing Lea's coat again and then looked at the door. Margaret stared at the door too. She wanted so much to do something to help locate Lea, and it was almost as if the dog wanted the same thing. It sparked an idea. She'd seen police dogs on the news tracking people. Could Duke accomplish such a task? She stared down at him again. "Do you want to give it a try, Duke? Can you help me find Lea?"

Duke let out a soft bark. His eagerness gave Margaret hope. She quickly slipped on her coat, hat, gloves and boots. She also remembered to put a flashlight in one of the deep pockets of her jacket. After she attached Duke's leash to his collar, she threw Lea's coat over her shoulder, opened the door and stepped out of the house. Duke, being the well-trained dog that Paul taught him to be, waited on the porch for Margaret to take the lead. Instead, she crouched down and presented Lea's coat for Duke to sniff again. After a quick inhale, Duke looked up for further instruction. Margaret pointed towards the street. "Find Lea, Duke! Find my sweet girl!"

Duke was ready for the challenge. Once down the stairs, he used his nose to investigate the snowy driveway. He moved faster when he got to the street. Margaret had to practically run to keep up with him. The snow and wind made the going harder, but neither woman nor beast was thinking about the weather. They were on a mission to find a loved one. It didn't take long for Duke to reach the end of Margaret's street. He continued his excited pace as they traveled the road that led out of town.

As the houses were left behind, tall, majestic trees lined the road they were on. The moon peeked from behind the clouds and swirls of snowflakes danced in the light. In spite of her worries about Lea, Margaret couldn't help but think about how beautiful the natural world could be. After her husband died, it had been her source of comfort. In the winter, she often walked at night. The darkness and deep stillness of the area helped her grieving heart forget itself for a bit.

But she wouldn't let herself imagine losing Lea. Instead, she focused on staying upright on the snowy road as Duke continued pulling her forward. With the wind buffeting her body and trying to snatch her breath away, she almost slipped a couple of times. But she had faith that Duke was on Lea's trail. When he slowed to a walk and began sniffing the shoulder of the road, she felt a glimmer of hope. "What is it, Duke? Did you find something?"

Duke pranced up and down the side of the culvert and answered her with happy yelps. Margaret got her flashlight out and edged as close as she could to the drop off. She searched the area, sweeping the light back and forth over the brush below her. A slight movement caught her eye. Targeting the flashlight's beam, she let out a little gasp. "Lea, is that you?"

Something stirred beneath the light. When Margaret called out a second time, a face looked up, blinking back with wide, frightened eyes. Margaret could hardly contain her relief. "Oh, thank goodness."

She was trying to decide what to do next when she saw headlights coming towards her. Moments later, Paul's truck pulled up alongside. As soon as the vehicle came to a stop, the passenger door opened and Matthew was immediately on the ground.

"Did you find her?" he asked. His anxious voice was loud and demanding as he came over to where she stood.

Margaret nodded and pointed to where her light was directed.

Matthew didn't hesitate. He started down the snowy drop off. Fortunately, it wasn't very steep. Once he was standing next to Lea, Matthew stripped off his coat and put it around her shoulders. He held it in place as he crouched down next to her.

Ned, Eric and Paul were soon out of the truck too. Everyone stared down at the two people in the ditch. Ned had brought along his own light. Its powerful illumination added to Margaret's weak beam. Like Matthew, Eric quickly took action. He half slid down the incline to join the couple.

The rescue effort went well after that with Ned remaining only part way down the incline. He seemed to know what to do and spoke in a steady-she-goes, but assertive tone. Matthew and Eric became the lower level crew, carrying out Ned's orders. After Matthew helped Lea to stand, both he and Eric supported her and helped her to navigate halfway up the incline. From there, Ned was able to get her up to the road.

Margaret remained next to Paul, watching it all. She was impressed with how quickly things were resolved. Lea was soon in the truck and being ferried back to warmth and safety. She and Paul had elected to return on foot with Duke leading the way.

As they walked side by side, Margaret liked Paul being there. It gave her a chance to talk to someone who knew a lot about people's physical and emotional states. "Thank goodness, Lea doesn't seem to be too bad off. I'm sure she's half frozen, but when she looked at me, she seemed to know me."

Paul continued at a brisk pace. "She has three fine doctors there for her. I think she'll recover very nicely."

Margaret stopped and grabbed for his arm. "You're worried about her, aren't you?"

Paul shook his head. "My opinion doesn't matter."

"What do you mean? After all those years of being a successful—"

"Those years are behind me," he said flatly.

"How can you say that? You have so much knowledge and experience."

"I'm retired. Don't you know what that means?" Paul asked.

"No, I guess I don't."

"It means I've stopped doing what I used to do. Now, let's change the subject. Tell me how you found Lea."

Margaret smiled and looked at Duke. "I didn't find her. Your dog found her."

Paul's eyes flashed a brighter blue, and he went over to where Duke was standing a few feet away. "Did you hear that, Duke my boy? You're a hero."

Margaret joined them and stroked Duke's head. As she did, she felt a slight tremor in his body. "We better get him home, Paul. I think he's cold."

Paul started walking again. "He's old, like me. He can't take the weather like he once could. When we get home, I'll put him to bed and keep him warm."

They didn't talk the rest of the way back. Margaret used the silence to reminisce. During a very difficult situation at the Ferguson mansion, Paul was supposed to come to the rescue. After all his efforts ended in failure, he became very depressed. She also remembered her part in the whole affair. She'd taken her anger out on Paul. She'd done that same thing earlier that day. She regretted both occasions. She could only hope to make it up to him, to let him know he was appreciated. But glancing at Paul's face and seeing the hard set of his jaw and his furrowed brow, it might be quite the task.

Thirteen

ERIC AND NED SAT in Matthew and Lea's living room. With Matthew tending to Lea, they were waiting to make sure she was alright. Eric drummed his fingers on the arm of his chair and glanced around at his surroundings. He appreciated the Howell residence. It had all the modern conveniences so much of Elkville lacked. Even though it had been built on a small lot, the two-story house had sufficient space. The lower level had a generous living room, a large kitchen, a decent size dining area and a half bath. The upstairs had three bedrooms, a full bath and a master bath. All in all, it was the newest and nicest house in Elkville. With the improvements that Paul had made, his home was the second nicest.

Eric wished his mother would allow him to fully update her residence. Most of its rooms still had old wallpaper and worn carpeting. But Margaret insisted that she was fine with the house as it was.

Eric had come to the conclusion that his mother was a very, stubborn woman. He hadn't realized just how stubborn she was until his father died. He'd been so busy dealing with his dad's willfulness that he didn't notice much else.

Eric's father refused to take heed when Eric warned him about his health. He'd been a difficult man right up to the end. Just thinking about it could still make Eric's stomach knot up. But the past was past. He shook off the feeling and turned his attention to Ned Finney. "Thanks for putting Matthew and I up at the clinic, Ned."

Ned looked up from the magazine he was paging through. "Will you be coming back tonight?"

"No, my mom is insisting on me staying with her. I think this incident with Lea has shaken her a bit."

"About Lea, I mean Mrs. Howell, what do you think made her run off like that? She seemed fine whenever we've talked."

"I guess you've talked quite a bit since she's very involved with the clinic."

"Yes, it was always about the clinic, the finances and that sort of thing. I've never gotten to know her personally. Maybe you could clue me in."

"I don't think Lea's personal life is any of your business."

"It will be if you or Matthew aren't around, and she gets upset again. I know that she has Paul and Margaret, but if she does something and hurts herself—"

Eric didn't want to think about Lea hurting herself. But Ned had a point. "I got acquainted with Lea when I hit her with my car." He paused, waiting for a reaction from Ned, but the younger man didn't say anything. Eric cleared his throat and continued. "It was a rainy night, and she ran out into the street. I couldn't stop in time. Lea wasn't badly hurt except for one problem. We've never understood why, but she lost her memories, and they've never come back."

"Your mom and Lea seem very close."

"With no identification and no memories, Lea had no one we could contact. She became part of our family. The sister I never had, and the daughter that Mom always wanted. Over time, as Lea accepted a life without a past she could recall, she made peace with herself. Things were going well until her father traced her whereabouts. It was only natural that Lea's parents and Matthew wanted to take her home."

Ned's brows edged up. "What happened?"

"Things didn't go well. Lea wasn't the same person she'd been when she was engaged to Matthew. She didn't even recognize him when he came to Baltimore. Matthew was overwhelmed by it all. After losing the woman he loved and finally locating her, he was shocked when she didn't want to go back to Chicago with him or her parents. Sometime later, they reconciled and were happy, but only after some very traumatic events."

"The events you talked about earlier this evening, the things that Paul was involved in?"

"Yes, that's right."

"So do you have any idea about what caused her to suddenly go walking in the snow tonight?"

"No, but we both saw her when we got her out of that ditch."

Ned put his magazine aside. "She looked traumatized," he said quietly.

The sound of footsteps on the stairs interrupted their conversation. Matthew came walking into the living room.

Ned and Eric both stood up.

"How is she?" Eric asked.

Matthew's shoulders relaxed a little. "She's better."

"That's a relief," Eric said.

"Yes, it is," Ned said as he walked to the small foyer and grabbed his coat. "If you need anything, I'll be at the clinic."

Matthew walked over and stuck out his hand. "Thanks for your help, Finney."

"You bet," Ned said as he gave Matthew's hand a firm shake. After that, he turned and quickly let himself out the door.

Eric stared after him. "Ned seems to be in a hurry."

"Maybe he knows not to wear out his welcome."

"Matthew, you're not jealous, are you? Because there's no way that you have to worry about Lea."

"I guess not, but there's something about Finney that feels off."

"How so?"

Matthew rubbed his temples. "Forget it. It's late. Go home and get some sleep."

* * *

Ned left Lea and Matthew's house and climbed into his truck. When his thoughts kept going back to Lea's past, he forced himself to ignore them. That information belonged in a patient file, one that he could refer to if Lea ever came under his medical care.

Lea Howell had to remain an acquaintance or at most, a friend. He couldn't let his attraction for the beautiful, petite brunette ever blossom into anything more. Lea was a married woman. Any romantic ideas about her could not be entertained.

He was doing very well with managing his feelings earlier that evening. After being invited to dine with Paul, he'd gone into Margaret's kitchen to tell Lea about the new arrangement. After he delivered his message, he was ready to turn and leave. Lea didn't let that happen. She took hold of his hand and smiled. She told him how wonderful he was in rescuing Matthew and Eric. It was an embarrassing moment that was even more awkward when he had to be the one who pulled his hand away.

It was the story of his life. He had to be the one who always put on the brakes. It was as if everyone else had permission to say or do what they wanted. Lea could smile and grab his hand. Matthew could yell out whatever he wanted to yell out. But for Ned, it wasn't like that. He was the one who had to ignore his feelings and never, never act on them.

His father had sat him down and told him why it was the right thing to do. Feelings didn't mean anything. They were like the sound of a tea kettle whistling. They were there to tell you that the water in the pot was boiling. So a person simply turned off the flame. They weren't troubled about the sound or thinking something was wrong. They took the kettle off the burner.

Growing up, Ned sometimes poured out his childish feelings to his father. How he was mad at the kid at school who bullied him. How a teacher had reprimanded him unfairly. His father never rushed his complaints. He sat and listened. He'd tell Ned his feelings were normal. He'd explain they were also useless, to dismiss them like he'd dismiss a wasp at a picnic.

John Finney walked his talk. He was even tempered and calm. He only let his feelings matter one time. Ned's mom ran off with another man, and Ned's dad fell apart. Later, as he slowly tried to put his life back together, the story of an unfaithful wife became a powerful example of why a person didn't let his feelings matter.

Ned would always remember the day his father came into his room to apologize. Ned was eight years old.

"I haven't been much of a father lately. I've been short with you, and I haven't given you the time you deserve. Your mother is gone, but we are both going to go on with our lives, living them with courage and determination."

Ned took the opportunity to question why life had taken his mother from him. Wasn't he a good enough son? Wasn't his father a good enough husband?

John Finney didn't answer at first. He went to the window and stared out for a long time. When he eventually came back to where Ned was sitting on the bed, he let out a heavy sigh.

"Your mother leaving has nothing to do with your goodness, Ned. She simply let her feelings matter so much that she thought she needed a different life. Do you understand?"

Ned didn't understand, but he nodded anyway. He had to, for his father's sake. He couldn't disappoint someone he looked up to. And more importantly, he couldn't do anything that might jeopardize his bond with his father. Ned didn't have anyone else.

All the hurt of his mother running off, all that pain had to be stuffed away. All the tears he'd shed at bedtime when there was no mother to tell him goodnight, all those tears had to be dried. The kettle had whistled, his mom had run off, and now his father said it was time to go on with their lives.

Ned did his best to do just that. But sometimes his feelings got the better of him. He didn't know if he had the strength needed to simply take the kettle off the flame. Those were the times he threw himself into his work. He took on extra shifts in the ER. He ran for miles and worked out. And yet, as hard as he tried, the feelings were always there.

Recently, they'd centered themselves around Lea Howell. But after seeing Lea looking so forlorn in Matthew's arms, the attraction was waning. If he had to deal with an emotionally troubled individual, he didn't think he'd be able to manage it. He had enough to do keeping himself straight.

Still, he'd probably fall for someone else eventually. According to his father, desire for what you couldn't have was just another feeling. For Ned, it was something he wished he could banish. His life would be so much simpler if he didn't have to deal with his desires.

* * *

After testing the icy waters of an insane moment, Lea was back home. Her bed was soft, and the room was toasty. The best thing of all was Matthew holding her. His warmth had helped her body to stop shaking and her teeth to stop chattering. Even her mental numbness had begun to thaw. She'd come back to herself, not completely, but at least her heart could connect to Matthew again.

She leaned into his shoulder. "I'm so sorry. I didn't realize what was happening to me."

Matthew pushed aside a stray bit of hair from her eyes. "I'm sorry I wasn't there for you. Instead of trying to understand what you were going through, I thought I didn't matter anymore."

Lea put her hand on Matthew's broad chest. She needed to feel the strong, steady beat of his heart. She needed to feel the strength housed in the vessel. She hoped it would help her when she confessed one of her deepest fears. "I'm scared it could happen again, Matthew. I'm scared of who I am."

Matthew pulled her a little closer. "We'll find a way through whatever is frightening you."

"Are you sure? Maybe I'm possessed. Maybe that horrible person I once was will destroy everything we have."

"That's not going to happen."

"How can you be sure? Tonight, when I thought about what I'd been doing, how I've been driving you away, it was such a shock that I lost it. I just started walking. I didn't know what else to do."

"When I found out you were missing—"

"That's just it. I keep scaring you. I'm sure I scared Margaret and Eric too. But I don't want to do that."

"We're a team, Lea. This is something we can work out together."

"I don't understand why you still care. You've been through so much already."

"None of that has anything to do with who you are. The real you is loving and beautiful, but you have to believe that."

"You don't know what it's like when the other me takes over. She's so cold and unfeeling. I think she wants to hurt you." As soon as she said it, her body started shaking again.

Matthew gently rocked her back and forth. "Don't try to figure that out now. You're exhausted. You have to rest."

"I'm afraid to go to sleep. What if I wake up, and you're gone? I couldn't blame you for saving yourself if you came to your senses and left."

"I'm not going anywhere. I'm staying right here with the person I almost lost."

Lea paused and stared up at him. "I never asked, but how did you get those scratches on your face?"

Matthew smiled. "Let's just say that me and that mountain outside had a go, but I'm fine. And I have you. That's all I care about."

Fourteen

TERESA WOKE UP early on the day of her trip. She'd had a good night's sleep and was on the road before the morning rush hour. It was a beautiful day to be traveling, and her rented Toyota SUV was a dream to drive. It also had a good sound system. All she had to do was sit back, listen to tunes on the radio and watch the miles slip by. She couldn't believe how much she was enjoying herself. It had been a long times since she felt so free and relaxed.

A high point of the morning was stopping by a diner for breakfast. The food was good, the service cheerful and she liked the diner's retro look. With black and white tiled flooring, red booth seating, and vintage Coca Cola signs on the walls, the quaint diner made Teresa feel like she'd leap-frogged back in time.

After a leisurely meal, she went to the ladies room and had a pleasant surprise waiting for her. Stopping in front of a full length mirror, she noted that her smile was open and carefree. Most of the time, she wore a serious expression. It came with her job and the stresses of caring for people who depended on her.

But she was on vacation now. It was a liberating thought that prompted her to remove her hair tie. Shaking out her shiny, thick, red locks, she was pleased with the way her hair cascaded past her shoulders. It made her feel lighter and younger. Her sun glasses added a finishing touch that was bold and exciting. She didn't know if it was a good thing, but a bit of her teenage wild side stared back at her.

When she got back on the road, she was in a cheerful mood. As the miles rolled by and her cares were left behind, she felt like she was at the beginning of a wonderful adventure.

Her spirits were slightly dampened when Eric called. He acted as if all was fine, but she sensed an underlying anxiety. When she asked him if everything was okay, she found out that Lea had had a bad moment the night before. Without going into details, Eric said they could discuss it later. Teresa kept the call very short. She didn't want Eric noticing how happy she was. She wanted to surprise him when she pulled up in front of his mother's house.

After five hours of driving, she reached Blacksburg, Virginia. It wouldn't be long before she'd be traveling the mountain roads to her destination. After she pulled into a gas station and filled up the tank, she purchased a few snacks at the station's convenience store. Before she went any further, she needed to check the weather forecast. Hopefully, the entire area would be blessed with a continued warming spell.

She took out her phone to check the weather app and sighed. Her phone battery was dead. She'd been having battery problems the last couple of weeks, but she hadn't had time to have the phone checked out. She'd have to ask around about the conditions of the mountain roads. She might have to stay the night in Blacksburg. But first, she'd find a phone she could use and call Eric. She didn't want him to do what he often did, worry excessively.

Fifteen

ERIC SAT AT the kitchen table, ignoring the sandwich his mother had placed in front of him. How could he eat when he was sure something was wrong? When he talked to Teresa, she wasn't herself. It was almost as if she barely had five minutes for him. She'd never acted like that before. But there was more to it. He had a pain in his gut that told him to be on the lookout for danger.

"Aren't you hungry, Eric?" Margaret asked as she brought over a pitcher of ice tea.

Eric pushed his plate away. "It's Teresa. I'm worried about her."

Margaret sat down and stared at him with probing eyes. "I thought you said you talked to her a couple of hours ago. Did she say something was wrong?"

Eric got up and went to the back door. "No, but that doesn't mean anything." He paused, trying to control his rising anxiety.

"What's going on?" his mother asked.

"You know I get these premonitions."

"What about them?"

Eric braced himself against the door frame. Trying to explain his intuition to someone was like trying to describe what air felt like when you caressed it with your hands. "Please, Mom, not now."

"Has everything been alright with you and Teresa?"

Eric turned and stared back. "Yes, of course. Why would you ask me that?"

"Because last night, before Lea ran off, she told me that she and Matthew had been having a lot of quarrels. I didn't have any idea about their problems."

"Matthew mentioned the same thing when we were driving here."

"That's such a shame," Margaret said.

Eric turned and looked out the back door window again. He was distracted from his concerns by the back yard. After the snow melted, the grass would start growing. Once it did, it could get out of hand very quickly. In the past, he'd tried to give his mother money to hire someone for the job, but she always found better uses for what he gave her. The thought of coming back to knee-high weeds was just another reason why he was irritated with Elkville.

"Eric, maybe you're still upset over what happened yesterday, and that's why you're having these feelings. Why don't you try to call Teresa again?"

Eric returned to the kitchen table. "You might be right. I didn't sleep very well last night. I'm sorry for being in a foul mood."

"Yesterday was terrible for all of us. First, I was worried about you and Matthew's safety, then Lea, and finally Paul."

"What's Paul's problem? I thought he loved it here."

"Now that the clinic is finished, I don't think he feels very needed." Margaret blushed. "I was short with him when he tried to talk to me."

"So was I, but he can be so darn irritating."

"What do you mean?"

"He can't just be a friend. I feel like he constantly wants to put me on his couch."

"Not anymore. Last night he essentially told me he felt old and useless."

"Great, I hope we don't have to start worrying about him doing himself in. Thank goodness Matthew was there to talk some sense into him the last time he acted all weird."

"Eric, are you going to hold on to your resentment of Paul forever?"

"Am I supposed to forget that he nearly sent us all to the looney bin when we were at the Ferguson mansion?"

"He meant well, I'm sure."

Eric headed out of the room. "Let's not talk about it. I'm going to call Teresa."

"Tell her that I send my love," Margaret called after him.

Eric picked up the landline phone in the living room and tried to connect with Teresa's cell. He waited and listened, but his call never went through. He made more calls hoping to locate her at her Baltimore office or the hospital where she worked. The results were distressing. Teresa wasn't where she was supposed to be. His wife had handed over both her patients and his to some colleagues. Just as he was hanging up with one of them, Margaret came into the living room.

"Did you get hold of her?" his mother asked.

"No, I've been told she's on vacation. Her friend, Joan Whittaker, is helping Teresa out by looking after her patients."

"I don't understand."

"I don't either. I only know what Teresa told Joan. She explained that she was going to visit family, and that she was looking forward to the drive to Elkville."

"Teresa's coming here?" Margaret asked with excitement.

"Yes, and that's a problem. I don't want her driving on those mountain roads."

The phone rang before Eric could decide what to do next. He picked it up, hoping that it might be Teresa. When he heard her voice, he relaxed a little. "Teresa, where are you? Are you alright?"

Teresa's answer wasn't one Eric wanted to hear. His voice went up in volume when he replied. "What? You're in Blacksburg? At a motel? What motel? What's your room number?"

While Teresa related her plans and information, Eric held his breath. He imagined the worst. What if her car went off the side of the mountain like the SUV he'd been driving? What if she died, and he lost the woman he loved with all his heart? As his fears played out, Teresa was cheerfully telling him about the nice motel she was in and how she was looking forward to her drive to Elkville the next morning.

Eric managed a response. "No, you can't come here! Go back to Baltimore."

His orders weren't well received. Teresa began to get irritated, and she insisted she wanted to see him. Eric couldn't stop the panic that grabbed hold. He wasn't one to raise his voice, but his words came out in a loud, demanding way. "You're being completely unreasonable, Teresa! Just do what I'm asking!" As soon as he issued the statement, Teresa's end of the conversation went dead.

Eric turned to his mother. "I can't believe it. She hung up on me."

"Can you blame her? You should have heard the tone you took. If I didn't know better, I'd think I was listening to your dad when he was shouting at someone."

It was the last thing Eric wanted to be told. "Thanks a lot, Mom. Now, I'm turning into my father." But he couldn't worry about his performance. He had to do something before his wife had an accident.

He went to the hall and grabbed his jacket. "I'm going next door. I have to speak to Matthew."

* * *

Matthew was quite proud of himself. He'd fixed a very nice brunch for Lea. His egg omelet had included shredded cheese, sautéed onions, and bell pepper. It was topped off with a dollop of sour cream and herbs. He'd never been much of a cook, but he'd been doing some practicing in Chicago. He decided he'd help out with the food preparation when Lea was busy studying.

His efforts had paid off. Lea seemed to like her meal. Recently, she'd become a picky eater, but she ate almost everything he'd put on her plate. Afterwards, she smiled and told him she was satisfied and sleepy. Matthew was happy that she was relaxed enough to catch a few more winks. When she went upstairs to nap, Matthew decided to clean up the kitchen.

He started by putting the dishes in the dishwasher. It was probably the only dishwasher in Elkville except for the one in the clinic's kitchen. It was a nice convenience.

Matthew had never wanted to own a home in Elkville, but he had to admit he was beginning to like the one Raymond had built. All the kitchen appliances were top of the line. In fact, he had more to work with than he had in his apartment in Chicago. Hopefully, he and Lea would someday buy a house in the suburbs of the city. But first, they needed to restore some balance and stability in their relationship.

A forceful knocking on the front door made Matthew grab for a dish towel and wipe his hands as he went to answer it. The day had begun so nicely with Lea snug in his bed. He hoped nothing would spoil the mood. He opened the door and found Eric waiting on the small front porch. Matthew didn't get a chance to greet him or to invite him in. Eric started talking as soon as the door opened.

"I need to borrow your car," Eric blurted out. His voice was forceful and insistent. "I have to drive to Blacksburg and stop Teresa from ending up in an accident."

Matthew stared back. "Could you slow down?"

"I need your car!"

Matthew noted Eric's intense eyes. When the guy panicked, he looked like he was ready to go into battle. "Come in and tell me why you think your wife is in danger."

Eric didn't move from where he was standing. "I don't have time. Just loan me your car, okay?"

Matthew grabbed Eric's arm and pulled him inside. "Eric, you have to calm down. I don't know about Teresa's problem, but you'll do yourself in if you go off in your condition."

Eric yanked his arm away. "Never mind. I'll borrow Paul's truck."

Matthew blocked the door and crossed his arms. "You're not going anywhere unless you talk to me."

Eric took in a breath and scowled back. "Teresa called from Blacksburg. She wants to join me in Elkville and plans to drive here tomorrow. I can't let her do that."

"Why? A lot of the snow is already melting. By tomorrow, the mountain roads will probably be fine."

"You don't understand. I have this terrible feeling about Teresa's safety."

"Is this one of those eerie hunches you get?"

"Yes."

"How accurate are they? Do they always come true?"

Eric shook his head. "No, but I can't take a chance."

Matthew knew it was no use trying to change Eric's mind when he got an idea stuck in his craw. "Alright, but you're not driving down that mountain. I'll call Ned Finney and ask him to take you."

Eric's frown eased a little. "I guess that's reasonable. I know where Teresa's staying."

* * *

Lea had barely closed her eyes when she heard the sound of someone's raised voice. She was sure it belonged to Eric. She got out of bed, concerned that there might be something wrong with Margaret. Thankfully, she felt more herself. After a restful night with Matthew next to her, she had renewed hope that together they'd work things out.

She quickly slipped out of her pajamas and put on jeans and a charcoal grey sweatshirt with the Chicago skyline on the front. It was a favorite of Matthew's as far as sweatshirts went. She hurried downstairs, but by the time she reached the lower level, Eric was gone. She walked into the kitchen and saw Matthew wiping down the counters. She went over to him and tapped his shoulder. "Thank you for a delicious omelet."

Matthew turned and smiled. "I thought you were still sleepy."

"I guess I wasn't as sleepy as I thought I was, especially when I started thinking about you."

"What were you thinking?"

"Remember our honeymoon? How we spent so much time in bed?"

Matthew's eyes lit up. "I do remember."

"We could have a mini honeymoon here. What do you think?"

Matthew threw his dish cloth aside. "I think you're right."

Lea took his hand and pulled him towards the stairs. "Then follow me, Doctor Howell. We have some catching up to do." Halfway there, she paused. "By the way, did I hear Eric's voice?"

"Yes, he stopped over. He's convinced himself that he should check on Teresa."

"But Teresa is in Baltimore."

"No, she drove to Blacksburg. Eric found out she plans on driving here tomorrow. He thinks the roads are still too dangerous."

"So what does he plan to do?"

"I called Ned Finney and arranged for Ned to get him to Blacksburg."

"And then?"

"I don't know. Eric didn't wait around to say anything more."

"Well, he's in good hands. Ned is very capable."

Matthew pulled her close. "About last night and what I said about Finney. I'm sorry, Lea. My comments were ridiculous."

Lea smiled. "I've already forgotten them."

* * *

If Ned was going to drive down the mountain, he wanted to be prepared. The snow was melting on the road, so he didn't think chains were necessary, but his snow tires seemed like a good idea. He only wished his passenger didn't look so uptight. "Matthew said something about how you had a feeling that you needed to check on your wife."

Eric sat in his seat, staring straight ahead. "Yes, that's right."

"Are we talking about intuition?"

"Why? Don't you believe in such a thing?"

"Feelings come and go all the time."

"So you think it's crazy that I'm doing this?" Eric asked.

"I think it's what you believe is true so you probably don't have a choice, but I stick to facts." After a long pause, Ned glanced at Eric again. "I have a question for you. Did you ever think about taking the clinic job in Elkville and carrying on what your father started?"

Eric laughed. "Not a chance. How about you? Did you want to follow in your father's footsteps?"

"My dad's a forest ranger. It's an okay job, but it's not for me."

"Do you get along with your father?"

Ned shrugged. "Sure, he's a great guy."

"You're lucky."

"Yes, I guess I am."

"So why did you decide to practice in Elkville?" Eric asked. "With your resume, you could have gotten a job just about anywhere."

"Maybe I like a challenge, something different than the norm."

"You came to the right place."

Ned gave Eric a confused look. "Like I said, it's been pretty quiet since I arrived."

"I hope that doesn't change while you're gone. Not with Matthew as a backup."

"He looks like he can handle himself."

"Oh, he can do that, but you don't want to listen to him complain if there's a problem. When he had to deliver Betsy Campbell's baby, I didn't think we'd ever hear the end of it afterwards."

"Was it a difficult birth?"

"No, not at all. But attending a hefty, mountain gal, squatting in the back of a filthy pickup truck freaked him out."

"Are we talking about Donny Campbell Jr.'s wife?"

"Yes, why do you ask?"

"She came to see me last week. She's due soon."

Eric let out a gasp. "Oh please, lord, don't make Matthew deliver that baby too."

Sixteen

TERESA UNLOCKED HER motel room and pushed open the door. With Eric's words still fresh and hurtful, she tossed her suitcase a few feet into the space, stomped inside and slammed the door shut. She couldn't believe her wonderful day had suddenly turned so dismal. She couldn't believe Eric could talk to her in such a harsh, demanding tone.

She was angry and wanted to cry at the same time. If she wasn't welcome in Elkville, maybe Eric wouldn't be welcome in her bed. The thought made her eyes fill with tears. She loved Eric more than she thought possible. She didn't want anything to come between them. But maybe she was kidding herself. Maybe something had already come between them, and she'd ignored the signs.

Eric had never been totally forthright about his life. He kept everything bottled up inside. He avoided any kind of communication that concerned his mother and father issues. On the other hand, he was totally involved with his mother. Being his wife was another matter. Teresa realized she came second when it came to Eric's priorities.

The day before, she'd been so concerned for his safety. It took all of her determination not to give into her fear. Eric seemed oblivious to that fact. He'd even forgotten to call her when he first got to Elkville.

She swiped a tear from her cheek and crossed her arms. "You know, Eric, you could have at least had Lea or Matthew call me. But why should I be surprised?"

Teresa rarely visited Elkville with Eric. She stayed behind in Baltimore and took care of his patients instead.

She sat down on the bed and fell back on the firm mattress. All the thoughts running through her head weren't helping. She was only getting more miserable. Her mood had shifted dramatically from earlier in the day. She'd been so happy during her trip to Blacksburg. So why was she letting Eric's behavior spoil all that? Was she supposed to

76

forsake her adventurous spirit because Eric was being a jerk? She didn't think so. At the same time, she didn't want to overreact.

She got up and undressed, determined to put aside her emotions. A hot shower would help. She walked to the bathroom and stopped in front of the mirror. When she saw a strikingly, beautiful woman staring back at her, she was surprised to think of herself in those terms. She'd believed in taking care of her body, but vanity wasn't something she entertained. There were so many things that were more important than her looks.

Before she met Eric, lots of guys had tried to tell her that she was gorgeous, but she'd dismissed them. She wasn't interested in their opinion or maybe she was too busy to have time for such frivolous advances. Had she been too quick to decide that the physical part of life wasn't that important?

She and Eric had an amazing connection in the bedroom, but she had never really let herself express that drive that she'd once felt. As a teenager, the desire to let go and break a few rules was just beneath the surface. Even so, she felt herself lucky when she was taught how to control her behavior. It could have gotten her into a lot of trouble.

The teacher who mentored her told her how to cultivate a better life. Teresa needed to throw away the outrageous clothes and surrender her defiant attitude. She needed to describe herself with new adjectives like studious and hard working. In other words, she needed to grow up and act like an adult.

She pulled the shower curtain back, turned on the spigots and adjusted the water temperature. When it felt just right, she stepped into the shower and stood under the cascading water. She welcomed its ability to soothe her emotions. She wanted it to blot out the talk she'd had with Eric.

After a long soak, some of her usual steadiness returned, and her anger began to fade. She toweled her hair and combed it out, all the while reminding herself of what she'd almost forgotten. No matter how fun it was to enjoy herself on a road trip, it was just a passing fancy.

Maybe, she had to forget putting her hair down and listening to music that aroused her sensual nature. She'd spent more than half of her life building a meaningful career. She'd met and married the man of her dreams. Surely those things were more important than a few minutes of feeling the unbridled side of her personality.

As for Eric's behavior, she was probably just indulging in self-pity. She was bringing up all of his faults instead of concentrating on how good and giving he was.

She picked up the pendant setting on the vanity and put it back on. She stared at the mirror, leaned in and looked at herself more closely. Completely nude except for the ruby pendant, she began to question the events that brought her to where she was. Her life began to replay in short clips, how she'd been a parentless child, how she'd trained to be a physician, how she'd fallen in love.

The most important part of it all was that she'd always had a sense of self. She was the one constant that she could depend on no matter what. Even if the going was hard, she managed to have faith in herself. The thoughts made her smile. She didn't have to give up anything. It was okay to be both the wild child and the responsible adult. Both were parts of who she was. Each had their place.

She lifted up her chin and shook out her long, thick, fiery-red hair. As a peaceful feeling took hold, she walked into the bedroom area and looked at the bed longingly. She'd been up very early to get on the road. The idea of sleep called to her. After a nap, she'd go out for a meal. She slipped under the covers and closed her eyes.

* * *

Eric found the trip down the mountain to be a completely different experience than the one he'd had the day before. Instead of being confronted by a raging blizzard, he could enjoy the warm, sunny day. Ned's relaxed attitude helped too. The man didn't go along with concepts like intuition, but Ned was so at ease at the wheel that he made the drive seem effortless.

By the time they got to Blacksburg, Eric was feeling better about everything. Perhaps he'd been wrong about his fears concerning Teresa's safety. Perhaps, like his mother suggested, he was still spooked by the previous day's events.

After Ned dropped Eric off at Teresa's motel, Ned continued on his way to refuel. They'd agreed to meet back at the motel a little later. Eric went in search of Teresa's room. He was getting excited about seeing his beautiful wife. She'd let him know that she wanted to be with him in Elkville. It was unexpected news. Eric couldn't understand why anyone would want to visit a place that was so run down and depressing. Not that Teresa had ever complained about the times she'd been there. But he'd assumed she was being her sweet, accommodating self when she claimed she was okay with the small settlement.

When Eric found Teresa's room, he was immediately nervous again. An apology was definitely in order after the way he'd behaved on the phone earlier. Thinking that he sounded like his father was a horrible and frustrating idea. He knocked on the door with hopes that Teresa could forgive him. When there was no answer, he knocked more forcefully a second time. "Teresa?"

Standing there, waiting and wondering what Teresa would say to him, he blurted out his feelings. "Teresa? I'm so sorry." He put a hand to the door and called out in his most sincere voice. "Can you forgive me?"

Finally, the door opened just a crack. "Eric? Is that you?"

Eric noted the sleepiness in Teresa's voice. "Did I wake you?"

The door opened a little wider, and Teresa peeked out, but most of her body was hidden by the door. "I must have been dead to the world," she mumbled.

Eric stood in place, wanting to get whatever was coming over with, sort of like an errant school boy who was standing outside the principal's office. "Can I come in?"

Instead of giving him an affirmative answer, Teresa hesitated. "Give me a minute," she said and closed the door again.

Eric's anxiety inched upwards. Teresa was usually so open, but that wasn't the case now. What was going on? Had he hurt her in a way that was so unacceptable that she wouldn't forgive him?

The door opened again before he had a chance to totally evaluate himself. He stepped into the room watchfully, not knowing quite how to go forward. He and Teresa had never had a serious quarrel. Was one brewing now? He hoped not.

Teresa walked over to the side of the bed, grabbed a pillow and held it in front of her. "Have you come here to make sure I return to Baltimore, Eric? Is that it?" she asked.

Eric didn't know how to answer her. It was like his wife had become someone he didn't quite recognize. Her voice was guarded, and she even looked different. Maybe it was her hair. He'd seen her with it down, but it had never been so free of any restraint. And her eyes had become bright and intense instead of soft and serene.

He approached her cautiously, like he would a wary deer he encountered in the woods. "Teresa, please, I don't want you to go anywhere."

Teresa squeezed the pillow even tighter. "That's not what you said when we talked. So if you don't want me to be a part of your family, just tell me now."

Her response made Eric step closer. "Is that what you think?"

"What else can I think? When you're with your mother in Elkville, it's like I don't exist."

Eric closed the distance between them and took hold of the pillow. He pulled it out of Teresa's grasp, threw it aside and took her hands. "You have it all wrong. I adore you. You're so perfect just as you are. I don't want that to change. But if you get mixed up with my family and Elkville, I'm afraid it might."

Teresa blinked back several times and finally lowered her eyes. "I want to believe that, but—"

"But I've hurt you, haven't I?"

Teresa lifted her gaze again. "Yes, you have. Whether you meant to or not, you've shut me out of your life."

Eric brought his hand up to caress Teresa's cheek. "Then that's got to change. Because it's the last thing I want."

Teresa gave him a tentative smile. "Are you sure you're ready to open up and let me in?"

Eric laughed. "I want that more than anything, but if you find some bats in my belfry, promise you won't go running for the hills."

"Is that what frightens you?"

"Of course. I grew up in a forgotten, desolate place with a father who didn't have a clue. What if I'm a chip off the old block and don't know it?"

Teresa's face brightened. "If I see any bats, I promise to let you know."

Eric took her hands again and stood back. "I meant it when I said you're perfect. But you're not only the most beautiful woman I've ever seen, you're sweet and open and always there when I need you. I don't understand why you picked me to be your husband."

Teresa gave him a sideways glance. "Hmm. Maybe you do have a few bats flying around."

Eric's body stiffened. "Really?"

"Come with me," Teresa said as she led him into the bathroom. She stopped in front of the mirror. "Tell me what you see."

"I see you, an exquisite example of the feminine, standing next to someone who can't get it together, who's lacking in everything that defines a strong, confident example of the masculine."

"So let me ask you a question. When did you last have your eyes checked?"

Eric shrugged, trying to come up with a date. "I don't remember exactly, maybe a year ago. But I don't know how my vision has anything to do with us standing here."

Teresa giggled. "Of course it does. You have a problem, Eric Lloyd. And I'm sorry, but you just asked me to tell you when I think something's wrong."

Eric swallowed hard. "Yes, I did, and I'll do what I promised. Fire away."

"Your ability to see clearly is compromised in the extreme. Because when I look in the mirror, I'm standing next to the only man who met my qualifications for a partner."

"What qualifications?"

"I wanted a man who's loving, generous, kind, compassionate and smart. You, Eric, get top marks in all those departments. I wasn't worried about my guy's looks, but, my goodness, check out the mirror, Eric. You're so handsome that I almost didn't want to go out with you."

"Why?"

"Because most extremely, handsome guys are in love with themselves. They don't have a lot of affection left over for a mate. That's not the case with you, thank goodness."

Eric felt his face redden. "I'm flattered."

"Now for the negatives."

"Can't we stop with the extremely handsome part?"

Teresa eyed him thoughtfully and smiled. "Eric, I love you, faults and all, but you asked me to be truthful. So here goes. I also wanted someone who's flexible, a person who's not so obstinate. Those you have to work on, not as a doctor, but as my husband."

Eric pulled back his shoulders. "You have quite a list. I'm relieved to know I'm only coming up short in a couple of departments."

"Oh, that reminds me. There is one item I forgot to mention. You excel in that one too," Teresa said as she began to unbutton her top. It was one of Eric's old shirts that she liked to sleep in.

Eric was too distracted to look at her. He was going over his shortcomings, wondering if he'd ever get top marks in all of Teresa's categories. He caught himself not paying attention and looked up. "I'm sorry, but I didn't catch that last thing you said."

"Eric Lloyd, you're quite irresistible in one area," Teresa teased as she let the shirt drop to the floor.

Eric's jaw dropped too. He'd been told not to stare, but he couldn't help it. If the Creator had beauty in mind when he made women, Teresa was the result. "You take my breath away," he finally gasped.

Teresa put her arms around his neck. "Do you know how happy I am that you're here with me?"

Eric grinned back. "Do you know how much I want to be here?" he asked as he leaned in to kiss her. His lips barely touched Teresa's when there was a knock at the door.

Teresa pulled away and glanced at the front of the motel room. "Who could that be?"

Eric turned with a scowl. "I'm sure that's Ned Finney. He was very accommodating when asked to drive me here."

"Then I better get dressed," Teresa said as she dashed to the outer room and rummaged through her open suitcase. She quickly gathered up some things and hurried back to the bathroom. "Let him in while I'm getting ready."

Eric bulked at the idea. "Couldn't I tell him to go away for a while?"

Teresa kissed his cheek. "I've heard very good things about him. It'll be nice to finally meet. In fact, let's all get a bite to eat. I'm starved."

Eric trudged out of the bathroom and closed the door behind him. "Fine, but he's just a nice guy with a good resume."

Teresa called back. "Great, I'll be out in a jiffy."

Seventeen

AN UPBEAT RESTAURANT was located a few blocks from Teresa's motel. It wasn't as quaint and charming as the diner where she'd had breakfast, but the people at the motel recommended its food.

Sitting in one of its booths, Teresa tried to pay attention to her honey garlic salmon and kept getting distracted by the two men who were dining with her. Eric and Ned were both extremely attractive. However, their eyes were particularly captivating.

Eric's were the palest of blues and had an other-worldly quality. Ned Finney's were a darker, grounded blue that twinkled back at her when he spoke. Eric's eyes could look distant, like he was counting stars. Ned's gaze flashed out a clear message that said, "I'm a child of the Earth, totally present and accounted for."

Teresa took a bite of her salmon and washed it down with a sip of ice tea. "So tell us about yourself, Ned."

Ned smiled. "Not much to tell. I grew up, decided to be a doctor and here I am. How about you?"

Teresa traced a finger over the condensation on her glass. "Similar story. I grew up, decided to be a doctor and here I am," she said and looked at Eric.

Eric didn't hesitate. "I grew up, my father decided I should be a doctor, and here I am."

"Are you saying you didn't want to be a doctor?" Ned asked.

"I never thought about it," Eric replied. "I simply did what I was supposed to do."

Ned's eyes turned curious. "Do you like being a physician?"

"I don't know anything else," Eric said.

Teresa put her fork down and patted her mouth with her napkin. "Eric, I know your father was someone who was very controlling, and that he expected you to be a doctor. Are you saying his wishes are still influencing your decision to continue doing what you do?"

Eric stared down at his salad and pushed a tomato around. "Matthew told me that when I was slightly delirious at the Ferguson mansion, I talked about working in a pet shop."

Ned let out a friendly laugh. "Pet shop? I suppose that would be much less stressful."

"But you're so good at what you do, and your patients love you," Teresa said.

Eric speared some lettuce. "Thank you, I'm glad I can be of service."

"My dad never asked anything of me," Ned said. "I was told to do whatever I wanted. Sometimes, when I was younger, I resented him for that."

"I understand," Teresa said. "I grew up in foster homes, and the people caring for me were nice for the most part. But they were usually too busy to do much when it came to taking a personal interest."

Eric reached out and put his hand over Teresa's. "Whatever they did or didn't do doesn't matter. You're the best."

Teresa blushed. "That's very sweet, but I wonder about us."

"In what way?" Ned asked.

"Do any of us know who we really are? When I was driving here, it's like I left behind the person I think of as myself. I felt so happy and free to be enjoying a day without any obligations."

Eric leaned back and stared wistfully into space. "Sounds so right to me."

"But can we trust those kinds of feelings?" Ned asked. "Feelings have no real meaning any more than the wind has meaning. We can't allow them to direct our lives."

Teresa hesitated. "But Ned, feelings are what connect us to one another. I think they're very important."

Ned gave her a smile you'd give a child. "Sorry, Teresa, but you might be giving them way too much importance," he said as he stood up. "Now, if you'll excuse me, I'm going to grab a beer at the bar. Do either of you want anything?"

Teresa shook her head. "No thanks."

"Nothing for me," Eric said.

After she was sure Ned was out of earshot, Teresa looked at Eric. "What do you think about what Ned just said?"

"He's completely full of it. That's what I think. But my father would probably have loved his philosophy."

Teresa met Eric's eyes and appreciated her husband more than ever. He might be a stargazer, but his core-strength resided in his giving, devoted heart. She wondered about Ned Finney's ability to connect in the same way. "Eric, no matter what your father did or said, you didn't let him destroy your ability to love, and for that I'm so grateful."

* * *

Ned made up an excuse to get away from Teresa and Eric. He quickly walked over to a dimmer lit area where the bar was located. After he took a seat, he told himself to calm down. He could handle emergencies of all kinds, and yet certain things could get to him. After the conversation he'd had with the couple, he felt too warm and his body was on edge. He couldn't blame anyone but himself. If he'd kept his mouth shut, all would be well. Instead, he had to share his thoughts about trust and feelings.

The bartender came over. "What can I get you?" he asked.

"Do you have non-alcoholic beer?"

"Sure. Anything in particular?"

Ned shrugged. "You choose something."

After the bartender left, Ned rubbed at the tightness in his chest. His anxiety was acting up. It was an old pattern. Whenever he tried to defend what had been drilled into him since he was a boy, his body became apprehensive. Even if his father was right about feelings being useless, Ned had to back off when it came to trying to convince anyone else of that fact.

He glanced over at Teresa and Eric. They were holding hands. Ned could understand how Eric could be completely taken with his wife. Lea Howell was a beauty, but even Lea Howell couldn't match Teresa's knockout looks. Teresa was one of the prettiest women Ned had ever seen.

After going over his bleak track record with the opposite sex, Ned had decided that he had to be content living alone. He tried, but he was never able to give the women he dated what they wanted. Eventually, he stopped asking women out. His decision to remain single was painful, but his emotional angst was just another feeling that he couldn't let bother him.

He looked up when the bartender brought over his drink. "Thanks."

"Are you okay?" the bartender asked.

"What do you mean?"

"You keep rubbing your chest. Do you need a doctor?"

Ned took out his wallet and tossed some bills on the counter. "I am a doctor, and I'm fine."

The bartender squinted back and snatched up the money. "Just saying, you look a little off."

Ned ignored the remark and got up with the mug of beer in hand. As he carried it back to the table, all he could think about was returning to Elkville and hoping that he was needed there. Activity was his ally, and he was tired of nothing going on.

Once he was seated at the table, he glanced at Eric. "Just wondering about your plans."

Teresa spoke up. "Eric and I are going back to Elkville in the morning. We'll take my rental car."

"Thank you for giving me a lift," Eric said. "I appreciate it."

Ned smiled. "See that, Eric, all is well. Your wife is fine, and your anxious feelings were for nothing."

"What's he mean, Eric?" Teresa asked. "Did you think something was going to happen to me?"

Eric squeezed her hand. "Why else would I have acted like a person who'd taken leave of his senses?"

Teresa hugged his arm. "I wish I'd known."

Eric gave her a slightly wounded look. "You hung up on me, my darling, but I don't blame you. I didn't sound very rational."

"That's why we have to stick with the facts," Ned said as he stood up. He pulled out his wallet. "But let me buy dinner."

Eric stood up too. "Put that wallet back in your pocket, Ned. This dinner is on us."

"Thank you," Ned said. He glanced at Teresa. "It was great getting to meet you, Teresa."

"I'm glad we had a chance to get to talk," Teresa said.

Ned began backing up. "Well, it's time for me to get going."

"You're not going to stay and drink your beer?" Teresa asked.

"No, I'm driving back to Elkville."

"Tonight?" Teresa asked.

Ned nodded. "I think I better. Eric claimed that Matthew would lose it if Betsy Campbell goes into labor. But about the beer, I haven't touched it, so you're welcome to it."

Teresa laughed. "Why not? I haven't had a beer in a long time."

Ned passed her the mug. "Enjoy."

Teresa took a sip. "Strange, but it doesn't taste like I remember beer tasting."

Ned smiled. "Sorry to disappoint you. It's non-alcoholic. When I was ordering it, I realized I was going to be driving soon. I'm not a big drinker so it seemed like a good idea."

Teresa took another sip. "It's rather pleasant."

Ned turned and started to leave.

"Be careful on the road, Ned," Eric cautioned. "Most of the snow is gone, but still."

Ned waved an acknowledgement as he walked through the restaurant. By the time he exited the eatery, an antsy feeling was taking hold. It had been quite a while since he'd interacted with so many people socially. In his last job, he was too busy to make any real friends. Since arriving in Elkville, he'd experienced the exact opposite. He'd had nothing to do but treat minor ailments. He'd had an overabundance of free time.

Paul and Margaret seemed determined to keep him distracted. They were the first to invite him into their little circle. He relaxed and turned off his brain around the two of them. He let himself enjoy the home-cooked meals and small talk. It didn't require more of him than he wanted to give to a social outing.

Now that circle was expanding with people closer in age. Teresa and Eric were very friendly, but they were a reminder that some people had found love and happiness. It was evident in how they acted around each other.

He paused in the parking lot, enjoying the fact that the overhead light was burned out. The darkness gave him a chance to come back to himself. He could be in the middle of external chaos and be fine as long as he didn't buy into what other people were feeling. As long as he stayed in that neutral place, nothing could touch him.

Maybe that's why he didn't want to be with someone like Teresa. Maybe he didn't want a woman smiling at him with adoring eyes like Teresa did with Eric. If he was with such a woman, and she found out how incapable he was of returning her feelings, she'd leave him. Maybe that was why his mother left. His father probably never gave her what she needed. The thoughts aggravated the tightness in his chest.

He took out his car keys. It was time to stop thinking and get moving. He was about to walk to his truck when he heard the sound of a car. Wheels squealed and loud music filled the air as the vehicle turned into the parking lot. Before he had a chance to react, its head lights filled the darkness with a sudden, glaring brilliance. Time, that thing that he'd had too much of, slowed enough for him to have an unwelcome thought. Like Lea Howell, he was a person standing in the way of an oncoming car. Brakes squealed just before he felt the impact.

Eighteen

ERIC AND TERESA followed Ned's lead. They decided to leave the restaurant and return to their motel. Eric had just paid the check at the cashier's stand when he heard a woman's panicked cry.

"Help! I hit someone with my car!"

For the slightest moment, Eric couldn't move. He was back to a time when he'd had the same terror in his voice when he'd hit Lea. Teresa moved past him and hurried over to the woman who'd shrieked out her problem.

Eric turned to the cashier. "Call 911!"

Teresa held the young woman's hands as she questioned her. "Where did it happen?"

As soon as Eric heard the words "parking lot," he sprinted to the door. Running to the parking area, he saw a vehicle in the middle of a lane. It had its head lights on, and music was blaring from the interior of the car. He ran to the front of the old Chevy and saw someone on the ground. Teresa was right behind him. They both got to the stricken person at almost the same time.

"Oh my gosh, it's Ned," Teresa cried out.

Ned was trying to get up. "Just got the wind knocked out of me," he gasped.

Ned's announcement was overridden by the young woman who'd hit him. She'd returned to the scene and started screaming. "Please don't let him die! I didn't see him! You have to believe me!"

Eric turned to Teresa. "I'll stay with Ned, and you try to calm her down, okay?"

Teresa got up and went over to the young woman. Putting her arm around her shoulders, she guided the woman back towards the restaurant.

Ned was still trying to get up, but it was clear that he was in pain.

Eric immediately went into the role of a professional. "Don't try to move, Ned," he ordered in a stern voice. "If you're hurt, you're going to do more damage to your body. So lie still."

Ned lay back on the pavement. "Trying to catch my breath," he panted.

After Eric made a quick assessment of the situation, it was clear that Ned had sustained some bodily damage. How much damage? That was another matter.

* * *

Teresa and Eric sat in the hospital waiting area after being advised of Ned's injuries. Teresa nudged Eric. "Thank goodness he's only been badly bruised."

Eric crossed his arms. "I'm relieved for Ned but also for Elkville. If it had been anything more serious, the clinic might be in need of a new doctor."

"Eric, you said you had a feeling about something happening to me."

"What about it?"

"Is there any chance that you were worried about the wrong person?"

Eric frowned. "I guess it's possible. I knew it had to do with a car. The first person I thought of was you."

"How are you feeling now?"

"I feel okay. Whatever I felt has passed."

Teresa glanced down the hall and saw a nurse pushing a wheel chair towards them. "Eric, here comes Ned."

Eric got to his feet and stared at the person in the wheel chair. "He looks pretty beat up."

Teresa grimaced. "He is beat up. He was just run down by a teenager not paying attention."

* * *

Ned was wheeled to the hospital exit by a friendly nurse named Amelia. She tried to engage in small talk, but he had nothing to say. He had to make sense of what was going on. He didn't understand how his life could change so fast. He'd been fine for twenty-nine years. Then in less time than it took to shake someone's hand, he wasn't fine. While his mind tried to put the pieces together, the very things his father had warned him about, his feelings, were taking over. Doubt and fear were edging out the clarity he hoped to maintain.

Before he'd been injured, he'd been standing in a parking lot. He'd been reflecting on the relationship between Eric and Teresa, and how he didn't want that kind of connection. When Teresa reached out and touched Eric, he glowed. That kind of behavior centered around dependency. Just the thought of losing Teresa made Eric a nervous wreck. Ned could do without the touching if it meant losing all control in life.

And yet, without his consent, as he stood in that parking lot, he'd been "touched" anyway. A car "touched" him like some powerful, hand of fate, knocking him down with a force that took the breath from his lungs. After all his years of remaining on the outside of trauma, of keeping his feelings in a safe, neutral place, his reward was to be the object of a violent act.

His injuries weren't physically life-threatening, but being on the receiving end of an oncoming car threatened something just as important, his way of viewing his life. He'd always felt that his ability to stay calm and rational would keep him safe. To have that concept challenged sent his mind reeling.

He was brought back to the moment by someone talking to him. When he looked up, Eric was standing by his side.

"Teresa brought the car around," Eric explained. "Do you think you can stand up?"

Ned frowned, contemplating Eric's question. It seemed ridiculous until he tried to push himself out of the chair. A massive surge of pain from his upper legs and gut let him know his body had other ideas.

That kind of body pain was a shock, and something he hadn't known before. He'd rarely caught a cold growing up. And he'd been extremely fortunate when it came to accidents. He hadn't had any that were serious. People called him lucky, but Ned knew the real reason he'd fared very well in life. He made sure he was always prepared. More importantly, he had made an unspoken promise to himself to always remain calm no matter the circumstance.

He almost broke that promise when he wasn't able to stand up on his own. His body had always been his ally. It was strong, capable, and dependable. Until now. Now, its virtues had been replaced with a sickening weakness. The feelings took him back to childhood and his father's caution. Ned was supposed to accept things with dignity and calm. Even if Ned's mother was a drama queen, Ned didn't need to act like her. He needed to be stronger than that.

When he tried to get up again, Ned did his best to follow his dad's advice. He told himself he had to push through the pain. With great effort he succeeded. He was able to get to his feet, at least for a few seconds. He was about to commend himself when a terrible inner trembling took over and his strength failed him. He fell back into the chair with a heaving need for oxygen to still his panic. What was wrong with him? Did he have a low level of pain tolerance? Perhaps he'd made a bad decision when he refused the pain meds. Or maybe he was like his mother. It was a sickening thought that made his stomach turn over.

Whatever the problem, he didn't know how to handle what was happening to him. Fortunately, Eric seemed to sense what Ned needed. He reached out, offering his support. Ned had no choice but to accept Eric's help. If he was going to get into the car, his body insisted on it.

As soon as he grasped Eric's hand, he suddenly felt better, stronger. It was a new and unexpected experience. Ned's father was there for him growing up, but John Finney seemed to maintain a distance when they interacted. Sure there was the occasional pat on the shoulder, but the space between them was always there.

With Eric, it was different. It was as if Eric's hand was a conduit of sorts. It allowed Eric's strength to flow into Ned's hurting body. When Ned got a glimpse of Eric's eyes, he could feel what true caring meant. It meant Eric being gentle in how he helped Ned to slowly get to his feet. It also meant Eric supporting him as he wobbled step-by-step to the car.

The last challenge was getting into the SUV. Ned's deeply bruised legs protested. When he tried to lift one, a shout of pain told him that his body had gone as far as it was going to go. Its explanation was simple. He wanted too much from it. Didn't he understand that his legs were barely able to move?

Eric spoke up. "There's no hurry, Ned. Give yourself time to breathe. When you feel better, I'm here."

Earlier in the evening, Ned had dismissed Eric Lloyd as an uptight worrier who let his emotions overrule his actions. But in that moment, all he felt from Eric was his compassion. It shown not only in his eyes, but in the way he held himself, a man braced and ready to do whatever to help another person in trouble. He wasn't some pushover. Quite the opposite. He was what a dedicated, thoughtful doctor should be.

When Ned felt a little better, and with Eric's continued assistance, he was able to climb into the back seat of the car. While Eric buckled the seat belt around him, Ned took more breaths. He reflected on the journey he'd just taken from sitting in the wheel chair to sitting in the car. It was so simple a task, and yet it had taken everything he had to accomplish it. He was one step away from helplessness.

When Eric slammed the car door shut, the sound prompted a long forgotten memory that Ned didn't want to think about. On the day his mother left, her face looked so sad. She stood in his room and tried to reach out to him but failed. The only thing she seemed able to do was tell him to listen to his father. After that, she hurried from the room, slamming the front door on her way out. Ned had wanted to run after her, but his legs wouldn't budge. His body was frozen and stiff with grief. His mother had turned her back on him, and there was no way to stop her from leaving.

* * *

After they returned to the motel, Teresa sat on the bed going over the evening's events. They'd had quite an impact on Ned's attitude. After his accident, he didn't look like the confident man who had been at dinner.

Thankfully, they were able to get him a motel room close to the one she and Eric were staying in. Eric had helped the young doctor settle in. Eric had also stopped at a drugstore to fill Ned's prescriptions. While there, he'd purchased a few necessary items like toothbrushes and shaving accessories for both himself and Ned.

"Eric, I'm worried about Ned," Teresa called out.

Eric came out of the bathroom with a toothbrush in hand. "I've never seen a person's personality change so fast. When I was helping Ned into bed, he looked slightly traumatized. I know part of it is his injuries, but something else is going on."

"What could be the matter? He doesn't seem like the kind of person who'd react that way."

"I asked if he'd like to talk about anything, but he claimed he was very tired." Eric frowned. "I keep remembering what you said at dinner. You asked if any of us know who we are."

Teresa got up and walked over to Eric. She took his toothbrush out of his hand and put it aside. Standing on tiptoe, she kissed him lightly on the lips. "I think I know who you are."

"Hopefully you see me in a better light than Matthew. He accused me of whining and acting like a victim." Eric narrowed his brows. "I'm sure those aren't qualities you put on your list of requirements for a mate."

"Matthew says a lot of things."

"But I think he's right. I just have to figure out how to change."

"Do what you have to do but for me, aside from being so closed-mouthed, I think you're fine as you are."

"You do?"

"Yes, but Ned, that's another story. I think he's in trouble. First, he invalidates the idea of feelings. Next, he seems totally caught up in them."

"We do have a psychiatrist in Elkville. Maybe Paul Glass can hang out his shingle again."

"You said he's incompetent."

Eric's face flushed red. "I guess I was angry when I said that. Supposedly, he did help lots of people before he got to the Ferguson mansion."

"When we drive back to Elkville tomorrow, maybe you can pay him a visit and talk to him about Ned."

"I don't know about that. Matthew seems much better when it comes to communicating with Paul Glass."

Teresa laughed. "From the little I know about Matthew, he doesn't consider himself a great communicator."

Eric pulled Teresa close and smiled. "Let me tell you a little secret about Matthew. He acts like all he wants is to do his job and be left alone. But beneath all his bluster and complaining, he's very compassionate. I know he was there for me during the worst of my craziness."

"Then maybe Matthew could talk to Ned."

Nineteen

MATTHEW STRETCHED AND rubbed the sleep from his eyes. He felt more rested than he had in a long time. Lea had encouraged him to sleep in while she fixed breakfast, but he wanted to get his day started. It was a beautiful morning, and the sun was peeking through the slightly open blinds. He didn't think it was his nature to wake up happy, but when he thought about Lea, he even smiled.

The previous day they had reconnected in a way that made all the months of upset fade. They became lovers and best friends again. If the old patterns of Lea's personality came to the surface, they'd work together and do whatever to help Lea through it.

After having such an unspoiled day with Lea in their new home, Matthew had a thought he never imagined he could have. Perhaps Elkville wasn't all bad. Perhaps it could be a retreat of sorts when they needed to get away from their normal routine in Chicago.

He went to the closet, took a blue, button-down shirt off its hanger and slipped it on. As he was buttoning it, he could hear birds chirping outside in an old tree in the back yard. Lea had wanted to keep the tree even though the lot wasn't very big. She said it would be nice in the summer. They could sit outside under its shade.

Matthew wasn't an outdoor person, but he wanted Lea to be happy. Listening to the birds, he felt she'd made a good choice. Their chirps and tweets reminded him of the times in his childhood when he'd visited his grandfather's house. There were lots of birds there too, flying to and from bird feeders his grandfather filled daily. Matthew paused. His grandfather was a good man, someone Matthew could look up to.

The memory added a pleasant feeling to the morning as he put on a pair of light charcoal slacks and started for the door. He was looking forward to a hearty breakfast with Lea and spending another day with her in his arms. He was about to reach for the door knob when the room suddenly went dark. At first, he thought the sun had gone behind a cloud. But there were still rays of light coming through the blinds. That's when he realized the darkness was part of a vision that began playing out in his mind. The details were fuzzy, but the ominous feelings were so powerful that he almost lost his balance. He steadied himself as the vision passed as quickly as it came.

Before he had a chance to process what happened, the phone rang. Matthew answered it while he was still recovering from something that nearly derailed him. He was brought back to the moment by the sound of Eric's "worry voice" and bad news. Elkville's new doctor had been injured. Not badly in a physical sense, but Eric was concerned about Ned Finney's frame of mind. The guy wasn't acting himself. On the plus side, Teresa and Eric were doing well, and Eric was excited about his wife coming back to Elkville with him.

After Eric said goodbye, Matthew was determined not to let his day be ruined by Eric's concerns. It was unfortunate that Ned Finney wasn't handling his run-in with a car very well. However, Matthew knew how doctors could be. They often made terrible patients. He was betting Finney would be fine in a couple of days.

It was his waking nightmare that concerned him. He started out of the room trying to dismiss it like he'd dismissed Eric's news. He paused in the hall and inhaled deeply. The house was filled with the smell of fresh coffee, and he needed a generous portion of the stuff. It would help to snap him out of any negativity that was trying to take hold. After a firm reprimand to ignore his vision, he continued down the stairs. By the time he got to the lower level and walked into the kitchen, he felt a little better.

Lea was at the stove, scooping a hefty amount of potatoes onto a plate. She turned and smiled. "Good morning, sweetie."

Her voice was filled with the same playful excitement she had the day before. He did his best to sound just as upbeat. "Morning, Lea."

Lea put the plate down, turned off the stove and hurried over. "Matthew, what's wrong? You look so, so—"

"What?" He blinked back wondering at how transparent his feelings must be. Lea had tuned in immediately. That's when he thought about Eric and how the man had looked when he was worried about Teresa's safety. "I'm becoming Eric's clone," he moaned.

Lea took hold of his hand. "What do you mean?"

"Nothing, just ignore me. I'm probably reacting to Eric's phone call. He and Teresa are fine, but Ned Finney had an accident."

"That's awful."

"He's just shook up, nothing serious."

Lea's brows bunched with confusion. "But there's more, isn't there? I can see it in your eyes."

Matthew frowned. "You know how Eric has these premonitions? I think I just had one. Eric, with all of his nuttiness, has infected me."

Lea stepped back. "Before you go down that road, I thought you admitted to being intuitive too. You said you sometimes know things about a patient in the OR. You feel it before they're going to take a bad turn."

"That's different."

"How?"

"That's something that's appropriate to the moment. This is much more generalized."

"From what I know about the subject, it still falls into the same category."

"Fine, I'm crazy too. Is that what you're telling me?" Matthew asked.

Lea laughed. "Crazy is the last thing you are. But whether you like it or not, you are in touch with more than you know. It's what makes you so good at what you do."

"Whatever, I don't like what I'm feeling now."

Lea paused. "Remember, I'm here for you."

Matthew took her hand and kissed it. "Thank you. If everything goes to hell in this little pocket of the Appalachian wilderness, I'm going to need you by my side."

"You'll also have Eric. Is he coming back today?"

"Yes and Teresa is coming too. It seems she wants to be a part of all the fun Elkville has to offer."

Lea ignored his sarcastic tone. "Teresa is very sweet. It'll be wonderful to see her."

"It's a good thing she's so together and even tempered. She can balance out Eric's bouts of obsessive worrying."

Lea returned a teasing grin. "Well, don't you become obsessive, Doctor Howell. Forget everything and have some coffee and breakfast."

Matthew rubbed his stomach. "Just some coffee. I'm not very hungry."

Lea stared up at him. "You have to eat something. It'll help."

"You sound like Margaret."

"Is that a bad thing?"

Matthew sat down at the table. "I don't think you can help it. You're both nurturers."

"That's right, and I'm going to make sure you eat something," Lea said as she went over to a counter. She poured coffee into a large mug and brought it over to the table. "What about Ned? Is he coming back too?"

"Eric is driving Ned's truck back, and Ned is riding with Teresa. From what Eric said, Doctor Finney will be the first person to convalesce at the new clinic."

Lea frowned. "If he's been hurt, he should stay here."

"Here?" Matthew felt his stomach lurch. "Couldn't he stay with Paul?"

Lea gave him a pained look. "Are you still worried about my feelings towards him?"

"Of course not. It's just that we were having a great time together, just the two of us."

Lea smiled. "You're right. He can stay at Paul's house."

"Good, at least that's one small blessing." Even as he said it, Matthew felt an uneasiness settling in. It told him to enjoy himself while he could. Like it or not, his vision was trying to get him ready for something unwanted. He just didn't know what that unwanted thing was. He picked up the mug and stared at the two words printed on its side. He scowled when he said them out loud. "Happy Camper."

The day before, he'd trivialized Eric's fears. Now, with his own sense of doom circling overhead, the mug seemed to be mocking him.

Twenty

MARGARET STOOD WAITING at Paul Glass's front door with a loaf of banana bread in hand. She'd gotten up early and started baking. It was her way of handling life when it got to be too much. And life felt like that after the last couple of days.

When the door opened, Paul looked out with a slightly paint-splattered face. He was holding a paint roller. "Margaret, how nice to see you," he said in a quiet voice.

Margaret smiled. "It looks like I came at an inconvenient time."

Paul opened the door a little wider and gestured her in. "I was just about to take a break."

Margaret stepped into the living room and noted the half painted walls. "I like the color. It's a lovely muted aqua-green."

"You know your colors, but I'm not surprised. You were once an art student."

"Yes, a very long time ago." She looked around and didn't see the official house greeter. "Where's Duke?"

"I put him in an upstairs bedroom. I didn't want him exposed to the paint fumes. He doesn't seem to be feeling very well."

"I'm sorry to hear that. He and I are just beginning to get acquainted." Margaret held out the banana bread. "I thought you might like something I baked this morning."

"Thank you. Would you bring it into the kitchen? I'll cover this roller and serve some tea if you'd like. Earl Grey, right?"

Margaret followed Paul into his newly remodeled kitchen. "That would be very nice."

Paul wrapped his paint roller in some aluminum foil and glanced at Margaret. "I've found this keeps the roller from drying out."

Margaret put the bread on the table. "I have some bad news. Eric phoned last night and told me that our dear Ned Finney got hit by a car."

"Is he seriously injured?"

"No, but Eric called me again this morning. He said Ned hardly spoke at all. He's very withdrawn."

"That's too bad."

"You and I have spent a bit of time with Ned. He's always been so even tempered. What do you think is wrong with him?"

"Why are you asking me?"

"Paul, surely you must have treated lots of people who experienced that kind of trauma."

Paul filled the tea kettle and put it on the stove. "Like I told you before, that's all in the past."

"You're being unreasonable. If you can help someone—"

"I don't want to talk about it."

Margaret frowned. "I think your attitude is a little childish."

"And what about your attitude, Margaret? When you don't want to discuss something, you make it very clear that the subject is closed."

"If you're referring to my behavior the other night, I'm sorry. But what you're doing isn't right. By holding on to your hurt feelings you're punishing Ned, a person who might need your help."

"Do you want to talk about my hurt feelings?"

"Yes, if it'll get you to stop acting like this."

"I'll make a deal with you. First, you tell me about why you were so upset the night Eric and Matthew arrived."

Margaret looked away. "I was just mad at Eric, that's all."

"Why were you angry with him?"

"Because he treats me like, like—"

"Like what?"

"I don't know." Margaret pulled out a chair and sat down at the table. "I just feel like he thinks I can't handle my life."

"Welcome to getting old," Paul sighed.

Margaret had been staring at the checkered table cloth and looked up. "Is that how you feel?"

"How else am I supposed to feel?"

"Well, I don't know, but when I look at you, I don't think about your age. I think about how much wisdom you must have."

Paul came over and sat down at the table. "I think about the past and how different I used to be. I certainly didn't lack in confidence."

"I'm sorry."

"For what?"

100

Margaret clasped her hands. "We all blamed you for what happened at the Ferguson mansion, but it wasn't fair to put everything on your shoulders."

"You were right to blame me. I mishandled everything."

"Even if you did, what about all the people you've helped? Doesn't that fact count for something?"

"No, after my demonstration of total incompetence, I can't trust myself."

Margaret felt her heart go out to him. "I wish you didn't feel that way." When Paul didn't respond, she turned her attention to the scene outside the window. The mountains were in the distance. She'd stared at them so many times when she sat at her own kitchen table with her husband, Ricky. So many times, she'd tried to talk Ricky out of his need to confess his shortcomings. He never listened to her. She felt her breath catch. "Oh no! I'm doing it again!"

Paul got to his feet. "What is it. Margaret? You've gone all pale."

Margaret tried to catch her breath. "I just saw everything so clearly," she gasped.

"What did you see? Talk to me?"

"You've taken my Ricky's place. For most of my life, I lived with a man who felt like you do. He couldn't let go of his mistakes either. So he came here, and he brought his misery with him." Margaret stood up and glared back. "You've done the same thing! I can't escape people like Ricky. They just look like someone else! They look like you, Paul!"

Margaret turned and ran from the kitchen. When she got to the front door, she kept going. Paul had become a good friend, and she'd become very fond of him. She thought it was because he was so nice and helped to get the clinic built. But the clinic was her dead husband's dream, and Paul had taken his place in that respect too.

She dashed into the street. The rutted pavement was still sloshy with melted snow in some areas. She wasn't watching where she stepped and got her shoe wet when she put her foot in a puddle. It didn't matter. She had to get away from Paul and all his guilt. As she neared her house, she heard Paul calling after her.

"Margaret, please, let's talk about your feelings."

"No!" she yelled out. She'd talked to Ricky for forty years. It never did any good. Nothing ever changed. "Leave me alone!" she cried.

Tears of anger and self-pity streamed down her face and blurred her vision. She half tripped up her front porch stairs. But nothing was going to stop her from distancing herself from more unwanted pain.

She let herself into the house, shut the door and locked it. It had never been necessary to bolt the door before. But she had to find a way to shut out the men who insisted on telling her about their failings. A good part of her marriage was spent trying to help Ricky get beyond his. But her husband refused to release even an ounce of his wretchedness. It became the burden they shared to the moment of his death and beyond. Now Paul was confessing his sins, and she didn't want any part of them or Paul. Better to lock the door and keep him out of her life.

She hurried upstairs to her bedroom and tried to catch her breath. Paul was pounding on her front door, and it frightened her. She remembered how persistent Ricky had been. His demands haunted her dreams long after he died. They repeated over and over again. "I'm a failure, Margaret! Help me! Don't shut me out! I need you!"

Paul was becoming another Ricky. He'd acted so innocent when he followed her to Elkville. He claimed he needed the serenity of the mountains. What he really needed was a confessor, someone to listen to his inadequacies and self-blame. She put her hands over her ears as she recalled how hard it was to say no to her dead husband. Just the thought of what she'd endured had her mind scrambling for a solution. If necessary, she'd leave Elkville. She'd find solace in a place where she could start over. She'd lock her door and never open it again. The thoughts helped a little, but the tears kept coming.

Twenty-One

MATTHEW SAT IN one of the recliners in the living room. While Lea was taking a shower, he'd catch up on a little reading. He was enjoying a sci-fi thriller when someone started pounding on the door. He put the book aside, praying that it wasn't one of Ned's patients in need of a doctor. When he opened the door and saw Paul Glass standing outside, he was somewhat relieved, but he resented the intrusion.

"Can I come in?" Paul asked as he pushed past Matthew.

Matthew shut the door reluctantly. Two days in a row, people had turned up at his house, clearly wanting something. Didn't anyone understand that he needed time alone with Lea?

It only took a quick glance at Paul to answer that question. The older man was caught up in his own needs, not Matthew's. "How can I help you, Paul?"

Paul stared back with bent posture. "Don't worry about me. I'm here about Margaret. She came over to my place, and we were talking, and she suddenly got very distressed. Now she's locked herself in her house and won't let me in to speak to her."

Matthew crossed his arms, remembering his earlier vision. It had a dark and very melancholy feel to it. Afterwards, Eric called and said Ned Finney was an emotional mess. Now Paul was telling him that Margaret was distraught. Was his vision a premonition about the two events? "So what were you and Margaret discussing?"

Paul's face went red. "I was simply telling her that I was retired."

"And that's what got her upset?"

"Not exactly. She was concerned about Ned Finney. Eric told Margaret that Ned's not faring well, and Margaret thinks I should help him."

"You're a friend, Paul. Why wouldn't you help him?"

103

"You know why." Paul rubbed his brow and snorted out a breath. "Eric called me a quack, and it's true."

"So what does that have to do with Margaret?"

"She thinks I'm like her late husband, that I came here like he did, to run away from my guilt."

"Is she right?"

Paul shuffled over to the living room sofa and sat down. "Maybe, but I swear, I didn't think about it that way. I liked this place—"

"And you liked Margaret," Matthew said as he joined Paul in the living room. "Admit it. You've had a crush on her from the start."

Paul stared at the rug. "You know that's true, so stop badgering me."

"I'm not trying to badger you. I'm trying to understand why you're here."

Paul's head swung up. "Maybe I am like Margaret's husband, but I never wanted to hurt Margaret."

"Then get over yourself and start picking up the pieces of your life that you've been ignoring."

Paul shook his head. "You missed your calling, Doctor Howell. You have an uncanny knack for getting to the heart of a problem. With a little finessing and patience, you would have made a great therapist."

"That's the last profession I'd want. Listening to people recite all their crap day in and day out. That would be hell."

"I think that's exactly how Margaret feels. She had to listen to her husband all those years. And then I started in, doing the same thing, and she snapped."

"What do you mean 'she snapped'?"

"You didn't see how she looked at me. She was scared and took off like the devil was chasing her. I followed her back to her house, but she locked the door." Paul glanced up with penitent eyes. "That's how upset she is. She never locks her door."

"Eric should be home soon. He can talk to her."

"I don't think that's going to work. Margaret said Eric makes her feel old and useless." Paul stood up and stepped closer. "Please, for Margaret's sake, go over and talk to her."

"You said she locked her door. There is no way I'm going to go over there and break it down."

"You don't have to. I think the door to her kitchen is open."

"I don't want to invade someone's house," Matthew protested.

"If she was physically ill, you'd do something, right? This is the same thing. Left to herself, Margaret could sink into some horrible depression, a depression that might destroy both her and Eric."

Matthew glared at Paul. "Fine, I'll go, but I better tell Lea where I am. In the meantime, you need to go home. And once you're there, start getting your life back on track so we can all get some peace."

Without replying, Paul walked to the door and let himself out.

Matthew was about to check on Lea when she came skipping down the stairs. Her chestnut, shoulder-length hair bounced off her pink sweater, and she was smiling at him. Matthew whispered the first words that came to mind. "You are so beautiful."

Lea stopped in front of him and rubbed her hand over his unshaven cheek. "That shower was great. Now, it's your turn."

"I wish."

"What do you mean?"

"Paul was just here. He said he upset Margaret. Now, she won't talk to him. He's convinced that I need to go over and see how she is." Matthew paused. "But maybe you should be the one to check on her."

Lea shrugged. "I'll be happy to do that."

"Good," Matthew said as he headed for the stairs. "By the way, you'll have to use the back entrance. Margaret locked the front one."

"Margaret never locks her door."

Matthew looked back at her. "That was true until Paul got her all stirred up. I knew the guy was a menace five minutes after I met him."

"Matthew, please, that's a little extreme, isn't it? Paul does have his good points."

Matthew started up the stairs. "It's not his good points I'm worried about." When he got to the landing, he paused and called down to Lea. "I'm here if you need anything."

Lea blew him a kiss. "I'm sure everything will be fine. Margaret can just be a little high-strung at times."

* * *

Lea didn't quite believe what she'd told Matthew. Margaret could be more than a little high-strung. Margaret had two sides. She could be as tough as they came during a crisis, or she could quickly falter if an emotional nerve was bruised. Lea just hoped Paul had exaggerated his fears about the older woman.

She hurried from her yard to the neighboring property. The sun was out, warming the air and melting the few patches of snow that were left on the grass. It was hard to believe how quickly the weather had changed. It felt like spring again.

When she got to Margaret's back porch, she tried the door. It was unlocked. She let herself into the kitchen and smiled. The room was filled with the smell of something that Margaret had recently baked. Lea was sure it was something delicious. But where was Margaret now? "Mom, it's Lea!" she announced in a loud voice.

She continued to call out as she made her way through the lower level and quickly climbed the stairs to the second floor. "Mom, can you hear me?"

The creak of a door made her turn around. Margaret stood in her bedroom doorway. "There you are," Lea said. "I was worried when I couldn't find you."

"Hi, Lea."

Margaret's shaky voice and her red, teary eyes made Lea hurry over. She put her arm around Margaret's shoulder. "What's going on?"

Instead of answering, Margaret started crying. Lea let her go and grabbed some tissues from the dresser. "Matthew said that Paul did something to upset you."

Margaret took one of the tissues and blew her nose. "I can't blame Paul. I did at first because I was so ashamed of what my life has come to. But when I started to calm down, I had to put the blame on myself."

"I don't understand."

"When I moved back here, I focused on the clinic. I watched it being built and kept telling myself how things were changing for the better. But I know what I was really doing. I was hiding from the truth."

"What truth are you talking about?"

"Eric is right to think of me as an old woman who can't take care of herself."

"Eric doesn't think that about you."

"Yes, he does. The other night when I made that scene in front of everyone, he saw what I've come to. I resented it, but that was stupid of me. I need taking care of."

Lea stepped back and put her arms around herself. "I guess that means I need taking care of, too."

Margaret frowned. "Why is that?"

"I was worse than you that night. I ran out like an idiot and ended up in a ditch."

Margaret paused. "But look at you now. You're doing just fine. And from what you said when you called me yesterday, you and Matthew are better than ever."

Lea shrugged. "Maybe I'm hiding from the truth like you."

Margaret came forward with imploring eyes. "Lea, please don't let my behavior make you feel like that."

"But what if we find out that we're both defective in some way?"

Margaret stood up a little straighter and pursed her lips. "Maybe no one is one hundred percent. I thought Ned was an exception until Eric called and said the poor man was barely making it."

Lea returned a little smile. "So far, at least Teresa seems fine."

Margaret smiled back. "Teresa is one of a kind. Eric is very lucky to have her."

"But what about the rest of us? You said something about other people having to take care of us."

"I'm sorry. I got so upset that I said things I shouldn't. I'm feeling sorry for myself and blurting things out."

"Mom, no matter what, you seem just fine to me."

"I'm trying. I really am, but sometimes, when I look at myself in the mirror, I wonder."

"When I look at you, I see the person who took me in when I had nothing, not even my memories. I was in the hospital, feeling angry and lost, and you came to see me. You told me you wanted to take me home."

Margaret came over and gathered Lea up in her arms. "That's the day I became a mother for a second time. I finally got the daughter I always wanted. And I never once thought of you as defective. You were more beautiful and giving than I could have ever deserved."

Lea sniffled. "That's how you made me feel, like it was okay to be me. That's the way you are with all of us. And when Teresa and Eric get here—"

Margaret gasped. "I keep forgetting about them. And they're bringing Ned back too. I have to get ready."

"Do you think that Ned could stay with Paul?" Lea asked.

Margaret huffed out a breath. "Forget about Paul. Ned can stay here. I'll get the spare bedroom spruced up a bit."

"Lucky Ned, he couldn't be in better hands."

Margaret smiled at the compliment, but she seemed preoccupied with preparing for her arriving guests. "I have the other bedroom ready for Eric and Teresa. I bought that full size bed, but the room is so cramped now. They'll barely have room to move."

"They could stay with Matthew and me," Lea offered. "We have plenty of room."

Margaret's eyes brightened. "That would be wonderful, but I don't think Matthew would agree. I'm sure he wants some time alone with you."

"Maybe, but he can be very understanding."

Margaret let out an uncertain laugh. "I know that. I just don't want to be there when you tell him what you have in mind. He can look so dejected."

Lea agreed. "I always kid him about his pouting. He claims he's being introspective, but he's so easy to read."

Margaret started for the door. "It's getting late, and I need to get a meal started so it'll be ready when everyone arrives."

"I can help."

"No, go home and talk to Matthew. If he has a problem with Teresa and Eric staying with you, don't worry about it. I'll make do."

* * *

Matthew took a quick shower, shaved and dressed. He wanted to be ready when Lea came back from her mission of mercy. She might return with bad news about Margaret, a person she considered a mother figure. If that happened, he'd be there to support her.

But he had to handle things with that finesse Paul mentioned. He had to consider all the elements involved. First of all, there was Margaret's makeup. No matter how strong Margaret could be most of the time, Matthew had witnessed how fast she could fall apart given the right circumstances. When he and Eric arrived in Elkville after the snow storm, she was in the middle of one of her episodes. She was crying and looking stressed to the max.

"Maybe my premonition was about Margaret."

108

It made sense. Margaret was a central figure in Elkville. She and her husband were the ones who gave the area and its people a sense of security if someone was sick or injured. If his "everything's-falling-apart" foreboding were about Margaret, it could be bad. He could easily imagine Margaret's potential to be an emotional time bomb, just waiting to go off.

He rubbed his temples as he felt the first signs of a headache coming on. But his headache wasn't important. More than anything, he had to do whatever he could to stabilize the situation. "If she does blow her top, it could send Lea plummeting into a depression, too." He couldn't let that happen.

Lea returned home as he was getting his thoughts together. "How'd it go with Margaret?" he asked, trying to keep any emotion out of his voice.

Lea walked over and stared up at him. "You're worried, aren't you? You try not to show it, but I can see that you care about Mom."

Matthew rubbed his temples again. No matter what, his best course in keeping Lea happy and balanced was to remain agreeable. "Sure I care." It was true, but probably not to the extent that Lea cared. Margaret was a person he admired, but he wasn't emotionally attached like his wife.

Lea smiled. "She was very upset, but she's better now. In fact, she wants to have Ned Finney stay at her house."

Matthew felt his shoulders relax a little. "That's a great idea. Margaret loves to take care of people."

"There is one thing—"

Matthew's shoulders edged up again. "Yes?"

"Would it be okay if Teresa and Eric stay here? Margaret's house is so small."

Matthew let the idea sift through all the worries he'd been entertaining. From what he could tell, his chances of having a quiet, intimate day with Lea were nil. So why fight whatever she wanted. At least she'd be happy, and that was a good thing. As long as she was smiling, he knew she wasn't slipping back into her old personality. He leaned in and kissed her cheek. "Of course they can stay here," he mumbled.

Lea let out a little cry of delight. "That's so sweet of you! I was afraid you'd be disappointed. But look at how amazing you're being."

Matthew swallowed hard when another feeling of disaster flitted through his mind. It was gone almost as fast as it came, but it was enough to remind him about being on his best behavior. He heard himself asking a question. "Is there anything I can do to help before they get here?"

Lea's eyes practically glowed. "Yes! The guest bed needs to be made. I bought a sheet set and washed it, but I haven't put it on the bed. Now we can work together, just you and me, doing something as a team."

Matthew forced himself to sound enthusiastic. "Then we better get to it. We want Teresa and Eric to feel comfortable."

Lea hurried up the stairs. "Just think, Matthew! We're having our first house guests! I'm so excited."

Twenty-Two

TERESA WAS RELIEVED to pull up in front of her mother-in-law's house. It had been a very quiet, but very tense trip from Blacksburg to Elkville. Her passenger, Ned Finney, hardly said a word. When she tried to fill the airways with a bit of song from the radio, Ned apologized, but asked her to turn off the music. He said he didn't feel well and had a headache. Teresa glanced in her rearview mirror and saw that he'd removed his seat belt and was stretched out as much as possible. When she asked if he was in pain from his injuries, he claimed he was okay. She hoped it was true. He had a prescription, but she didn't know if he took any of it or not. Whatever the case, he looked miserable.

A bright spot was seeing Eric's vehicle in front of her on the road. In the past, when she'd been in the car with him, she'd worried about all the ups and downs as they weaved their way to their destination. But watching the way Eric drove Ned's truck, the way he took the inclines and the downgrades with ease, she decided he was a very capable driver. All and all, the trip went more quickly than she expected. If it hadn't been for Ned's unhappy presence in the car, she would have had the tunes blasting and probably had a great time.

When she arrived at Margaret's house, she checked on Ned before she got out of the car. He had fallen asleep, but his brows were still narrowed. She looked up and saw Margaret coming out of the house and waving to her. Her mother-in-law had a sweet smile on her face. It was a welcome contrast to Ned's fretful expression.

As she was about to open her door, Eric was there to open it for her. He had parked the truck and had hurried over to help her out. She put her finger to her lips when he was about to close the door. "Let's be quiet. Ned's asleep."

Eric nodded. "Good, it'll give us a chance to say hello to Mom. From the look on her face, she's very excited to see you."

111

After being with a gloomy Ned Finney for hours, Teresa treasured the happy feelings she had when Eric took her hand. He led her through an aging gate and up the broken sidewalk towards the house.

Margaret came down the porch steps with open arms. "It's so good to have you here, Teresa!"

Teresa smiled back. "I couldn't be happier. I feel like I'm part of the family when I'm here."

"Of course, you're family. I have two daughters now, you and Lea. I couldn't ask for more than that."

Eric stepped forward and smiled. "Don't forget you have a son too."

Margaret laughed and gathered him into a group hug. "I have two daughters and the best son ever."

They were soon joined by Lea and Matthew walking across the yard.

Lea waved as she approached the group. "Teresa, it's so wonderful to see you!"

Matthew smiled too. "Welcome to Elkville."

Margaret's eyes lit up even more. "Look at all of us standing here when I have a big dinner ready." She paused and glanced around. "But where's Ned?"

Teresa looked back at the car and saw that someone had opened the back car door. "Ned fell asleep on the drive here, but I think he must be awake now."

Eric turned and started for the car. "I better help him out."

Margaret whispered to Teresa. "How's Ned doing?"

"Not too well," Teresa said as she watched Eric give Ned a hand. Getting Ned out of the car went a little faster than getting him in. However, once the young doctor was on his feet, he started arguing with Eric.

Ned's voice was loud and demanding. "Just give me the keys to my truck so I can drive myself to the clinic."

"Ned, you're in no shape to be driving anywhere," Eric said.

Ned started for his truck. "Fine, then you can drive me there."

Eric followed him. "My mom is expecting you to stay for dinner."

Ned got to his truck, held on to the tailgate, and looked back at the group gathered around Margaret. "Thanks, Margaret, but I'm not hungry."

Margaret hurried towards the street. "Ned, please, won't you come into the house? You can rest for a little while."

Ned's breath was coming out in gasps as he slowly sunk to his knees. "Those pain meds didn't agree with me. I think I'm going to be sick."

Before Margaret reached him, Ned began vomiting on the street.

Margaret and Eric were both there to steady him as he continued heaving. By the time he finished, he'd broken out in a cold sweat, and his body was shaking.

Matthew joined the threesome. "Margaret, let Eric and I help Ned."

Margaret stood up and put her hand to her mouth. "The poor man looks like he's going to faint."

As she was commenting, Ned tried to stand up with Eric and Matthew assisting on either side. When he was upright, he successfully took a couple of steps, weaved back and forth, and passed out.

* * *

Ned woke up, opened his eyes and decided on three things. He was still nauseous. His body was still a source of pain. And he didn't recognize where he was. If that wasn't enough, when he thought about recent events, his embarrassment was off the charts.

The ride to Elkville was a horror. He was in the car with Teresa. She was being her caring self, and he acted like some pathetic loser. But he couldn't get beyond the misery he was in. His head throbbed and his stomach churned. It was everything he could do not to throw up. By some almighty grace, he fell asleep during the last half hour.

When he woke up, he realized he was back in Elkville. His first thought was to go home to the clinic. He only had to get out of the car, get in his truck and drive himself there. He did manage to get out of the car, but Eric refused to give him the keys to his truck. Then his nausea went ballistic, and he threw up. The violent heaving punished his battered torso. He tried his best to recover and ended up fainting. He'd never fainted before. That was another new experience.

"Ned, you're awake."

He looked to one side of his bed and saw Margaret Lloyd sitting in a chair.

113

"How are you doing?" Margaret asked.

He put a hand to his stomach. "Do you have any crackers? I'm told they're helpful when your stomach is off."

Margaret got to her feet, smoothed down her dress and smiled. "Yes, I'll get you some."

Ned started to push himself up into a sitting position. He was getting used to his body's protests and learning not to react to the pain as much as he had in the beginning.

Margaret helped steady him. "I'm so sorry about your accident."

"You know what my dad says, if you don't let circumstances hold you back, life goes on."

"That's a good way to look at it."

As soon as Margaret made the comment, Ned's stomach lurched. "Where's your bathroom?" he asked as he got to his feet.

Margaret gave him a quick glance and started out of the room. "This way."

Ned followed her, moving much faster than he had earlier that day. The hall was filled with the sound of people talking downstairs and the smells of dinner. Both the conversation and the smells made his swirling stomach worse. He had an urgent need to empty himself of everything. When he reached the bathroom, he slammed the door shut and threw back the little bolt that would keep him safe from intruders. His head was swirling too. He kept trying to use his father's formulas for life, to go on in spite of whatever came at him. But his body wouldn't listen to a word of it. He was soon on his knees again, heaving out bile. When it was gone, he started dry heaving. Maybe that was his fate, to stay on his knees forever.

He heard Margaret calling to him. Her voice became his mother's voice, calling to him when he was a boy. He was in the yard playing, and she was telling him to come into the house. He wished that just once he could see her again. If only he could, maybe he'd stop thinking about her. He wanted all the memories to go back where they belonged, in the past.

"Ned, are you okay?" Margaret asked.

"I'm okay," he called back. "Just need those crackers."

"I'll go get them," Margaret said.

Ned almost smiled. From her tone, he could tell that Margaret understood his need for a saltine. That need was real and immediate. If he didn't get something to control what he was feeling, he'd dry heave himself to death.

The thought was overly dramatic, and he would have laughed at himself if his gut wouldn't retaliate with more pain. Instead, he forced himself to stand. He was shaky again. He turned, took hold of the sink, and saw himself in the medicine chest mirror. He was shocked by how bad he looked, but it was just another feeling to be ignored.

He turned on the faucet and splashed some water on his face. It helped. After he dried off, he turned to the door and unlocked it. He couldn't understand why he felt so weak. When he was in the hospital, he heard people talking about a bug going around. Maybe he caught it. "Great, get hit by a car and now a bug. Gimme a break."

By the time he got back to his room, Margaret was coming in with the crackers. He let himself half fall into an old, faded-print upholstered chair.

"Feeling better?" she asked as she handed him a plate.

Ned picked up a cracker. "I think I know what's wrong with me. I caught that virus going round in Blacksburg."

Margaret retrieved a green and yellow knitted throw from the bottom of the bed and brought it over. She sighed as she covered his knees. "Stomach bugs can be terrible. No wonder you're feeling so bad."

Eric knocked on the door jamb and came into the room. He put a hand on Margaret's shoulder and looked at Ned. "How are you doing? Mom said you were sick again."

Margaret spoke up. "He says he thinks he has a bug."

Ned put the cracker back on the plate. "I've been lucky. I can't remember when I felt like this. I guess it'll make me more compassionate with my patients."

Eric turned to Margaret. "Mom, go down and eat. I'll stay with Ned."

Ned shook his head. "Nobody needs to stay. I'm fine now." He held up his plate. "Look, I'm eating something to settle my stomach. Now, both of you go, please."

Eric tugged on Margaret's arm. "You heard the man. Your dinner is getting cold. Let's go."

Margaret pulled away and approached Ned. She leaned in and was about to kiss his cheek. He pulled back just in time. "Don't get too close. I don't want you catching this."

Margaret stepped back, looking slightly chastised. "Alright, but I'll be back in a few minutes."

Ned watched Margaret and Eric leave with a sense of relief. He'd appreciated Eric's help in Blacksburg, but there was something about Margaret that overwhelmed him.

He picked up a cracker and forced himself to take a bite. He kept eating until he finished off two crackers. He felt drowsy again. If he could sleep straight through for a couple of days, his body would repair itself, and he could go back to being himself again.

Twenty-Three

PAUL TOOK THE paint roller off the handle and tossed it in the trash. He removed the trash bag from its stainless steel receptacle and took it out to the outdoor garbage can. He'd finished painting the living room. It was the last room in the house that needed his attention, and he wouldn't need the roller any more. Back inside, he got the worst of the paint off his hands at the kitchen sink and purposefully marched upstairs. He needed to get the little flecks of paint off his face and arms.

He stood in the shower scrubbing and shampooing. When he felt mostly paint-free, he got out, dried off and went to his bedroom. When he'd had the house remodeled, he made two of the small bedrooms into one larger one that included a good-sized closet. Sliding back its doors, he had to push aside the clothes he normally wore. He searched for garments he'd once worn before he retired. He found a designer shirt that cost a hefty three hundred fifty dollars on sale. The casual shirts he wore in Elkville ran about twenty dollars. He studied the Italian made shirt. It had the crisp, finished look that he'd once enjoyed wearing.

His slacks were at the far end of the closet. He grabbed a pair, an ink-blue favorite, off its hanger. His belt didn't take as much effort to find. It was with a number of others on a special belt hanger. He'd discovered the belt in a London shop, and thought it was a little expensive at over two hundred pounds, but he liked it enough to buy it. He'd put on a little weight since then and was grateful that it still fit.

He dressed and went to look for some socks. He found a cashmere pair that had set him back seventy five dollars. After he put them on, he realized how comfortable they were compared to the white crew socks he'd been wearing.

Once he moved to Elkville, he'd tolerated a lot of things. He'd tolerated too much. It felt good to return to his former attire and way

117

of conducting himself. Margaret was the one who gave him the good shaking he needed to understand that fact.

He was about to go downstairs and stopped next to Duke's bed. His companion was still under the weather. Instead of getting better, he seemed more listless. Duke barely looked up at Paul when he crouched down and stroked his head. "I have to leave for a bit, but I'll be back soon."

He closed the bedroom door hoping Duke wouldn't have to breathe in the lingering paint fumes. Once downstairs, he almost grabbed his winter jacket and decided he didn't need it. The spring weather was pleasant, and he was only going a couple of doors down the street.

When he got to Margaret's house, he knocked lightly on the door. After a short wait, Eric answered.

"May I come in, Eric? It'll only be for a quick visit. But I want to apologize to your mother."

Before he could say more, Margaret walked in from the living room. "Paul, I didn't expect to see you."

"I know," he said, stepping a little further into the space. That's when he noticed the people sitting in the living room. He gave them a wave and turned back to Margaret. "Dear lady, I wanted to say how sorry I am for upsetting you this morning. I also wanted to let you know that you were right about everything."

"I was?" Margaret asked.

"Yes, and I'm here to tell you that I'm moving back to Chicago. I've already inquired about a place to stay that takes pets, so I should be out of your hair within a few days." He reached out a hand to Eric. "Take care of your mother."

Eric hesitated, but finally took Paul's hand and shook it. "I will."

"Good, then I'll be going." Paul smiled at Margaret one last time, and quickly turned and let himself out the door. As he walked back to his house, he felt calm. He'd expected to feel devastated, and it didn't happen. In fact, when he thought about his options, possibly getting a teaching job at the university he'd once attended, he decided that he had everything to look forward to.

* * *

Margaret walked back into the living room and looked at Lea, Matthew, and Teresa. They were staring back with blank faces. "What just happened? Did everyone hear what Paul just told me?"

After a general nodding in her direction, Matthew spoke up. "Maybe Paul's falling apart again."

Margaret swiveled around and started for the door. "If you're right, Matthew, I better talk to him."

"I'll come too," Eric said.

Margaret looked at him. "That's very nice of you, Eric, but if Paul is in one of his moods—" She paused and glanced back at Matthew. "Maybe Matthew should come."

Matthew sat up in his seat. "Me?"

Margaret clasped her hands. "Please, Matthew, I know you'll say the right things."

Matthew reached out for Lea. "Lea, you know me. Tell Margaret she's got the wrong man."

"No, she's right," Lea insisted. "You have a knack for handling difficult people."

Matthew forced himself out of the confines of the sofa. "Okay, I'll go, but I don't know what to say to him."

Lea stood up and took his hand. "Remember when Paul was so depressed in Chicago? You wouldn't let him give up. He might need another pep talk."

Matthew grimaced. "He might need a lot more than that. Did you see how he was dressed? Was he trying to make a statement?"

"A statement about what?" Lea asked.

"He's making it clear that he's no longer part of Elkville for starters," Matthew said.

Teresa stood up. "I think you're right, Matthew. I haven't been around Paul very much, but when I've visited here, he's always been dressed in a way that made him blend in. It's almost like he wanted to leave everything about his past behind. Seeing him now, I think that's changed."

Margaret stepped into the living room. "This morning I accused him of following me here, and that I didn't appreciate it."

Teresa and Lea both went over to where she stood.

Lea spoke up first. "That's reasonable. Elkville is your home. Paul should have talked to you about moving here."

119

"Well, he did," Margaret said. "But he acted like it was only for a little while."

"He didn't give you any space," Eric added. "He bought the house two doors down and made himself right at home coming over all the time."

Margaret looked up at Eric. "So you think it was alright of me to be angry about him being so close? At first, with him helping with the clinic and all, it was fine, but now, now I don't know."

Eric's blue eyes became more focused. "Mom, you and I both agreed that we needed to rethink our lives. I don't think Paul being here has helped you to do that."

Margaret took a deep breath and let it out slowly. "Still, I'd like to talk to him before he does something that might not be for his best."

Matthew walked to the door. "Then let's go have that conversation."

Margaret grabbed his arm. "Matthew, go easy on him. I don't want him to feel completely unwanted."

"Do you want him to stay or not?" Matthew asked.

Margaret released his arm and bit her lip. "For the time being, I don't want to think about him at all. Is that selfish of me?"

Teresa took Margaret's hands. "If it helps, you're the last person I think of when I think of someone being selfish. Everyone needs to attend to their own needs first. Otherwise, they'll have nothing to give to those they love."

Matthew smiled. "Teresa, you're very good at this. Maybe you should go with Margaret."

Margaret latched on to Matthew's arm again. "No, Matthew, I think Teresa is very wise, but I need you right now."

"Why is that?" Matthew asked.

"Because you can be firm and uncompromising. And I need someone like that by my side if I'm going to believe in myself when I talk to Paul."

Twenty-Four

AS MATTHEW AND Margaret walked to Paul's house, Matthew had a sinking feeling that another crisis was brewing. But he wasn't surprised. Crisis was the theme of the day. First, he'd had a premonition that sent him into a panic. Next, he was told Margaret had a meltdown. Then Teresa and Eric pulled into town with the ailing Ned Finney.

Matthew and Eric had to literally pick up Elkville's bright, new doctor off the street when he collapsed. The guy wasn't just hurting, he wasn't able to stay on his feet. Afterwards, they got him tucked into bed and hoped he'd sleep and feel better with some rest. They thought they could relax for five minutes. They were wrong. The family barely had time to eat a meal and sit down in the living room when Paul Glass had come knocking.

The retired psychiatrist barged into Margaret's house with no warning, supposedly to ask for Margaret's forgiveness. If the guy had stopped with an apology, it would have been fine. He might even been given a piece of Margaret's freshly baked apple pie.

But no, Paul couldn't simply seek forgiveness. Paul had to tell Margaret how he was doing her a big favor by moving back to Chicago. To make things more theatrical, he'd dressed himself up like some puffer pigeon as if to show everyone who they were dealing with and how much he'd given up to live in Elkville.

Now, Margaret was worried about the man. But perhaps more importantly, Matthew sensed she was worried about herself. She was hanging on to his arm in a desperate sort of way. She'd even told him that she needed him to help her believe in herself. But it was up to Margaret to accomplish her goal.

Still, Margaret was a nurturer. He'd discussed that fact with Lea earlier. And nurturing was fine, even necessary at times. Without it, a baby would die. However, a line could be crossed when the nurturer became an enabler. From what Lea told him, Margaret confessed that she had crossed that line with Paul. But Margaret didn't stop there. She announced that she wanted to change. But how committed was she to her declaration? From what he'd experienced, people said lots of things and never followed through.

When they reached Paul's property, Matthew didn't know what he was supposed to do. If Margaret and Paul were quarreling, he wasn't about to get in the middle of their disagreement. Just as he was making that promise to himself, Margaret tugged on his arm.

"Matthew, why is Paul putting one of Duke's dog beds in his truck? Is he leaving already?"

Matthew shrugged. "I don't know why Paul does anything, but don't forget what you said to me, that you wanted to remain calm."

Margaret wasn't listening. She let go of him and rushed forward, calling out to Paul. "Paul, can we talk to you?"

Paul stopped and stared back. "I can't right now. I have to drive to Blacksburg. I have to get Duke to a vet. He's very sick."

"What's wrong with him?" Margaret asked.

"I don't know," Paul said, "but I came home and found him having trouble breathing."

"Paul, I'm so sorry. I feel like it's my fault that Duke is ailing. If I hadn't taken him out that night to find Lea—"

"Margaret, please, I don't have time to talk about it."

"At least let me go with you. I can keep an eye on Duke."

Paul hesitated. "You don't even like Duke."

"I've never been around dogs, but I'm grateful for what he did. So let me be there for him now, like he was there for Lea."

Paul gave her an anxious look. "I'm just so worried about him. He's all I have."

Matthew's brows narrowed as soon as Paul made the statement, "He's all I have." Those were words that no professed enabler, namely Margaret, could resist. It was the chum, the bone and blood, someone threw overboard to bait the fish swimming in the water. And Margaret was that fish. He quickly took Margaret's arm and gently pulled her aside. "Margaret, I have to talk to you."

Margaret's eyes met Matthew's for the slightest moment and flashed back to Paul. "Matthew, I have to help Paul. It's my fault that Duke is sick. It was so cold that night. I shouldn't have taken an old dog out in such weather."

Matthew bent down enough to look Margaret in the eye and gave her a little shake. "Margaret, you're doing it again. You're letting guilt get in the way of thinking things out."

Margaret pulled away. "Maybe so, but I have to do what's right for Paul and his dog."

"At least come back to the house and talk to your family first."

Margaret glanced at Paul's house. Paul was walking unsteadily down his sidewalk, carrying Duke. "Oh, dear lord, help him, Matthew!"

Matthew had no choice but to do as Margaret asked. Paul had a bad heart. He'd be having a heart attack next if Matthew didn't act quickly.

After that Matthew didn't have time to give the situation more thought. He followed instructions and got the ailing dog into Paul's truck. He helped Margaret get in the back seat next to the dog. He made sure she was belted in. He barely had time to close her door when Paul fired up the engine and started backing out of the driveway. At the last minute, as Paul's truck sped down the street, Matthew's mind started working again. He ran out into the road and yelled to Paul. "Where are you going? What's the name of the vet?"

Paul didn't hear him, or he didn't want to hear him. Instead, the man stepped on the gas, and the truck raced down the road. It barely stopped at the corner and kept going.

"Dammit, he's driving like a maniac!" Matthew wasn't one for cursing, but sometimes, it seemed the only way to vent his frustration.

He walked back to the Lloyd house, still trying to contain his emotions. Once inside, Lea and Eric rushed over to greet him.

"What's going on? Where's Mom?" Eric asked.

Matthew glared back. "She's with Paul Glass. His dog is sick, and he's taking it to a vet in Blacksburg. Your mother insisted on going."

Eric closed the distance between himself and Matthew. "Didn't you try to stop her?" he asked in a demanding voice. "I don't want her on the road with Paul Glass!"

Matthew didn't respond. If he let himself tell Eric what he was feeling, it wouldn't help the situation. He finally came up with his own question. "Have you ever been able to stop your mother, Eric? Have you once been able to talk some sense into her when she's determined to have her way?"

Eric backed off and averted his eyes. "I'm sorry. I should have insisted on going with her. As usual, I let Mom do as she pleased."

123

Matthew's only wish was to escape the latest Lloyd family saga. His dream would be to take Lea home and forget everything that was happening. But that wouldn't work. Family sagas, with all their pain, didn't just go away. Besides, he was a part of it now. He was committed to Lea, and Lea was committed to Margaret and Eric. They were her adopted family, and he had to be there for her. That meant standing where he was, in a small hall, and waiting for whatever happened next.

Lea put her arms around him. "I know you tried your best, Matthew. You always do."

Eric looked at Matthew. "Yes, she's right. I'm sorry for expecting something from you when it's my responsibility."

"I have a thought," Matthew said. "Paul took off before I could find out the name of the vet in Blacksburg, but it might not be too hard to get that information. We could go to Paul's house and check his recent calls. I'm sure he made one to Duke's vet."

Teresa had taken her place next to Eric and was holding his hand. "That's a great idea. And once we know where Paul and Margaret are headed, we could go after them."

Eric turned and looked at Teresa with eyes that clearly said he adored her. "I don't know about going after them. I don't know if it'll help. My mother has a mind of her own. She'll just resent me for chasing after her."

"Maybe we should all go into the dining room, have some coffee and talk about the best thing to do," Lea said.

The thought was a soothing balm to Matthew's frazzled nerves. "I could certainly use some coffee."

"Could I have some tea?" a voice called from the stairs.

Matthew looked up and saw Ned Finney making his way down, step by step.

Eric turned to give him a hand. "Are you feeling better, Ned?"

Ned smiled. "Yes, my stomach is finally settling down." He paused and stared at the group gathered in the hall. "Is everything okay?"

Matthew wasn't going to field that question. His nerves were like Ned's stomach. They were just beginning to settle. He wanted to forget what had just happened, not rehash it. He brushed the dog hair off his shirt and headed for the kitchen. "I'll put some coffee on while somebody brings Ned up to speed."

Teresa started for the kitchen too. "And I'll get Ned some tea."

Twenty-Five

TERESA WALKED INTO Margaret's kitchen and had to pause. Everything about the room reminded her of pictures she'd seen in a magazine article. It was about how people lived in bygone days. The stove, sink and work spaces had an antiquated look. Everything belonged in the past.

Matthew was at a counter, putting scoops of coffee into a coffee maker. It was one of the few things that looked like it belonged in current times. He glanced at her and held out a gallon of water. "Need some for Ned's tea?" he asked.

"Thank you, Teresa said, taking the water and pouring some into a kettle. After she put the kettle on to heat, she turned to Matthew. "It's been an interesting day. I've never been here when there's so much going on. It's helping me to understand Eric a little better."

Matthew switched on the coffee maker. "What do you mean?"

"When Eric gets off the phone with his mom, or he's been visiting here, he seems tenser than usual."

Matthew's brows shot up. "Tenser? If you're around this family or you've been in Elkville for a couple of days, you'll thank your lucky stars if you're able to put two and two together."

"That's exaggerating a little, right?"

Matthew grabbed some mugs out of a cupboard. "I'll let you form your own opinion."

"But Matthew, being a surgeon, you're used to stressful situations."

Matthew stepped a little closer. "When I'm in the OR, I bring everything I have to the table. I know how to handle just about anything that comes my way. However, this isn't the OR. We're in Elkville, an isolated place that breeds craziness. Anyone who dares to breach its borders better be prepared for that insanity."

Teresa found the tea and took out a tea bag. "It seems like a place that's fighting the ravages of poverty, that's all."

Matthew sneered. "From what I've experienced, a weapons testing ground is safer."

Teresa giggled. "Now I know you're exaggerating."

"Maybe I am, but I do know this much. If you've got any weaknesses before you come here, Elkville will ferret out those weaknesses. If you're already confused, lord help you. Either way, you'll find yourself on an emotional battlefield and not even realize it until the crap starts happening. Then it's too late. You become one of the walking wounded, trying to rescue the ones who have already fallen. You're binding up the bleeders and hoping they're strong enough for the next battle."

Teresa blinked back. She'd always considered Matthew to be well balanced and very competent. To hear him describe Elkville was a little scary. She didn't know what to say.

Matthew stared at the tea bag in Teresa's hand. "Is that for Ned?"

"Yes, what about it?"

Matthew handed her a mug. "I have a request. Don't make Ned's tea too hot. He'll be burning himself next, and we can't have that happen. We have to get him back on his feet and ready for duty."

"What duty? You mean his job at the clinic? He claims he's hardly been needed so far."

Matthew picked up the other mugs he'd set out. "It's called the calm before the storm. Pray that you're out of here before that storm hits."

Eric walked into the kitchen. "How's it going in here?"

"Just keeping our heads above the water line," Matthew said. "Now I better check on Lea and Doc Ned."

As soon as Matthew left, Teresa beckoned Eric closer. "Eric, I'm worried about him."

"About Matthew? Why?"

"He said some things that didn't sound too rational."

"Like what?"

"Like making sure Ned's tea wasn't too hot, that he might burn himself."

Eric moved to the stove as the kettle started whistling. "Is this boiling water for Ned's tea?"

"Yes, it is."

"Well then, here's what I think you should do. When you put the boiling water in the cup, only fill the cup half way. Put the tea bag in and let it seep. When you think it's strong enough, dilute it with cool water."

"Are you serious?"

"I'm just making sure you follow Matthew's instructions."

"But, Eric—"

"Please, Teresa, I know Matthew might sound a bit extreme, but he has a sense about these things."

"Okay, I'll do it for you," Teresa said as she put the tea bag in a mug and partially filled it.

For her sweet husband's sake, she'd play along with Matthew's suggestion, but she still had trouble giving any credibility to his description of Elkville. To think of the place as some sort of battlefield was too much of a stretch.

"Eric, how are you doing, you know, with your mom going off with Paul?"

Eric frowned thoughtfully and took a cookie jar from a cupboard shelf. He began putting cookies on a plate. "I've decided I have to resign myself to letting Mom live her life as she sees fit. Otherwise, I'll be fighting with her constantly."

"That makes sense. You can't make people change."

"For Mom's sake, I hope I'm doing the right thing." He looked at the cookies and then at Teresa. "I know we just ate a bit ago, but sweets seem to sooth people's nerves."

Teresa pointed to the coffee maker. "I think the coffee is ready. You can take it in too."

While Eric was serving the coffee, Teresa checked on Ned's tea. It looked like it was sufficiently steeped and cooled to an appropriate temperature. "I just hope Ned doesn't think it's too cold," she muttered as she took it into the dining room. She smiled at Ned when she served it. "Here's that tea you requested."

Ned picked up his mug. "Thanks, but don't get too close, Teresa. I might have some kind of stomach virus."

Lea was sitting at the other end of the table, next to Matthew. "I thought the nausea was caused by the pain meds."

"It probably was, but I'm not taking any chances," Ned said.

"Is your stomach still off?" Matthew asked.

"It's much better, so maybe there isn't a problem."

"Make sure to stay hydrated," Eric cautioned.

"This tea will help," Ned said as he brought the mug to his lips. He was about to take a sip when a car backfired out on the street. Ned jerked enough to spill his tea down the front of his shirt.

Teresa jumped too, but she quickly reached for some napkins and handed them to Ned.

"Sorry, I don't usually react like that." Ned patted himself down. "It's a good thing this tea isn't too hot, or I'd have to add another woe to my list of complaints."

Teresa looked at Eric to check his reaction, but Eric just gave her a shrug.

Matthew didn't seem as comfortable with the incident. His eyes were a bit too wide, like he was surprised that his advice would actually be needed. He stood up and looked around at the table's occupants. "Excuse us, but I have to talk to Eric about something."

Eric shrugged again, stood up too and followed Matthew out of the room.

* * *

Matthew let himself out of the house and held the door for Eric to follow him. Once they were standing on the front porch, he studied the wooden slat flooring. It looked recently painted a battleship grey. The color was appropriate. It matched his mood. He'd always known how to steer his life. There was always a feeling of certainty that formed the foundation of how he saw the world. Now, he was surrounded by a sea of doubt. He didn't know which way to steer anything. He thought he needed to talk to Eric about how he felt, but the feeling had passed. When he didn't say anything, Eric spoke up.

"What is it, Matthew? Why are you so quiet?"

"I'm contemplating my future and wondering if I'll end up working in that pet shop you once mentioned."

"That's a surprise."

"Yes, it's a surprise to me too."

"So why would you leave a career that means so much to you?"

"Because I'm drifting, and I can't afford to behave like that and still be responsible."

"Drifting? How?"

"I was in the kitchen with Teresa, and without thinking, I was telling her to be careful about Ned's tea."

"And it's a good thing. The guy would have burned himself."

"Yes, and I'm glad that didn't happen."

"But—"

"Eric, don't you see what's going on? I'm becoming like you!"

Eric stepped back and crossed his arms. "Well, I'm sorry that you find that so devastating."

"I'm not saying there's something wrong with you. Every person has to embrace who he is, but I'm starting to lose that ability. The Matthew Howell I know myself to be is disappearing!"

Eric let his arms fall to his sides. "Let's back up. Just because you had a spontaneous, sixth-sense feeling about Ned's safety doesn't mean you're not you."

"You're wrong. The real me doesn't have that kind of sixth-sense whatever. And if it happens when I'm on the job, I could spontaneously make the wrong move." He rubbed his forehead. "On top of it all, I'm getting one of those horrible headaches I sometimes get."

Eric smiled. "I remember when you had one at the Ferguson mansion. I helped you to get rid of it. I bet I could help you now."

Matthew quickly backed up. "Don't you dare touch me again. I think that's how all of this got started. Your mumbo-jumbo kind of healing did something to me, and I've been paying the price ever since."

"As I remember, your pain went away, and you felt happy afterwards."

"Exactly! But I'm not the happy type, Eric, and whatever you did has come to this! I'm having premonitions and telling Teresa how to make tea for Ned."

Eric stalled. "You had a premonition? What did you see? It wasn't my mother getting hurt, was it?"

"No, it was a general feeling of disaster, one that involved all of us."

Eric went over and leaned on the porch railing. "Then we better prepare ourselves."

"So you think what I felt was real?"

"Of course it was."

"So why are you saying we have to be prepared when we don't know what to prepare for?"

"You of all people should know the answer, Matthew. When you went to medical school, you learned everything you could about treating people, and you did it for a reason. You didn't know what was coming your way, but you tried to prepare yourself."

"I get that, but I don't know what the disaster involves. It could be anything. It might have already happened. Ned was injured, your mom and Paul had a falling out, Paul is leaving, and his dog is sick."

"That's true, but what you have to ask yourself is a simple question."

Matthew held up a hand and took a deep breath. He was almost afraid of what that question might be. He finally nodded. "Go on."

"Matthew, is the worst yet to come?"

Matthew didn't let himself think about the answer. Instead, he needed to get away from all of Eric's nonsense. A sudden blinding pain came to his rescue and nearly struck him down. It also succeeded in short-circuiting any further thought about topics he needed to forget. He grabbed for one of the porch columns to steady himself. When he was able to breathe again, his stomach was churning.

He stumbled down the porch stairs. "Ned's given me his stomach bug," he groaned. In the next breath, he threw up on the lawn. As he tried to stand, Eric took his arm.

"This isn't a bug," Eric whispered.

Matthew recovered enough to wipe the drool off his face with his handkerchief. "What?"

"I know things too. And I know you don't have a bug. But you're in no shape to think about that now. You have to lie down."

It was true. Matthew had confessed all his weaknesses to Eric, and it only made things more unmanageable. He had to retreat, to have time to forget everything. He didn't have much choice with his head trying to split open. "Tell Lea I'm not well," he instructed.

"Feel better soon," Eric said.

Matthew paused long enough to stare back at Eric. The man's slender build was set against the mountain range in the distance. The two didn't go together. Eric's clean-shaven face, fair skin, white-blond hair and genteel ways had nothing to do with the Appalachians. The vast range of mountains and the people who lived in its crags and valleys were the opposite of anything genteel. They had to be.

130

In a brief instant, Matthew had another vision of sorts. He glimpsed what those people's ancestors had gone through. When they dared to lay claim to a patch of the mountains, they did it without thinking about the consequences. Generation after generation paid a price for their desire to own something too vast to be possessed. As a result the mountains stripped them bare. To survive, they had to be as wild and stubborn as their environment.

Matthew felt like some great force was stripping him bare too, but he didn't want to end up wild or stubborn. He wanted to go back to civilization. He wanted to escape the foreboding and fear that had taken up residence in his psyche.

When he felt he could manage it, he turned and walked across the yard. He opened the door to the house that had been built by Lea's father. With all its modern conveniences, it was supposed to be a small oasis where he could feel comfortable and safe. The comfort part was true. He could find solace in the bed waiting for him, but the house and all its trappings couldn't protect him. Something as vast and untamed as the mountains was closing in, and no house was going to keep it from having its way.

His only choice was to recoup, to find the strength to push back his fears and to hold on to what was real for him. Otherwise he'd become as crazy as the people in the hills.

Twenty-Six

LEA DIDN'T KNOW how to help Matthew. His headache was so severe, he had to go to bed. When she tried to sit by his side, he told her that even her breathing was making the pain worse. He pleaded with her to leave him alone. That's when she knew she needed support and asked Teresa, Eric and Ned to come over.

The three of them were gathered in her living room. Teresa and Eric sat on the sofa and were anxious to do whatever they could. However, Ned was laid out in a recliner, sleeping again.

Lea took a seat close to where Teresa and Eric were sitting. She kept her voice low, not wanting to wake Ned. "I'm scared. I think that Elkville, this house, and my spending so much time here has been too much for Matthew. Maybe it's been too much for me. I completely lost it the other night."

"How are you doing now?" Teresa asked.

"Since Matthew and I talked about everything and reconnected, I feel more like myself. Actually, we were having a wonderful time together. Then everything fell apart today. Matthew fell apart."

"When I stopped over yesterday, he did seem fine," Eric said.

Lea sat up a little straighter. "Eric, I think you know something that you're not telling me."

Eric lowered his voice. "Did Matthew mention anything about a premonition?"

"Yes, how did you know?" Lea asked. "He said something about being afraid he was becoming your clone."

Teresa gave Eric a thoughtful glance. "When you say 'premonition,' are you talking about how you felt about me? You were afraid I might be involved in an accident."

Eric took Teresa's hand. "Yes, I've had those kinds of feelings most of my life. But knowing something bad is going to happen isn't for the faint of heart."

"I'm sorry you're burdened with that sort of thing," Teresa said. "It must be very hard."

"It is what it is. I've learned to accept it."

Lea sat back and thought about Matthew's reaction that morning. "I don't think Matthew has any intention of accepting what he saw."

"That's understandable. It can turn a person's world upside down," Eric said.

Teresa sat back and crossed her arms. "When we were in the kitchen earlier, Matthew went on and on about what was coming. He made me feel like we were in for a disaster if we stayed in Elkville."

"I wonder," Eric sighed. "Maybe Matthew's fears aren't about Elkville, but about himself. When we talked, he seemed worried about his career."

"That makes sense," Teresa said. "You said your feelings aren't necessarily specific. Like your feelings about me having an accident. It was actually Ned who had the accident."

Ned stirred in the recliner and opened his eyes. "Did I fall asleep again?"

Lea got up and went over to him. "Ned, how are you doing?"

Ned tried to sit up and groaned. "I can't keep my eyes open. I hardly slept last night, so maybe I'm catching up."

Lea smiled. "We have an extra bedroom, why don't you use it."

"I should get back to the clinic."

"Just stay the night and go back tomorrow."

Ned tried to move again and laid back. "Maybe you're right."

"Do you think you could eat something?" Lea asked. "I'm going to make sandwiches for everyone a little later."

Teresa came over. "And I'll help you."

Eric started for the stairs. "I'm going to check on Matthew."

"Thanks, Eric," Lea said. "I know you said he won't let you use your healing abilities, but—"

"Healing abilities?" Ned asked. "What's that about?"

Lea smiled. "Eric is a very gifted person, but most people don't believe in his gifts."

Ned glanced at Eric. "How does it work?"

Eric frowned. "It doesn't work most of the time, but on some occasions, I feel like I can help heal someone. It's not something I control one way or the other."

"That's unfortunate," Ned said. "I could use some help just getting out of this chair."

Eric walked over to him. "That I can do," he said, extending a hand.

Ned grabbed hold and slowly got to his feet. Once standing, he smiled. "I know I still look like an invalid, but overall, I feel a lot better." He rubbed his stomach. "I think I'm ready for more tea and maybe some crackers."

Lea started for the kitchen. "Follow me, and I'll show you where everything is. That way you can have whatever you want. That goes for you, too, Teresa. If you're going to be staying here, I want you to feel at home."

"I'll be back in a bit," Eric said as he went to the stairs.

Lea paused and looked back at him. "Thank you, Eric, you're still my angel, you know."

Teresa looked confused. "Eric's your angel?"

"Yes, he was there when I was like Matthew, caught up in my fears. When the darkness seemed to be taking over, Eric helped me find the light again. I'll always be grateful."

* * *

Ned followed Lea and Teresa into the kitchen. With each step he could feel his body getting just a little stronger. His emotions were balancing out too. Maybe it had to do with the people he was with. If he didn't worry about all the irrational stuff they talked about, he could enjoy how thoughtful and kind they were. He pulled out a chair from the table without too much effort, sat down and looked up at Teresa. She was smiling at him.

"What about some eggs and toast?" she asked.

Earlier in the day, Ned felt like he'd never want food again. But that had changed. He was hungry. It gave him a new appreciation of how fast bodies could heal. "Eggs and toast sound good."

As he waited for his meal, he watched the activity around him. Teresa was getting bread out of its wrapper, and Lea was at the stove, putting a kettle on. Both seemed content. He felt content too until he thought about Lea's remark. She'd called Eric her angel.

Ned had a distant memory of what an angel was supposed to be. When he was young, his mother gave him a little picture book about a lost baby angel. The book was already old and tattered. His mother probably found it at one of the garage sales she enjoyed checking out. But he liked the pictures in the book. They told the story of a sister and brother who helped the lost angel. Seeing the boy and girl together, Ned often wished he had a sibling he could talk to. He might have even mentioned the idea to his father. Then one day, the book was gone.

Looking back, Ned figured his dad probably threw it out. Thinking about his father from his adult point of view, Ned began to see John Finney in a different light. Was he really the wonderful father that Ned thought him to be? If he was, why did he leave the house when his wife was having a crying fit? Why didn't he do something to help her?

If only Ned could have been his mother's angel, like Eric was for Lea, things might have been different. In his young heart, he did want to be there for her, but he didn't know how. Her world of tears often swallowed her up. She'd shut her bedroom door and wouldn't come out for hours. Ned heard her crying, but he was too little to know how to rescue her.

He was snapped out of his memories when Teresa brought over a plate of food. But the feelings of sadness didn't go away. He wondered why his mother never tried to visit him. He never got a clear answer when he asked his father about it. He stared down at his eggs and felt his stomach tighten. He looked at Teresa. "Thanks for making this for me, but maybe I'll only eat the toast."

Teresa returned an easy smile. "Do whatever you feel is best."

Lea came over and put her hand on his shoulder. "I'm glad you're staying here tonight."

Lea was touching him again, and it felt uncomfortable. Did she want something? "I don't quite understand why you're being so nice."

Lea smiled. "Because I like having family around."

"But I'm not family."

"Maybe not technically, but Margaret and Eric told me I was family shortly after they invited me into their home." Lea withdrew her hand. "I liked the idea, but maybe that was just me."

135

"It's very kind of you to think of me that way, but my dad is my family." Ned forced himself to his feet. "Sorry, but I think I need more sleep. Maybe you could show me the bedroom you want me to use."

Lea frowned and nodded. "Of course."

Once he was assigned his room, Ned shut the door. He had let himself indulge in old memories again. It didn't help. It only aggravated his body. He lay down in his bed and promised himself he wouldn't do it again. He closed his eyes, wanting sleep, but there was a knock on his door. "Come in," he called out.

Teresa opened the door and brought over tea and toast and a side of cherry jam. She put them on his nightstand. "Just in case you change your mind," she said.

After she left, Ned sat up and took a bite of the toast. It seemed to help steady his body. He put jam on the remainder of the toast and continued eating. He was determined to get his strength back and return to the clinic so he could be on his own again.

* * *

Eric sat in the shadows of Matthew's room. There wasn't much light, but his night vision was excellent. He could see Matthew's chest as it rose and fell.

When he first entered the room, Matthew's breath was more erratic. Eric's initial instinct was to help ease the situation. But he sat down instead. Matthew had made his wishes known. It was a hands-off kind of case. Eric wouldn't dare override Matthew's orders.

As he made himself relax, he also stilled his mind. Being empathetic, he'd learned that thoughts could sometimes be as damaging as a physical violation. Angry thoughts had an energy that could be felt as surely as a hand slapping you. So perhaps, if he could sit with Matthew with a quiet mind, one that only entertained thoughts of harmony and composure, maybe they could bring a bit of peace to the hurting surgeon. After all, Matthew might not like it, but Eric was sure Matthew was empathetic too.

Eric's stillness took him back to childhood. He'd known how to soar as a boy. He'd sit in the woods, and his mind would let go of its bodily confines. He'd feel himself leaving behind his mother's constant busyness, and his father's obsessive need for control. He'd enter something that felt a little like a pleasant dream. It could be so enticing that he wished he could remain in the dream and never return home. But hunger and not wanting to worry his mom were strong motivators.

Enjoying the quiet in Matthew's room, he was tempted to soar again, to leave the current problems with his mother and his failures behind. He decided against it. He wasn't a child anymore. He was a man now, and he had to find a way to do more than soar in the heavens. He had to find a way to bring a bit of the peace and serenity of the heavens back into his life.

* * *

Matthew thought he heard someone come into the room, but he didn't dare move or open his eyes. Perhaps it was Lea, coming to check on him again. He couldn't let himself think about it. It wouldn't help his throbbing head.

After a few minutes, his tense muscles eased just a bit. He'd been battling the pain and realized he was probably aggravating the problem. He forced himself to breathe, not in gasps, but with longer, calmer inhalations. It seemed to help.

As his body settled a little, the feeling that he wasn't alone came back. He barely opened his eyes and was grateful that the blinds were shut and the curtains were closed over them. It left the room in relative darkness. If there was anyone in the room, he decided it didn't matter. He had to focus on only one thing, reducing the stress in his body. When he began to feel a little drowsy, he was encouraged. Sometimes he could sleep off a monster headache.

He closed his eyes again and thought he heard someone breathing. Or was it his imagination? He didn't care. His lids felt too heavy to open them again. Sleep was calling to him, and he had every intention of going with it.

Twenty-Seven

FOR MARGARET THE trip to Blacksburg was very troubling. She'd had time to think about how she conducted herself with Matthew before she left. After Paul's visit to her house and his announcement that he was moving, she'd asked Matthew to be there for her, to help her make good decisions when she talked to Paul. But she hadn't listened to the surgeon any more than she'd listened to Eric. Without any hesitation, she insisted on having her way.

Matthew asked her to slow down and discuss the best course of action, but Margaret didn't have any idea about how to slow down. Her entire married life was one of constant activity. And the activity had an urgency to it. That urgency dictated an order of importance. First and foremost, her family had to be fed, the house had to be clean, and she had to support her husband in his role as a doctor. Each day started out the same and ended the same. She got up, tended to things that needed doing and dropped into bed feeling worn out each night.

Nothing changed when Eric moved away or when her husband died. Somehow, she always found something to do. The house still needed cleaning even when there was no one there to dirty it. She still baked and gave her goods to neighbors. If she had to sit in the evenings, she'd read books or knitted blankets with complicated patterns that kept her mind engaged.

Paul's attitude wasn't any better than hers. He refused to listen to her or Matthew. He insisted on leaving for Blacksburg in a complete panic. Once on the road, he didn't slow down. Needless to say, she found his fast driving very uncomfortable. By the time they got to Blacksburg, her nerves were frayed, and she wasn't happy. But she couldn't blame Paul. She was the one who just had to go along with the man. "Just like I went along with my Ricky no matter what," she whispered silently.

Once they arrived at the vet's office, things became more orderly. The people who were there to take care of Duke were calm. They helped Paul get the dog out of the truck, and then asked that Paul and Margaret remain in the waiting room while they ran some tests.

At least Margaret made one good decision. She borrowed Paul's cell phone and called her house to talk to Eric. She wanted to let him know she was fine. When she didn't get an answer, she called Lea's house. Eric was there, but he wasn't available. He was sitting with Matthew. The man had taken ill with one of his headaches. After that, her conversation with Lea was short.

"Yes, Lea, I'm fine. Yes, I'll call again later when I know how Duke is. Don't worry about me. Like I said, I'm fine."

She handed the phone back to Paul knowing she'd just lied. She wasn't fine. She was worried about herself. Would she ever stop her busy mind from calling the shots? Would she ever slow down and make decisions that didn't scare her loved ones? Would she ever take their feelings into consideration when they disagreed with her? So far her track record was pretty dismal. Was there any hope that it would improve? It scared her when she thought about her future. More than anything, she wanted it to be different than her past.

* * *

Paul sat next to Margaret, trying to get a handle on his emotions. They were totally out of whack. Sure he could make an excuse and say it was because of Duke. But that wasn't what fueled his actions before the Duke crisis.

He'd let himself act the fool. Dressing up, marching over to Margaret's and telling everyone how he was moving away was ridiculous. He hadn't acted that childishly since he was a little boy. What was wrong with him? How did he let himself get to a point in life where he could behave like that?

After Margaret borrowed his phone, he looked at her, not with a glance, but he really looked at her. Her face was twisted and her hands were knotted together in stress. He'd been telling himself that he liked her as a friend. That was true, but he kept denying the fact that he'd never been able to let go of his deeper feelings. But they were obvious. Matthew even called him on it.

139

But if he really cared about Margaret, would he be acting like he was acting? Absolutely not. He knew better. His mother had taught him how to behave when he was still in short pants. And a person didn't punish another just because they were angry.

He cleared his throat, stood up and looked at Margaret again. "Margaret?"

"Yes?" Margaret asked.

"I want to apologize for everything. My behavior today was inexcusable."

"You weren't the only one who was inexcusable, Paul."

Paul studied the floor. "You were right about me. I left my practice because my pride was damaged. And I moved to Elkville for all the wrong reasons. Now, my actions have come to this. I've hurt you and myself. And I don't know how to fix any of it."

Margaret nodded. "My life feels like a mess that I'm never going to get straightened out."

Seeing the sadness in Margaret's eyes and hearing the desperate tone of her voice, Paul remembered all the patients he'd had in the past. He remembered being there to help them find themselves again. He wanted to do that for Margaret. "Don't give up hope, dear lady. Believe in yourself."

Margaret scowled at him but didn't answer.

Paul tried to straighten his shoulders a little. They'd been hunched and stiff ever since he'd left Elkville. He could tell he'd failed to help Margaret feel better, and he needed to do something useful. "I'll be right back. I'm going to check on Duke."

After talking to the doctor in charge, Paul returned to Margaret to relay what he'd been told. "Good news, they think Duke is going to be okay, but they want to keep him overnight, just in case."

Margaret got to her feet. "Good, at least your dog is going to live."

"Yes, so I'll drive you back to Elkville, but I was wondering if we could first stop for something to eat."

"Alright, but I better call Lea again and let her know what I'm doing."

* * *

Paul took a large bite of his fish fillet sandwich, chewed a little and swallowed. He hadn't eaten since breakfast, and he was hungry. He'd chosen fast food so that he could get Margaret home as soon as possible. Margaret didn't seem hungry and only wanted an iced tea.

She looked at him with a frown. "You don't have to bolt your food, Paul. I'm not in that big a hurry."

Paul wiped his mouth and took a sip of water. "I feel bad about not letting you even have time to talk to Eric before you left. I acted like an idiot."

"Eric should be happy to be rid of me with the way I behave."

"Margaret, please, don't say that. Eric is one of the most devoted sons I've ever met."

Margaret grabbed her napkin and dabbed her eyes. "Is that supposed to make me feel better?"

"Everything I say is wrong, so I better keep my mouth shut," Paul said and picked up his sandwich.

Margaret sniffled. "You don't have children. You don't know what it's like to have a son like Eric. Every time I see the hurt in his eyes, it breaks my heart."

Paul put his sandwich down. "Why do you feel like that?"

"Because I'm the one who raised him. I'm the one who didn't pay attention to his feelings when he was a little boy. He grew up without a mother or father who had room for his emotional needs. Now, he's ruined."

Paul couldn't help but smile. "Think what you want, but I don't believe that for a minute. Eric might have a few issues, but he's working them out. And he has a wonderful wife who'll be there for him when he needs encouragement."

Margaret squeezed the napkin in her hand. "Do you think he'll be okay?"

"Yes, in my personal and professional opinion, I think Eric will do just fine."

"Your professional opinion? I thought that was all behind you."

"So did I, but I'm reconsidering my decision."

"When you return to Chicago, do you think you'll go back to doing what you did before?"

"I'm not sure, but I might do volunteer work. Goodness knows there are a lot of people who can't afford that kind of help otherwise."

"I wish I could go back to something."

141

"What do you mean?"

"All I know is being a wife and mother in a little forgotten part of the world."

"You could help out at the clinic. You learned a lot as a doctor's wife, and I'm sure Ned could use an assistant."

"No, I don't want to do that kind of thing anymore."

"Why is that?"

"Because I'll go to my grave never feeling like I had a life I chose."

"But you did choose, Margaret. You chose to be a wife and mother."

"Maybe, but that's behind me. I want something different. I just don't know what it is."

"Did you ever think that's the perfect place to start? Sometimes not knowing exactly what you want opens up countless possibilities."

"I don't need countless possibilities. I just need a direction that feels right."

"You'll find it."

"How can you say that when I'm sitting here not knowing up from down anymore?"

"You survived a difficult past because you're a strong woman. That strength will carry you through these times. But I would advise you to give yourself a breather. Sometimes, things like knowing what you want take time."

Margaret dropped her gaze and sipped her iced tea. When she looked up again, she sighed. "Oh goodness, I don't know if I can do what you're suggesting. The idea of waiting and giving myself time scares me. I have something inside that says I have to keep going. I don't know anything else."

Paul smiled. "I have an idea."

"What now?"

"Maybe you need to get away from Elkville too."

"I tried that. I moved to Baltimore and lived with Eric. It didn't change anything."

"Margaret, come with me to Chicago. Let me take you to concerts and plays. Let me get you out of what you've known for so long and introduce you to another world, the world of art and culture. After a month, you can see if you feel differently."

"Paul, if you think it's going to change how I feel about you—"

Paul shook his head. "No, I don't think anything of the sort. I simply had an idea that you've been in a rut, and a change would do you good. It might help Eric too."

Margaret raised her chin a little. "How's that? How would my going to Chicago have anything to do with my son?"

Paul's enthusiasm had been on the wane for quite a while. Now, it was resurrecting itself. His voice was more animated when he spoke. "Be an example for Eric. Show him that you're open to new ideas. Show him that you can enjoy yourself. Because that's what he wants. He wants you to be happy."

Margaret hesitated. When she spoke, her voice had an iffy tone. "I guess that makes sense."

Paul put a crispy fry in his mouth. He forced himself to chew it slowly. He took another sip of water and hesitated. When he brought his eyes in line with Margaret's, he knew he was doing it again. He was letting himself want more from life, from Margaret, than he should. But that wasn't right. He had to think of what was best for her. "Margaret, I don't want to tell you something that puts pressure on you. I'd like to show you a city I love, but I don't want to be pushy. So please do whatever it is that makes you feel better."

Margaret brushed a crumb off her side of the table. "Thank you, Paul. I'll think about what you said."

Twenty-Eight

MATTHEW WOKE UP, opened his eyes and stretched. He felt almost one hundred per cent again. His head was pain free, and the dark mood he'd been in had vanished. He looked at the clock and had to look again. "Eight in the morning?" He managed to sleep for nine hours straight. The last he remembered, Lea had climbed into bed around eleven the night before. He'd already been sleeping and was starting to feel better. Lea insisted that he go back to sleep, and he did, with Lea in his arms.

She was missing from his bed now, but he knew their connection was there. He sat up with a renewed sense of well-being. He inhaled deeply and smelled coffee and something else. Had Lea been baking?

He got up, went directly to the shower and let the hot water further restore his body. Any tightness in his muscles was soon gone. After shaving and dressing, he was ready for the day. He went down the stairs with a spring in his step and followed his nose to the kitchen.

Everyone was gathered around the table. When the house was built, it didn't include a separate dining room. Rather, a good-sized area off the kitchen served as a general dining area. A hutch and a rectangular table that could accommodate eight people occupied the space. Eric and Teresa looked comfortable sitting next to each other on one side of the table, Ned was on one end, and Lea sat across from the Lloyds.

"Good morning, all," Matthew said as he walked over to a counter.

Lea turned to greet him. "How are you feeling?"

Matthew poured himself a mug of coffee. "I'm doing well."

Lea smiled. "You're just in time for breakfast. We have biscuits, gravy and scrambled eggs. Come and sit down."

Matthew went over to Lea, kissed her cheek and took a seat. He was in luck. The table was filled with platters of food, and he was ready for a good meal. "You've been busy, Lea."

Lea looked at Teresa. "I had help. I found out that Teresa is a whiz when it comes to baking."

Teresa laughed. "As Eric will tell you, I rarely bake at home. I don't usually have the time."

Eric held up a buttered biscuit. "Your secret is out now, my darling wife."

Matthew scooped some eggs on his plate and grabbed a biscuit. "Looks great."

Ned glanced at Teresa, than Lea. "Everything is delicious. Thank you both. I think I'm finally getting back to normal."

Matthew was about to take a bite of eggs and looked at Eric. "How's your mom? I presume she's returned from Blacksburg."

Eric nodded. "She and Paul got back last night. Lea asked her if she wanted to join us for breakfast, but she said she'd see us all later."

Matthew chewed thoughtfully and sipped some coffee. "And Paul's mutt? Is he still with us?"

Lea nudged Matthew's arm. "His name is Duke, and he's at the vet's."

"Mom says the veterinarian thinks he'll be okay in a couple of days," Eric said.

Matthew was about to have another bite of biscuit and paused. "Thank goodness for that. If Paul loses that animal, he'll probably fall apart."

Ned pushed his plate away and stood up. "I better be going. I have a job I've been neglecting."

Matthew waved to the young man and silently said a prayer of thanks. He could relax. Elkville had its doctor back.

* * *

After Teresa and Eric left to return to Margaret's house, Lea took some serving dishes off the table and put them on the counter. Matthew was loading the dishwasher, and she tapped his shoulder. "Maybe you should let those go."

Matthew turned and looked at her. "I thought you liked to keep the kitchen tidy."

Lea smiled. "I do, but we have the house to ourselves for a while, and I thought—"

Matthew stared back. "Yes, go on. Explain what you have in mind."

She put her hands around his neck. "Oh, I'll let your imagination do that."

Matthew's eyes brightened, and he returned a sly smile. "Do you think you can handle my imagination?"

"From my experience, I believe I can."

Matthew laughed. "From my experience, I agree."

Lea took his hand and started out of the kitchen. "I'm just so happy that you're feeling good again. Eric is truly a wonderful friend."

"Eric?" Matthew asked.

"Yes, he sat in your room for a long time."

Matthew stopped short and crossed his arms. "I gave Eric specific instructions not to interfere."

Lea smiled. "Don't worry. He didn't use his healing abilities. He just wanted to be there in case you needed anything. Wasn't that nice of him?"

Matthew walked over to the couch and sat down. "I guess so, but still."

Lea followed and sat down next to him. "What is it?"

Matthew reached for Lea's hand this time. "I don't know, but ever since he helped with my headache at your parents' house, I wonder about everything. I don't feel like myself anymore."

"In what way?"

"I know you don't remember us before you ran off, but we were different people."

Lea pulled her hand out of Matthew's and stared down at her lap. "I guess we were. According to my diary, I've changed completely." She looked up at Matthew. "But I thought you liked who I am now."

"Of course, I do. You're not the problem. I am. I woke up this morning and almost started whistling. Where did that come from? I've never whistled in my life."

"Not even as a child?"

"Well, maybe, but I'm not a whistler now."

"I don't think I understand what you're getting at. Is this about that premonition you had?"

"Yes, being happy, having premonitions, that's not the person I used to be or want to be now."

"Matthew, I think you have a trust issue."

"Maybe you're right. We're sitting here, and a part of me wants to take you upstairs and make love to you. But there's another part that says I'm fooling myself. That we'll no sooner think all is well and good when something horrible will swoop in and—"

"And I'll run off again?"

Matthew turned away. "Maybe. All I know is if that happened and I didn't have the old Matthew Howell to fall back on, I couldn't handle it."

Lea put her hand on Matthew's again. "This is a pretty weird situation. I'm scared of my old self, and you're scared of your new self. We make quite the pair."

Matthew gave her the briefest smile. "I guess it does sound ridiculous."

Lea stood up. "Let's forget it all and take advantage of what we have now, a few hours to ourselves."

Matthew got to his feet. "Teresa said I exaggerate. Maybe she was right."

Lea started for the stairs. "I think so. You've had all these bad feelings, but nothing bad really happened. Ned was actually lucky that he wasn't seriously injured. Now, he's back at the clinic. Margaret got upset with Paul, but when I spoke with her last night, she seemed okay. Even Paul's dog is recovering. All in all, things are fine."

Matthew rubbed his temples. "I hope you're right."

Lea was about to put her foot on the first step when the doorbell rang, followed by a hard knock. She turned, went to the door, opened it and saw Eric standing on the porch.

"Sorry to bother you, Lea, but Ned just called. He says he can use some help."

"What kind of help?" Matthew asked.

"When Ned got to the clinic, there were people waiting. From what he can tell, two of them have knife wounds, and there's a child who keeps screaming when Ned gets near him."

Matthew grabbed his jacket and started for the door. "I guess things aren't fine after all," he grumbled.

Eric looked at Lea. "While we're gone, could you talk to Mom? She seems very preoccupied, but as usual, she won't tell me anything."

* * *

Lea walked over to Margaret's house thinking about Matthew and hoping he didn't get another headache. She was sure he was going to be challenged at the clinic. He didn't have any experience around children.

As she climbed Margaret's front steps, she reminded herself that she had to put aside her concerns for Matthew. If Margaret was having more doubts about herself, Lea had to be ready to support her. When Margaret came to the door, the older woman managed a smile and quickly invited Lea into the living room.

Lea sat down on a well-used, upholstered chair. Margaret seemed unsure, with her hands clasped in her lap, and her eyes staring straight ahead. Lea didn't know what to say. Even more importantly, she didn't want to say the wrong thing.

She rubbed her hand over the arm of the chair. Its flowered fabric was faded and worn. Margaret looked worn too. Lea offered a hopeful smile. "I was happy to hear that Paul's dog is going to be alright. From what Matthew said, Paul was very worried about him."

Margaret nodded. "I can't imagine what Matthew thinks of Paul and me. We looked like we'd taken leave of our senses when we left for Blacksburg."

"You must have been worried about Paul and his dog."

Instead of agreeing, Margaret's eyes became wistful and sad. "Did I ever tell you that the chair you're sitting in was my Ricky's favorite? So many nights he'd come home absolutely drained. He'd sit in that chair reading, trying to catch up on what was going on in medicine. Of course, he and I both knew it was useless. How could he keep up with so many advances happening? But he never stopped caring. He said he might read something that could mean life or death for one of his patients."

"He was very dedicated."

"Yes, but what good did it do?" Margaret asked. "He'd patch up people, and they'd go back to their same lives. Today, most of them are as poor as ever."

"We've talked about an outreach program, but I don't know if it's right for me at this point. I want to spend more time with Matthew."

"It's not right for me either. It might sound selfish, but I want to do something else with my life."

"There's nothing selfish about that."

Margaret's eyes sparked just the slightest. "So you think it's alright if I leave Elkville?"

"What? Leave? You?"

Margaret drew her lips together in a pinched sort of way. "Do you think that's wrong? Should I stay here and help with the clinic?"

"No, it's not that. I'm just surprised. You always said this is your home. That's why you moved back, isn't it?"

"I came back thinking I needed time to sort things out. It hasn't happened. In fact, the only thing I've sorted out is that I'm not happy. I'm old, bad-tempered, and stuck."

"I don't agree with how you see yourself, but if you need a change, where would you like to go?"

"Paul invited me to go to Chicago. He said the change of scenery would help me to see more of my options."

"Are you going to accept his invitation?"

"Maybe."

Lea smiled. "I'd love it if you did go to Chicago. We could see each other whenever we wanted. In fact, we have a two bedroom apartment. You could stay with us for as long as you liked."

For the first time since Lea came over, Margaret laughed. "Wouldn't Matthew love that? Me moving in with you two. The man would have a stroke."

"Matthew works a lot. While he's gone, you and I could have fun together."

Margaret giggled softly. "That's all very nice, but if Paul wants me to come to Chicago, he's going to have to make arrangements for where I'm going to stay." She sat up a little straighter. "I'm sure he can afford it, and I think he needs to think about someone besides himself for a change."

Lea sat back in her chair. "You've given this idea some serious thought."

"When Paul first mentioned it, I wasn't interested. But I've had time to consider it. I think it might be exactly what I need."

"Have you talked to Eric about your thoughts?" Lea asked.

149

"No, but this might be a good time for that kind of conversation. With Teresa at his side, he might be more receptive. But no matter what, if he approves or not, it's not up to him."

"I have a thought. Why don't I fix a nice dinner for everyone? Afterwards, when we're all fed and content, you could tell Eric your plans."

"That's very sweet of you, Lea. But I don't want to burden you with making a big meal."

"I have everything I need for lasagna. It wouldn't be any trouble."

"If you have dinner for all of us, I insist on bringing over a salad and dessert," Margaret said.

"Great, and we can ask Ned over too, but maybe we shouldn't include Paul. It might be easier to have a conversation about you going to Chicago without him there."

Margaret nodded. "Yes, you're right."

"Does Paul know you're considering his idea?"

"He's waiting for my answer."

Lea laughed. "If you go off to Chicago with him, it would be his dream come true."

"Lea, please, I'm not going off with him. I'm visiting Chicago, that's all, and Paul will simply be my tour guide."

Twenty-Nine

AS SOON AS Matthew walked into the clinic and heard a man cursing, a tearful woman pleading, and a child screaming, he knew why he'd chosen a career as a surgeon. His role removed him from chaos. In the operating room, he had a calm, orderly place to work. He was even willing to take cases that most surgeons turned down. But he wasn't willing to put himself in the middle of bedlam.

Teresa and Eric dived right in. They went over to where Ned Finney was trying to calm an older man and a young woman. Matthew noticed the child who was hiding in a corner and crying. He wasn't very old, maybe four or five. He was very thin, probably mal-nourished from the look of it.

Watching the tears run down the child's face, Matthew thought about himself when he was a youngster. He was at his aunt's house. She was a cranky, old woman who made it clear that she didn't like children. She really didn't like him when he came in from outside crying after he'd fallen and skinned his knees. The old gal was quick to come up with a remedy. He could still hear her yell out an order to his mother. "Shut that boy up with a cookie!" Matthew had to smile. The cookie worked. He stopped crying.

"Maybe it'll work with this kid," he said as he went to the kitchen. After rummaging in the cabinets, he found some oatmeal raisin cookies. They were probably ones that Margaret had given Ned. He grabbed one for the little boy and one for himself. After all, the child wasn't the only one who was upset.

He returned to the main area of the clinic and walked over to the bawling child. The boy cried even louder at Matthew's approach, but Matthew quickly crouched down. He'd watched some nature programs that offered suggestions. "Make yourself smaller and avert your eyes. You'll be less frightening to the wildlife."

151

He added a component of his own. He took a bite of cookie, trying to ignore the boy's crying and enjoy a moment of respite. After a little while, the boy began to calm down. Without looking at the child, Matthew held out the second cookie. There was a brief moment of hesitation, followed by the flash of a small hand relieving him of the tempting sweet.

It was a very strange experience. Matthew had never bonded with a child before, but there was something about the situation that they shared. Neither of them wanted to be there, and both were grateful to have a cookie to dull their pain.

After he finished his treat, Matthew knew he had duties to perform. He wasn't there to hand out cookies. He was supposed to be helping the two people who'd been injured. He gathered from what he overheard that the man was the boy's father. The woman was his sister. He looked at the child. "Sorry, young man, but I have to help your relatives."

When he started to get up, the little boy burst into tears again. But he wasn't only crying, he was reaching out to Matthew with arms that weren't only thin, they were bruised and shaking.

Matthew looked over at Teresa. She was standing back from where Ned and Eric were attending to their patients. "Teresa, can you come over here?"

Teresa hurried over. "Yes, what is it, Matthew?"

"I think this child wants to be held."

"Oh, of course," she said as she approached the youngster.

As Teresa came closer, the little boy started screaming louder than ever. With fresh tears on his dirty cheeks, he looked up at Matthew with outstretched hands.

Teresa backed up. "I think he wants you, Matthew."

Matthew had no choice. He couldn't stand the screams so he crouched down again. "You're making a mistake, kid. You want Teresa. She's a very nice lady."

He was still talking when the little boy stopped crying and began to scoot his way forward. Grabbing onto Matthew's knee and pulling himself up, he was able to latch on to Matthew's shirt.

Teresa smiled and said the last thing that Matthew wanted to hear. "Matthew, I didn't know how good you are with children. You've made a friend."

Matthew put his hands around the little boy. The boy's body was like that of a bird. His bones were small and light. Holding him carefully at arm's length, Matthew didn't know what he was supposed to do next.

The little boy didn't seem confused at all. He reached out again.

Matthew finally took the hint and stood up with the child holding on to him. What else could he do? After looking at the boy more attentively, he shook his head. "I think you need a bath."

The little boy paid him no attention. He leaned into Matthew's shoulder and started to suck his thumb.

Teresa maintained her distance from Matthew and his new "friend." She brought him up to date on the condition of the injured adults. Their knife wounds were superficial. The young woman said her mother was the one wielding the knife. She already had a dozen kids, and she was intent on not having any more. When her husband got drunk and tried to have his way with her, the woman made her point by stabbing him. The daughter was injured trying to be a referee. They'd both be going home after their wounds were cleaned and dressed.

Since Eric and Ned were attending to the boy's family and the child had stopped crying, Matthew felt a sense a relief. He wasn't needed after all. With the thought of going back home beckoning him, he decided to put the little boy down on a chair and leave. But the child had a different idea and wouldn't have it. Matthew looked at him and shook his head. "You're quite the clinger, aren't you?"

Finally, he was forced to take a seat. The little boy eventually fell asleep in his arms. When it was time for the child to return home with his family, he fought his sister's attempts to take him from Matthew. She had to forcefully accomplish the task.

Matthew should have been thankful, but all that he could do was worry about what would become of the little boy.

Afterwards, Eric seemed to know what Matthew was going through. "We can't provide permanent solutions, but we helped his father and sister. As for the child, at least you gave him one good memory of the outside world."

Matthew was left with one good memory too. The little boy had stopped sucking his thumb long enough to smile up at him. It was a smile he'd long remember.

Ned stood in the middle of the clinic's treatment area and appreciated the quiet. His two patients had left and so had Teresa, Eric and Matthew. But the sounds of crisis still filled Ned's mind. In some ways, the sounds were nothing new. He'd worked in an ER. Hurting people were part of the job. He listened to their moans and groans, to their anger and lashing out and all the different ways they expressed their pain. But the people who came to the clinic were different.

Maybe the difference was simply that he'd been on his own when he first encountered the three individuals. He arrived at the clinic and found them waiting at the door. Two of them needed him to bind their wounds. Perhaps, if he wasn't still recovering from his own injuries, he would have been more capable of handling the group. As it was, the first thing he had to do was try to quiet the argument between the father and daughter. It was obvious that the father had been drinking. He was also combative when the daughter tried to get him to understand that he needed medical care.

Ned had to admire the young woman. She'd sustained injuries herself, and yet she put her father's injuries and wellbeing first. While the two of them were arguing, a small child was huddled close by, looking terrified. When Ned tried to talk to him, the boy's fear escalated, and he started screaming. The father responded by cursing and even attempting to strike out at the child, but the daughter was able to intervene.

Ned called for backup shortly after that. But if that backup hadn't been available, he wondered if he would have been able to handle the crisis successfully. Even if his determination was there, his body wasn't up to the task. He'd forced himself to hang on and help care for his patients, but now he didn't have the energy to do anything but go to his bed.

He lay in his room wondering about the days ahead. What if they were like the one he'd just had? The father he'd treated took repeated swings at Ned. The young woman was adamant in wailing out her woes, and a screaming child completely shut Ned out when he tried to come close.

Fortunately, he'd had helpers. Eric was there to keep the drunken father from delivering his blows. Teresa calmed the daughter, and

Matthew quieted the screaming child. But what would happen when that support team was gone? How could he deliver the care people needed when another crisis arose?

When he arrived in Elkville, things couldn't have been rosier. He was strong and healthy, and he had people around him who acted as if they were there to make sure he succeeded. Both Margaret Lloyd and Paul Glass embraced him with dedication and friendship.

How quickly that had changed. His health had been compromised, and Paul Glass was leaving the area. That meant that there was only one person in Elkville he could count on if he needed help again. Margaret Lloyd might have seemed a little too attentive the day before, but he had a different perspective now. He needed her.

Once Teresa, Eric and Matthew left, Margaret Lloyd was the only person who stood between him and a potentially disastrous situation.

* * *

Paul made his second trip to Blacksburg on his own. The vet's office had called and said he could take Duke home. Happily, when he saw his canine friend, Duke seemed much better. The dog even greeted Paul with enthusiastic tail wags and eager doggie kisses.

On the return trip to Elkville, Paul was overjoyed to have Duke with him, but he missed Margaret's company. The day before, as they drove back home, Paul felt hopeful. There was a chance Margaret might come to Chicago with him. The thought made the return trip extra special. Margaret sat in the passenger seat and every time he looked at her, he smiled inwardly. For quite some time, he'd tried very hard to forget his attraction to the woman. Now it was back, and it was as strong as ever. He could only hope that she'd take him up on his offer to show her more of the world.

When he returned home the next day with only Duke for company, he had to give himself a good inner shaking. Pining away over Margaret wasn't helpful. He'd been happy before he met her, he could be happy again. The remainder of his afternoon was spent tidying up the house. Paint, tarps, and other tools he'd used in remodeling were stowed away in a back shed.

Once the place was neat and orderly, he surveyed his possessions. About the only things he'd take with him to the city were his clothes.

155

Other than that, he'd leave the house as it was. In fact, as he was going through the rooms, he had an idea. Instead of selling the house, he'd keep it. He'd make the home available to people visiting. People like Teresa and Eric, or even Lea's parents, should they ever come to Elkville, would have a place to stay. Or perhaps, Ned would prefer living in a house rather than at the clinic.

The thought made him smile. That's when he realized he missed doing something to help others. He missed his practice. It's like he'd gone through a period of mourning, and now he was coming out on the other side. It made sense. He'd had his ego heavily assaulted when he'd made mistakes at the Ferguson mansion. He'd gone through a period of doubt and remorse. He'd even moved to Elkville thinking he was ready to retire. Was it true?

He approached a hall mirror and took a long, hard look. His hair was grey and he had some wrinkles, but all in all, he was staring at a man who could still serve. It was a welcome thought that started to fill up that space called loneliness. With a new sense of excitement, he started to make more definite plans for his move. He was determined to go forward, with or without Margaret.

Thirty

RETURNING FROM THE clinic, Matthew walked into his house, sniffed the air and smiled. Lea was making an Italian dish, he was sure of it, and he loved Italian food. He followed his nose to the kitchen. Lea was leaned over, checking something in the oven. He wondered why she was wearing a dress, but his mind soon moved on. "What is my lovely wife making?" he asked from the doorway.

Lea shut the oven door and rushed over to him. "Matthew, I have so much to tell you."

"I have something to tell you too," he said with a smile. "I had a very interesting experience at the clinic. There was a little boy there, and I managed to get him to stop crying. Afterwards, I thought about us, about how you might be pregnant, and how we might have a little boy of our own someday."

Lea frowned. "Oh Matthew, I'm so sorry. When I went over to see Margaret, I remembered the pregnancy test you brought. It was still at Margaret's house. When I checked, I found out I'm not pregnant after all. My period is just late or maybe I skipped it. I think it's because I was so stressed out for a while."

Matthew hesitated. He hadn't expected to feel so disappointed by Lea's news. Up until that afternoon, he didn't know if he wanted a family or not. But that had changed. "I'm sorry, too," he said.

"I just had a thought," Lea said as she put her arms around him. She leaned into his chest. "Trying to get pregnant could be lots of fun."

"That's true."

"But for the time being that will have to wait."

Matthew kissed the top of her head. "What's going on?"

Lea pulled away and smiled. "Tonight, we're having everyone over for dinner."

"That's nice, I guess."

"But I didn't tell you the reason for the dinner."

Matthew noticed how Lea's eyes were suddenly bright, like a child's eyes when they were very excited. "With that look on your face, I'm almost afraid to ask."

Lea grinned. "I can't help it. Margaret has some big news for everyone. She's going to accept an invitation from Paul Glass to go to Chicago. Of course, she's only going as a friend."

"Paul Glass? Chicago? For how long?"

"I don't know. Margaret said something about moving away from Elkville."

"Of all the people, she's chosen to go with Paul? He's someone who has caused a lot of problems in the past, especially for Eric. He's going to go ballistic."

"I hope not. I hope he's happy for his mom."

"What about you? Do you think this is a good idea?"

Lea gave him an inquisitive look. "Why not? It's going to be perfect having Margaret close again. At first, I was so happy I even told Margaret she could stay with us."

"With us? But Lea—"

"Don't worry. Margaret refused. She says that she expects Paul to provide a place for her to stay."

Matthew tried to take it all in. Lea seemed to be thrilled by Margaret's latest decision. But what about Eric? The guy talked a good game about letting his mother do whatever, but Matthew had his doubts about the latest. He wondered if he and Eric would soon be reversing roles. The night before, he'd had a killer headache. He could just imagine that Eric had his headache waiting in the wings.

* * *

Ned felt a lot better physically by the time he arrived at the Howell residence for supper. His appetite was back. He polished off a large plate of lasagna, a generous amount of salad, and a couple of glasses of iced tea. Afterwards, when everyone retired to the living room, his body was content, and he even felt better about the clinic job.

As usual, his father's advice came to mind. He should have never bought into his fears and let himself become so depressed earlier that day. It was almost laughable now, but before he'd come to the Howell's for dinner, he'd soothed himself with a promise. If things got really bad, he could call Lea's dad and tell him to find a new doctor for Elkville.

But that was nonsense. He wasn't a quitter. He'd always made sure to follow his father's example. When John Finney was fighting a fire, he didn't back off until the last whisper of a flame was extinguished. Ned was proud to think that he'd been just as dedicated.

Besides, he wasn't alone in his job in Elkville. Even if things got rough, he had a permanent ally, one he could depend on. Margaret Lloyd told him that Elkville was the only place she knew. She'd lived there for most of her adult life. From the way she talked, she'd probably die there. Happily, she was a strong, healthy woman, and he imagined she'd live in Elkville for many more years.

It left him with a wonderful feeling after a wonderful meal. With everyone chatting around him, he settled into a comfortable recliner, feeling sleepy again. A little smile replaced the scowl he'd worn earlier. He'd almost closed his eyes when Lea said something to him. He sat up more attentively. "Could you repeat that, Lea? I didn't hear what you said."

"Ned, this is a little difficult."

"Yes, what is it?"

Lea glanced over at Matthew before she continued and smiled at her husband. When she looked back at Ned, the smile was gone. She stared at him with serious, intent eyes. "Remember how we talked about an outreach program for Elkville and its surroundings?"

Ned blinked away any sleepiness when he heard Lea's tone. It sounded apologetic. "Go on."

"I'm sorry, but that's not going to happen. Matthew and I would like to start a family, and I want to spend my time in Chicago from now on."

Ned was disappointed by Lea's news, but he'd been prepared for her change of mind ever since she had her mini breakdown. Still, he'd hoped that she would visit the clinic off and on. Seeing the way she was latched on to Matthew's hand, he doubted that would happen. "That's understandable. I wish you and Matthew the best."

Margaret stood up before Ned completed the sentence. "I have some news too," she said as she looked at her son. "Eric, I hope you don't take this the wrong way, but I'm leaving Elkville. For starters, I'm going to Chicago with Paul."

The announcement hit Ned as brutally and unexpectedly as the Chevy that ran him down in Blacksburg. In spite of his ailing body, he was on his feet in an instant, and he was shouting. "What? You're leaving too?"

His outburst was so immediate and so loud that Eric didn't get a chance to respond to his mother. Both of them turned to look at him.

"Yes, I am," Margaret said.

Her words, her tone and the way Margaret looked at him so innocently, triggered something Ned had never felt before. It was as if she'd sliced him open and poured acid on a festering wound. The trauma was so all encompassing that he couldn't help but scream out in pain. "How can you be so cruel, woman? Don't you care about anyone but yourself?"

Eric was instantly on his feet too, putting himself in front of Margaret. "You can't talk to my mother like that, Finney!"

That's when Ned's world began to fall apart. He heard the word, mother, and he wasn't only angry, he was instantly sick. He groped around, trying to breathe, trying to get control, and failing. "Where's the bathroom?" he yelled. "I'm going to be sick!"

Someone grabbed his arm and pulled him along as he tried to help himself. But he kept hearing the little boy screaming in the clinic, and he knew that he was screaming too. Screaming for a mother that abandoned him. Screaming at a father who didn't stop her. Screaming at all the crap he forced himself to endure and keep enduring during those painful years growing up. It was all coming up at once in waves of nausea. So much had been hidden away, and he couldn't keep it inside anymore.

He didn't know how he got there, but he realized he was leaning over a commode, vomiting. But it didn't feel the same as when he'd vomited before. This emptying was fueled by an inner violence that had taken hold of him. It was almost as if something inside of him wanted to do away with him, to finish a job someone else had started.

As the food and bile kept coming, his memory returned to a time he shouldn't have remembered. In some long ago past, he'd heard voices. People lashed out at each other. Snatches of what they said weaved in and out of the sickness in his body. Finally, the words formed a clear message. His mother and father had never wanted him. But he came along anyway. His mother tried to cope and couldn't. His

160

father raised him, but he did it because it was a duty he attended to, just like being a fire fighter was a job he performed.

After his revelation, Ned felt like he didn't know how to go on and collapsed in a heap. Again, he felt hands on his arms, pulling him upright. He didn't care about where he was going.

He didn't belong in the world, and he couldn't care about anything anymore. As he lost touch with the real world, he entered a dream state. He was in his truck, ramming his foot against the gas petal, flying off the edge of the mountain. Falling, crashing, and moving into a black void.

* * *

While Eric and Matthew tended to Ned in an upstairs bedroom, Teresa, Lea and Margaret sat in the kitchen. Teresa and Lea insisted on being there for Margaret. She was grateful for their support. "Girls, I feel just terrible. I think I caused that young man's mental collapse."

Lea gave her an understanding look. "Ned must have big issues. Take it from one who knows. So even if you activated that response, he needs to address whatever he's not dealing with."

Teresa nodded. "You're right, Lea. Before he got hurt, we had dinner together. I was a little shocked at what he told Eric and me. He essentially dismissed feelings. He said they didn't matter. For him, facts were the only things that counted."

Margaret cradled a cup of tea that Lea had handed her. "I don't think he's running from his feelings anymore. When he was yelling at me, his eyes were full of anger. But there was more. I think he's battling a lot of pain."

Eric came walking into the kitchen. "Are you talking about Ned?"

Margaret looked up. "Yes, how's he doing?"

Eric went over to the coffee maker. "It's going to be a long night."

"Has he calmed down?" Teresa asked.

Eric brought a mug of coffee over to the table and sat down. "I don't know about that. At one point he said he hates all of us."

"Why would he say that?" Lea asked. "He seemed fine at dinner. He ate everything on his plate."

Eric sipped his coffee. "All I know for sure is that he's not helping his body. Just as he starts to heal, he seems to have some emotional problem that sets him back again."

Margaret reached out for Eric's arm. "Before we talk anymore about Ned, I want to say how sorry I am about the way I made my announcement. That wasn't right."

Eric put his hand over hers. "I wish we could have talked about it privately, but after seeing Ned in action, I can only guess you were trying to prevent me from making a scene."

Margaret took a tissue out of her pocket. "I don't think I can leave after tonight. Ned obviously felt I was someone he could depend on."

Teresa held up a hand and looked at Eric. "Honey, I'll respect your wishes, but if you wouldn't mind too much, I'd be willing to take some time off and help Ned for a while. In the meantime, maybe Lea's father could find him an assistant."

Eric's eyes widened in surprise. "Really, Teresa? You want to stay here?"

"Yes, when I was at the clinic today and saw the desperate need for care, it inspired me. Now I want to do something to get the clinic off to a good start."

Margaret smiled. "That is so sweet, my dear Teresa, but you don't know what you'd be getting into."

"Maybe not," Teresa said, "but I'm willing to give it my best."

Lea sat up and bit her lip. "If you stay, I'll stay too, at least for a little while. Matthew and I are on a good page. I think he'll understand."

Matthew appeared in the kitchen doorway. "What will I understand, Lea?"

Lea got up and went over to where Matthew stood. "Matthew, your premonition was right. This place is falling apart. Now, Teresa has volunteered to stay and help Ned out for a while. I want to stay too. Not for that long, but just until things stabilize."

Matthew crossed his arms. "I can't leave you in this crazy place. We're just getting our lives back on track."

Lea's brows narrowed. "I'm sorry, but I'm part of the reason Ned is in the condition he's in. He thought he had support from Paul and Margaret and me. After recently being hit by a car, he's hurting and feeling abandoned. If this place is crazy then he needs people to help him cope. I want to be one of those people."

Matthew uncrossed his arms and rubbed his brow. "Lord help us all, Lea, you have abandonment issues too."

"Matthew, please, I have to do this. People were there when I went off the deep end. So I won't leave until I know Ned's going to be alright."

Matthew stared at her with sharp, focused eyes. "Then what choice do I have but to stay with you."

"But you hate this place," Lea said.

"I hate it with a passion, but I love you more than I hate Elkville, so there it is."

Eric got up and went over to Teresa. "I feel the same way about you, Teresa. If you stay, I'll stay too. We can both make the necessary arrangements back home."

"But you feel the same way as Matthew," Teresa insisted.

"It doesn't matter," Eric said. "Things could get out of hand here, and I refuse to let you face that kind of situation alone."

Margaret stared at Matthew. "Should someone be with Ned?"

"I gave him something, and he's sleeping for now," Matthew said.

Teresa stood and leaned into Eric's shoulder. "Matthew, about that premonition you had—"

"What about it?" Matthew asked.

"You said something about the walking wounded taking care of the fallen. Are we the walking wounded you talked about?"

Matthew let out a sulking laugh. "Please, Teresa, don't ask me something like that. My head is already spinning."

Margaret got up from the table and pushed her chair in. "My head is spinning too. We've had a very emotional evening, and we've all said a lot of things about what we should do. So maybe we should get a good night's sleep and see if we feel the same tomorrow."

Thirty-One

IT WAS STILL very early morning, and the smell of fresh coffee filled the kitchen. Eric was enjoying his first cup of the day. Matthew sat across from him. "I'm grateful that both of us got some rest," Eric said. "I didn't think Ned would sleep so soundly."

Matthew shrugged. "The guy really lost it, but we got lucky."

"How do you feel about staying here for a couple of weeks?"

"I don't have a choice if Lea's welfare is at risk. Fortunately, I took off two weeks already. I'll have to call my partner, Ralph, and extend that time if need be. Hopefully, he'll be able to handle the case load."

"I'm sure Lea appreciates your support. And I have to admit, I'm grateful too. You have a calming presence. The way you helped that little boy was impressive."

"It was no big deal. I gave him a cookie, and he shut up."

Eric laughed. "You have no idea how hard it can be to establish that kind of rapport with a kid from the hills. I've tried."

Matthew got up to refill his cup. "How about you, Eric? You've had some rough times when you've come back here."

"I don't know. I'll have Teresa with me this time. It'll be a new experience."

Matthew was about to sit down again, cup in hand, and paused. "Hear that? The upstairs shower stopped."

"When I was leaving my room, I noticed Ned's bed was empty and heard the water in the bath. He must be feeling better."

Matthew sat down and studied his mug. "We better come up with a game plan before he comes down."

"What do you have in mind?"

"First of all, is he in any shape to return to the clinic? If not, we'll have to work out a schedule for manning the place."

"I think that at least two of us should be there when needed."

"Sorry to tell you this, Eric, but you're the key player now. You know these people. Teresa and I don't."

"That's not a problem, I'm used to long hours. I'll be there for both of you."

"That's generous of you."

"Matthew, give me a break. I know how hard you work."

"Yes, but I'm going to cut back on my hours. If Lea and I are going to have a family, I want to be there for her and our kids."

Ned came walking into the kitchen. His black hair was still wet and curly, and his face unshaven. "Morning all."

Eric smiled. "Good to see you up and about, Ned."

Ned returned a scowl. "I feel like I've returned from the bowels of hell. Thank you both for being there while I was acting like an escapee from the looney bin."

Matthew frowned. "How about now?"

Ned came over to the table, started to pull out a chair and paused. "My body feels like somebody took a phone book to it, but I'll be okay."

Matthew tapped his head. "How about—"

"Oh, you want to know if I still feel like a raging madman," Ned said. "No, I don't, but after last night, I can't be sure of anything."

"Do you know why you reacted the way you did?" Eric asked.

"It all happened so fast," Ned said. "Everything was okay and then your mom said something about leaving, and I lost control."

Eric crossed his arms. "Have you been worried about being on your own with the clinic?"

Ned's blue eyes narrowed. "I guess I was concerned after I found out I'm not the tough guy I thought I was." He stared at Eric. "But you warned me, didn't you? The night you arrived, you gave me the impression that this place would be more than a challenge. And you were right. Yesterday, I couldn't manage a couple of injured people and a crying kid."

Eric averted his eyes. "I apologize if I acted like a jerk that first night. As for yesterday, you did fine."

"Yes, with three people helping me. But that won't be the case when everyone leaves. That's why I'm going to call Mr. Ferguson. I'll stay and do my best until he finds a replacement."

Matthew sipped his coffee. "So you're leaving Elkville?"

"Look, it's not just the job." Ned said. "I'm not dependable. I probably have screwed up genes."

"How so?" Eric asked.

"My mother walked out when I was eight. I was a good kid, but I assume she couldn't handle the strain. If I'm like her, I'm in serious trouble."

"You have an excellent track record in the ER," Eric said.

Ned held his midsection. "That's all behind me."

Eric protested. "I think you're being too hasty. Just because you lost it last night doesn't mean you're finished. It can happen to anyone."

Ned looked away. "I don't know. You guys were there. I went straight off the grid."

"You must have felt overwhelmed," Eric said. "I've been there. Right, Matthew?"

Matthew chuckled. "Yes, indeed. Talk about going off the grid, Eric really—"

Eric quickly interrupted. "So try to hang in there. And you'll have help. Teresa, Matthew and I are staying on until things settle down."

Ned hesitated and then gave Eric a hopeful look. "I guess I don't have anything to lose."

"If you've been stressed, you could talk to Paul Glass," Matthew said.

Ned stiffened. "You guys called him a quack."

"That was just our experience," Eric said. "But he did have an excellent reputation before we met him."

Ned scowled. "So did I. I was fine until I rescued you two."

Eric ignored the remark. "The point is that you need to talk to somebody. We're not shrinks, but we might be able to help."

"Practically speaking, even if you stay, I think you need an assistant at the clinic," Matthew said. "So call Ferguson and see what he can do."

Eric smiled. "And we'll be here for a couple of weeks until better arrangements can be made. What do you think?"

Ned's eyes brightened a little. "I appreciate it." He rubbed the stubble on his face. "I'll go back to the clinic for now. Hopefully, there won't be any stab victims waiting, and I can get presentable."

Matthew stood up too. "Come back around nine. We'll have breakfast and work out some details."

Teresa woke up, thought about the night before and smiled. When she'd made a commitment to help out Ned, it felt so right. But she wasn't the only one who wanted to be there for him. Lea was quick to volunteer her time. Matthew and Eric followed suit. It was like they were all coming together as a family. And a family was something she'd always wanted and never had growing up.

By the time Teresa got downstairs, Lea was already in the kitchen. She was busy taking some plates out of a cupboard. Since Eric considered Lea his adopted sister, Teresa thought of Lea as a sister, too. It was another reason to feel happy. "Good morning, Lea. What can I do to help?"

"Morning, Teresa," Lea said with a smile.

Teresa hurried over. "Let me take those plates. Do you want me to set the table?"

"That would be great. While you're doing that, I'll get breakfast started. I'll make scrambled eggs again if you don't mind. And Margaret just called. She's already made a double batch of cherry muffins that she's bringing over."

"That sounds so good. How many of us will there be?"

"With Margaret and Ned, there'll be six."

"Where are Matthew and Eric?"

Lea pointed out the kitchen window. "They're on the porch. It's a beautiful day. The air is good for them."

Teresa looked out and smiled. "You have a great deck, and I like the patio set."

"Yes, my dad did a great job with everything."

"And look at our two guys, sitting there and looking all serious."

Lea peeked out the window too. "Both of them have already showered and are ready for the day. They wanted to help me with breakfast, but I told them they could help another time. Margaret will be here any minute."

"I didn't realize how late it was. The bed was very cozy, I slept like a baby."

"I'm glad you did. You're supposed to be on vacation."

Teresa took some silverware out of a drawer. "I don't think so, not with the Ned situation. By the way, where is he?"

"Matthew said he went back to the clinic, but he'll be here for breakfast."

"Hello?" Margaret called from the foyer.

"We're in here," Lea replied.

Margaret came walking into the kitchen holding a large, covered basket. "Morning."

Lea put a carton of eggs on the counter and hurried over. She kissed Margaret on the cheek. "Good morning, Mom."

Teresa came over with a greeting too and hugged Margaret.

Margaret beamed back smiles. "Just look at you two beautiful girls. My goodness, Eric and Matthew are very lucky men." She held out her basket. "Where do you want me to put these muffins?"

Lea pulled away the basket's red and white checkered cloth. "Look at these, Teresa. Don't they look and smell yummy?"

Teresa took in a deep breath. "Yes, they're going to be delicious. Do you want me to put them on the table?"

"You bet, and I'll get those eggs going," Lea said.

As Teresa carried the freshly baked goods to the table, she felt her heart do a little leap of joy. She was getting a chance to interact with Lea and Margaret in a way that brought them all closer, and she couldn't have been happier. She didn't care what Matthew thought, she was opting for a more positive attitude about her time in Elkville.

* * *

After Ned shaved and made himself presentable for breakfast at the Howell's, he had time to sit and reflect in his private quarters at the clinic.

Eric and Matthew had asked him to reconsider giving up his job. But they didn't know all the facts. When he fell apart the night before, it wasn't a small fall. He'd gone over the side of a ten story building. Some saving grace had been there to catch him before he hit pavement, but was it enough to save him for very long? Earlier, he'd held out his trembling hand to demonstrate his physical condition. His body was stressed and anxious. But his physical state didn't compare to how he felt on a much deeper level. No one could see how broken he was inside.

He could hardly believe it himself. For most of his life, he'd been going along blindly, thinking his foundation was rock solid. His father was proud of him. Ned had graduated at the top of his class in medical school. Afterwards, he handled all the stress of working in the ER day in and day out. Surely those were facts that meant all was well with him.

"I've been a fool," he muttered.

What he didn't know during those uneventful years is that he hadn't been tested yet. All seemed well as long as no devastating storms battered his shores. It was only when he was vomiting his guts out that the truth came up too. Memories stored in some dark place came gushing out along with the bile and undigested food.

"I never wanted him!"

His father, who never raised his voice when Ned was older, had shouted out the words to Ned's mother. Her response was just as caustic. "And you think I did?"

Ned had called Margaret cruel. He'd heard himself say it. But reflecting on what he'd learned later, he knew she wasn't the woman he was yelling at. He was screaming at the person who bore him. Ned's mother tried to hide her feelings as he got older. She even cried over him before she abandoned him, but tears meant nothing. His mother was sobbing over her own unhappy life.

He looked at the clock and realized it was time to leave for breakfast. As he headed out the door, he remembered how Eric and Matthew had encouraged him to take another chance on himself. He didn't know if he could do that. His foundation wasn't rock solid anymore. His house had been built on sand. He vaguely remembered hearing a story about such a structure. No matter how well built they were, they didn't survive when the storm hit. There was nothing there to hold them up when the sand was washed away.

If another storm hit his foundation, he didn't know if he'd survive. Maybe the bright, clever boy who graduated early and excelled in everything he did, might end up weaving baskets instead of mending bodies.

Whatever the case, he had to put an end to his irrational outbursts for the time being. People were trying to help him cope. At least that's what they told him. It's what he kept repeating to himself as he drove to the Howell's residence.

169

When he arrived, he was greeted by a smiling Teresa. She ushered him into the kitchen. Everyone was seated at the table and smiling too. The room was sunny, and the smell of good food and light conversation filled the air. He should have been buoyed up by it all, but something didn't feel real. The scene was too bright, too cheerful. It reminded him of something he'd seen in a movie. But he'd never really believed those movies that ended with the message that all was well. Working in the ER, he knew all about domestic violence and how brothers ended up shooting each other.

Still, the people around him, Teresa, Lea, Margaret, Eric and Matthew, were supposedly there on his behalf. Lea had even mentioned something about being family. But were they all lying to him? His parents tried to cover up the truth. Were the people seated around him doing the same? Was he simply someone's burden again?

No matter what Matthew Howell said earlier that day, the man didn't want any part of Elkville. Neither did Eric. Both men had made that clear that first night when they stayed at the clinic. They hated the place.

As for Lea and Margaret, the women had announced what they wanted the night before. Both of them wanted to leave. So that left Teresa. Teresa might be the exception in the group. But she was probably staying because she pitied him.

So there he was, with a pile of food on his plate, right back where he'd started. He was the problem someone had to deal with. He was trying to cope with that fact when Lea asked him a question.

"Ned, I know you're close to your father. Do you think you should call him and let him know about your accident?"

Teresa chimed in. "Lea's right, Ned. I'm sure getting hit by that car was traumatic. Perhaps, if you talked to your dad, it would help."

Ned had to steady himself, especially when he wanted to answer the women with the truth. "My father doesn't give a damn about me. I'm a mistake he's had to live with. Nothing more."

But he couldn't say those things. He had to remind himself that he was being tested again. And this time, he would not let his emotions call the shots. He had to get through the relentless hell that his life had become. He had to get through breakfast without going off the edge of another building.

He looked at Lea and Teresa and tried to smile. "Thank you both, but my father is a very busy man. He doesn't need to know about something as trivial as a few bruises."

Teresa frowned. "Is that how you think of your injuries? As trivial?"

Ned paused and thought about what to say that would put an end to the questions. "You were there, Teresa. I'm sure you were told that my injuries weren't serious."

Eric took Teresa's hand. "I think what Lea and Teresa are trying to say is that we're concerned. If we can make life easier for you—"

Ned cut in, trying to stop the conversation from going any further. "You've already done more than you should. Staying here and babysitting me is a sacrifice you shouldn't have to make."

Matthew spoke up. "Look, Ned, you never planned on having an accident."

Margaret smiled. "I agree with Matthew. Something like that can happen to anyone."

Ned sucked in a breath, used all the strength he could muster, and gave the people around the table what they wanted to hear. They wanted to be told they were doing the "right thing." It's what people called their lies when they had to do what they hated. He tried to smile again. "You're all being kind. In fact, Margaret, you've been nothing but gracious since I got here. And I'd like to apologize for the things I said last night. My ranting had nothing to do with you. I can't imagine how much you've given to others over the years. So follow your desires and—"

He had to pause. He almost said, "Follow your desires and stop being a martyr, woman." Instead, he said. "Follow your desires and go to Chicago."

Margaret smiled. "That's very kind of you. But even if I leave, I won't hesitate to return if you need a helping hand. Is that understood?"

Ned nodded. "Yes, ma'am. I understand."

And he did understand. He understood how she wanted him to think of her as a sweet, caring person. In truth, all she really wanted was for him to be okay so she could let go of her guilt. If she left, it'd be a good thing. There'd be one less person torturing him with their self-deception.

Margaret pointed to his plate. "Ned, do you think you could eat a little more? You need food if you're going to get your strength back."

Ned stood up. He was swearing inside, cursing himself for accepting a breakfast invitation at the Howells. If he needed more pain in his life, he'd throw himself in front of another car. He started to move away from his chair with another apology. "I'm sorry. I'm not hungry. I better get back to the clinic."

* * *

Margaret waited until Ned left the kitchen and then turned to the other people around the table. "Poor thing didn't eat a bite. I'm worried about him."

Eric spoke up. "I know, but did you hear what he said? I think he wants you to stop worrying and do what's best for yourself. I want that too."

"So you wouldn't mind if I took some time away?"

"I think you need time," Eric said. "So go to Chicago with Paul for a couple of weeks. While you're gone, we'll be here to take care of our ailing Doc Ned and the clinic."

Margaret folded her napkin and put it on the table. She looked up at Eric and then at Teresa, Lea and Matthew. "Perhaps Eric has a point. There's no reason I need to stay here. Ned couldn't be in better hands than with the four of you."

Lea smiled. "Does Paul know you might go with him?"

"No, not yet," Margaret said. "So I think I'll go see him and break the news."

Matthew tapped a finger on the edge of his plate. "Margaret, I've been wondering why there's been so little happening at the clinic."

Margaret sighed. "Elkville and the surrounding area have been without a doctor for quite a while. People have learned to take care of their ailments as best they can. But I'm sure as time goes by that will change. My husband certainly had enough to do."

Eric let out a curt laugh. "You forgot to mention something else. It takes time to build up trust with the locals. People here don't take to strangers too quickly."

Matthew grabbed another cherry muffin. "If they want to keep to themselves while I'm here, that's fine with me."

172

There was a lull in the conversation, but Eric broke the silence. "So much has been happening that it seems like a long time ago since Matthew and I went off the road coming here. But I'm finally getting the rental car out of the ditch. I called a tow truck, and they're taking care of the problem today."

Teresa gave him a satisfied look. "You don't need your rental anyway. We have mine. Isn't that perfect?"

Eric smiled broadly. "It's perfect that you're here."

Teresa's green eyes glowed brightly as she looked at the people around the table. "I know there have been some rough spots, but all in all, I'm very happy I came. And I'm excited about the prospect of a few patients stopping by the clinic. I can't wait to go over and see what's happening."

Eric stared back. "I better come with you."

Teresa shook her head. "I'll call you if I need help, but I don't want to overwhelm Ned."

Margaret got up and started for the hall. "And I better go and talk to Paul."

Thirty-Two

PLEASANT TEMPERATURES WARMED the air as Margaret walked to Paul's house. She hadn't seen or talked to him since their trip to Blacksburg. Knowing that she was going to tell him her big news prompted both anticipation and apprehension. She couldn't know what her future held. Would she discover something new and exciting about herself in Chicago? Or would she find there was no escaping her rigid mindset?

When she knocked on Paul's door and he opened it, she was relieved to see that Paul looked more relaxed. Duke was also there to greet her. She petted his furry head and was genuinely happy to know he was on the mend.

Paul invited her in, and she immediately noticed a change. There was no sign of any tools or painting items lying around like there had been for months. "You've been busy, Paul. The place is as neat as a pin."

Paul led the way to the kitchen. "Let me get you a cup of freshly made coffee and bring you up to date on my progress."

Margaret sat down at the table. "I have things to tell you, too."

Paul poured coffee into a cup and brought it over to Margaret. "Would you like to go first?"

Margaret blushed. "For starters, I think it would be nice to go to Chicago with you."

Paul smiled. "That's wonderful news. I hadn't expected you to want to come."

"Why is that?"

"Sometimes it's very hard to try something new. You should be proud of yourself. I think you have an adventurous spirit."

"Here's some news that isn't wonderful," Margaret said. "Ned Finney got extremely upset last night."

"What happened?"

"It was horrible. He started yelling and then got so sick that he couldn't stop vomiting. It took both Eric and Matthew to calm him down."

"Is he better today?" Paul asked.

"Thankfully, he seemed more himself this morning. But he doesn't know if he can continue on as Elkville's doctor. So Teresa, Lea, Eric and Matthew are staying here for a couple of weeks to help out."

Paul grabbed the back of a chair with both hands and leaned on it for support. "You told me to help him, and I was too stubborn to listen, Margaret."

"I don't know if it would have helped. He didn't seem willing to share much before the incident last night. And even now, I know he's still in a bad way, but I think he wants to isolate himself."

"When I talked to him before all this started, he behaved so confidently," Paul said. "And from what I know about his background, he's never shown any indication of emotional disorders."

Margaret sighed. "After all of Eric's problems with his father, I was relieved when Ned told us that he and his dad were on great terms. But today when Lea and Teresa encouraged him to contact his father, he said he didn't want to do that."

"Where is Ned now?"

"He's at the clinic."

Paul sat down at the table and clasped his hands. "Do you think it would help if I talk to him?"

"It couldn't hurt."

"Then I'll go over to the clinic later today."

"Good." Margaret brightened a little. "Now tell me your news."

Paul gave her a hasty glance. "Well, I've arranged to rent a place in Chicago. It's not where I want to live permanently, but it'll do until I find something I like better." He looked up and smiled. "There's even a separate apartment upstairs that was probably used for a mother-in-law."

"Good, it sounds like it will be just what I'll need while I'm there."

* * *

Teresa had been at the clinic for a couple of hours, but there wasn't much for her to do. Ned took care of the few people who came and went with minor complaints. Teresa was impressed with the way Ned interacted with his patients, but she could see that he wasn't doing very well himself.

After an elderly man with arthritis said goodbye and left the clinic, she came over to where Ned was filling out a patient file. Sitting behind his desk, he looked pale and worn. "Are you hungry?" she asked. "I'd be happy to make you something."

Ned put his pen down and sat back in his chair. "You don't need to be here, Teresa. Go home and enjoy some time with your husband."

"Are you saying you don't want me here?" Teresa asked. "It's just that I wanted to spend some time getting to know more about the clinic."

"Why?"

"Because I like what this clinic is all about, bringing healthcare to people who probably feel forgotten. What about you, Ned, why are you here?"

"At this point, I don't know. I called Mr. Ferguson and told him I'm ready to move on."

"I thought you were going to consider staying until you felt better."

"Feeling better isn't going to change anything."

"What do you mean?" Teresa asked.

"From what you've said, you seem to know how to deal with feelings," Ned said. "I've never had any use for them. Now, I know why. The only thing they do is tear you apart and leave you wishing you were never born."

Teresa saw the way Ned's hand shook as he spoke. "But Ned, feelings can let us know when our thinking is off."

Ned huffed out a mocking laugh. "My thinking was crystal clear until that car hit me. But it did me a favor. It forced me to see the truth."

"What truth?"

"Everything people do is just for show. They're all pretending."

"What people are you talking about?"

"Never mind." Ned pushed himself out of his chair. "I'm tired. I'm going to lie down. If someone needs me, I'll be in my room."

Teresa watched Ned make his way out of the office. She suspected that his body was hurting, but he had defiance in his uneasy steps. He reminded her of an exhausted soldier who had to keep on fighting. She thought about Matthew's warning. He'd spoken of people being on an emotional battlefield. She decided to think more positively about Ned. No matter how he looked, she was sure he was going to be able to weather his emotional storm. He just needed time to heal.

She started for the kitchen. She'd make some lunch whether Ned was hungry or not. He might change his mind. Before she had a chance to check out the refrigerator, she heard someone come into the front entrance of the clinic. When she went to investigate, Paul Glass was standing in the waiting area.

Paul smiled. "It's nice to see you, Teresa. How are you?"

Teresa lowered her voice. "I'm okay, but I'm very worried about Ned."

"That's why I'm here. Margaret said he wasn't doing well."

"He seems very depressed. He's even told Lea's dad that he's not staying."

"Maybe I can talk to him."

"He just left to go to his room and rest. But if you think you could help him—"

Paul nodded. "I'll do what I can."

***

Paul walked through the clinic reminiscing. He'd been so excited while the structure was being built. He often found himself on the phone with Raymond Ferguson, giving him a detailed report of what was going on. It was satisfying to be a part of something so meaningful.

Once the building was completed, Ned Finney arrived. The young, energetic man filled the space with a sense of what medical care was all about. Coming from a job that centered around the workings of a busy ER, Ned was friendly enough, but he wasn't used to sitting around.

Paul took advantage of the slow pace to visit the clinic. He and Ned became friends of sorts. They talked about the needs of the surrounding area, and Paul even found himself offering ideas of his own.

Then Lea ran off on that snowy night when Eric and Matthew first arrived. When Paul saw the small, fragile woman at the bottom of a ditch, all he could think about was the first time he'd seen her. It was at the Ferguson mansion, and he'd been called in by her father. He was

177

supposed to help her, to pull her out of a very dark place. Lea did make an astounding recovery, but that recovery had nothing to do with Paul.

Instead of being an instrument of healing, he didn't seem able to help at all. It was the opposite. Everything he did seemed to make matters worse for Lea's parents, her fiancé, Margaret and Eric. It was such a horror show that he gave up on himself.

Seeing Lea in that snowy ditch brought up all the pain he'd tried to leave behind. His dog, Duke, had been a hero when he found Lea, but Paul only felt his failures more acutely. It was a paralyzing feeling that made him redouble his efforts to stay retired forever. Thankfully, that feeling was waning. He'd begun to reconsider his calling.

He walked through the beautiful new clinic, hoping he'd rounded a new corner in his life. His response to the Ferguson case was childish and immature. He had to take another chance on his abilities as a psychiatrist.

When Margaret first asked him to talk to a struggling, injured Ned Finney, Paul had refused. Standing at Ned's door, knowing that Ned needed help, he had to recover his confidence and go forward.

* * *

Ned was just nodding off when he heard someone knocking. If only he could get in a twenty minute power nap, he was sure he wouldn't be so tired. It might even improve his mood. He forced himself to sit up on the edge of his bed. "Yes, Teresa, what is it?"

"It's Paul. Can I come in?"

Ned felt his jaw stiffen. What did Paul Glass want? Even if they'd had a sort of friendship going a few days before, a lot had changed since. "Come in," he ordered.

Paul opened the door, came striding forward and smiled. "Thought I'd drop by and see how you're doing. I was told you had an accident."

"I'm recuperating," Ned said. "How about you? I hear you're moving."

Paul pulled over a desk chair and sat down. "Yes, I'm returning to Chicago. I might even start up my practice again."

"A sudden decision, isn't it? A week ago you were interested in how everything was going at the clinic. What happened?"

"I suppose it's as simple as this. I changed my mind."

"So the clinic means nothing to you. Is that what you're saying?"

Paul shifted in his seat. "No, it's not like that. I just—"

"Because you talked a good game when we were getting to know each other. There were all those discussions about the people in the area and how to implement some plans to help them."

"Yes, well, I don't think I'm needed here after all. So I might as well move on."

"That's a bunch of BS from my perspective, Paul."

"I don't know what you mean."

"Face it. You do whatever it is that takes care of your own needs. If that means up and leaving, that's what you do. You don't worry about the stuff you spouted off to others, but some people took your involvement seriously."

"Are you talking about yourself?" Paul asked.

Ned glanced around the room. "Since I don't remember anyone else being a part of those discussions, what do you think?"

Paul looked down as if he needed to study the carpet. "I see what you're getting at."

Ned forced himself into a standing position. With all the recent violent vomiting, his abdominal muscles were very painful again, but his anger and resentment were overriding his physical woes. "So why are you here, Paul? Do you want to help poor Ned so you can skip out of town thinking you performed a kind act?"

"Margaret said you had a difficult time last night. I thought you might want to talk about it."

"You thought wrong. I'm tired of people like you, people who believe they care. They rush in and play nice. Then they're gone."

Paul stood up. "I wish you didn't feel that way, Ned. And I'm sorry if I've disappointed you or let you down."

"You let yourself down, Paul. So go."

Paul scowled. "Teresa said you're leaving too."

"I may be leaving, but I'm not lying to myself. That's the difference between you and me."

Paul started for the door and turned. "I can't believe this is happening."

Ned glared back. "Are you saying you can't face the truth? Sorry."

Paul took some hurried breaths. "I don't know, Ned. I thought I was on the right track. I thought I was doing the right thing—"

"What's right about coming here? If you cared, you would have been there when I got back to Elkville. But no, you didn't even give me a thought. Everything's about you, Paul. When you came to Margaret's house the other day, I was standing in the hall upstairs. I heard your little speech about leaving town. Apologizing like you really cared. But the only thing you cared about was protecting your self-image. I heard the effect you had on everyone afterwards. Margaret got so scared she ran off with you to Blacksburg. Do you have any idea how stressed Eric sounded after that?"

Paul put a hand against the wall. "I wasn't thinking clearly. I'm sorry."

"And now you're here, trying to help me?" Ned shouted. "Give me a break."

Paul grabbed his chest and started to stagger. "You're right, I—"

Ned went on instant alert. "Paul? Are you alright?"

Paul dropped to his knees. "Can't . . . breathe."

Ned rushed over and started yelling for help. "Teresa, get in here, now!"

Thirty-Three

RAYMOND FERGUSON TOOK his private plane to Blacksburg, Virginia, rented a car and headed to a tiny settlement named Elkville. Whatever was going on in the isolated community wasn't good, and he was determined to find out what the problem was.

He'd done his best to make changes that would improve the quality of life there. He'd sunk a good deal of money into a clinic and hired a very competent, young doctor to man it. He'd also built his daughter a house in Elkville because she liked to visit Margaret Lloyd, a woman Lea thought of as a second mother.

Lea was his one and only offspring, and he'd almost lost her. She'd been a difficult child and an even more difficult adult. However, the reason for Lea's emotional problems eventually came to light. Raymond came to understood how he had failed in his job as a father. The Lloyd family helped Lea to escape the downward spiral of emotional chaos she'd found herself in. Unfortunately, a short time later, Raymond had almost lost Lea a second time.

Paul Glass, an eminent psychiatrist, had assured Raymond he'd be able to intervene, but Paul failed to do as he promised. In fact, he made the situation worse. Raymond had to thank Eric and Matthew for coming to Lea's rescue. Both were good men. Now, they were in Elkville, along with Teresa Lloyd, trying to hold the place together.

As for Paul Glass, he had recently redeemed himself a little. The retired doctor had been a valuable resource while the clinic was being built. He was Raymond's watchdog and reported back anything of importance. But Paul hadn't told Raymond about the incident with Lea and how she'd panicked and run off. He hadn't been told about Ned Finney's accident either. It was only when Ned Finney called to resign his position that Raymond realized something was seriously wrong.

When he contacted Lea for more information, she didn't hold back. She brought him up to date on all kinds of turmoil he didn't know about, including information on Paul Glass. The man had had a minor heart attack, and he'd spent a couple of days in a Blacksburg hospital. Afterwards, he decided to go to Chicago and consult with his own doctor.

Hearing about all that had happened, Raymond decided to take a trip to Elkville. He needed to personally evaluate what needed to be done to improve the situation. He also wanted to check on his daughter. Lea had sounded okay when they spoke, but he wasn't taking any chances. He hoped and prayed she was doing alright.

By the time he pulled into Elkville, his nerves were on edge. He knew how to drive, but he didn't bother when he was in Chicago. He had a chauffeur to get him from one place to another. However, he'd decided he could manage the trip to Elkville. He hadn't realized how scary driving in the mountains could be when he was the man behind the wheel.

He was a little wobbly-legged when he got out of the car in front of Lea's house. Of course, the house also belonged to Matthew, but Raymond knew the surgeon wasn't too fond of the idea of owning property in Elkville. On the plus side, Raymond could not have picked a better husband for Lea.

* * *

After months of pursuing her business studies and doing very little in the kitchen, Lea was once again enjoying cooking and baking. Tonight she was preparing a nice meal for her dad. He was coming to Elkville for a visit.

Matthew offered to help Lea in the kitchen, but she suggested he get caught up on his reading instead. The simple meal of roast chicken, mashed potatoes and a salad didn't require much effort. She'd come a long ways since she'd first learned to peel potatoes. Thinking back, she had to laugh at herself. She'd made the task so much more complicated than it needed to be.

She was both excited and a little nervous about seeing her father. So much had happened recently that was distressing, including Paul

Glass collapsing at the clinic. Luckily, Ned and Teresa were there to help. And Eric soon joined them.

In the following days, Ned, who was already on shaky ground, was even worse after the incident. He blamed himself, claiming he'd said things to Paul that prompted Paul's attack.

Matthew stayed in the background as much as possible. He seemed to think his job was to make sure that Lea remained as stress free as possible. But it was hard not to be upset. She felt for everyone involved.

When she heard a knock on the front door, she was about to answer it, but Matthew was already on his feet before she had a chance. He might have urged her to remain calm, but she noticed he was definitely jumpier than usual. It probably had to do with his premonition. He seemed very concerned when his description of future events actually started to come true.

Lea turned down the flame on the stove and hurried into the foyer just as Matthew was inviting Raymond in. "Dad, it's so good to see you. Welcome to Elkville."

Raymond seemed very pleased by her greeting and smiled broadly. "Look at my gorgeous girl!" he said as he gave her a warm embrace. After he let her go, he held out his hand to Matthew. "How are you, Matthew?"

Matthew gave Raymond's hand a firm shake and a weak smile. "Hanging in there, Raymond."

Lea grabbed her father's arm and led him into the living room. "Dinner is almost ready. Do you want to sit down and talk to Matthew for a bit?"

"Yes," Raymond said, "but I'd like to wash up first."

"Of course," Lea said.

While Raymond was freshening up, Lea returned to the kitchen with Matthew following her. When he spoke, he used a low, quiet tone. "I hope that your father doesn't plan on staying very long."

Lea was about to open the oven door and hesitated. "I thought you liked my father."

"I do like Raymond. That's why I wish he hadn't come here."

Lea frowned. "I don't think I know what you're getting at."

"Lea, he's not the healthiest guy around, and I don't think he looks the best. I think that drive took it out of him."

Lea slipped on some oven mitts. "He looks okay to me. You're worrying too much," she said as she opened the oven door.

Matthew came over immediately. "Lea, please, let me take that bird out. It's heavy, and you could burn yourself."

Lea stood back and handed him the oven mitts. "Matthew, you have to relax. You're getting edgier by the day. If you're not careful, you'll get another one of those headaches."

Matthew put on the oven mitts and lifted the eight pound bird out of the oven and onto the tile counter. When he spoke again, his voice became a whisper. "I'm getting edgier by the day because every day it's something new to deal with. I couldn't believe it when Paul keeled over. It was dominoes after that. Margaret got very upset again thinking she shouldn't have pushed him in to talking to Ned. And of course Eric's worries about Margaret escalated. It's like the Ferguson mansion fiasco all over again."

"I see your point, but Dad just got here, so let's forget all that and have a nice meal."

Matthew removed the oven mitts and handed them to her. "You're right. I'm sorry."

Lea put the mitts aside and put her arms around Matthew's waist. "You have to stop obsessing about what's gone wrong."

Raymond walked into the kitchen. "Did I miss something?"

Lea let go of Matthew and smiled at her father. "The only thing you missed is my wonderful husband worrying too much."

Raymond went over to Matthew and patted his shoulder. "Is she right, Matthew? Are you worrying too much?"

Matthew's face went slightly red, but he quickly recovered. "I'm fine, and I'm looking forward to dinner. Lea's been very busy making your favorite meal."

Raymond rubbed his hands together. "I'm starving. I had an early lunch that didn't stick with me. I'm on a diet, you know. Lost twenty pounds. But while I'm here, I'm going to enjoy Lea's cooking."

"And baking," Matthew added. "She made an apple pie for dessert."

Raymond's eyes lit up. "I'm so proud of all the things you can do, Lea. I hope you know that."

Lea hugged her dad. "Thank you. Now go talk to Matthew for a couple of minutes while I finish up in here."

Raymond started out of the room and paused. "I wanted to ask about Paul. How's he doing?"

"I guess he's okay for now," Matthew said.

"And what about Eric and Teresa? I thought Lea mentioned they were staying here."

Lea began basting the chicken. "They are, but they're having dinner with Margaret."

"I want to get together for a meeting with Ned at the clinic tomorrow morning," Raymond said. "I'd like you to be there, Matthew. I want Eric and Teresa there too."

"But for now, Dad, let's relax and enjoy ourselves," Lea said.

* * *

After dinner with his mother and Teresa, Eric sat on the living room sofa and stared at Duke. The dog was dozing in his bed. Eric had never imagined that he'd see a dog living in his mother's house. But with Paul being away, Margaret was taking care of his pet. Strangely enough, she didn't seem to mind too much.

As he thought about their canine guest, Eric listened to the sound of dishes and pans being washed. He'd tried to help clean up after supper, but his wife and mother insisted he leave the kitchen. He could tell Teresa was enjoying getting to know her mother-in-law. Since her arrival in Elkville, Teresa had been the happiest of the group during all of the recent, troubling events.

Eric wished he could be just as happy, but he found himself getting moody instead. It was difficult to see his mother trying so hard to help herself, only to have circumstances foil her attempts. She'd made a decision to explore Chicago and what happened? Paul Glass had a heart attack. That was bad enough, but Margaret felt she was instrumental in bringing about his problems. Eric wanted and needed to reach her and help her to move on in her life, whatever that meant.

He found his mood shifting a little when his mother and Teresa came walking in from the kitchen. He had a surprise for his mother. Earlier that day, Eric had discussed a possible plan with Teresa. Once everyone was seated, he spoke up. "Mom, can we talk about something?"

Margaret was just settling into her chair. "What do you want to talk about?"

Eric glanced at Teresa who was sitting next to him and back at his mother. "Teresa and I want you to go to Chicago. But you don't have to stay with anyone. We want to rent a place for you to live, a place where you can feel that you're on your own."

Teresa nodded. "I agree. Paul's heart attack is unfortunate, but it shouldn't stop you from doing something you want to do. In fact, having your own place might work out so much better for you."

Margaret blinked back. "I don't know what to say. I haven't done anything like that since I went to art school in Baltimore. But it would be so expensive. You can't afford that sort of thing."

Eric smiled. "Teresa is an amazing person when it comes to budgeting and saving. And we can't think of a better way to spend our money than giving you that chance you deserve to try something different."

"What if I don't know what to do with myself? You'll have squandered your money."

"That's not true," Teresa said. "Any kind of adventure is good for a person's soul."

"And you'll have Lea and Matthew close if you need some family support," Eric said.

Margaret looked over at Duke. "What about Paul? I'm the one who told him to talk to Ned. But from what Ned admitted, he resented Paul's visit and said some things—"

"I'm sorry about Paul," Eric said, "but the man's supposed to be a professional. I'm sure he's faced lots of patient hostility."

Teresa nodded. "Paul should have known that Ned wasn't doing well. So if he reacted to whatever Ned said, then he has to take responsibility for his heart attack."

Margaret bit her lip. "Still—"

Eric edged forward in his seat and gave Margaret a stern look. "I want you to stop always blaming yourself for everything. You've been doing it with me, and it's not helping. You have to see me as strong and resilient. With you and dad as my parents, being tough has to be in my makeup."

Margaret laughed. "You can be quite stubborn and determined."

"Just like you," Eric said. "But I'm beginning to see that as a good thing. I couldn't have wanted a better mother."

Margaret scowled. "Now let's not get carried away."

"I mean it," Eric insisted. "My upbringing wasn't the easiest at times, but I always knew how much I was loved. Now, I need you to believe in me."

Margaret looked away and sucked in a breath. When she returned her gaze to Eric, she nodded. "I'll try, Eric, but maybe I have to believe in myself first."

"And we want to help you do that," Teresa said. "I promise, if I see you doubting yourself, I'll let you know." She blushed. "That is, if you think that would be helpful."

Margaret smiled. "I might have a hard time accepting your help when my feelings get going, but I want something better for all of us, Teresa. So do what you think best. And that goes for you too, Eric."

Eric sat back and put his arm around Teresa. "Look at us, talking things out with each other and making plans. What could be better than that?"

Thirty-Four

A COUPLE OF days after a mild heart attack, Paul had felt well enough to fly to Chicago. The doctors in Blacksburg were good, but there was some discussion about how Paul should go forward with his heart condition. He decided to see his own doctor. His Chicago based physician was one of the best in his field.

Once Paul arrived back in Chicago, he was pleased to book himself into a very nice hotel. It was expensive, but he needed a touch of elegance to help lift his mood. He kept thinking about how Ned had called him out on all his faults. He wanted to believe Ned was wrong, but the more he pondered the points Ned made, the more he agreed with Ned's assessment.

Ned wouldn't even be in Elkville if it weren't for Paul. Paul had been the one who pushed for a clinic. He was the one who talked Raymond Ferguson in to building it. All the time, Paul told himself that he wanted to help the unfortunate souls in the surrounding area. But in truth, he was trying to impress Margaret. If he'd really cared about the clinic, he would have gotten involved when Ned had his accident. He would have helped the young man out at the clinic. In truth, he cared about his dog a lot more than he cared about Ned Finney.

In retrospect, Paul had to question his ability to care about others, period. Maybe it's why his heart gave out. Maybe when the truth was put in front of him, his heart couldn't bear it.

It was a terrible thought to dwell on, and he pushed it aside. For his body's sake, he had to focus on something more positive. He walked over to the generous window in his hotel room. Chicago's skyline during the day was magnificent. At night, it was a shimmering palette of color and delight.

He loved the city. Day or night, Chicago's amazing buildings and architecture were inspiring achievements of creativity and splendor.

188

Unlike sleepy, little Elkville, the city had been built for people who were fully engaged with life. It had a hustling-bustling vitality that excited the blood. He wanted Margaret to experience the city too. He wanted to show her all the wonders that were there to enjoy. He wanted her to feel what it was like to be part of something so big and grand.

As soon as he thought of the woman, he thought about the last time he'd seen her. While he was in the hospital in Blacksburg, Margaret, Teresa and Eric had come to visit him. Matthew and Lea stayed in Elkville with Ned, but the Lloyds were kind enough to be there for him. They brought their well-wishes as well as Paul's toiletries and some of his clothes. Their kindness was appreciated. He had what he needed for his stay in Chicago. He was sad when Margaret said goodbye. Again, he had to remind himself not to get upset.

He retreated from the window and walked over to his bed. He tired easily after his heart attack and had to rest. He undressed and climbed onto the luxurious, king-sized mattress. As he lay on the silky, pale grey sheets, he tried, but he couldn't keep his mind from wandering back to Elkville. He wondered what was happening there. Since his encounter with Ned, how was the young doctor doing? Ned had a lot of unresolved issues, and Paul hadn't helped to resolve them. From what Margaret and Eric told him, Ned's reaction to Paul's visit and heart attack compounded Ned's dim take on life. It wasn't a happy thought to have when Paul was trying to give himself a break and go to sleep.

Thirty-Five

RAYMOND WOKE UP early and immediately thought about the previous evening that he'd spent with Lea and Matthew. After a delicious meal, they sat in the living room. Raymond had asked Lea about something she'd told him, something that scared him. He wanted to know more about why she'd run off again.

His daughter had been so candid in how she answered him. She shared the fact that she'd been slipping back into her old personality. While she was talking about it, Matthew held her hand. He didn't interrupt Lea as she spoke, but Raymond could see how Matthew stiffened when she talked about her feelings. Like Raymond, the surgeon's fear was there. They both loved Lea and neither wanted to lose her.

As Lea went on with her story, she confided that the last few months, she'd made her business studies and Elkville's interests a priority. As she invested almost all her time in the outer world, her connection to who she really was began to weaken. On the evening that Matthew arrived in Elkville, she'd been so frightened by the thought that she could lose herself again. It sent her into a panic, and she ran off. It was a pattern she'd used in the past.

Thankfully, this time her extended family was there for her. Before she got very far, they were there to pull her back into a world where she was safe and loved. She told Raymond that it felt like she was coming home again.

Now, Raymond was faced with another person who was trying to run away. That person was Ned Finney. He'd personally interviewed the young doctor and found him to be exactly what he thought Elkville needed. Smart, friendly, and self-assured, Finney inspired Raymond with his professionalism. The young man's physical appearance matched his excellent qualifications. With thick, black hair, piercing

190

blue eyes and handsome features, he was the kind of guy that women swooned over. But Ned Finney didn't seem interested in swooning women. When Raymond had his investigator look into Finney's private life, he learned that the man didn't date or even get out with friends. All in all, he didn't sound like a very well-rounded individual.

Raymond ignored that fact because Finney did have something that Raymond valued. Finney's record indicated that he could hold the line when that line was threatened. He could be steadfast and stable under extreme circumstances. He was the kind of man Raymond hired to help him run his business. And, Raymond wanted Finney to run the clinic in Elkville.

But Ned Finney was doing what Lea did. He was trying to handle his problems by running from them. Raymond wasn't going to let that happen. He'd been lax with his daughter when he should have stopped her tantrums early on. If he had, she would have been forced to talk to the doctors he hired. In Ned's case, he had to provoke the man's ability to fight for himself, to snap him out of his depression with some pressure.

He'd called for a meeting at the clinic that morning. When he arrived at the facility, Ned Finney, Teresa, Eric and Matthew were waiting for him. They were seated in folding chairs in the treatment area.

Raymond came into the space with certain expectations about Finney. He had thought he'd see a man who was recovering from an accident. He didn't expect to see someone who looked like he'd been brutalized. It was a shock to find he barely recognized the man who sat scowling up at him.

Ned's handsome features were gaunt and guarded, and he sat in a hunched way that looked like he was collapsing in on himself. But it was Finney's eyes that told Raymond just how much Finney had changed. Finney's icy, blue eyes were not the friendly ones Raymond remembered. But he recognized the look and what they were telling him. Lea's eyes had once conveyed a similar message. In one glance, his daughter could inform him that she resented him with every bone in her body.

Finney's look wasn't as hostile, but it was still a harsh reminder of those heart-breaking days with Lea. After suffering from an abusive childhood that Raymond had stupidly ignored, Lea's sweetness had been replaced by anger and a desire to lash out. They had both gone through years of torment and misery before Lea got the help she needed.

Raymond didn't know what Finney's problem was, but he refused to let the young man end up a victim like his daughter. Calling in his own ability to hold the line no matter what, he prepared himself for what he had to do.

After greeting the group of people who were waiting for him, Raymond sat down on one of the folding chairs. Before he said anything more, he took out his reading glasses, opened a folder he'd brought with him and took out a document. "Recently, I got a call that confused me," he said. "The person I hired to man this clinic told me he wanted to leave. However, I'm looking at a contract that plainly states that Benedict Michael Finney has agreed to staff the Elkville clinic for a period of at least one year." He took off his glasses and looked at Ned. "And you, sir, will not back out of that contract. Is that clear?"

Ned started to protest. "I called you because I'm not capable—"

Raymond cut him off. "Save the excuses, Finney! You will live up to your obligations, or you will pay the consequences."

Ned's pale face turned red. "What consequences are you talking about?"

Raymond stood up and stared down at Ned. "If you don't live up to the terms of our contract, I will see to it that you never work in the medical field again. I will personally make it a point to destroy your career so completely that you won't be allowed near a bedpan."

Ned stood up too. "You can't do that. My record is untarnished."

Raymond moved closer to Ned and poked a finger in Ned's heaving chest. "I could care less about your untarnished record, son. With my money, power and connections, it'll be worth less than a coffee receipt. In the meantime, you look pathetic. So get some help. You have three doctors sitting here, use them and get yourself looking presentable again." He turned and started out of the room. "This meeting is over."

Raymond walked to the front entrance with steady steps. He just hoped his instincts about how to handle the situation would work out as he planned.

* * *

When Ned forced himself to go to the meeting with Raymond Ferguson, his appetite was nonexistent, and his energy level was just enough to keep him on his feet when he walked from his bed to the clinic. As for his mental state, he just wanted to be left alone, especially after Paul Glass's visit. Ned had finally allowed himself to say what he thought and the result was Paul having a heart attack.

Ned was left feeling he was in a no-win situation. He couldn't live with himself if he kept quiet, and he had to worry about damaging someone else if he spoke up. He was trapped in some horrible sea of chaos. He knew how to battle disease and fight to save a life after an accident. He had practical tools at his disposal. But he didn't know how to fight the feelings that had taken over. The anger was there, but to express it seemed useless. He'd always tried to help people, not hurt them, like he had in Paul's case. He hoped Raymond Ferguson wasn't another Paul. He couldn't handle another person acting like they cared when they didn't even know him or what he was going through.

After Teresa, Eric and Matthew arrived at the clinic. They were helpful in setting up some chairs. Other than that, not much was said. Ned figured everyone was thinking the same thing. Ferguson would come in, tell Ned he'd have a replacement very soon, and the meeting would end.

But that's not what happened, except for the meeting being short. Ferguson did most of the talking. Ned was told that there would be no replacement. No matter what condition Ned was in, Ferguson didn't care. Ned had to remain at the clinic and do his job.

Ferguson's demands didn't make sense. He could find a new doctor for the clinic. The salary was great, and so far there wasn't much to do. But Ferguson was adamant. The man wanted what he wanted, period.

After Ferguson left, Ned stood in place, trying to take in oxygen, trying to understand what just happened. He could still hear Ferguson yelling at him, bullying him. When he tried to defend himself, Ferguson got more abusive and insulting. Ned's entire hard won career was dismissed with a few words.

It felt like the final storm had hit Ned's unstable foundation, and he didn't have the strength to withstand the force that wanted to take him out.

Teresa came over and reached for his arm. "Ned, are you alright?"

Ned didn't answer her. How could he? His mind wasn't working anymore. He turned and walked back to his room. After he locked his door, he collapsed on his bed.

* * *

Eric watched Ned retreat from the room and turned to Matthew and Teresa. "Has Raymond Ferguson taken leave of his senses? Doesn't he understand anything about this situation?"

Matthew shook his head. "Lea and I told him Ned was depressed, and Raymond made a comment. He said he knew how to handle men like Ned, men who were fighters. Once they were goaded enough, they often came back to themselves. When he made the statement, I had no idea he was going to put his idea into action."

"Ned is beyond fighting," Teresa said as she swiped a tear from her cheek. "Did you see the look on his face? I've known kids in foster homes who looked like that. One was a friend who ended up killing herself."

Eric put his arm around Teresa. "We won't let that happen to Ned."

"Teresa's right," Matthew said. "Raymond is a complete idiot if he thinks intimidating Ned is going to be helpful."

Eric agreed. "He looks like death warmed over, but I don't think it's only a physical problem. It's like he's given up on himself."

Teresa sniffled. "Just before my friend committed suicide, she looked so lost. She'd been in so many foster homes."

Eric held her a little closer. "Ned said he came from a stable background. That's what's confusing."

Teresa stared up at him. "He also said his father never asked anything of him, but was it true?"

"I don't think so," Eric said. "He had to get that idea that feelings don't matter from someone."

Matthew crossed his arms. "If his father drilled that idea into Ned, I'd say that's asking a lot."

"It didn't work with me," Eric said. "But I think I was more aware that something was wrong. My father's anger and demands made that obvious. In Ned's case, if his father treated him well, he probably didn't question what he was being taught."

"Maybe that's what he's doing now," Teresa said, "questioning what he was told."

Matthew grimaced. "If twenty nine years of feelings are coming up all at once, I think we know what the problem is."

"He shouldn't be left alone," Teresa insisted.

"Maybe not," Matthew said, "but a loner is a hard one to handle. I've been there."

"I'll go check on him," Eric said as he walked to the back of the clinic. When he got to Ned's room, he knocked on the door, waited and knocked again. He tried the knob and looked back towards the clinic. "Hey, guys, he's locked himself in."

Teresa and Matthew walked back to join him.

Matthew paused and looked up. "If this is a regular interior door, there's probably a little key somewhere." He fingered the trim over the door and smiled as he held up a small thin item. "Here we go," he said as he put the key in the knob. A moment later the lock was undone.

Teresa pushed the men aside and hurried into the room. Eric and Matthew followed close behind.

Teresa was calling out as she rushed to the bed. "Ned? Are you alright?"

Ned was face down on the covers, but he raised his head. "Is it a patient?"

Teresa knelt down. "No, I'm worried about you? We all are."

Ned stared at her with questioning eyes. "Why?"

Teresa put a hand on Ned's cheek. "You're so hot."

"Go away," Ned moaned.

"You have to talk to us," Teresa insisted. "So we can help you."

Ned was just as insistent. "Talking doesn't work. Just need sleep."

Teresa scowled at Eric with flaring-green eyes. "I don't care if I have to stay here the whole year he's under contract, I'm not letting anything happen to him."

Eric stared down at Ned and felt like he was seeing himself. They both had fathers who taught them to believe in crazy ideas. Ned appeared confident and a little full of himself when they'd first met, but now Eric understood why. It was the way Ned had learned to survive. But life seemed determined to expose his vulnerability. Ned was fighting some powerful, inner monster. It looked like he could lose the battle if he didn't get some help. "Don't worry, Teresa, I'll be right here with you. And when I talk to Ferguson, I'm going to let him know what a complete jerk he is."

Eric meant every word he said. He might hate working in Elkville, but it didn't matter anymore. Raymond Ferguson had thrown down the gauntlet, and if Ned was too sick to pick it up, Eric would take up the challenge. He refused to give in to the dictates of another man who was incapable of knowing how to treat other human beings.

Matthew put a hand on Eric's shoulder. "Nobody's staying here. Raymond's going to tear up that contract or else. In the meantime, let's do what we can to get Ned back on his feet so he can walk out of this place."

Thirty-Six

WHEN MATTHEW TALKED about the "walking wounded" in his conversation with Teresa, he wasn't sure what the words meant. But when he arrived home from the clinic, feeling drained, he wondered if they applied to him. He'd taken some heavy emotional hits since his arrival in Elkville.

First, there was Lea running off and the thought of losing her. It scared him, and that fact didn't sit well. He needed to know he could take on whatever came his way. Next there was the crying child he'd met at the clinic. He couldn't put the boy out of his mind. He sometimes woke up in the middle of the night, wondering if the boy would grow up with all his teeth and bones intact.

Finally, there was Ned Finney. The guy wasn't a kid. He was a fellow doctor. But when Matthew and Eric were helping to get him settled in his bed, Ned's flushed face was young and innocent, just like the little boy's. A few days before, Matthew had a chance to observe Ned when he was treating the boy's drunken father. The young man was compassionate and caring even though the boy's father had tried to get in a number of punches.

Ned was a dedicated doctor. It wasn't fair that Raymond Ferguson came barging in and terrorized him so viciously. The older man's heavy handed tactics delivered a terrible blow to Ned's already precarious self-image. Matthew could only hope that Ned could be pulled back from whatever dark place he was in.

Matthew was feeling pretty dark himself when it came to Raymond Ferguson. When he let himself into his house, he heard Lea and Raymond in the kitchen. Not knowing how to express his anger, he tried to steady himself for the coming conversation.

As soon as he walked into the kitchen, Lea got up from her tea and came over. "Good, you're home. What took you so long? Dad said the meeting was a short one. Did a bunch of people show up at the clinic?"

Matthew loved Lea, but he wouldn't hide his feelings. "Teresa took care of a few. Eric and I were busy trying to stabilize Ned."

"Ned? I know he's been hurting, but—"

Matthew looked at Raymond who was sitting at the table. "He's doing more than hurting after this morning."

Raymond got up and came over. "What's going on? Did he finally put on his fighting gloves?"

Lea stared at Raymond. "What do you mean, Dad?"

Raymond took Lea's hands and squeezed them. "After all the mistakes I made with you, I didn't want to make any with Ned Finney. I wasn't going to let him run and maybe keep running. I told him I'd hold him to the contract he has."

"You did more than that," Matthew said. "You told the man to either stay put or you'd ruin his career."

Lea pulled her hands away from Raymond's grip. "Ruin Ned's career? Why would you do that?"

"The young pup started to think he'd do what he wanted," Raymond said. "So I had to apply a little more pressure to make sure he got the message."

"What kind of logic is that?" Matthew asked. "That young pup was already down, and you came in and kicked the hell out of him."

Lea sucked in a breath. "Oh my goodness, Matthew, is he going to be okay?"

Matthew looked away. "I don't know. I think he's lost hope, and he won't talk to us."

"I'll go back to the clinic," Raymond said. "I'll tell him I found a replacement."

"It's too late for that, Matthew said. "He's not going to trust you after this morning."

Raymond averted his eyes. "I don't know what else to do."

Lea looked at Matthew. "When I felt lost, it helped to know someone cared. I bet that's what Ned needs too."

"People do care," Matthew said. "Teresa and Eric care so much that they're willing to stay here until Ned's contract is up."

Raymond wandered back to the table and sat down. "I've made a hell of a mess, haven't I?"

Matthew looked at Lea. "We have to get Ned to eat something. Some broth might be the ticket. Do you think you could make some soup with the leftover chicken from last night?"

"Yes, I'll be happy to do that. And I'll personally take it over to him."

The doorbell rang and Matthew looked at Lea. "While I get that maybe you could get started on the soup."

Matthew went to the door mumbling to himself. "What now?" was on his lips when he opened the door. The young woman who'd been stabbed was on the stoop.

"Doctor Howell, sorry to bother you," she blurted out, "but the folks at the general store told me where you live. Can I come in?"

Matthew nodded and opened the door. "You're name is Mary, right?"

Mary nodded.

Matthew waved her forward. "Let's talk in the living room."

Once they were seated, Mary clasped her hands and took quick glances at Matthew. "I been in Blacksburg since I was twelve. Auntie took me in when my dad—" She paused. "I lived with auntie and went to school. Some folks were nice to me. They taught me how to talk proper, and I even got a job. I had to come back to help out. Ma's been poorly since Jacob. Now, she's got real bad."

"Is the little boy you had with you the youngest child in your family?" Matthew asked.

"Ma didn't want no more after him, but it's been hard when my pa gets to drinking."

"Is your brother alright?"

Mary looked at her lap and twisted a button on her sweater. "He's always bawling. Pa slaps him, but it don't do no good."

Matthew sat up more attentively. "Mary, is he hurt?"

Mary stared back with eyes that held nothing but sadness. "Not bad yet. So I brought him here."

"Here?"

Mary pointed to the door. "Jacob's in the truck."

Matthew jumped up and hurried to the door. He didn't want to care about the dirty, little boy from the hills, but it was too painful not to care. He had to find out if the boy was still among the living. When he got to the old truck on the street and looked through the window of the cab, he didn't see anyone. There was no one in the truck bed either.

Mary came up behind him and opened the passenger door and pointed again.

Matthew peered in and saw a small heap on the floor. "Jacob?"

Mary leaned into the truck and pulled back an old blanket. "Boy, wake up," she said as she grabbed hold of some small arms. "Come see that nice man you liked."

Once she was holding the child, Mary looked up at Matthew. "Can you keep him, just 'til I go back to Blacksburg? Auntie will take him in."

Matthew wasn't quite sure what took place in the next few minutes. He did hear himself agreeing to take Jacob. And he found himself holding the little boy again and carrying him into the house. After that, things were a bit of a blur. Lea was there, in the middle of it all. She was excited and asking questions about the little boy he was holding. But Jacob wouldn't have anything to do with her. He clung to Matthew, burying his head in Matthew's shirt and refusing to open his eyes.

* * *

Margaret hurried over to Lea's house as soon as she'd been told she was needed. Earlier, she got off the phone with Paul. He'd flown to Chicago to consult with his own physician. She hoped he'd be alright, but she put aside her concerns when she let herself into Lea's house. A child was crying. But what child would that be? "Lea?" she called out.

"In the kitchen, Mom," Lea called back.

Hearing the cries escalate into screams, Margaret rushed to the kitchen and stopped short. She couldn't believe what she was seeing. Matthew was trying to dislodge a little boy who was clinging to Matthew's shirt. Lea was standing back with a hand over her mouth.

As soon as Matthew saw Margaret, he called to her. "Margaret, he won't let go of me!"

Margaret stood where she was, trying to think. Lea had told her that Matthew had tended to a child a few days before. "Matthew, try to stay calm," she said in a quiet voice. "If he's the boy I think he is, this house and everything he sees is all new and frightening. It would be best if you take him into a dimly lit bedroom and just sit with him. He'll probably calm down once he sees nothing is going to hurt him."

Lea gestured to Matthew. "Come with me. You can stay with him in our bedroom."

Matthew did as he was told, but as he passed Margaret, she saw his eyes. They were almost as panicked as the child's.

Margaret walked over to the kitchen table where Raymond was sitting. "Good to see you, Raymond," she said. "Lea said you arrived yesterday."

Raymond looked up at her. His jowls were sagging with regret. "It was a mistake. It was all a mistake. I should never have come."

"Why did you come?" Margaret asked.

"I built a clinic. I hired a great doctor. I expected that was the end of it. But a few weeks after my doctor arrives, he's ready to leave. What was I to think? I had to check it out for myself."

"What did Ned tell you when you talked to him?"

Now Raymond's head was sagging too. "I didn't talk to him. I told him how it was. He had a contract. He couldn't walk out."

Margaret's shoulders tightened. "But the man is sick. He's hardly able to see more than a patient or two, and he's exhausted."

"I understand that now, but from what Matthew said, it's too late to do anything about it."

"Is Ned's condition worse? Is that what you're telling me?"

Lea came back into the room and answered Margaret's question. "After what dad did, he's very ill."

Margaret turned to face Lea. "Maybe I should go over to the clinic."

"I don't know about that. Eric and Teresa are there for now. From what Matthew said, they're trying to keep Ned quiet. Talking to him might agitate him even more. But you can help me make some soup for him. I just got started when we had an unexpected visitor."

"You mean the little boy?"

"His sister brought him here. She was afraid her father might hurt him. She's hoping we can care for him for a little while."

Margaret held herself. "Ricky and I tried to take a child in once. He was such a little thing and clearly mistreated. But his father wouldn't let us keep the boy. He came to our house, all mad and determined. I tried to protect the boy, but his father took him from my arms. There was nothing I could do to stop the man when he stormed out of the house. When Ricky came home, he asked where the child was, and I told him." Margaret gasped out a shaky breath. "Poor thing never survived the winter."

"Oh, Mom, you don't think that will happen to Jacob, do you?"

"Jacob?" Margaret asked.

"That's the boy's name. He didn't make a peep until Matthew tried to set him down. Then he started screaming and holding on to Matthew. I think Matthew was scared too. He's never had to deal with children."

Margaret sniffled, wiped her eyes and glanced upwards. "Well, I don't hear Jacob crying anymore. So I guess whatever Matthew did, it was the right thing."

Lea gave Margaret an anxious look. "Matthew's tired. He hasn't been sleeping well. I think everything that's happened is wearing him down. He's already worried about Ned. Now there's little Jacob too. Matthew wouldn't have taken him in if he didn't care."

Margaret got up and went over to Lea. "Now you listen to me. Matthew is strong, and he has you. But you have to have faith in him and yourself."

Raymond came over too and reached out to Lea. "I'm so sorry that I've made things worse."

Lea sighed. "It's not what you wanted to happen."

"I'm starting to feel like Paul Glass," Raymond said. "The man made some terrible blunders, and I cursed him for it. Now I'm cursing myself."

Margaret steadied the shakiness that was trying to undermine her resolve. Lea looked like she needed someone who was reassuring by her side. Her advice to the young woman could be applied to herself. "Talking about mistakes doesn't change anything. We have to pull together and put things right. Lea, let's make that soup for starters. And Raymond, do you know anything about helping in the kitchen?"

Raymond smiled. "I didn't always have money. While my mother worked, I cooked for my brothers and sisters. I wasn't too good at it, but no one starved."

"Then wash up," Margaret said. "You can make a salad to go with the soup. And I'll bake something for dessert."

"Before we start, Mom, can we take a peek and see how Matthew is doing?" Lea asked. "I don't want him to think we've forgotten him."

"That's a good idea, but let's be very quiet about it."

Margaret followed Lea up the stairs, relieved that Jacob hadn't started crying again. It was a good sign that the child felt more secure. They paused in the hall, and Lea took a quick look into the master bedroom. She pulled back and smiled at Margaret. "Look at them," she instructed.

Margaret took a hasty glance into the bedroom and smiled too. Matthew was stretched out on the bed sleeping. Jacob was asleep next to him, with one hand on Matthew's chest. It was a picture of calm and serenity that gave Margaret hope in the middle of all the turmoil going on.

Thirty-Seven

NED WOKE UP, opened his eyes, and took stock of his body. His headache was almost gone, and he felt better. He started to move his arm and realized he was hooked up to an IV. He noticed Teresa in a chair by his bed. She was reading. He didn't know why, but seeing her made him breathe a little easier. "Teresa, what time is it?"

Teresa looked up at him and smiled. "It's almost five o'clock. You had a very good nap."

"I must have slept all day."

"You needed it. And I'm happy to report that your fever's down."

Eric came walking into the room. "Look who's finally joining the land of the living."

Ned blinked back. "Have you two been here all this time?"

Teresa put her book aside, stood up and stretched. "Of course, we have. You don't think we'd leave you, do you?"

Ned didn't know what to say. He'd never had people care about him like the twosome in front of him. "I don't know what happened. I was so tired, I must have crashed."

Teresa took Ned's hand. "Raymond Ferguson's visit got to all of us."

Hearing Ferguson's name brought back thoughts of the morning meeting. A moment of intense anxiety about his future followed. But when Ned looked up at Teresa's beautiful face, the whole fiasco didn't seem quite as alarming. "Don't worry about me. I'll find a way to get through this mess."

Eric sat down on the side of Ned's bed. "You're not alone. Teresa and I have already made up our minds. We'll stay here with you and make sure you get through this year."

Ned frowned. "You can't do that. You both have practices in Baltimore."

Teresa squeezed his hand. "We're not leaving you, Ned. That's the bottom line."

"Why? Why would you care about a person you hardly know?"

Teresa paused. "You didn't seem comfortable when Lea mentioned something about family. But take it from someone who grew up in foster homes, whoever you're with is your family."

Eric glanced at Teresa. "Actually, this is an opportunity for Teresa and me to work closely with one another. I'm looking forward to it."

"You detest Elkville," Ned protested.

"Everything feels different when you're with people who matter to you," Eric said.

Teresa nodded. "And you matter too, Ned."

Ned pushed himself up into a sitting position. "I don't know what to say."

Eric stood up. "Instead of talking, why don't we all have some dinner that Lea and Margaret dropped off?"

"The chicken soup smells so good, Ned," Teresa said. "Do you think you could try a little?"

Ned rubbed his stomach and felt the first snatches of hunger he'd had in a while. "I guess so."

"Good," Eric said. "If you're up to it, we can all eat in the kitchen."

Ned frowned. "Wouldn't you rather have dinner with Lea and Matthew or Margaret?"

Eric laughed. "No, I found out they have their hands full. The three of them and Raymond are dining with a very vocal dinner guest."

Teresa giggled too. "Remember the little boy who was crying while you tended to his father and sister?"

Ned did remember the boy. It was hard to forget him. "That kid was small and skinny, but he did have a good set of lungs. What about him?"

"His name is Jacob, and his sister asked Matthew to take him in for a few days. Now, according to Lea, Jacob has attached himself to Matthew. He has a screaming fit if anyone gets too near, or if Matthew tries to put him down."

Ned couldn't help himself and smiled too. "And I thought I had problems. Matthew Howell, the big tough guy, is stuck with a screaming child? I'm glad we're eating here."

The battle of clean versus dirty was fought before dinner. After Matthew took a good look at Jacob's appearance, he had to take a stand. The child's face and hands were beyond dirty. Matthew doubted they'd been washed in days.

If he was going to eat dinner with Jacob in his lap, helping himself to Matthew's food, Matthew decided a hand washing was in order. Jacob seemed to have other ideas.

The simple act of Matthew putting the boy's hand under a faucet and running water was met with deep resistance and another screaming fit. At least Lea was there to help. As Matthew held Jacob's fisted hand, Lea lathered it and tried to wash most of the grime away. The process was repeated with the second hand. A warm washcloth to the face and arms came next. More screams followed, but Matthew was just happy to see some of the dirt come off.

When the experience came to an end, Matthew made sure to give the little boy a piece of cookie as a reward. Jacob gave him a pathetic scowl, but he did accept the peace offering.

Feeling rather triumphant after the battle, Matthew was pleased when he noticed Jacob eyeing the food that Lea and Margaret put on the table. It was the first time that Jacob had greeted his new situation with anything but fear.

However, Jacob was cautious about trying anything. When he was given his own bowl of hearty chicken soup, he balked. He wasn't about to taste the stuff until Matthew took a spoonful and pronounced it delicious. Jacob seemed satisfied enough to try it too. But he was particularly interested in the buttered biscuits. When he started stuffing his mouth with one, Matthew tried to caution him to slow down, but Jacob seemed to think it was his only chance to fill up. He downed two in a row and reached for a third. Matthew had to move the basket aside before the child could grab it. Jacob screamed out his protest, but Matthew remained firm. "I'm sorry, Jacob," he said, "but you have to take your time, or you'll get sick."

That's when Jacob gave Matthew the most woeful look that Matthew had ever seen. It was like he'd crushed the little boy's small heart. The look was almost enough to make Matthew let Jacob have his way, but he had to do what was best for the child. In an effort to sooth the situation, he found himself rocking the little boy. It was an instinctual response that worked. After a few minutes, Jacob calmed down and put his thumb in his mouth. Later, he refused any salad, but he wasn't shy about the chocolate cake.

A few minutes after Jacob finished his dessert, he fell asleep in Matthew's arms. Matthew dusted a crumb off the boy's newly washed face. It was the face of a cherub. It was hard to believe the small child could have such a temper.

* * *

During dinner, Lea was too distracted by Matthew and Jacob to pay attention to her food. Margaret and Raymond seemed to feel the same way. They all sat at the opposite end of the table. They didn't dare get any closer for fear of prompting another crying fit. All three were intent on observing the interaction between man and boy.

Lea was impressed with her husband. He could be curt and even abrasive around adults, but he was very patient with Jacob. Lea knew how much patience it took to interact with the boy.

Before dinner, Lea had been called to duty. She helped to wash Jacob's hands. She couldn't believe how strong the frail child could be when he didn't want to do something. Matthew tried his best to be careful in how he held the boy's arm. Lea did her best to wash Jacob's small fist. As she rubbed the dirt off his face with a soft, wet cloth, she wondered about herself.

Her father said she was very stubborn as a child. She figured she didn't have a choice. According to her diary, she'd been subjected to daily torment by a demonic nanny. Perhaps Jacob had faced a similar adversary. Whatever the case, she hoped the child knew she and Matthew wanted what was best for him. She also had a new appreciation for the man she'd married. If they had a family someday, Matthew would be an excellent father.

But what about her own father? That morning, Raymond had demonstrated a very ruthless side of himself. But when she glanced over at him at the table, he didn't look ruthless. He wore that forlorn expression she'd seen when they were together at the Ferguson mansion.

That was a difficult time for everyone. In her father's case, his marriage fell apart, and he didn't know what he could do to stop his wife from leaving him. The man was a whiz at business, but home and hearth were his downfall. Happily, Lea's parents reconciled and were learning to communicate. She hoped her father found a better way of going forward with Ned and the clinic situation.

* * *

Raymond sat at the kitchen table, finishing his iced tea. "Lea and Margaret, I want to thank you both for a delicious meal."

"And you did a great job with the salad," Margaret replied.

Raymond smiled. "I enjoyed being part of the kitchen team." He glanced at Matthew. After quite an emotional meal, the man looked relieved that Jacob was asleep. "I also want to say that I'll be driving back to Blacksburg in the morning."

Lea spoke up. "You could stay a little longer, Dad."

Raymond sat back and let out a sigh. "I came to Elkville wondering why there were so many problems, and I've made things worse. It's best that I get out of everyone's hair."

"What about Ned?" Matthew asked.

Raymond reached into his pocket and put an envelope on the table. "I wrote a letter of apology, and also stated that I'll find a replacement. He should be able to leave before too long."

"That was decent of you," Matthew said. "I'm sure he'll appreciate it."

Raymond stood up. "It's been quite a day. I think I'll turn in and get an early start tomorrow."

Lea stood up too and gave him a hug. "I can fix you some breakfast in the morning. What time are you leaving?"

"No reason for you to get up, my darling daughter."

"Oh please," Lea protested.

"Alright, I'll say 'goodbye' before I leave, but I want to be on the road by six thirty."

Margaret pushed back her chair and got to her feet. "Have a safe trip home, Raymond. I'm sorry things turned out the way they did."

Raymond looked at the little boy in Matthew's arms. "I've learned a lot in the short time I've been here. If Ned had wanted to stay, I realize he'd be up against quite a challenge. Hearing about this child's family and seeing how frightened the boy acts, this is not an easy place."

"No, it's not," Margaret said. "But you did try to make it a better place by building the clinic."

"That's true," Lea said.

Raymond smiled. "At least I got that right."

Margaret excused herself. "I have to go home and check on Duke, but I'll be back in a little while."

Raymond watched her leave. "She's a very good friend, Lea."

Lea hugged Raymond's arm. "And you're a very good dad. You not only built the clinic, but you also gave us a beautiful home." She looked at Matthew. "Isn't that right?"

"Yes, Raymond, it's very nice," Matthew said.

Raymond gave the surgeon a nod and started out of the room. As he made his way up the stairs, he felt a little less guilty than he had earlier. Still, it would be a long time before he tackled a problem with someone like Ned without outside advice and better planning. He was just lucky Teresa and Eric had been there for Ned. When they called Lea before supper, they said the man was eating and his attitude was better.

* * *

After her father left to go to bed, Lea looked over at Matthew. "What are we going to do about Jacob tonight?"

Before Matthew could answer, the little boy woke up and started to wipe the sleep from his eyes. He looked around and frowned. For the first time, he let go of Matthew and slipped off of his lap. Grabbing himself, he stood on wobbly legs doing a little dance.

Lea smiled. "I think someone needs to use the bathroom."

Matthew stood up and took Jacob's hand. "It's about time. He hasn't gone since he got here. Come with me, young man."

This time Jacob seemed not only willing but eager to follow Matthew to the powder room. While they were gone, Lea began to clean up the dishes. She was removing her father's plate from the table and thought about how she'd become much closer to him recently.

He'd definitely made a mistake with Ned, but he was trying his best. Lea was sure of that.

She thought about Margaret too. The woman had hurried from the house like she was on a mission. Lea knew Duke probably needed some attention, but there was a look on Margaret's face that Lea recognized. Margaret was up to something.

Matthew was holding Jacob's hand when they came back to the kitchen. Lea was finishing loading the dishwasher and looked over at them. She saw the smile on Matthew's face. "How'd it go?"

"Jacob wasn't sure about our facilities, but he got the idea fast enough. And afterwards, he actually let me wash his hands."

"My goodness, that's quite an improvement in a very short time." Lea beamed broadly at Jacob. "What a good boy you are."

"Jacob gave her the smallest indication of a smile and then buried his eyes in Matthew's pants leg."

A moment later, Margaret announced she was back and hurried into the kitchen. Lea saw the pleased look on Margaret's face. "What's going on?"

Margaret held out a shopping bag. "Guess what I have for Jacob?"

Lea came over and took a small shirt out of the bag. "How adorable!"

"It belonged to Eric when he was about Jacob's age. I gave away most of his things, but I kept a few special items in the bottom of my cedar chest. I forgot about them until now."

Lea checked out more of the clothes and looked at Margaret. "Mom, I don't see any size labels. Did you make these?"

Margaret blushed. "I did, but I'm afraid they don't look store bought."

"You did a great job. They're better then what you get at a store."

"I studied the Sears catalog and tried to find fabric and patterns that matched the clothes I saw."

Lea held out a navy blue sailor shirt with white piping. "What do you think, Matthew? Isn't this the cutest?"

Matthew took the shirt and inspected it. "Nice job, Margaret." He looked down at Jacob and showed him the shirt. "What do you think, Jacob? You have new clothes."

Jacob stared at the shirt, almost touched it, and pulled back. He gave Matthew a questioning look.

"It's okay. It's for you," Matthew said.

Jacob grabbed the shirt, held it guardedly and stared up at Margaret.

Margaret came a little closer and crouched down. She took more shirts and pants out of the bag. "These are for you too," she said as she tried to hand Jacob the bag.

Jacob turned instantly shy, backed up, and hid behind Matthew.

Matthew took the bag from Margaret and helped her up. "Thank you. That was very kind."

"I've always loved children, but I couldn't get pregnant after Eric," Margaret said. She turned to Lea. "But lo and behold, I was eventually blessed with this sweet girl."

Lea came over and kissed Margaret's cheek. "And you have Teresa now too."

"I'm so happy that she insisted on coming here. She told me she feels like we're all becoming family."

"Teresa has the right idea," Lea said. "She called a bit ago and told me that she and Eric are staying with Ned at the clinic tonight."

"Is Ned doing alright?" Margaret asked.

Lea crossed her arms. "Teresa says he's better, but she doesn't want to leave him by himself. I guess she's had some bad experiences with depressed people getting worse when you don't expect it."

Matthew stifled a yawn. "It's been a long day. Maybe we should turn in."

"I'm ready," Lea said. "It's not that late, but I'm surprisingly tired. Plus, I want to be up early to see my dad before he leaves."

"And I still have to take Duke for a little walk," Margaret said as she headed out of the kitchen.

After Lea showed Margaret to the door, she turned to Matthew. "I've been thinking. Maybe we could make a bed for Jacob out of sofa cushions."

"Where should he sleep?" Matthew asked.

"At least for this first night, I think he should be in our room."

Matthew groaned. "Our room?"

"Yes, otherwise he could get very scared."

Matthew looked down at the child attached to his leg and shook his head. "You get the sheets, Lea, and I'll bring up the cushions."

The phone rang before Lea got to the stairs. "I'll get it," she announced. After she answered the call, she held out the phone to Matthew. "It's your partner, Ralph."

Lea waited for Matthew to finish his conversation. If Ralph was calling, it probably involved one of their patients.

Matthew hung up and looked at her. "I have to go back to Chicago. Ralph's got a surgery that's really iffy, and he needs me to be there."

"When would you leave?"

"Your dad can drive us to Blacksburg in the morning, and I'll fly back to Chicago with him."

Lea looked at Jacob. The child was sucking his thumb with half-closed eyes. "What about our little house guest?"

"He'll have to manage without me. Besides, he has you and Margaret. It'll be a chance for him to bond with more people."

"I don't know, he's still very—"

"Lea, I don't have a choice. Ralph wouldn't ask me to come back if it wasn't necessary. A person's life is on the line."

Thirty-Eight

THE FIRST PALE light of dawn was making its way into Ned's room. He'd had such a peaceful night that Raymond's visit the day before felt like a distant dream. Maybe it was Teresa and Eric's presence that changed everything.

Ned lay in his bed letting himself remember the meal he'd shared with the couple. There was warmth in their eyes, not only for each other, but for him. They were willing to give up everything to be there for him. Their gentle caring was the opposite of everything he'd been experiencing recently.

For days, his stomach had been fighting food, just as his mind fought the feeling that life was meaningful. He kept thinking about his father, the man he'd looked up to as his hero, and how that man had never wanted him. His father taught him that feelings didn't matter because that was the kind of world his father lived in. There was no love there, only duty and responsibility.

But when Teresa urged him to take a sip of soup, Ned knew that she wasn't there because she had to be. Eric was often quiet, but he didn't have to say much. The light in his eyes and his gentle mirth let Ned know that not everyone was like his father. Not everyone only acted out of responsibility.

After dinner, they talked. Teresa shared some of her childhood experiences, and so did Eric. They were so open about their feelings that Ned was able to talk a little about his own. Ned expected them to leave after that, but Teresa made it very clear that they weren't going anywhere. The couple bunked out in the room that Matthew and Eric had used the night they arrived.

Their presence was comforting, and Ned fell asleep with a full stomach and a much more peaceful mind. The feeling was still there as he faced another day. But there was more. He felt like his strength was finally coming back.

* * *

When Eric awoke in the twin bed, he knew it was still early. There was barely any light. He felt rested and ready for the day. Teresa was tucked in close to him. Sometime during the night, she had climbed into his bed. The bed wasn't as roomy as the one they normally slept in, but that wasn't a problem. It only meant they were closer than usual as they slumbered.

A thought about their future crossed his mind. He didn't know how they'd get along without their jobs in Baltimore, but in that moment, he didn't care. He nuzzled Teresa's hair, taking in the scent of lavender and rosemary. Having Teresa so close and thinking about their commitment was exciting. And he hadn't felt excited in a long time. It wasn't that he disliked his life in Baltimore, it's just that the routine never seemed to change.

Being partnered with Teresa felt new and quite extraordinary. They worked so well together. He got a chance to experience a side of Teresa he normally never saw. When she committed herself to something, her strength was inspiring. His mother said he could be determined too. With Teresa by his side, he felt his fortitude getting even stronger.

He smiled when Teresa began to stir. "Good morning," he whispered.

Teresa let out a happy sigh. "Good morning, my sweet husband."

"Are you ready for a new day in Elkville?"

Instead of answering, Teresa giggled a little.

Eric played with her hair. "What is it? Did I say something funny?"

Teresa managed to turn enough to look at him. "Do you know you sometimes have a distinct, southern drawl?"

Eric hesitated. "Is that bad?"

"I love the sound of your voice and the way you say things. It's like you're soothing me with your words."

Eric smiled and kissed her cheek. "Well, then, maybe I won't try to get rid of my accent completely."

"I hope not. It's part of your charm."

Eric heard the sounds of plates rattling and drawers being slammed shut. "Someone's in the kitchen."

"Ned must be up. That's a good sign."

"Yes, but I'm enjoying being here with you," Eric said as he pulled Teresa closer.

"Are you as happy as I am?"

Even in the dim light, Eric could see Teresa's sparkly, green eyes. "I couldn't be happier."

"Good," Teresa said in a firm, assertive tone. "That means that Matthew's forecast of doom and gloom is on the wane."

"I certainly hope so," Eric said.

* * *

Matthew got out of bed as quietly as possible and showered. He hadn't wanted to wake Lea or Jacob. The little boy was still sleeping on the makeshift bed they'd made for him.

Matthew came out of the bathroom to get dressed and saw that Lea was already up and ready for the day. She kissed him before she went downstairs to get some sandwiches packed. She insisted that he and Raymond have food for their trip.

By the time Matthew got downstairs, the smell of coffee filled the house. When he walked into the kitchen, Raymond was already there, cradling a mug at the table. He smiled when he saw Matthew.

"So I hear I'm going to have company going back to Chicago."

"Yes," Matthew said. "By some stroke of luck, my trip and yours were timed perfectly."

Raymond sipped his coffee. "I've always believed in luck. It's saved my bacon on a number of occasions."

Lea came over and handed Matthew his coffee. "I'm going to miss both of you."

Matthew leaned in and kissed her. "I didn't think I'd ever say it, but I wish I didn't have to leave Elkville, not with you here."

"And little Jacob," Lea said. "He's going to be heartbroken if you don't say 'goodbye' before you leave."

"Do you think I should?" Matthew asked. "He's sleeping so peacefully. If I wake him, and—"

215

Raymond spoke up. "Lea's right. That's one thing I learned when she was little. It's best to tell a child what's going on, even if they don't like it."

When it was time to leave, Matthew did as he was advised. He went back upstairs. He hesitated before he woke Jacob. The little boy looked so small and helpless curled up under his blanket. He'd slept through the night, but his face didn't look entirely peaceful. He seemed to be dreaming about something unpleasant and made little sounds of distress.

Matthew knelt down and shook his shoulder. "Jacob, wake up. You're dreaming."

It took a moment for the little boy to open his eyes. When he did, he was still frowning. After staring back and slowly becoming more aware, he rubbed his eyes with his fists. He looked up at Matthew and held out his hands. He wanted Matthew to pick him up.

"I'm sorry, Jacob, but I can't. I have to go. I'm leaving on a trip. I'll be back as soon as I can. While I'm gone, you have to be a good boy."

Jacob continued to stare at him and reached out more forcefully.

Matthew did the only thing he knew to do. He had to leave and stood up. "Goodbye," he said as he started out of the room.

Jacob began screaming before he got to the stairs. They weren't the screams of an angry child. They were the cries of helplessness and panic. Matthew forced himself to quickly go down the steps, telling himself he had to do what he was doing. But the sound of Jacob's plaintive cries were impossible to shut out.

Lea was waiting for him at the door and shrugged. "You did the right thing," she whispered.

He hugged her and gave her a kiss. "I'm so sorry to leave you like this," he said.

Lea nodded. "Try not to worry. Maybe Jacob will let me be there for him. In the meantime, go back to Chicago and help Ralph with his patient. He's depending on you."

Before Matthew could leave, Jacob started scooting down the stairs with tears running down his face.

Lea took action and opened the door. "You better leave now. It's not going to help if he latches on to you again."

Matthew kissed her one more time and quickly left the house. As he walked to Raymond's car, he could hear Jacob's cries escalating.

Eric's morning at the clinic started out well. Ned seemed in better spirits. He even ate breakfast without being coaxed. However, before the clinic opened, there was a call from Margaret. She was at Lea's, and they had a problem with Jacob.

When Eric arrived at Lea's house, his mother greeted him at the door. Margaret was wearing her anxious face. Growing up, Eric had seen that face whenever Margaret was afraid or couldn't handle something on her own. "What's going on, Mom?"

Margaret grabbed his hand and pulled him into the foyer. "Matthew had to leave this morning. He had to go back to Chicago for an emergency. Now Jacob is inconsolable. At first, he just screamed. Lea tried to talk to him, but he ran away from her. Now, he's hiding in Lea's closet upstairs. I thought maybe you could find a way to reach him."

Eric looked up and saw Lea coming down the stairs with a tear stained face.

"Eric, what are we going to do?" Lea cried. "You should have seen that poor child. He tried to get out the door and go after Matthew. I was able to stop him, but my touch seemed to terrify him."

"I'll go up and see if I can help," Eric said. "But before I do that, tell me how you're doing, Lea."

"When Jacob was pounding on the door and screaming, I could feel how desperate and alone he is, like everything he counted on was gone."

Margaret gave Eric a questioning look. "Jacob only got here yesterday. How could he be so attached to Matthew?"

"You know the homes some of these children come from. The kids don't have anything. There's no safety or security in their lives. They're just trying to survive. When Matthew showed Jacob that something else was possible, the boy probably gave himself over totally to Matthew's care."

Lea sniffled. "And now Matthew's gone."

"But we're here," Eric said. "It might take time and patience, but we can show Jacob that he can depend on us, too."

Lea nodded and dried her eyes. "I forgot to tell you that he wet himself when he couldn't get the door open. I tried to help, but he scrambled up the stairs and hid in the closet."

Eric tipped up her chin. "Are you ready to give it another try?"

"Yes, of course," Lea said.

"What should I do?" Margaret asked.

"Why don't you run a warm, shallow bath while we get Jacob out of the closet?"

* * *

Lea stood watching as Operation Closet Rescue commenced. It started with Eric picking Jacob up. When the little boy went into an all-out panic, Eric didn't let him go. The holding part continued until Jacob wore himself out and started sucking his thumb.

Next came undressing the child. Lea was happy that she could help, but she almost cried again when she saw how thin and fragile the little boy was. She and Matthew had noted the bruise marks on his face and arms the night before. When his clothes were off, it was obvious that his entire body had been mistreated.

By the time Eric got Jacob into the tub, the boy was trembling from head to toe. Lea was there to quickly wash him off, and Margaret had a warm towel waiting to dry him. Afterwards, he was dressed in the clothes Margaret had brought over. Jacob's own torn shirt, pants and underwear were put in the wash. After they were clean, the child could wear his own things if he wanted.

Since Jacob continued to tremble even though he was dressed, Margaret warmed another towel in the dryer to keep him warm. She also instructed Eric to go to her house and retrieve her rocking chair. She said the rocking motion helped to sooth Eric when he was sick as a child.

Lea asked to hold Jacob while Eric was getting the chair. She sat on the sofa with the little boy cradled in her arms. His face was buried in the towel, and he wouldn't look at her, but it didn't matter. In that brief moment, feeling his small, shivering body against hers, she went from being a caretaker to knowing she could mother this child with all the love in her heart.

Margaret sat next to Lea and looked at her knowingly. "My darling girl, you can't let yourself get too attached. He doesn't belong to you. He'll soon have to go back to his own family."

Thirty-Nine

AFTER ERIC LEFT to help with Jacob, Teresa tidied up the treatment room in anticipation of patients stopping in. She was encouraged by the way Ned was coming back to himself. The previous morning, after Raymond Ferguson's meeting, Ned had collapsed. Teresa was so worried about his condition, she'd committed to staying for a year in Elkville. Yet today, Ned said he felt well enough to catch up on paper work.

Teresa wondered how Ned could go from being so ill to acting almost normally a day later. Was Ned really okay, or was he in denial? The phone interrupted her musings. Before she could pick it up, Ned answered it. She heard Ned's raised voice a number of times. When there was only silence, she figured Ned had ended the call. She walked to his office and looked in. "Is everything okay?"

Ned stood up. "Everything's fine, but I'm finished here. I think I'll lay down for a bit. Call me if anyone comes in."

Teresa nodded and watched Ned leave the room. He used his desk and the wall cabinets to steady himself as he went. Teresa wondered who could have caused him to look so shaken. After she heard the door to Ned's bedroom close, she went to the desk. She was about to check the caller ID and hesitated. Was it an invasion of Ned's privacy to do something like that? She was tempted and almost pressed the button when the phone rang again. She quickly answered it. "You've reached The Lloyd-Howell Clinic. How may I help you?"

A man responded. "Is Doctor Finney there?"

Before Teresa could say anything, someone picked up the extension. "You can hang up, Teresa," Ned instructed. "This is a personal call."

"Of course," Teresa said as she put the phone down. In the same breath, she decided that she had to find out what was going on. With

220

Ned's health at risk, she had to know as much as possible about what was distressing him. At least that's what she told herself as she crept out of the office and hurried down the hall.

She stopped outside of Ned's room and listened. Ned was yelling out something again. The only word that she could catch was the word, dad. There was silence after that, and she quickly returned to the treatment area. She didn't have to check the caller ID after all. She was sure Ned's caller was his father, John Finney.

She didn't know what to do next. She didn't want to confront Ned. He probably needed time to process whatever had gone on between him and his father. She decided to check on Jacob instead. She called Lea's house and Eric answered.

"Teresa, am I needed at the clinic?" he asked.

Teresa frowned. "I was just calling to see how Jacob is doing."

Eric let out a heavy breath. "Not too well."

After Eric explained the situation, Teresa felt for everyone trying to be there for the little boy. Nothing they did seemed to help. He was withdrawn and miserable. Eric said the child was probably grieving over losing Matthew's comforting presence.

"If there's anything I can do, let me know," Teresa said. After she said goodbye to Eric, she heard the buzzer on the clinic entrance door. "Good, a patient," she mumbled. She was grateful to be distracted after the news about Jacob.

A man's frantic cry rang out from the waiting area. "Baby's comin'!"

From the urgent tone of the person doing the yelling, Teresa could tell she should get some backup. She ran halfway down the hall towards Ned's room. "Ned! I need you!" she shouted and ran back to the waiting room.

* * *

Ned jumped up from his bed as soon as he heard Teresa's shout. He'd been trying to settle his nerves after a couple of calls from his father. He was disappointed with himself. He'd said things to his dad that shouldn't have come out the way they did, but he meant every word. He never wanted to see his father again. As he hurried for the door, he

221

had to forget his own problems. It sounded like there was an emergency to attend to.

When he got to the treatment area, he saw Donny Campbell Jr. and Teresa helping a very pregnant woman. Ned had forgotten that Betsy was due to have her child at any time. It looked like that time had arrived.

Ned went to the sink to wash his hands and snap on some gloves. But when he looked over his shoulder, Betsy was already going into a squatting position. "Oh no," he groaned.

He remembered Eric's story about Betsy Campbell's first delivery in the back of an old pickup. It seemed that Matthew Howell had been scared out of his wits by the thought that the child would land head first on the filthy bed of the truck. In this case, Ned could only imagine that the baby's head would be jettisoned onto the tiled floor of the clinic.

He rushed over to Betsy and made a quick dive to put his hands under the woman as she was bearing down. It wasn't a moment too soon.

Forty

WHEN MATTHEW ARRIVED in Blacksburg, he was grateful that the trip down the mountain was uneventful. Raymond Ferguson did a competent job behind the wheel. On their way to the airport, Matthew made a call to Lea. He wanted to check on her and Jacob.

After Matthew ended the call, Raymond glanced over at him. "How is Jacob?" he asked.

"According to Lea, he's a mess. Thankfully, she has Margaret and Eric there to help deal with the situation."

"I'm sorry to hear that."

"There was some good news at the clinic. Betsy Campbell gave birth to a nine pound, eight ounce, healthy baby girl."

Raymond smiled. "That's at least one positive. How about Ned Finney? Did you find out any more about him?"

"Yes, it seems he was well enough to play 'catch the baby' when Betsy gave that final push."

Raymond's jaws tightened. "I wish Lea could have had a better start when she was born. The nurses said she cried a lot in the nursery. But I couldn't worry about her with her mom in such bad shape. Rita almost died giving birth. I was so worried about losing her that I didn't have time to think about my daughter for a couple of days."

Matthew thought about losing Lea and grimaced.

Raymond continued. "I'm so grateful that Lea has you. And little Jacob seems to think you're pretty special too."

"Maybe, but now he's paying the price for that connection. Lea says she's been holding him, and so have Eric and Margaret, but Jacob won't even look at any of them."

"Maybe he just needs time," Raymond said. "But no matter what, after your stint at the hospital in Chicago, you can use my plane to quickly get back to Blacksburg."

223

"That's kind of you, Raymond."

"I have to do something to ease my conscience. So go back as soon as possible and take care of the flock, Matthew."

"I've never thought of myself as a shepherd."

"Maybe not, but I think some people do."

"Like who?" Matthew asked.

"Like Paul Glass. He says you held things together at the mansion and afterwards too."

"Paul Glass doesn't know what he's talking about."

"Doesn't he? Or do you want to believe you can separate yourself from others by pretending he's wrong?"

Matthew stared straight ahead. He did not want to be anyone's shepherd. He did not want Jacob depending on him. But from the way things were shaping up, he didn't have a say in the matter, at least for the time being.

* * *

Margaret came over to where Lea was sitting and looked at the child in her lap. He had a pinched expression and was still sucking his thumb. On the plus side, he'd stopped hiding his eyes. Margaret held out her hands. "Let me take Jacob while you go eat that sandwich in the kitchen."

Lea cuddled the little boy. "Jacob, you have to eat something too."

Margaret could see that Jacob wasn't paying Lea any attention. Still, he wasn't crying. Maybe that was the best he could do. She took the little boy from Lea's arms and stepped back so that Lea could get up.

Lea stretched and rolled her shoulders. "I wish Eric didn't have to leave. I think Jacob responded a little more when Eric held him."

"He'll be back. He just wanted to check on Teresa and Ned." Margaret smiled. "And of course he wants to see the baby."

"Little baby Teresa," Lea said. "That was sweet of Betsy to name her daughter after our Teresa."

"Yes, it was. Now let's get you some food," Margaret said as she carried Jacob to the kitchen. She glanced back and winked at Lea. "And let's see if we can get this little guy to have a biscuit."

Lea caught on at once and went to the counter. She picked up a newly made, buttered biscuit. "You mean one of these?" she asked, holding it out to Jacob.

For the first time in hours, Jacob looked up more attentively. He seemed even more interested when Lea broke off a piece of the biscuit and put it in her mouth.

"Yummy," Lea said with a smile.

Margaret walked over to the table and sat down with Jacob in her lap. "Why don't you bring those biscuits over here, Lea?"

Lea did as she was told and sat down too. She pushed the biscuit basket within Jacob's reach before she began to eat her grilled cheese sandwich.

Margaret followed Lea's example and broke off a piece of biscuit and ate it. "You know, Lea, these are so tasty."

Jacob shifted in her lap and sat up. He was still sucking his thumb, but he was also eyeing the biscuits.

Margaret broke off a big chuck this time and put it on the table. "So Matthew said they got to the airport okay?"

Lea patted her lips with a napkin. "Yes, he and Dad are probably in the air by now."

"How did Matthew sound?"

"He's been worrying, but I couldn't lie about our little guest. So I imagine I added to his problems."

Margaret looked down just as a small hand grabbed the piece of biscuit. "Well, I think you're going to have something better to report the next time you talk to him."

Lea's eyes brightened as Jacob chewed and swallowed his bite. Instead of going for more biscuit, he held out his hands to Lea.

Lea grinned back and stood up. "You want me to hold you, pumpkin?" she asked as she took the little boy from Margaret.

Margaret winked again. "Maybe he wants some of your cheese sandwich."

Lea sat down, settled Jacob on her lap, and held up a half of her sandwich. Jacob came alive instantly and grabbed it with both hands. He began stuffing it in his mouth. Lea gave Margaret a look of concern. "I hope he's not going to make himself sick."

Margaret was wondering the same thing. "For the time being, I think we have to let him do whatever he wants. He definitely needs to eat."

225

Lea nodded and smiled again as she offered Jacob some of her iced tea. "I bet you're thirsty, too."

Jacob took hold of the glass and began to down its contents. When he came up for air, he let out a loud burp.

Margaret and Lea both laughed.

"Goodness, I'm impressed," Lea said as she tried to wipe Jacob's mouth. He frowned and pushed her hand away. He seemed to have other ideas and reached for another biscuit. Lea looked at Margaret. "I didn't think Jacob would come around like this. What a surprise he can be."

Margaret felt a wash of relief replace the strain of the last few hours. "I'm always surprised by children. They seem to be so much more resilient than adults."

"Mom, I have an idea. Let's have a big supper for everyone. Ned sounds like he's better. And I'm sure Teresa and Eric would enjoy a family meal. We'll celebrate a new baby in the world, and a little boy who's back to enjoying his food."

The phone rang just as Margaret was agreeing to Lea's idea. She got up to answer it in the living room. She smiled when she heard who was calling. Paul had probably phoned her house, got no answer and called Lea's next. "Paul, how wonderful it is to hear from you."

After a short conversation, she came back into the kitchen. "Paul says to say 'hi' and give you his best, Lea."

"He's in Chicago, having some tests, right?"

"Yes, but he said he called to ask about Duke, and I told him all was fine." Margaret paused, thinking about how she was actually enjoying Duke's company. An easy-going animal, he was always happy to see her when she passed by his bed. She'd even started taking his bed up to her room at night so he could be close."

"Did you tell Paul that Matthew is in Chicago?"

"Yes, and he sounded enthusiastic when I mentioned it. I think he's lonely."

"Do you miss him?"

Margaret sat down and sipped her tea. "Yes, I do. I've gotten used to having him here. But I guess that's changing."

* * *

226

After Paul hung up the phone, he sat in his hospital bed thinking about Margaret. When he chatted with her, she sounded happier than she had in a long time. Her voice was animated when she told him about how she was helping Lea and Eric with a frightened, little boy, and how their efforts were working. With lots of TLC, the boy was doing much better.

Paul wished he felt better too. So far, his tests results had been encouraging, but the news didn't raise his spirits like he thought it would. Even if he didn't have to have bypass surgery, he still had a heart condition that needed watching. And since he believed that body and mind were connected, he needed to do more to address some underlying emotional issues. But when he thought about Ned's comments about his shortcomings, he felt stuck.

However, Margaret did mention something that gave him hope. Matthew Howell was in Chicago. In the past, Matthew had been helpful when Paul needed to talk about things. Perhaps, he'd call the straight-forward man and see if he could stop by and chat for a while.

Forty-One

LEA STOOD IN the living room, holding the phone close to her ear. "Matthew, I don't like the idea of you staying at my parent's place. I know how depressing you find it. You already have enough on your mind without that."

Matthew's answer was delivered in a low voice. He'd told Lea he didn't want to be overheard. "Look, your father insisted on it. I think he's trying to be very accommodating. He also wants his chauffeur to take me back and forth to the hospital. When it's time to return to Elkville, he's having his private plane take me to Blacksburg."

"Yes, but so much miserable stuff happened when we were at the mansion. That house has bad vibes. Now, you'll be there by yourself. I'm worried about you."

"What can I do? Your father tries to act like he's fine, but he could be another Paul Glass, especially after the Ned fiasco. I refuse to be the cause of a heart attack."

"I appreciate your concern about my dad. Still—"

"There's Paul too. He wants me to visit him in the hospital."

"Why is that?"

"I don't know. But I have to go into the city anyway to consult with Ralph. Since I was able to get here so quickly, the surgery has been rescheduled for tomorrow morning. So I guess Raymond's offer to chauffeur me around will come in handy."

"At least Jacob is doing well. He's decided that he wants Margaret and me to hold him. It's a bit tricky since we're trying to prepare a nice dinner."

"Sounds like he wants to be near the food."

Lea laughed. "Yes, Margaret has him balanced on her hip while she's stirring the gravy, and Jacob is watching everything we do with very intent eyes."

"I don't know anything about kids, so I can't comment. Listen, I've got to go. I'll call you again when I get a chance."

Lea said goodbye to Matthew and put the phone down just as Teresa, Eric and Ned were coming in the front door. She smiled. "Hi everyone, are you ready for dinner?"

"You bet," Eric said as he walked towards the kitchen. "I better check out what you and Mom have been up to."

Teresa came over and hugged Lea. "Whatever we're having smells fantastic."

Ned walked in from the foyer. "Thank you for the invitation, Lea."

"So glad you could make it," Lea said as she went over to him. "It'll give you an opportunity to get to know Jacob. But I better give you some advice."

"What's that?"

"To get on his good side all you have to do is share your food."

Ned smiled. "He's a little chow hound?"

"Totally, but it has made it easier to get him out of his shell."

Teresa gave Lea an excited look. "Lea, show me what to do. I love kids, and I'd love to get to know Jacob."

"Well, to start with, don't approach him. Let him get to know you first," Lea said. "But for now, let's all get seated and enjoy our meal. We're having pot roast and mashed potatoes."

* * *

Ned sat at the table, remembering the last time he'd been at the Howell's for breakfast. It seemed like a long time ago. Since then, a lot had happened, both good and bad. Fortunately, it was easy to forget all of it with Jacob around.

The boy had changed drastically from the first time Ned saw him at the clinic. He was clean and tidy. Instead of looking like a waif off the streets, he was dressed in a blue, checkered shirt and brown pants that Margaret had made for her son when he was little. Jacob's hair was still overgrown, but it had been combed enough to look much better. And best of all, he wasn't screaming.

Eric held him during the first part of the dinner. Jacob had his own meal but when he wanted something on Eric's plate, he looked up with big, brown eyes and whined. Eric tried to resist Jacob's whimpers, but he soon let Jacob have his way. Teresa, who sat next to Eric, tempted Jacob with some apple juice. Since Eric wouldn't allow Jacob to drink his coffee, Jacob did accept Teresa's drink proposal, but he refused her offer to hold him.

After the main course, Jacob made it clear that he wanted Lea's attention and moved to Lea's lap for dessert. Finally, when he'd eaten his fill, Jacob reached out to Margaret. It seemed she'd been assigned the duty of rocking him as he fell asleep.

Ned was amazed at the little boy's ability to get what he wanted. "Jacob has a good thing going," he commented to Eric.

Eric smiled. "Yes, but if you'd seen him this morning, you'd be like me, just thrilled that he's not withdrawing anymore."

"What did you do that changed his mind?"

"We held him and kept holding him."

Ned looked down and rubbed the white linen tablecloth, but he didn't know what to say.

Eric seemed to notice his reaction. "What's going on?"

"I realize I wouldn't know how to handle a case like that."

Eric shrugged. "It's not exactly a case, is it? It's what you do when a child is hurting. You hold them and let them know you're there for them."

"Do you?" Ned didn't remember ever being held, not in the way that Eric described. But until that moment he didn't think about what he'd never been given. The thought stirred up all the feelings he'd had after talking to his father. He got to his feet. "Excuse me, but I'm tired. I need to get back to the clinic." He looked at Lea and Margaret. "Thank you for a great dinner."

Eric stood up too. "I'll go back with you."

"No, please stay. I'll be fine."

"Ned, you're leaving so soon?" Teresa asked.

Ned felt his stomach tighten. "Yes, but you and Eric need to stay here. I'll see you in the morning."

Teresa immediately stood up. "No way, we're staying at the clinic, remember?"

"What?" Ned mumbled. Teresa was talking to him, but the only thing he could think about was his father. When the man called that morning, John Finney had spoken and acted as if everything was just as it had always been. But Ned told his father the truth. Except for a biological connection, they meant nothing to each other.

He walked out of the Howell kitchen without saying anything else. Eric and Teresa were on his heels, trying to talk to him, but nothing they could say would change the facts. Teresa had mentioned family, but Ned didn't feel like he could understand that word anymore than he could understand the concept of holding a child. They were speaking a foreign language that didn't compute.

A terrible thought slipped in as he walked towards the front door. It felt like a report card of sorts, one that graded him as a human being. He stopped short, turned and looked at Teresa, then Eric. "Do you know what I just realized? I'm not like you people. I can't process what you process. It's the reason every girl I dated eventually bailed. So stop your worrying. There's nothing to be done. I'll find a way to go back to being some kind of automaton, heal some sick people, and hopefully keep these damnable feelings from coming up anymore."

He turned and started to open the door when Eric grabbed his arm and swung him around. "What now?" he asked.

Eric held on to his arm. "Ned, no matter what you think. There's nothing wrong with you."

Ned wanted to believe him, but his father's words were burning inside of him. After he told his father that they were finished, John Finney didn't shout or protest. He was very calm when he delivered his response.

"Ned, haven't I taught you better than to let your feelings get out of hand. Now stop, take some breaths and get a grip. Then we'll talk about why you're spouting such insanity."

Ned had slammed down the phone, trying to shut out the words, but maybe he needed to accept his father's diagnosis. His mind was slipping. The evidence was there. He was swimming in emotions, yelling at his father and unable to properly think anymore. His mother had abandoned him. Now, he couldn't even depend on his mind to move him forward.

Teresa reached out too. "You look exhausted again, Ned. Let's go back to the clinic, and you can rest."

Ned stared at Teresa and took a moment to study her face. How beautiful and perfect it was. After his latest discovery, one that pointed out all his inadequacies in knowing how to relate, he knew he'd never have someone like Teresa in his life. Instead of feeling sad about that fact, he accepted it. He had to accept everything coming at him. What else was there to do?

After he got back to the clinic, there was a message on his machine. It was from his father wanting him to call him back. Ned deleted the message and climbed into bed. He didn't want to do anything but sleep for a very long time.

Forty-Two

MATTHEW HAD A pleasant trip from the Chicago suburbs to the city. Raymond's chauffer, Joseph, was an older gentleman who kept his eyes on the road and any small talk to a bare minimum. When they arrived at Matthew and Ralph's office, Matthew felt clear headed and able to concentrate on being brought up to date on Ralph's patient. The case was complex, but Matthew had faith in Ralph's abilities and his own.

After meeting with Ralph, Matthew climbed into the limo feeling less confident about the next item on his agenda, visiting Paul Glass. On the way to the hospital, he gave himself specific instructions to keep his feelings in check. He needed to remain in a neutral mindset, but it was a difficult task under the circumstances.

Paul's bungling track record was growing longer. His latest failure was Ned Finney. The man had finally opened up and let himself express his feelings with the psychiatrist. And what did Paul do? Paul gave in to all his personal crap instead of simply listening to Ned. But Paul didn't only give in to his crap, he had a heart attack on the spot. Afterwards, Ned walked around in a daze of guilt.

Still, it wasn't any of Matthew's business, so why was he letting himself get involved? His job was to visit Paul for a few minutes and let Joseph drive him back to the Ferguson mansion. Well, he wasn't going to actually stay in the "big house" as Lea called her parent's home. Earlier, while talking to Raymond, he'd had a brilliant idea. He told Lea's father that he wanted to bunk out in the guest cottage.

Set away from the main building, the guest house was beautifully furnished in light, restful colors and airy modern furniture. The last time he'd slept there, Matthew found the place to be a soothing refuge after staying in a room in the mansion. Most of the mansion was furnished in dark, heavy antiques. For Matthew, the décor was downright morbid. His spirit soared when he realized he had options.

He used thoughts of sleeping in a pleasing cottage to distract his mind as he made his way to Paul's hospital room. Once there, he knocked on the door and let himself in. Paul was watching television and didn't notice Matthew until he approached Paul's bed.

Paul smiled as soon as he saw Matthew and turned off the television. "I'm so glad you could make it," he said in a friendly voice.

Matthew was about to reply when his most recent argument with Lea came to mind. They were in Margaret's kitchen, and Lea said something about his terrible bedside matter. It was enough to make him pause. He used the moment to remind himself that he was a doctor, and he was visiting a person who was trying to recuperate. He put out his hand to Paul and forced himself to act appropriately. "How are you doing?"

Paul shook Matthew's hand. "I don't know."

Matthew waited for Paul to continue. But the man didn't say anything more. "Was there a reason you wanted to see me?"

Paul got right to the point. "I want your advice. If you were me, with a bad ticker, a reputation that's fallen in ruin, and people resenting you, what would you do?"

The loaded request made Matthew weary. He pulled up a chair and sat down. "I haven't any idea."

"Don't give me that, Matthew. You have very definite ideas about life and people. Tell me what you're thinking."

Matthew was thinking about how nice it would be if he was at the guest house, stretched out in a recliner, relaxing. But one look at Paul's intense eyes told him he needed to come up with something. "Maybe you should be asking another question. What do you want?"

Paul shook his head. "I can't have what I want."

"Can you be more specific?"

Paul averted his eyes. "Let's just say I know what I don't want, and that's to be alone. I guess it's why I panicked when Duke got sick. He's about the only thing I have left."

Matthew didn't know what to say. He'd come to the hospital with so many judgments. But listening to Paul, his thoughts turned inward. If he hadn't taken a chance on love, it could be him sitting in that bed someday. Even with Lea in his life, he'd been complaining when things didn't go the way he wanted. Why didn't he appreciate that people cared about him? Even if the worst happened, and Lea forgot him again, he did have support from his friends. But to have nobody, to be in some hospital, all alone and facing a heart giving out, that was a tough one.

Matthew sat up straighter and stared at Paul. "You're a shrink. How in the hell did you get yourself in this mess?"

"Ned answered that one. He said I put my own needs first, and that I don't really care if I hurt others in the process."

"And you agree with him?"

Paul lifted his head and looked at Matthew. "I didn't want to admit it when he said it. Still, you can't live a lie forever." Paul rubbed his chest. "My heart made sure I got the message."

Matthew shifted uneasily in his chair. He didn't want to hear Paul's sad story and scowled back. "All I can say is your heart didn't take you out. So you have another chance to—" Matthew paused, not knowing how to complete the thought.

"To do what?" Paul demanded. "Go on, tell me what I should do."

Matthew glared back. "I don't know. That's up to you. Besides, I think we've had a similar conversation before." Matthew stood up. "Look, I need to go. I have to get up early for surgery."

"Right, you have a life," Paul said with a frown. "I appreciate your stopping by."

Matthew ignored Paul's sulky tone and started out of the room. He almost made it to the door, but he had to turn and give Paul a piece of advice that he couldn't keep to himself. "Improve your listening skills. Ned Finney needed someone to hear him, not shut him down."

Paul's scowl deepened. "At one time, that's what I did. I sat with people and listened."

"What changed?"

Paul's gaze turned reflective. "I had all this knowledge. I went all over the world trying to learn what to do to help people. I think that's when I stopped listening as much."

"There you go, Paul," Matthew said as he continued on his way. "Start listening again."

* * *

After Matthew left, Paul could still feel the man's energy. Matthew could be a prime example of a person in charge of himself. It was only when Matthew let himself give into his fears about Lea that his presence was diminished. Happily, from what Paul knew, the two of them were doing well.

Paul had once felt a lot like Matthew. He was comfortable with himself and his desire to help people. When he was a child, his father died. It closed off his heart when it involved an intimate relationship, but when it came to people in general, he didn't have a problem being open and compassionate.

In those days, he was determined to be the best doctor he could be. He wanted to ease the suffering of others. He often simply sat and made sure he was present with a person who was hurting. He could understand their need to unburden themselves. He was often told that his presence brought a sense of calm.

Back then, he believed in the true nature of people. He could see them for what they were, innocent in the deepest parts of themselves. They were the grown-up children who'd been taught to judge themselves so harshly that they came to him wanting relief and forgiveness. He listened to their stories and helped them to know they could forgive themselves.

Over a span of decades, he began to lose touch with his own innocence. He kept seeking more knowledge, more techniques to help and heal. People's problems, instead of people, became a prime focus. He began to believe it was what he brought to the table that was important. His knowledge began to matter more than what his patients were telling him. As his reputation grew, he often forgot that healing always came from within the person themselves.

He hoped he could connect with his innocence again. But was it too late? Was he so mired in his falling-from-grace story that he would never feel hopeful again, or have a chance at self-acceptance? Judging from the look Matthew gave him, he needed to try.

Maybe that was why Matthew was able to do his job as a surgeon. He brought his extensive knowledge to the operating table, but he never lost sight of the fact that he was only giving his patient another chance. Once that patient left the OR, it was up to the person to continue the healing process themselves.

Paul chuckled. Maybe Matthew was right in not having much interaction after that. How many people wanted to be told the truth, to know that they were responsible for taking the gift he gave them and using it properly?

That's where a person like Paul came in. He could listen to all the reasons people felt unable to help themselves. He could gently assist them in finding ways to change their mindset. He could help them complete their road to recovery.

Paul lay back and thought about how it would feel to be that person. Could that role be the one that would help restore his sense of self? He'd have to give it some thought.

Forty-Three

AFTER WORKING HIS normal shift in the field, John Finney returned to the park cabin he'd been assigned to use during his stay. He had to contemplate what action to take in regard to his son, Ned. First off, he called his boss and explained that he was taking emergency leave. His boss was immediately concerned. Was something wrong? John had never taken that kind of leave before. Hell, he'd barely ever taken sick leave. If there was one person who could be depended on, it was John Finney.

John's voice was deliberate and composed when he gave his answer. His son needed him, and John had to fly to the East coast. He didn't go into any further explanation. When he disconnected, he let his phone drop on a side table. He'd just had one of the worst days of his life.

His morning started early. He was sipping a freshly brewed cup of coffee when he decided to call Ned. They usually talked every couple of weeks, but he hadn't heard from Ned since his boy's first days in Elkville. John understood that his son was probably adjusting to the small community and needed space. But they rarely went this long without talking.

Even though it was a work day, John called the clinic number he'd been given. Ned picked up almost immediately. But as soon as Ned answered and knew who his caller was, he blurted out things that John was unprepared to hear. Before he could find out what was going on, Ned hung up. John called the clinic again. A woman answered, but Ned soon picked up too. The woman was dismissed and after a brief conversation, Ned dismissed John too.

John didn't know how to handle what he'd been told. How could his son never want to see him again? Had the world turned upside down over night? Was it really Ned on the other end of the line? It couldn't be. Ned never spoke in a surly, hateful voice. His tone was kind and thoughtful, and his smile could brighten John's day when he was exhausted after fighting a fire. Ned was John's pride, and if he allowed himself the emotion, Ned was his joy.

John went to his job in spite of the talk he'd had with Ned. No matter what, he had to be the person who never let others down. And it was the final day of advanced wilderness training for a number of people who needed more hands on experience. He was able to carry out his duties by refusing to think about his conversation with his son. It was only when he got back to the cabin that he allowed himself to remember every terrible word that Ned had said to him. He also called the clinic again and got the message machine.

John sat down at the table in the cabin's tiny dining area and opened his laptop. He needed to check airline schedules. With a bit of searching, he found a mid-morning flight out of Salt Lake City. It included one stopover and would take six hours to reach its destination. Once there, John would rent a car. He'd probably stay the night in Blacksburg. He wanted to be rested and clear-headed when he confronted his son.

After he bought his ticket, he put off packing. He'd fix himself something to eat instead. It had been a long day, and he was tired and hungry. He was only forty-eight years old, and he was fit, but the recent confrontation with Ned was having a devastating effect. He had to take care of himself if he was going to be there for his son.

He'd tried so hard to raise Ned properly and to give him a background that was better than his own. But he'd known so little about raising a child, and he'd been so young. Ned came along when he was nineteen. He was going to college and working two part-time jobs to make ends meet. He tried his best, but there were times when he worried that he wouldn't put food on the table or pay the rent. Luckily, he was smart. He graduated early and got a decent job by the time Ned was old enough to notice his surroundings. His boy never knew how poor they were during those first years.

Ned grew up thinking it was normal to live in a decent house, to have enough food and to wear clothes that were like those of the other boys. "He was spared," John sighed. "He never knew how I grew up."

When Ned became a doctor, John felt like he was home free. He'd done it. He'd successfully raised a brilliant human being, a bright, giving person who would contribute to society.

But Ned didn't sound brilliant on the phone. He didn't even sound fit. His words were loud, but there was a breathless sound to his voice, like his lungs weren't working properly.

John could only hope that Ned was just having a very bad day, but deep down, he knew he was kidding himself. He hadn't been a successful parent after all. He'd failed Ned, just like his own father had failed him.

Forty-Four

MATTHEW WENT INTO an early morning surgery feeling rested. The evening before, he'd had a quiet, uneventful, late dinner with Lea's parents. Lea's mother, Rita, was on her best behavior, and Raymond was cordial, but quiet. He let Rita talk about her latest interests. The petite woman was branching out. She was learning about jewelry design and even thinking about starting a company of her own someday. After dinner, Matthew excused himself and went to bed.

It was a good thing that he was in excellent form the next day. The surgery was a challenging one. There were unexpected complications that could have claimed their patient's life. However, both he and Ralph were well versed in handling dicey situations. No matter, Matthew never got used to a person's life force slipping away. When he emerged from the OR in midafternoon he let out a sigh of relief to be on the other side of such an extremely, demanding situation.

Ralph looked worn too when he asked Matthew if he'd like to get something to eat. Matthew would have preferred to return to the Fergusons and call Lea, but he could tell from the look on Ralph's face that the man had more than a meal in mind. He accepted the invitation to dine at the hospital cafeteria.

As they carried their food to a corner table, Matthew realized how hungry he was. It didn't take him long to finish off a tuna sandwich. Ralph seemed just as intent on plowing through a chicken Waldorf salad. Afterwards, Matthew sipped his bottled water and thought about their office manager, a woman named Nicky. The former nurse had befriended Matthew after Lea disappeared. Later, Ralph got to know her, and the two of them hit it off. Matthew hadn't heard much about their relationship lately. "So how are you and Nicky doing?"

Ralph sipped his iced tea thoughtfully. "I didn't think I wanted a relationship after my divorce." He paused. "Then Nicky came along."

Matthew studied the little smile that was slowly taking over Ralph's somewhat serious face. "Yes, go on."

"Can you believe it, Matt? Nicky and I are getting married."

Matthew chuckled. "It's about time. You couldn't find a finer woman than Nicky. Congratulations."

"It's one of the reasons I asked you to lunch. I want you to be my best man."

"I'd be honored," Matthew said. "But I thought you had a brother—"

"I do, but we're not close. It's the reason I thought of you. I know we don't do too much socializing now that you and Lea are together, but I sometimes think of you as the son I never had. I always wanted a family, but my ex couldn't have children."

Matthew frowned. "You've been very good to me, Ralph. Thank you."

"I also have something else I want to discuss. Ever since you called and asked for time off in Elkville, Nicky and I have been talking. You said the young doc that your father-in-law hired wants to leave. If he can stick it out for a year, we might have a solution."

"Do you know someone who wants to work in a place that time forgot?" Matthew asked.

Ralph stared at his hands. "I figure I'm going to retire in a year or so."

Matthew put his water down on the table and leaned in. "Why? You're still perfectly capable at doing what you do."

"Perhaps, but I know it's what's best." Ralph glanced up and smiled. "Don't get me wrong. I've loved my work. And of course I won't leave until we find someone you approve of as a new partner."

Matthew couldn't understand it, but he felt like someone punched him in the gut. Until that moment, he simply thought of Ralph as his partner. But Ralph was right about their relationship. Ralph meant more to him than just a business associate. "What about you? What will you do? Go fishing with Nicky?"

"Spending time in the outdoors, fishing and hiking, is a great way to relax." Ralph's smile broadened. "It's why I brought up Elkville. When I retire, Nicky and I might be interested in staffing the clinic."

Matthew's body stiffened. "You and Nicky in Elkville?"

"We don't know for sure. At some point in the future, we'll visit and check the place out."

"Ralph, there's nothing there, nothing."

Ralph shrugged. "There are sick people, right? Otherwise why would Raymond Ferguson build a clinic?"

Matthew sat back and crossed his arms. "I can't believe I'm hearing this."

"You look upset, Matt, but don't worry. Everything will remain the same for our practice for most of the coming year."

* * *

Lea was happy for Matthew. When he called, he said that things went well with Ralph's patient. She had good news too. Jacob had a nice morning and enjoyed both his breakfast and lunch. He didn't scream very much and was much more willing to cooperate. Matthew sounded like he was pleased with the little boy's progress. When Lea asked when Matthew would be returning, he said he'd be back the next day. "I miss you terribly," she said as they were getting off the phone.

Margaret looked up from where she was sitting on the sofa. She had Jacob in her lap and was showing him a picture book. "How's everything with Matthew?" she asked.

Lea sat down next to Margaret. "He says he's fine, but I feel like there's something bothering him."

Margaret gave Jacob a little hug. "He can't be worried about our little boy. He's doing so well, and he seems so interested in Eric's old children books."

"Mom, remember what you told me. We can't let ourselves think of Jacob as 'our boy'."

"No, of course not," Margaret replied. "I just love kids, that's all."

Lea smiled. No matter what Margaret said, Lea could see how much she adored little Jacob. Of course it didn't help that he was dressed in clothes that Eric had worn when he was a little boy. "I had a thought. Let's take Jacob over to the clinic to visit with Teresa, Eric and Ned."

Margaret perked up. "That's a splendid thought. The more he can do and see, the less afraid he'll be."

Lea reached out for Jacob. "Come with me, pumpkin. You drank a lot of milk at lunch. Let's get you to the bathroom before we leave."

Instead of letting Lea take him, Jacob slipped off of Margaret's lap and ran towards the powder room.

Margaret gave Lea a pleased smile. "Look at him. He's already getting used to being here and following directions. I think he's very bright."

Lea headed for the powder room. "Yes, but it's hard for him to reach the faucets to wash his hands. I better make sure he's safe on the stepstool I put in there to help him."

"And I'll run home and get some cookies to take to the clinic."

Later, when they were all ready for their trip to the clinic, Jacob was anxious about getting into the car. After Margaret was seated in the back and urged him to join her, Jacob finally let Lea help him climb in too. However, he hunched down in the floor space. Margaret and Lea both had to slowly convince him to sit next to Margaret. She also gave him a book to look at, and it seemed to distract him from the ride.

Teresa and Eric gave them a warm welcome once they arrived at their destination. Ned came out of his office briefly, said hello and excused himself. He said he had some paper work to do.

Jacob made his feelings known by clinging to Lea while she talked to Teresa. But Teresa seemed to understand what to do. She invited Lea into the kitchen. The smell of freshly made muffins filled the air.

"I went to the little store here and got some ingredients," Teresa said as she took a container out of the cupboard. She opened it, took out a muffin and put it on a plate. After she showed it to Jacob, she put it back on the counter and held out her hands. Jacob was used to the drill by this time and reluctantly let go of Lea's sweater. Once Teresa had him in her arms, she rewarded him with a good sized chuck of a chocolate chip muffin. Instead of stuffing it in his mouth, Jacob took a bite and chewed it thoughtfully.

"I hope he likes it," Teresa said.

Lea watched Jacob hesitate before taking another bite. "I guess he's not as hungry as he was at first. Besides, he had a big lunch."

Jacob finally took a deep breath and shoved more of the muffin into his mouth. After he swallowed it, he started to whine and point to the refrigerator.

Lea acted as his interpreter. "I think he wants something to wash it down."

Teresa rocked Jacob as Lea got out some juice and poured it into a cup.

"He loves apple juice," Lea said as she handed the cup to Jacob.

Jacob guzzled down the juice in great gulps and suddenly started to choke.

Lea immediately grabbed the cup and nearly panicked when Jacob didn't seem able to get any air. Thankfully, he started coughing a moment later. Ned must have heard Lea's cry of alarm and came running in, followed by Margaret and Eric.

Jacob continued to cough with gasping breaths in between. When he finally reached a state of relatively normal breathing, his face was red, and he looked tired. He laid his head on Teresa's shoulder to rest.

Lea held herself and sighed. "Thank goodness, he's alright."

Ned took out a clean handkerchief and wiped the drool off of Jacob's chin. "He looks like he's going to be just fine. Aren't you, Jacob?"

In a surprise move, Jacob straightened up and reached out for Ned. Ned glanced around, looking confused, but then he carefully took the little boy from Teresa. Jacob knew what to do after that. He immediately pushed his head into Ned's shoulder and began to suck his thumb.

Ned blinked back at Jacob and at the group gathered round. "I didn't expect this to happen."

*　*　*

Ned couldn't believe it when Jacob reached out to him. He didn't have any experience when it came to holding children. But having the little boy in his arms felt very natural.

Eric had explained what to do with Jacob the night before, but Ned didn't get it. He thought it took some special ability to care that way for a child. But he quickly changed his mind as he held Jacob. The feelings Ned thought were missing in him were there after all. He realized how easy it was to care deeply about the little boy.

When Ned noticed Jacob starting to fall asleep, he was concerned and looked at Lea. "I don't think kids his age sleep this much."

Lea carefully lifted Jacob's shirt. "Look at him, how thin he is and how bruised. He's trying to recuperate from a lot." She paused and gave Ned a compassionate smile. "And so are you, Ned."

Ned thought about the comparison and knew it fit. His body was healing, but the bruises were still there. There was also the deeply bruised part of his mind that kept him from feeling at peace with himself. But holding Jacob, at least he knew some parts were working just as they should.

Forty-Five

AFTER HIS FLIGHT from Utah to Virginia, John Finney sat in a Blacksburg motel room drumming his fingers on the arm of his chair. He almost wished he'd made the trip to Elkville that afternoon. But something told him to wait for a new day to dawn.

He needed to be emotionally steady and in charge of himself when he surprised Ned. If his son was still having a problem with their relationship, John would be able to deal with the situation in a calm, rational manner. After a lifetime of practice, it shouldn't be that hard to do. However, the nervous movements of his fingers and the upset in his stomach told him otherwise.

No matter how he tried to relax, he kept asking himself the same thing. Where had he gone wrong? He reviewed his actions as a father with the same unbiased focus that he gave a personnel file on one of the people he supervised. But when he examined Ned's childhood, he still didn't understand what the problem was.

He'd prided himself on always being there when Ned needed him. No matter how long his day at his job, he always made sure to help with Ned's homework or lend an ear when Ned wanted to talk about a problem.

After his ex-wife ran off, he tried to be both the mother and father his boy needed. He not only took over duties in the kitchen, he prepared himself to feed Ned properly. He read books on nutrition and learned how to prepare a balanced diet. He served fish once a week, never fried their food, made tons of salads and steamed countless pounds of vegetables. On days off, he tackled the house. He kept it clean and orderly even though he found vacuuming and scrubbing floors to be his least favorite activities.

"I did it all, Ned. I tried to give you everything you needed to succeed in life. What could I possibly have done to make you feel this way?"

247

When he'd exhausted his mind with his questions, he knew he should go out for a bite to eat, but he had no appetite. He turned on the television instead. Maybe he'd get sleepy and go to bed early. Hopefully, when he woke up in the morning, he'd feel renewed. He'd take a shower, go to breakfast, and hit the road to Elkville.

* * *

It was near dawn, but still dark outside when John Finney forced himself out of his chair. His body was stiff and unresponsive as he made his way to the bathroom. He had to get ready for the day.

Sleep had never come. No matter how tired he was, he couldn't rest. During the long hours spent half-staring at the flickering screen of the television and not paying attention to the programs, he hadn't only thought about his son's childhood, he'd thought about his own. He'd revisited memories he'd refused to think about for over thirty years.

They weren't nice memories. The hell he'd shut out for decades was just as vivid as when he'd lived it. Everything he remembered was everything he'd tried to spare Ned. And he'd succeeded. There was no alcohol in Ned's upbringing. There were no beatings. No rages that left him whimpering in a corner. No empty shelves in the kitchen cupboards.

By the time John was old enough to be on his own, he felt as empty as those cupboards. The only thing he knew for sure was that he wasn't going to be like his father. When he met Ned's mother, she was a lot like John. Both had lost their way. Neither had a guiding compass to help them navigate that thing called a relationship.

John did have a sense of duty towards their son. Just like he later learned how to prepare a nutritious diet for Ned, he tried to provide a proper environment. He read child parenting books from the library whenever he had any spare time. He'd also taken a few psychology courses in college. Piecing together the knowledge he gleaned from different sources, he attempted to raise a child.

When he'd first seen his newborn son in the hospital nursery, he was so scared that all he wanted to do was run. That's when he set up rules for himself. Like it or not, a helpless baby was depending on him. There would be no shouting, no violence, and no irresponsibility of any kind.

At times, he did shout at Ned's mother, but even that eventually stopped. If he had to, he'd leave the house until the flares of temper he felt inside were doused. Eventually, he was able to mold himself into a person who had no resemblance to Ned's grandfather.

John succeeded in carrying out his rules, but the willpower involved, the determination took more than he thought he had to give. Between his jobs and college studies, he felt like he was already working at full capacity. But no matter how overwhelmed he was, he had a wife and baby. So he did what he had to do. He was that soldier who faced another battle despite his weariness. When his wife was having one of her emotional meltdowns, he changed his son's diaper and fell asleep giving him his bottle.

"And it's all come to this," he said as he looked at himself in the bathroom mirror. After staring for a long moment, he grimaced. "My lord, I look like him," he whispered. He kept a picture of his father in his wallet. His father had once been a handsome man, but he literally drank himself to death. The picture was there as a reminder. John would never let himself sink to the depths of insanity that claimed his parent.

He opened his toiletry bag and retrieved a razor and shaving cream. As he lathered his face, he wondered if all his self-imposed rules and all his struggles had been for nothing. He had renounced his father, and Ned renounced him. Did a person's actions count for anything if they still arrived at the same miserable destination they tried to avoid?

By the time he finished shaving, he'd nicked himself several times. He ignored the pain just like he'd ignored all the pain in his life. But he could not ignore his son's harsh words. They cut deep. He had a wound that needed attention, but John wasn't the doctor in the family. Ned was.

But would Ned even notice what John was experiencing. Maybe not. And maybe that was a good thing. Maybe John had it all wrong. Maybe Ned shouldn't care. The boy had his own life to live. It was John who had to do the right thing. If he truly wanted what was best for his son, he had to let him go if need be.

When he left the motel room, he didn't have a good feeling about what was coming. He got behind the wheel of his rental car and started the engine. Whatever happened with Ned, he wanted to get it over with.

Ned sat at the little table in the clinic's kitchen with Teresa and Eric. They had just finished a simple meal of eggs, toast and coffee. Ned was getting used to having breakfast with the couple. They were all getting to know each other in a way that allowed for easy smiles and even light-hearted teasing from Eric.

"Can you believe this guy, Teresa?" Eric asked. "The man pronounces himself an automaton, and the next day he becomes little Jacob's life size teddy bear. I didn't think the boy was going to let Lea take him home."

Teresa laughed. "I got to hold Jacob for two seconds before he decided who he really liked."

Ned could feel his face flush. "Believe me, I never expected that."

"I told you that there was nothing wrong with you, Ned," Eric insisted.

Teresa got up and carried her plate to the sink. "I wonder if there'll be more people showing up at the clinic today?"

Eric sat back and sipped his coffee. "We did have a few more yesterday. I think word is starting to spread."

Ned cleared his throat. "I want to thank you both for putting up with my moods. I've seen other people fall apart, but I never expected to be a person who couldn't maintain some kind of balance."

Teresa came back over to the table. "I know you've said that feelings have no place in your life, but look at the three of us. We're happy just being friends. Is there anything wrong with that?"

"I hope not," Ned said.

Eric took another sip of coffee. "Sometimes people are afraid to be happy because they think they're fooling themselves, and it won't last. But to me, that doesn't make sense. I'd rather be happy some of the time than constantly trying to control life and being unhappy."

"Is that what you think I'm doing, trying to control life?" Ned asked.

"I don't know," Eric said. "Only you can answer that."

The doorbell to the clinic sounded before Ned could think about Eric's comment. "I guess it's time to start our day."

Eric took a last swallow of coffee. "I'm ready."

Teresa smiled. "So am I. Let's go see who our first patient is."

Ned held up a hand. "You two stay here for a few minutes. I want to start feeling like I can handle this job without backup."

Eric looked at Teresa. "You heard the man. I guess we have to have a second cup of coffee."

Ned glanced back as he was leaving the room. "Go easy on that coffee, Eric. Too much isn't good for your health."

Eric smiled. "Yes, sir, Doctor Finney, I'll only have a half a cup."

Ned smiled too as he walked to the front of the clinic. It was nice to have friends like Eric and Teresa. He straightened his white lab coat and reached for the door. When he opened it and saw his father standing in front of him, he couldn't move. "Dad? What are you doing here?" he finally asked.

"I wanted to see you," John said.

Ned felt like his brain wasn't working properly. He spat out one word. "Why?"

"Can I come in?" John asked.

Ned opened the door a little wider and stepped back. "I guess."

John moved past him and walked into the treatment area. "This is a nice facility, son."

Hearing his father use the word, son, switched on Ned's brain. He suddenly remembered all the feelings he'd recently had about his place in John Finney's life. "Please, you don't have to call me that," he said.

John turned and stared at him. "Why wouldn't I want to call you my son, Ned?"

Eric and Teresa came walking in from the hall. "Who do we have here, Ned?"

John looked at Eric and held out his hand. "I'm John Finney, Ned's father."

Eric walked over and shook his hand. "I'm Eric Lloyd and this is my wife, Teresa."

Teresa smiled and shook hands too. "So nice to meet you, John."

John smiled back. "Are you friends of Ned?"

Ned stepped forward. "Yes, they're friends and colleagues. Now, tell me why you're here, Dad."

John seemed at a loss for words. "Why are you acting like this? Did I do something, Ned? If I did, just tell me what it is."

Ned glowered back. "Don't act like you care. All these years you did what you had to do. But you can finally be rid of me, is that clear?"

"No, it's not clear. You're not making any sense."

"You mean I'm being irrational because I can feel things. And I want to go on feeling. I don't want to end up like you, a person who never knew how to love anybody. I thought I was the robot, but it's you, Dad, who won't feel anything. That's probably why my mother left. You drove her away with that crap about feelings not mattering. You probably never touched the poor woman or ever gave her any kind of love because you don't know how to love."

John looked down and took a hasty breath. "I see. Well, it sounds like you have it all figured out. So what can I say?"

"There's nothing to say," Ned replied. "Go back to that existence you call your life, and I'll get on with mine."

John nodded and seemed to be trying to steady himself. After a moment, he nodded again. "If that's what it'll take to make your life better, Ned, then so be it." He turned to Teresa and Eric. "It was nice to meet you both. I'm so glad Ned has someone he can depend on."

"Let me walk you out," Eric said.

John took another breath. "Thank you."

Ned watched his father turn to leave and nearly ran after him. He'd said things that might be true, but that's not what he wanted. He wanted to be like Jacob. He wanted to be held by the person who raised him, the person he'd thought of as his family. He wanted his father's arms around him. He wanted his father to tell him he wasn't only wanted, but he was loved. But John Finney didn't have the capacity to love anyone. Love didn't exist in his world.

* * *

Eric knew enough not to interfere in the discussion between Ned and his father. However, he did observe John Finney's reaction to the things that Ned said to him. The man barely held it together. When he offered to show John Finney out, he hoped to have an opportunity to learn a little more about how John was doing. As they exited the building, Eric followed the man to his car. "Mr. Finney?"

John stopped and looked at him. "Yes?"

"I don't know what kind of relationship you have with your son, but—"

"I think Ned made our relationship very clear. He doesn't want me in his life."

"Yes, but—"

"Look, Eric, I have to get going," John said as he climbed into his car. He started the engine and rolled down the window. "Could you do me a favor?"

"What's that?" Eric asked.

John took out his wallet, removed a slip of paper and gave it to Eric. "Could you give this to Ned? His mother recently contacted me, and I wanted Ned to know how to get in touch with her. Tell him I would have given it to him sooner, but I wanted to explain a few things before I did. Now, that's not going to happen."

"Are you sure you don't want to try to talk to Ned again?"

"No, he seems to know what he wants."

"Are you okay with that?"

John paused. "I want what's best for my boy. I always have, but I guess I didn't get it right. Help him if you can, Eric."

"I will."

Eric watched John's car back out of the small parking area, turn towards the street and keep going. When he went back into the clinic, he saw Teresa waiting for him just inside the door. "Where's Ned?" he asked

"He's in his office." Teresa shut the door to the treatment room. "What did you and his father talk about?"

"Not much. He seems resigned to Ned's decision to part ways."

Teresa frowned. "Goodness, he looks like an older version of Ned, but not much older. He must have been very young when Ned came along. And his energy felt similar too. He seemed like a nice guy."

Eric sighed. "I got the same impression, but he didn't want to discuss what happened." He held up the paper that John Finney gave him and opened the door. "I have to give this to Ned."

Teresa followed him into the treatment room. "What is it?"

"It's the information Ned needs to get in touch with his mother."

* * *

After he left the clinic, John started driving back the way he'd come, back to Blacksburg. Before he got very far, he pulled over and turned around. He decided to continue up the mountain instead. He needed to find a place where he could come to grips with the feelings he felt stirring. They'd been denied for years, but he knew resisting them had been for nothing. In fact, Ned seemed to think they didn't exist. If he only knew how wrong he was.

John was his father's son, and no matter how much he'd changed his way of handling life, he still had the same passionate nature beneath it all. He needed to find a place on the mountain that offered solitude and privacy, a place where he could vent his anger and sooth his heartache.

Fortunately, he'd brought along his camping gear on the outside chance that Ned and he could spend some time together like they used to when Ned was younger. Since that wasn't going to happen, he'd camp out by himself. While he was letting himself purge what needed to be purged, he'd decide if life was still worth living.

Forty-Six

MATTHEW WAS GRATEFUL to Eric. His friend had driven down to Blacksburg to pick him up after his return from Chicago. When they arrived in Elkville, Matthew experienced one of the weirdest feelings he'd ever had. He was relieved to be back. No, it was even weirder than that. As they passed the run down houses on the street where his own home was located, Paul's old fence and Margaret's aging two-story felt like the familiar images he needed.

After Eric dropped him off at his house, he even had a slight smile on his face as he walked up to the front door. Lea and Jacob would be waiting for him. He was where he wanted to be. He opened the door, stepped into the foyer and looked into the living room. Lea was sitting on the sofa with a picture book in her hand, and Jacob was sitting next to her. As soon as Lea looked up and saw him, she smiled.

"Matthew, you're back!" she called out.

Jacob was in motion at once. His brown eyes were wide as he slipped off the sofa. "Pa!" he called out as he ran towards the foyer.

Matthew had never heard the boy speak before. He'd been afraid that maybe the boy had a speech problem. Now, the truth was ringing out, loud and clear.

"Pa!" Jacob repeated as he ran up to Matthew with arms outstretched.

Matthew picked him up and held him close. "So you still remember me?"

The answer was obvious. Jacob's small arms were around his neck and his body was pressed so close that Matthew could feel the boy's small heart beating against his chest. Soon, Lea was there too, hugging them both.

The happiest moment in Matthew's life was putting a wedding band on Lea's finger at the altar. This moment was a close second. He had a family! As soon as he had the thought, he had to backtrack. That idea was wrong and had to be corrected. He had a beautiful wife. The little boy who was invading his heart wasn't his.

"Jacob, I'm not your pa," he announced to the little boy.

But Jacob didn't seem to be listening. He was clinging to Matthew just like he had the first time Matthew held him.

"Did you hear him, Matthew?" Lea asked with excitement. "He's never spoken until now."

"I was just thinking the same thing," Matthew said.

Lea grinned. "Now we know who his favorite is, don't we?"

"Lea, we have to face facts. When his sister comes for him—"

Lea bit her lip. "I know. I keep reminding myself that I can't get too attached. But it's getting harder and harder to think of giving him back."

Matthew wasn't one to avoid difficult subjects, but he didn't want to think about it. "Let's talk about it later."

Lea wiped her tears away with a tissue and smiled again. "I bet you're hungry. I have a special treat warming in the oven."

Matthew sniffed the air. "Turkey?"

"Yes!"

Jacob pulled away slightly and sniffed the air too. "Ttt?"

"Turkey," Matthew repeated.

Jacob tried again. "Ttt . . . torkie."

Matthew couldn't help but smile. "That's pretty good!"

Jacob flushed a bright red and hid his eyes in Matthew's shoulder.

Lea stared up at the little boy and frowned. "Maybe he's never spoken because he doesn't know how to pronounce the words."

Matthew agreed. "But he seems willing to learn."

Lea grabbed Matthew's arm and pulled him forward. "That can wait. Let's eat?"

Jacob straightened and pointed towards the kitchen. "Torkie!"

Matthew laughed. "I see his appetite hasn't changed."

* * *

Ned couldn't stop thinking about the paper his father left for him. Two pieces of information were written on it. The name, Judy, and a telephone number. After he'd been wondering for decades if he'd ever be in contact with his mother again, he could call her.

He almost picked up the phone several times over the course of the morning, but it was late afternoon before he had the courage to actually do it. He'd just severed all ties with his father. It was a fact that could tear him apart if he let himself give in to his emotions. If he called his mother and things didn't go well, he'd have no one left.

He decided he couldn't be a coward. He told Teresa that she and Eric would have to take care of any patients who came into the clinic while he talked to his mom. Both Teresa and Eric gave him encouraging smiles. After that, he went to his room, shut the door, and phoned the number on the paper. He paced back and forth as he listened to the rings on the other end. Just as he was about to disconnect, a woman answered.

Ned had to swallow hard before he could speak. "Mom?"

"Who is this?" the woman demanded.

"This is your son, Ned."

There was a long silence before the woman spoke again. "Ned, is it really you?"

Ned nodded a few times. "Yes."

Another long silence. "I gave your dad my number and wondered if you'd call."

Ned didn't know what to say next. "How are you?"

The woman laughed. "I'm sober. I haven't had a drink in almost a year."

Ned had to swallow again. "That's good."

"How's your father?"

"He's okay, I guess."

"What do you mean?"

"We've had a falling out."

The woman let out a big sigh. "Why? John is the best guy I've ever known. Why would you have a falling out?"

Ned's hand closed tight around the phone. "Mom, did he drive you away?"

"What?"

Ned could barely ask the next question, and it came out in a breathless sort of way. "Did he hurt you?"

The woman let out a mocking laugh. "Hurt me? Are you kidding? I'm the one who hurt him."

Ned took a breath and became more forceful. "I don't understand."

257

The woman sniffled. "How could you think that about John? He nearly killed himself trying to give us both everything he could. But I was too screwed up to appreciate a good man." There was a long pause and more sniffles. "Listen, Ned, can I call you back some time. I have to go."

"Yes, please, call me anytime," Ned insisted.

"I'm sorry about everything," the woman whispered just before the phone went dead.

Ned quickly sat down on the bed. He had to grab for the night stand to steady himself. According to his mother, he had it all wrong. She seemed to think John Finney wasn't the bad guy that Ned had thought him to be.

There was a knock on the door, but he didn't have the energy to respond. A moment later, the door opened and Eric peeked in. "Just thought I'd check and see how it went."

Ned looked up and shrugged. "I don't know."

Eric came over and sat down next to Ned. "How's your mom?"

Ned let out a weak laugh. "She says she's sober."

"Did you know she had a drinking problem?"

"Look, I don't know anything about my mother."

"Okay."

"All I know is that they didn't want me!"

"How do you know they didn't want you?" Eric asked.

"I heard them!"

"How old were you?"

"Maybe three."

"And your parents came in and told you they didn't want you?"

"No, I think they were fighting, and I heard them."

"Maybe they meant they didn't want the pregnancy. How old was your dad when he became a father?"

Ned shrugged again. "He's forty-eight now, so I guess he was—"

"Nineteen," Eric said. "That's pretty young to have a baby."

"I didn't think of it that way. But it doesn't matter. The man never once told me he loved me."

"Neither did my dad."

"Really?"

"Is that why you're so angry at your father?"

Ned stared at the floor. "At this point, I'm not sure."

"Did your dad take care of you after your mom left?"

"Yeah, he did."

"Maybe that was his way of telling you he loved you."

"I thought you said people were supposed to hold a child, like you did Jacob."

"Yes, but that's not always the case. When I was growing up, my dad didn't behave like that."

"What was he like?"

Eric's brows came together, and he crossed his arms. "He was a no-nonsense 'take it like a man' sort of guy."

"So how did you learn anything different?"

"You've met my mom. She's very loving."

"I don't think my mom had much time for me."

"Did she work?"

"I don't think so." Ned paused and thought about his early life. Even with his mom around, it was usually his dad who came home from work and fixed the meals.

"What about when you got upset or angry?" Eric asked. "Did he yell at you?"

"No, he'd didn't do much of anything. He just waited until I asked him about what was bothering me. Then we talked." Ned stared at Eric. "You met my dad. What impression did you get?"

"I think he cares about you."

"If he cared, why didn't he stay?"

"I don't know, Ned. I haven't met many people like your dad. Maybe it's not his way to argue but to accept what you want."

"That's kind of lame, isn't it?"

Eric got up. "I don't know your dad, so I can't answer that. I can only tell you that he looked upset when he was leaving."

"My dad doesn't get upset."

Eric started for the door and paused long enough to look back at Ned. "I may not know your dad, but I know when someone is upset, and your father was definitely upset."

Ned remained sitting on the bed after Eric left. He didn't want to believe that his father could possibly be hurting over their meeting that morning. It was so much easier to hang on to his feelings of being the injured party. But as he thought about the look his father gave him, he did remember the distressed frown on his father's face. And his dad's blue eyes held a sadness that Ned remembered from when he was a boy. He'd never paid attention to such signs of pain because the couple of times he asked about what was going on, his father quickly smiled and told him that all was well.

But maybe things weren't okay. Ned's mother confessed that she had hurt her ex-husband. Then there was the part about how hard Ned's father had worked to care for them. Was it just because he felt responsible? Ned didn't know the answer, but it suddenly seemed very important that he talk to his father and learn the truth.

He grabbed the landline phone and dialed his father's cell. It had been hours since the man left for Blacksburg. Surely, he'd have cell coverage once he arrived there. When he didn't get an answer, he felt his temper taking over. Was his father punishing him by not picking up? If that was the case, Ned would call on the hour, every hour, until he got the information he wanted and needed.

* * *

After John left the clinic and started driving up the mountain, he hadn't gone that far before he realized how little energy he had. His last week in Utah was spent teaching people about what to do in extreme circumstances. There were long hours and tiring exercises involved.

But he didn't get a break. He'd had his conversation with Ned and all the worry that followed. The night before he left for Blacksburg had been spent pacing the floor. The following night wasn't any better. He hadn't paced, he sat in a motel chair, but he hadn't slept. Then there was the emotional strain on top of it all.

It was all catching up with him. His mind was a hamster wheel of repeating thoughts that went nowhere, and his body was demanding that he rest. When his eyes started to blur, he had to pull over. He found a small side road not too far out of town and parked on the shoulder. He figured if he could get in a good nap, it would be enough to restore him. Putting his seat into a reclining position, he closed his eyes. Moments later, he was asleep.

When he woke up, it was twilight and someone was tapping on his window. He sat up and looked out. There was enough light to see an old man standing outside the car. He was gesturing to John.

John had a good sense about people, and the old man looked harmless. Perhaps he needed John's help. He opened the door and started to get out. That's when he realized his body wasn't its usual responsive self. His movements were slow and stiff.

Once John was out of his vehicle, the old man started walking. When John didn't follow, he stopped and waved him on. After his meeting with Ned, the last thing John wanted was somebody else's problem, but he'd never been one to refuse his help when it was needed. He followed the old man deep into the woods.

When they finally arrived at an old shack, the man opened the door and waved John forward. John nodded and entered the small dwelling. It was dark inside, and he couldn't see anything with night gobbling up the last rays of the sun.

The man moved past him and a few moments later a kerosene lamp lit up the room. John cleared his voice. "Can I help you?"

Instead of answering, the old man pointed to a chair by the fireplace. There didn't seem to be any problem with the old man, and John was ready to decline. "I better be going," he said, hoping he could find his way back to his car in the dark.

The old man had other ideas. He came over, took John's arm and pointed to the chair again. John shook his head, but the old man was insistent.

"Do you need something?" John asked.

The old man smiled and pulled him towards the chair. That's when John decided that the old fellow might just want company. He was probably lonely. John didn't feel lonely. He'd just lost his son, and he existed in a terrible void. After forty-eight years of struggle, his body was worn and his mind was out of ideas about how to be the man he was supposed to be. He'd tried to make his role as a father meaningful. He tried to provide an environment that was safe for his son to grow up in and thrive. But Ned looked anything but happy. There was a bitterness in his words and expression that John couldn't understand or know how to change.

He had to stay in the moment. He was in an aging shack with an old man who wanted him to stay. Why should he resist? He didn't have anything better to do with his time. He walked over, sat down in the rocking chair and let himself forget everything for a few minutes. On the plus side, it was a comfortable chair, one that seemed to welcome him into its confines, like an old friend inviting him to relax. He rested his hands on its arms and noticed how smooth they were. Perhaps they'd become that way after years of someone rubbing the wood as they rocked.

The old man had started making a fire and tiny flames took hold of the kindling. The man had a slow, gentle way about him that ran counter to the normal, frenzied pace of the world. His calm manner was almost mesmerizing and so were his eyes. When he looked at John, they glowed with the light of the fire like bright, glassy doorways to worlds beyond the one John normally experienced.

He sat back in the rocking chair and let out a deep sigh. He felt sleepy again. His eyes started to close, and he didn't fight the feeling. He let the room slip away and started to doze.

When he woke up, the first thing he did was inhale deeply. The smell of something tempting was his reward. As he came awake more fully, he realized someone was shaking his shoulder. He opened his eyes and saw the old man. He was holding out a chipped soup bowl.

John sat up, surprised to have someone serving him a homemade meal. He cooked for himself, but this was a treat. "Thank you," he said as he took the bowl.

The old man sat down in a second rocker on the other side of the fireplace. He leaned over and retrieved his own bowl. John wondered if the old man had a wife at one time. He could just imagine that the two of them ate by the fire.

The old man began to slurp his soup with so much enthusiasm that John didn't hesitate. He tasted the soup too. It was very hot, but delicious, and he did a little slurping of his own. After he finished his meal, the old man took his bowl. John thanked him again. "That was a very fine meal. The best I've had in a long time."

John started to get up. "I better leave before it gets any later."

The old man shook his head and stared back with such an insistent frown that John decided he better stay put. The old man was probably right. It was a dark night in a heavily forested area. To find his car would be very difficult. He sat back and resigned himself to spending the night.

When he felt like he could go to sleep again, he questioned why he was having difficulty staying awake. He supposed he was making up for the sleepless nights he'd had recently. Or perhaps, sleep was a soothing agent that helped him to forget Ned and the anger that spoiled his son's handsome face. He began to watch the fire and a short time later, he fell asleep in his chair.

Forty-Seven

WITH MATTHEW BACK in town, Margaret felt like her extended family was all gathered in one place. Enjoying the thought, she wanted to host a nice breakfast for everyone. Paul wasn't there, but at least Duke was in his dog bed next to the stove. At first, she refused to consider having a dog in her kitchen, but she was growing very fond of Duke. Having him close began to feel natural.

She'd made one of her favorite recipes, cheese, potato, and egg casserole. Teresa was her kitchen helper, and Eric's job was to get everyone seated around the table and pour beverages. She took the casserole out of the oven and placed it in a wicker casserole basket. "What do you think?" she asked Teresa who stood by watching.

"I think it's going to be yummy," Teresa said. "And I love the dish holder."

"Eric bought it for me some years ago after he watched me trying to serve a hot casserole dish and nearly burning my hands."

"Do you want me to put it on the table?"

"Yes, please, put it in my seat so that I can serve everyone."

Teresa picked up the basket. "This is so nice, Mom. I love us being together like this."

"Me too," Margaret said as she followed Teresa into the dining room. She was carrying another basket with iced, cinnamon rolls she'd made earlier. Once she was seated, she looked around the table. Eric and Teresa sat on her right, with Ned next to Teresa. Lea and Matthew were on her left. Jacob sat on a very thick dictionary next to Matthew. The little boy complained at first, preferring a lap. However, after a brief struggle, he settled down. It helped that Lea had put some pieces of home canned peaches on his plate. While the others chatted, he was interested in spearing the peaches with his fork. Margaret was pleased to see that he was attempting to use a utensil instead of his fingers.

After everyone had a portion of the casserole and a roll, Margaret sat back to try her breakfast. She was satisfied that she'd prepared a tasty dish.

Eric agreed. "As usual, you've outdone yourself, Mom," he said.

Everyone else at the table chimed in except for Jacob. He was busy attacking his cinnamon roll. There was a minimum of conversation while they ate. When everyone's appetite was satisfied, Margaret smiled. "I think you were all very hungry."

Matthew sat back and patted his stomach. "I think I more than ate my fill. I'm stuffed."

Jacob had been watching Matthew and sat back too. "Tuffed," he announced.

Everyone looked at him and smiled.

"He's talking," Teresa said. "How wonderful."

Lea spoke up. "You should have seen him when Matthew came home yesterday. He was so happy that he even called Matthew 'Pa'."

Matthew straightened. "Yes, but I tried to tell him otherwise."

Lea ignored him and leaned forward to look at Jacob. "Jacob, tell everyone what you had for dinner yesterday."

Jacob swallowed a last bit of roll, but he didn't say anything.

Matthew leaned over in his direction. "Say turkey."

Jacob blushed and finally spoke. "Torkie."

Teresa clapped her hands. "Well done, Jacob! You're so smart!"

"Yes, you are," Eric said.

Margaret wiped a tear away. "He's such a little angel, isn't he?"

Matthew frowned. "I don't know if he's achieved angel status yet. He had another screaming fit when Lea tried to comb out a few tangles after his bath."

Lea blushed. "I tried to be careful, but he must have a very tender scalp."

Margaret looked at Eric. "I know someone else who did a little screaming when his hair was tangled. Of course when Eric was very small, he had a lot of curls."

Eric reached over and patted Margaret's hand. "That's more than enough information about my childhood, Mom."

Teresa shook Eric's arm. "I'd love it if our children had curls."

Eric turned to Teresa and put his arm around her shoulder. "I think they're going to have your beautiful red locks."

"Not to change the subject," Matthew said, "but how are things going at the clinic, Ned?"

Margaret had noticed that Ned had barely spoken during the meal except to thank her for the invitation. "Yes, Ned, are more people coming in."

Ned shrugged. "A few, but we're over-staffed to be sure. Teresa and Eric need to take some time off."

Teresa smiled broadly. "Eric and I have thoroughly enjoyed working together. Whatever the future brings, I hope we can continue."

Margaret saw Ned look at his watch and frown. "Are you worried about something, Ned?"

"I need to go back to the clinic and phone my dad."

"Did he get back to Blacksburg yet?" Teresa asked.

"I don't know. I called him a dozen times, but he never answered."

"That's a bit worrying," Margaret said. "I'm sure he has good phone reception in Blacksburg."

"Maybe he's having phone problems like I did," Teresa said. "I forgot to charge my phone, and Eric couldn't reach me at first."

"You don't know my dad," Ned said. "He probably has the words, 'Be prepared,' tattooed on his body somewhere." He shook his head. No, maybe he just doesn't want to talk to me."

"I don't believe that, Ned," Eric said. "When we spoke, I got the feeling that he wants to connect, but he didn't want to push you."

"Then why isn't he answering my calls?" Ned asked.

Matthew cleared his throat. "Do you think he could have had an accident on the mountain?"

"I thought about that," Ned said. "So I called all the hospitals in Blacksburg this morning. His description didn't fit any recent accident victims."

Matthew continued. "I hate to say it, but what if he went off the mountain like Eric and I—"

Ned cut in. "No, my dad's an excellent driver."

"But what if he wasn't himself?" Teresa asked. "He looked pretty shaken when he left the clinic yesterday."

Ned scowled. "Eric said something similar, but I guess I didn't notice."

Teresa gave him an understanding look. "You were upset too."

Ned stood up. "I have to find him."

"I have an idea," Eric said. "The folks around here don't miss much. Let's ask around and see if anyone saw his car leave town."

"Eric's right," Margaret said. "Elkville might look sleepy, but if a stranger does anything, I can guarantee somebody's watching."

* * *

It was morning by the time John woke up. He'd been in such a deep sleep that he didn't know where he was. He looked around and finally remembered meeting an old man and spending time with him the night before. The dim light of a lantern had been replaced by sunlight streaming through the window. He sat up and stretched. It was nice to feel rested.

He looked around for the old man and saw him lying on his bed on the other side of the room. John was surprised that the old timer wasn't up and about. He didn't look like the type to sleep in so late in the day. "Good morning," he said.

When the old man didn't respond, John started to get up and realized that he had an old quilt draped over him. He quickly threw it aside and hurried over to where the old man lay. "Hey fellow, are you sick?" he asked.

The old man looked up at him with watery, blue eyes and smiled. He didn't have anything to say, but he seemed to be having a hard time breathing. John grabbed for his wrist and felt his pulse. It was barely perceptible. "I need to get you to the clinic in Elkville."

With great effort, the old man slowly reached out. He put his hand on top of John's and smiled again.

John patted his shoulder. "Hang in there." While he was telling the old man to hold on, he was already trying to figure out how he could get the help he promised the guy. He didn't know how to get back to his car or how to transport the man.

The old man slowly rocked his head back and forth as if to say he knew what John was thinking.

"Don't worry," John insisted. "I'll find a way."

The old man gave John a final smile just before his chest stopped rising and falling.

John didn't let himself panic. He was well-versed in CPR. If he could just get the guy breathing and his heart going, the man would have a chance.

He didn't know how long he tried to reverse the hold of death, but in the end, his efforts were useless. Once again, he'd done his best, and it wasn't good enough. He tried to distance himself from the sadness in his chest. He didn't know why the feeling was so intense when they barely knew each other. The answer was simple. He'd been clinging to the man's caring and kindness. Now it was gone, and the shack was as empty as John's life.

Sadness soon turned to grief at what had been lost. He'd been hanging on, trying so hard to make life mean something, and he couldn't do it anymore. All he could feel was the loss of everything he held dear. It shook his bones and plunged inward, twisting his gut and tearing at his heart. The thought of never seeing his son again was suffocating, and he forced himself to breathe.

When his emotions were spent, he remained at the old man's bedside, not knowing where else to go. In the end, practicality took over. He decided he'd drive back to Elkville and report the old man's death to the authorities. He wandered out into the daylight, not knowing which way to go. The shack stood in the middle of a small clearing and was surrounded by thick woods. The forest floor was littered with dead wood. He looked for a trail that the old man might have taken, but he didn't see a path.

He stopped and regrouped long enough to settle on a direction. His steps had to be slow and halting as he made his way through heavy brush and decaying trees. When he stopped briefly, hoping he was headed in the right direction, the wind ruffled some fallen leaves. It carried the faint smell of smoke. John turned around and saw flames in the distance. The shack was on fire.

"Oh lord, no!" He'd forgotten to make sure the fireplace embers were out before he left the fragile structure. There was also the quilt that he'd flung aside. It lay close to the fireplace. One of the half burned logs could have rolled out and set the thin coverlet on fire.

He turned around and ran as fast as he could, tripping on hidden tree limbs, getting up and running again. He kept thinking about the old man lying on the bed and the scene shifted. It was his father lying there.

He'd always told himself that his father drank himself to death. But in truth, his father had been a smoker whose lit cigarette set his bed on fire. His father had been too drunk to save himself.

Whenever John had let himself think of his father burning to death, he got sick. The man had beaten him so many times, but when his father was sober, he held John in his arms and wept. It was those times of being rocked and loved that played out against the horror of the beatings. In the end, there weren't any answers. He left home confused and angry.

No matter, he couldn't bear the idea that his father had burned to death. Maybe that explained why he fought forest fires. He knew how lethal fire could be. Now, he had to save the old man from the flames.

By the time he got back to the shack, his lungs were heaving. Kicking the door open with his foot, a wall of heat hit him, trying to drive him back to safety. He entered the structure anyway, unaware that he wasn't thinking clearly. His emotions had overridden the rational thinking that kept his life on course, the thinking that Ned claimed drove him away.

One glance around the room told him that the shack couldn't be saved. The kerosene lamp had toppled off the blazing side table by the fireplace, spilling its contents over the floor and setting the room ablaze. The chairs by the fire had become dry kindling, consumed by flame and falling apart.

He rushed to the bed, trying to put out sparks of flame that were trying to claim the bedclothes. He tried to lift the old man's body, but his lungs were filling with smoke. He couldn't breathe or manage the man's dead weight. Everything was out of control. The fires and intense heat were about to claim him as their next victim. He was in the nightmare he'd had for years, trying to save his father and failing.

Choking and gasping for breath, he had to retreat. He stumbled to the door and beyond to the outside. He fell to his knees, hoping to get some air before he passed out. He didn't know how long it took for him to revive a little, but once he was well enough, he forced himself to keep going. He had no choice. Sparks of flame and ash were settling on the brush and dead wood around the shack. He had to put the flames out before the entire woods caught fire.

As the fire from the burning structure roared and flying embers landed on him and around him, he became that robot that Ned accused him of being. Not thinking, just doing what he had to do, he fought the countless flare-ups that threatened the area. When he was sure he'd put them all out, he fell into a heap. As for the shack, it had been poorly built to begin with, hardly fit for human habitation. Now all that remained was charred wood and the stone fireplace.

He stayed put until he was sure that there were no active embers left. After that, he started for his car again. Fighting his way through the patches of brambles, he didn't dare stop. If he did, he wouldn't have the strength to get up. It seemed like forever before he got to his car. The door was still open and the keys were in the ignition. How had he been so careless? He got in and tried to start the vehicle, but it refused to turn over. He had no choice but to walk back to Elkville.

By the time he got to the main road, he was running on sheer willpower. He limped along, coughing and wheezing, every step a struggle. It was only an inner strength that didn't let him stop. It went beyond his body's staying power and drove him forward. And yet, he didn't know why. There was nothing waiting for him. He might have had a reason for pushing so hard in the past, when he had a family, but not anymore.

He thought about the old man he'd met and wished with everything he had left in him that the old man hadn't died. But the truth had to be faced, and he had to be satisfied with the memories of their brief time together.

They were sweet memories that softened the pain that had hold of his body. Everything hurt. But he almost smiled when he remembered how the old man had found him and taken him home. How the old man looked at him and given him a meal. His blue, compassionate eyes were comforting when John's world was falling apart.

He thought about sitting next to the fireplace in the dim light that bathed the room. He'd liked the feel of the rocking chair. As he remembered its soothing motion and gave himself fully to the memory, the chair became his father's arms. They were around him again as he staggered forward. His father's voice filled his mind. "I love you, son."

John had learned to ignore his father's words because they didn't mean anything. They were spoken when his father was sober, but they certainly didn't ease the pain of the drunken beatings.

John never repeated those words to Ned. It was a man's actions that were supposed to speak for themselves. But it wasn't true in Ned's case. Ned didn't seem to know anything of the sort. As soon as John had the thought, the grief was back, sapping his will to keep going.

Forty-Eight

NED SAT IN his office chair, staring at the phone. He didn't know what to do. Eric had questioned the people in Elkville, trying to get some information on his father. No one had seen his vehicle take the road to Blacksburg, but that's the only information Eric could get. Ned wondered if his father had driven further up the mountain. If he did, there was no way of telling where he was.

The bell to the clinic rang several times and interrupted his worries. With Teresa taking the day off, Eric was out front and could take care of whoever needed medical care. Still, Ned didn't want to shirk his duties and decided to check on what was going on. When he walked into the treatment area, a tall man was talking to Eric. He didn't look like a local. He was dressed too well. Ned wasn't an expert when it came to clothes, but the man looked like he was wearing a designer shirt and expensive jeans.

Ned walked over when he saw the distress on the man's face. "What's going on?"

The guy started explaining at once. "I was just saying that I picked up this guy on the road. Almost ran over him coming around a curve. Poor bastard looks like he came out of the bowels of hell."

"Is he out in your car?" Eric asked.

The man nodded. "Yeah, he is. Damn, it was hard getting him in. He was so disoriented. Then he passed out."

"Let's go check it out, Ned," Eric said as he headed for the door.

Ned followed on Eric's heels. His first thought was that he hoped the guy's condition wasn't too serious. The clinic's facilities hadn't really been tested when it came to a bad situation.

He stood back and let Eric take the lead. With his emotions all over the board, he didn't know if he was at his best. After Eric opened the passenger side door, he looked back at Ned. "Let's get him into the clinic."

270

Ned started forward but froze when Eric hesitated and gestured for him to stop.

"What is it?" Ned asked.

Eric turned and gave him a look of deep concern. "Ned, I just had a better look at the man in the car. I think it's your dad."

"My dad?" It was the last thing Ned expected. His father was missing, but John Finney knew how to take care of himself.

Ned pushed Eric aside and checked out the man in the passenger seat. The man's identity didn't register at first. It was only when Ned allowed himself to see beyond the dark soot, burns and scratches, that he recognized his father. It was such a shock that he grabbed his father's shirt and shook him. "Dad! Dad!"

Eric took hold of Ned's arm and pulled him away from the truck. "Calm down," he ordered in a stern voice.

"It's my father!"

"I know, but you have to listen to me!"

Ned was trying to follow directions, but he'd never been so scared. "Is he dead?" he cried out.

"No, but you have to control yourself and do as I say. Go back into the clinic and call Matthew. I'll get the man who brought your dad in to help me."

Ned was nodding but he was also trying to look at his father. Was Eric right? Was his dad breathing?

Eric gave him another order. "Get moving!"

Ned swiveled round and ran back into the clinic. When he got to his office, he forced himself to focus on what he was supposed to do. He found Matthew's number, called his home phone and waited anxiously. He could barely speak when Matthew answered. "It's my dad," he said in the most composed voice he could muster. "You have to come to the clinic immediately!"

After he put the phone down, Ned forced himself to breathe. It helped. With more oxygen, his head felt a little clearer, and he was able to consider the situation with less panic. He was a very competent ER doc, and he wanted to be there for his father. It was a great thought, but when he looked at his hands, they were shaking. Hell, he'd been shaking off and on since his accident in Blacksburg. He had to get a handle on his fear. There was only one problem, he didn't know how. He didn't know how to take back all the terrible things he'd said to his father.

That's when he knew he was doing it again. He was giving in to all the crap running through his head. But what good did it do to dwell on his failings? Was beating himself up going to help his father?

He pushed himself out of his chair, clenched his fists and made a decision. He'd been behaving like he didn't have a choice in how to conduct himself. But scared or not, shaking or not, he had to find a way to act like a son John Finney could be proud of.

He walked briskly to the treatment room and went directly to the sink. After washing his hands and putting on some gloves, he went over to where Eric was caring for his father. "Tell me what to do, and I'll try my best to carry out your orders."

Eric stared back. "Are you sure you can handle this, Ned?"

"I'm his son, aren't I? I'll handle whatever I have to handle."

Ned's father stirred slightly and half opened his eyes.

"Dad!" Ned immediately leaned in close. It was such a relief to see his father awake that his heart raced with unexpected joy. "It's okay, I'm here."

His father tried to speak, paused and tried again. "Love you, son," he whispered in a hoarse voice.

"I love you, too," Ned said. And he meant it. All the hurt he'd been nursing didn't matter anymore. He just wanted his father back. Still, he had to forget his role as a son and assume the role of a doctor. He gave his father an encouraging look. "We'll talk later, but for now, you have to be quiet and let us take care of you. You need to conserve your strength."

His father half-smiled and closed his eyes.

* * *

Matthew sat in the clinic kitchen, drinking coffee at the table, along with Eric and Ned. He looked at Ned and studied the man's grim expression. "Ned, if you're worried, your dad is going to be fine. He's pretty beat up, but he's a strong man, very fit."

Ned glanced up. "Thanks Matthew, but I'm not worried about my dad, I'm worried about me."

"Taking care of a relative can be a challenge," Eric said, but you didn't let your emotions get in the way of delivering the care your father needed."

"I pulled it together," Ned said.

Eric smiled. "You and your dad are a lot alike from what I've observed."

Ned shook his head. "No, that's not true. When I was bandaging his hands, I knew that he was always there for me. But when my emotions got triggered, I became some kind of idiot who flat out rejected him. And he didn't do anything wrong. I was the one making up the problems."

Eric frowned. "Don't be so hard on yourself."

"I'm not," Ned answered. "I know that's not going to help anyone. I'm just trying to understand what happened to me so that I can correct my behavior."

Matthew chuckled. "Raymond Ferguson called you a young pup. And maybe he had a point. You've probably spent half your life studying and preparing for your career. You haven't had time to handle emotions."

Ned pushed away his half-full mug. "That's true. High school was all about getting the grades and that didn't stop when I went to college or med school."

"It's interesting," Eric said. "My father triggered every emotional button I had when I was growing up. In your case, it seems your father tried to protect you from being emotionally upset."

Matthew drained his mug. "My father was a total jerk, but I didn't let him run my life. I shut him out early on."

"No matter what, I think all of us turned out okay," Eric said. He looked at Ned. "You went a little haywire for a while, but you're willing to learn from your mistakes. That's what it's all about."

"How do you feel about your father now, Ned?" Matthew asked.

"It's like all my crap was a bad dream. I just want him to know how much I love and respect him."

"You've come a long way, my friend," Eric said.

Ned scowled back. "How's that?"

"You once told Teresa and me how feelings didn't matter. Now you're using the word, love."

Ned's face went instantly red, but he finally smiled. "I guess I have made quite the journey, but I don't think I'm capable of ever going the whole way."

"The whole way?" Eric asked.

Ned stared down at his clenched hands. "Both of you have beautiful wives. I'll probably end up being a bachelor forever."

Eric and Matthew exchanged glances and both began laughing.

"What's so funny?" Ned asked with annoyance.

"You haven't found the right woman, that's all," Eric said.

"And when you do, that's when you'll find out what a real challenge is about," Matthew added.

"Are you trying to scare me, Matthew?" Ned asked.

"Just sharing what I know," Matthew replied.

Eric patted Ned's shoulder. "Don't listen to him. Relationships can be great."

"Absolutely," Matthew said, "as long as you're willing to drop every belief you ever had about yourself. You also want to use the phrase, 'Yes, dear,' whenever you're talking to your partner."

Eric's eyes widened. "I've never once heard you say, 'Yes, dear' to Lea."

"You two can be quite the pair," Ned said as he got up. "Now, if you'll excuse me, I'm going to check on my dad."

"Don't go shaking him again," Eric said with a teasing smile. "Let him sleep."

Ned started for the door. "Yes, Doctor Lloyd, I'll try to behave myself. And as for you, drink a bottle of water instead of another cup of coffee."

After Ned left the room, Eric looked at Matthew. "He can be a bossy type."

Matthew got up and went to the counter. After he refilled his mug, he looked at Eric. "Maybe he's right, Eric. Maybe you do drink too much coffee."

Eric got up and refilled his mug too. "This from the man who probably bleeds the stuff."

"But I'm not the high-strung type like you. That's the difference."

"Oh lord, that's ridiculous, and you know it."

Matthew sat back and crossed his arms. "I'm just relieved that John Finney wasn't too badly injured, and his son is coming to his senses. Maybe we can all relax at long last."

"This has been quite the trip. First, the snow storm, then—"

"Stop," Matthew ordered. "I don't want to rehash any of it. I want to sit here and let my mind go blank."

"Just one more question," Eric said. "What are you going to do about Jacob when his sister comes to get him?"

Matthew glared back. "Didn't I just tell you I want to relax?"

"Sorry, I'm worried about the kid."

Matthew looked away. "So am I."

"By the way, I guess Teresa and I will start spending our nights at your house since Ned's dad is here. But as for meals, we'll eat at Mom's."

"I'll let Lea know. She'll be happy to see more of you two."

"Lea's a very social person, but what about you?" Eric asked. "I bet you never expected to have a child in your care plus house guests coming and going constantly."

Matthew shrugged thoughtfully. The idea of hosting Eric and Teresa didn't seem to matter one way or the other anymore. "I haven't had time to think about it, but I suppose I'm starting to get used to having my home turned into a boarding house."

Forty-Nine

JOHN WOKE UP and remained very still. He'd been dreaming, and if he didn't move, he had a chance to remember his dreams. There was the distant feeling that he'd been wandering forever, trying to get somewhere and feeling like he'd never arrive. After reviewing the dream, he decided to let it go and open his eyes. After a few blinks, he saw Ned sitting in a chair by his bedside, sleeping. But where was he, and what time was it?

Checking out a side table, he saw a clock. Six in the morning? How long had he been asleep? And where was a bathroom? He didn't want to wake Ned, but he needed to find one.

He was about to get out of bed when he noticed that he was hooked up to an IV. But why? Had he been sick?

He was about to push back the cover when he saw his bandaged hands. That's when memories of the fire flooded back in. "And the old man died," he whispered to himself. More disjointed images wanted his attention, but he decided to ignore them.

Easing himself out of the bed, he barely got to his feet when he nearly tipped over. After steadying himself, he took stock of his body. It was hurting in a lot of places. But nature was calling, and he had to continue his quest for a place to relieve himself.

"Dad? What are you doing out of bed?"

John looked over and saw Ned get up and rush around the bed. He started to say he was okay when he realized his throat was sore. He finally got out the words he needed to convey, but his voice sounded raspy. "I'm fine, Ned. Just need to use the—"

"You're not fine," Ned protested as he reached out and took John's arm. "I thought I might lose you."

John saw the look of panic on Ned's face. "Maybe you're right," he croaked. "Don't feel my usual self."

"Take it slow," Ned ordered, "and I'll get you to the bathroom."

John almost insisted he could navigate on his own when his body had other ideas. He nearly faltered, and Ned took on a more assertive role. "You have to hold on to me, Dad. Your body's been through a lot."

As soon as Ned gave him the order, John felt like he was holding on too. He was holding on to the old man when the old man was dying. It brought up so much sadness, that his voice broke when he spoke. "I couldn't save him, Ned."

Ned hesitated. "Save who?"

John clamped his jaws shut to keep his grief from escaping. Was he talking about the old man or his drunken father? He was so confused, he didn't know which was true. He shook his head and held on to Ned as uncertainty settled in and clouded his thoughts. It was accompanied by an acute weakness in his body. He had no choice but to let Ned guide him to his destination.

By the time he made the trip to the bathroom and back to his bed, he was exhausted. Ned hovered over him once he was under the covers. He tried to say more, but he could only whisper a word of thanks before he shut his eyes and sleep spared him any more memories.

* * *

After getting his father back to bed, Ned checked his dad's vitals, looked over his meds and made sure his IV was doing its job. Once he was satisfied that all was well, medically speaking, he sat down in the chair by his father's bed and allowed himself to think about the way his father was behaving. He came to a horrible conclusion. Something was going on that shouldn't be going on. And it all started when his dad came to Elkville.

When Eric and Teresa came into the clinic around seven o'clock, Ned was ready to deliver his news. "I don't care about what Raymond Ferguson says or how it affects my career, I'm getting my father out of this place and never stepping foot in Elkville again."

Eric stared back but didn't say anything. Teresa came over and gave Ned a look of concern. "Why? Why do you feel like that?"

277

Ned lifted his chin and glared at Eric. "You and Matthew warned me about this place when you first got here. I should have listened. Instead, I ignored what you said and ended up falling apart. Next, my dad, a man who's perfectly sane and healthy, comes here, and he falls apart. Well, as soon as he's well enough, I'm getting both of us the hell out of here."

Teresa sighed. "Ned, you're acting like some exterior force is out to get you. Isn't that a little far-fetched?"

Before Ned could answer, John began to thrash around in his bed and mumbled in his sleep. "Can't save him!"

Ned quickly went over and shook him gently. "It's okay, Dad, you're dreaming." When his father half opened his eyes, Ned smiled at him. "Go back to sleep."

After he was sure his father was sleeping again, Ned turned to Teresa and Eric. "It's been this way all night. Whatever happened on that mountain must have really freaked him out."

Eric came over. "Ned, if you want your father to get better, you have to believe in him and in yourself. And as far as what Matthew and I said, we were just letting off steam, nothing more."

Ned rubbed his temples. "I just don't understand it. My dad's never acted like this before."

"Maybe, but here's the bright spot," Eric said.

"What's that?" Ned asked.

"Your dad fights forest fires, right? If this happened somewhere else, you might not be able to be there for him. At least, here, in this little clinic, he has what's most important in his world. He has you."

Ned kept rubbing his temples. "I'm trying to be there for him."

"And you're doing a great job," Teresa said. "But it's only been a few days since you were ill, remember? So go get some sleep, and Eric and I will look after your dad."

Ned hesitated and scowled back. "Fine, but promise you'll call me if anything changes."

"I promise," Teresa said.

* * *

Matthew came out of a deep sleep when he felt someone tugging on his hand. He opened his eyes and saw Jacob standing by his bed. "Yes?" he groaned.

Jacob tugged on his hand again. "I 'ungry."

Matthew looked over at Lea. She was still sleeping. Neither of them had a peaceful night. Jacob could be a noisy sleeper who often moaned and groaned. He could be quite loud at times. Matthew looked back at Jacob and put a finger to his lips. "Shh, let's not wake Lea."

Jacob stuck out his lower lip and rubbed his eye with a balled fist, but he seemed to understand Matthew's explanation and waited quietly.

Matthew knew there was only one thing to do, get up and feed the child. As quietly as possible, he got out of bed and slipped on some clothes. Afterwards, he took Jacob's hand and started for the door.

"What time is it?" Lea called from the bed.

Matthew turned around and looked at his beautiful wife. He wished he could climb back in bed with her, but that wasn't going to happen. "It's a little after eight, and I'm going down to fix some breakfast. But you can sleep in."

Lea sat up a little. "Are you hungry?"

"No, but our friend is."

Lea smiled. "Are you sure you don't want me to fix something?"

"I'm sure," Matthew said. "Now, go back to sleep. You'll need your strength for later. Remember, we let Jacob's bath go until this morning. And we have to tackle his fingernails this time."

Jacob pulled his hand out of Matthew's as soon as he heard the word, fingernails. It seemed he had a real problem facing nail clippers.

Matthew continued out of the bedroom, shaking his head. He wondered if he was up to the task of keeping Jacob clean and groomed. An entire morning in the OR didn't seem nearly as difficult as dealing with Jacob's shrieks of resistance when he didn't want to do something.

He was about to start down the stairs when Jacob called out. "Pa!"

Matthew turned. The little boy was holding out his hand again, wanting him to take it. "Sorry, I forgot you have a problem with stairs."

Once they got to the kitchen, Matthew headed to the counter to get a pot of coffee going. Before he could get things started, Jacob was yanking on his pants leg. "What is it?"

Jacob pointed to the refrigerator. He definitely wanted his breakfast. Matthew was about to insist that Jacob wait, but when he saw the child's sad face, he stopped himself. "Fine," he muttered. After

279

he got out some eggs and bread, he gave Jacob an annoyed look. "You, young man, are a taskmaster, do you know that?"

Jacob returned one of his rare smiles, a smile that always made Matthew worry. He didn't want to think about what would happen when Jacob had to leave. The little boy was smart, but he wouldn't understand why he couldn't stay with Matthew and Lea. And Matthew didn't know if he could cope with Jacob's screams when his sister took him away. He'd always considered himself to be pretty tough, but he'd never had to care so much about a child before. He started whipping up some eggs and put some bread in the toaster.

Jacob was eyeing everything Matthew did. "Tanks," he said, smiling again and grabbing Matthew's leg in a hug.

Matthew let out a heavy breath. The little boy was learning some manners, but what use would they be if he ended up with his abusive father again? He started scrambling the eggs and glanced down at Jacob? "How did we get ourselves in this situation?"

Fifty

MARGARET WAS JUST returning home after going out for a stroll with Duke. She heard the phone as she walked through the front yard. Hurrying up the porch stairs with Duke in tow, she let herself into the house. She got to the phone before it stopped ringing. "Hello!"

"Hello, Margaret," Paul said.

"Paul, how good to hear from you."

"You sound kind of breathless."

"I was coming home after walking Duke. So how are you?"

"I'm out of the hospital. But I wanted to check on everybody there."

"Oh my goodness, Paul. We've had quite a time here." She told Paul the latest in what had happened recently and waited for a reply.

Paul sounded concerned. "I'm sorry to hear about all the problems you've had. And I'm sorry about my behavior, Margaret. I messed things up with Ned. He needed someone to talk to, and I only made things worse."

"Yes, I'm afraid he's been so confused about everything, especially about his father. But I know he's a caring person."

"When his dad is better, please tell him that he can use my house if he needs a place to stay. Would you do that?"

Margaret nodded. "I will. Anyway, what have you been doing?"

"Hopefully, I'm getting my life back on track. For starters, I've been looking in to volunteering at the hospital I was at."

"That's a splendid idea."

"Do you think so? Can this old dog learn to behave himself?"

Margaret looked down at Duke. He was lying next to her with his head on her foot. "Old dogs can be very good friends, Paul."

Paul paused. When he spoke, his voice was soft, just above a whisper. "I miss our chats and tea, Margaret."

"Me too," Margaret said. "Call me again soon."

After she put the phone down, she went to her front window. An old truck was pulling up in front of Lea and Matthew's house. After it stopped and a young woman got out, Margaret let out a gasp. "I bet that's Jacob's sister!"

* * *

Matthew was demonstrating the mechanics of nail trimming to Jacob, and he was using Lea as his model. "Look here, Jacob, and see how Lea's smiling while she's getting her nails all fixed up."

Jacob stood several feet away with his hands behind his back. He seemed interested, but he was also displaying his "I don't think so" look.

The doorbell interrupted the session, and Matthew got up to answer it. He leaned into Lea before he left the bedroom. "I hope I did a decent job on your nails."

"You did," Lea laughed. "Now I wonder how good you are with nail polish."

"Excuse me, but I think that's way beyond my comfort zone," Matthew said as he headed for the stairs.

When he got to the door, he realized his shirt had gotten wet during Jacob's bath. The little boy was beginning to like the water, and sometimes did some unexpected splashing. Matthew decided getting doused was better than having to hear Jacob's screaming. He pushed back some hair that had fallen across his brow and opened the door. He stepped back as soon as he saw who it was. "Mary!"

Mary stood in place and gave him a shy smile.

Matthew collected himself and opened the door a little wider. "Please come in."

Mary crept into the foyer and waited as if she didn't know what to say.

Matthew gestured her into the living room. "We can talk in here. Please, have a seat."

Once Mary was perched on the edge of the sofa, she hunched her shoulders and finally looked at Matthew. "Sorry I haven't been back sooner for Jacob. Ma's been real bad, and I didn't dare leave her."

"Why hasn't she come to the clinic?"

Mary stared down at her tightly clasped hands. "After Jacob come into the world, Ma got worse and worse. She don't leave the cabin no more. I think she's 'shamed of what's become of her."

"Mary, if she's ill that's nothing to be ashamed of."

Mary shrugged, but she didn't reply.

"We have a lady doctor at the clinic now. Do you think your mother would talk to her? Mary, you got your dad there. Maybe you could do the same for your mother."

"I could try, but she don't listen much or leave her bed. But it's Jacob I come to talk 'bout. Thank you for takin' 'em in."

"My wife and I are happy to help. In fact, we've become very fond of your brother."

Mary blushed. "You like that bawlin' boy?"

"Yes, Lea and I like him very much."

"I'm grateful to you, but I can't git the boy to Blacksburg, so I'll have to fetch 'em home."

Matthew felt his chest tighten. "Mary, do you think we could keep him here until your mother is better?"

Before Mary could answer, Lea came into the living room with Jacob in her arms. He was sucking his thumb with half-closed eyes.

Mary looked at Lea and Jacob and smiled broadly. "Well look at that!"

As soon as Mary spoke, Jacob came out of his sleepy mood, looked at his sister and started crying into Lea's shoulder.

Mary immediately averted her eyes. "See that? He's a troublesome child."

Matthew stood up. "Mary, this is my wife, Lea. Lea, this is Jacob's sister, Mary."

Lea came over and held out her hand while holding on to Jacob. "It's so good to meet you, Mary."

Mary nodded at Lea. "Nice to meet you too."

Jacob started crying louder and reached out to Matthew.

Matthew quickly gathered up the little boy in his arms and stepped back. "Jacob, it's okay. This is your nice sister who's trying to look out for you."

Mary's eyes welled up with tears. "It's mighty hard, with Ma so sick, and Pa drinkin' more and more."

Lea sat down next to Mary and put an arm around her shoulders. "Mary, let me get you a cup of tea."

"I don't wantta be no bother."

Lea squeezed Mary's shoulder. "It's no bother at all." She looked up at Matthew. "Why don't you read Jacob one of those little books he likes, and Mary and I will be in the kitchen getting some tea."

While Lea took care of Mary, Matthew held Jacob close and phoned the clinic. Once he got hold of Eric, he explained the problem. "Jacob's sister is here and wants to take Jacob back home with her. She says her mother is very ill, but the woman doesn't want to come to the clinic. What do you think about you and Teresa making a house call?"

When Eric agreed to help, Matthew felt a little better. He went to the kitchen to talk to Mary with Jacob clinging to him. "Mary, that woman doctor, Teresa, and her doctor husband would like to help your mom. Would you be willing to let them follow you back home?"

Mary studied her cup of tea for a long time, but she finally nodded. "That's very good of 'em."

"Is it alright if we keep Jacob here for a while longer?" Matthew asked.

Mary stared at Jacob with narrowed brows. "You'd do that for us?"

Lea spoke up. "We're happy to have him, Mary."

Mary nodded again.

Matthew grabbed a set of car keys off the black metal key holder mounted on the kitchen wall. "I have to go to the clinic and keep an eye on things while Teresa and Eric are gone. Mary, could you follow me to the clinic?"

Mary agreed and stood up.

Matthew went over to Lea and tried to hand off Jacob, but the little boy stubbornly refused to let go.

Lea put her hand out for the keys. "Why don't I drive us, Matthew? I'll stop in too."

"Good idea," Matthew said.

* * *

Lea arrived at the clinic with Matthew and Jacob. After Teresa and Eric left to check on Mary's mother, Lea went to the kitchen to fix Jacob a snack. She tried to be as quiet as possible. Ned had been up the night before with his dad. He was taking a quick nap while Matthew visited with his father.

Lea looked down at Jacob. He was shadowing her as she cut up apple slices for him. "You have a very nice sister," she said. Jacob put his thumb in his mouth and backed away. Either he didn't agree, or he didn't understand her.

Lea took the plate of apple slices over to the table. "Alright, we won't talk about your family. Instead, let's sit down, and I'll read you a picture book while you eat. How about that?"

Jacob followed her over and tried to climb up on the chair.

Lea began to look around the kitchen. "Oh, you need some kind of booster seat."

While Lea was searching, Jacob managed to hoist himself onto the chair. By the time Lea came back to the table, he was kneeling on the seat and eating an apple slice.

Lea smiled. "Good for you, Jacob. You solved your own problem."

Jacob held up his apple slice triumphantly.

Lea was about to start reading when the phone rang. "I'll be right back," she said as she hurried to Ned's office to answer it. She was happy when she heard Margaret's voice on the other end. Margaret was asking if Lea needed any help. Lea told her about the latest and that she was fine for the moment. She ended the call and was going back to the kitchen when she heard Jacob scream.

* * *

Jacob's scream was loud enough to have Matthew running from John's bedside to the kitchen. He got there just in time to see Lea picking up Jacob off the floor. "What happened?"

Ned showed up too, looking half awake. "What's going on?"

Lea's face was panicked. "Jacob fell off the chair."

With Jacob continuing to scream, Matthew tried to take him from Lea, but the little boy kept crying and looked away.

Ned stepped forward. "Looks like he's protecting his hand."

John came limping in. "Is a child hurt?"

Ned turned and looked at him. "Dad, get back in bed," he ordered, then stared at his father with narrowed eyes. "And you took out your IV?"

John laughed. "You worry too much, Ned. Now let me have a look at the young one. I've had some experience with children."

"When?" Ned asked.

"Raising you."

"I was never sick."

"You fell and hurt yourself a few times," John said as he went to Jacob and touched his wet cheek. "Give me your watch, Ned."

Ned frowned. "My watch?"

"Yes, please," John said.

Once Ned did as he was told, John presented the watch to Jacob. "It's a nice timepiece, isn't it? It was a graduation present I gave my boy. Do you like it?"

After a moment, Jacob's furrowed brows eased a little, and he stared at what John was holding out to him. With a few more sniffles, he grabbed for the watch with the hand that hadn't been damaged.

Lea smiled at John. "You have a way with children."

John glanced at Ned. "Ned turned out alright," he said and returned his attention to Jacob. He touched the boy's wrist very lightly with a bandaged hand. "No apparent swelling yet. He's going to be fine."

Ned came over to John and grabbed his arm. "Now, can you please go back to bed?"

"I'll make a deal with you, son, I'll get some rest if you promise to do the same thing. You look exhausted."

Ned tugged on John's arm. "I'm okay. You're the one who must have battled the devil."

"Maybe I did," John said quietly.

As John was leaving the kitchen, Jacob called after him. "Tanks."

Matthew was impressed. With John helping out, Jacob calmed down very quickly. He even let Matthew have a closer look at his wrist.

"Is he going to be okay?" Lea asked.

"Yes, I think he's got a slight sprain at most," Matthew said. "But—"

Lea cuddled Jacob a little closer. "What is it, Matthew?"

"We've got a new problem. I don't know how we're going to get that watch away from him."

Fifty-One

ERIC WOKE UP early. He'd had trouble sleeping after his trip to check on Jacob's mother the day before. When he saw the condition of the family's dwelling and the impoverished conditions that they lived in, it brought back a lot of bad memories from childhood.

The helpless feeling was back too. He'd watched his father give his life to the people living in the area. Yet Jacob's family was still no better off. Jacob's mother had neglected her health for years and was paying the price. She was a very sick woman. She needed to be admitted to a hospital in Blacksburg. At the least, she needed to come to the clinic in Elkville. However, she stubbornly refused to consider either option.

Teresa tried to talk to Eric about his feelings, but he didn't know how to explain what was going on. It was as if his entire childhood felt tainted and the feelings were coming back to haunt him again.

After getting dressed, he excused himself and drove to the clinic. When he walked into the clinic kitchen, John Finney was sitting at the table. The man looked much better. "Couldn't sleep?" he asked.

"I've been in that bed long enough," John said. "What about you?"

"Too much thinking." Eric walked over to the counter and poured himself a fresh cup of coffee. "Thanks for making the coffee."

John laughed. "I had to get a cup before Ned decides I shouldn't."

"You too? He's been on me to drink more water."

"Ned's a terrific son, and I'm sure he's a fantastic doctor, but he's always had a tendency to be a bit controlling."

Eric took a seat at the table. "I'm surprised he's not around."

"He'd be right here if I hadn't insisted he go to bed. He's been hovering over me like I could die any second. From now on, I won't dare get sick or injured when he's around."

287

"My mom accused me of hovering. But I was just very concerned. So I guess I can't blame Ned. He cares about you."

"I know that, but I still don't understand why he got so mad at me."

"I think a lot of emotion got stirred up when he got hit by that car in Blacksburg."

John sat up straighter. "He what? He got hit by a car?"

"Oh lord, I should have let him tell you about that."

"When did it happen?"

"A couple of weeks ago. Nothing was broken, but he was badly bruised from his chest to his knees. He had to have help just to get into a car."

John looked away. "My poor boy. No wonder he's so upset. He must not think he can confide in me."

"John, can I ask you something? Ned says you told him that feelings didn't matter. Do you believe that?"

John stalled and shook his head. "I grew up with a very emotional father, and I suffered because he couldn't deal with his anger and frustration. I wanted to spare Ned what I felt. I guess I went overboard, but that didn't mean I didn't have feelings for Ned." He looked up at Eric. "I loved my son with every breath in my body. I'm sorry he didn't feel that."

"But the two of you talked, right?"

"Yes, I always tried to be there, but I must have failed anyway."

Eric crossed his arms. "Teresa and I want a family, but the whole idea of children and how to raise them is starting to scare me."

"I wish I could tell you it's easy, but it's not. I don't think I've ever met anyone who said they had the perfect childhood. But I can say this much, Eric, you've turned out very well. You're a kind, compassionate man."

Eric smiled. "So are you, John, and so is Ned."

John's eyes turned thoughtful. He picked up his mug with two bandaged hands and took a sip. "What you just said gave me an idea. When I was raising Ned, it was all about not doing what my dad did, but that approach was probably the problem. If I could have simply had faith in the love I had for my boy, he might have been better off."

Eric felt his chest tighten. His thoughts about the impoverished people in the area and how their conditions never changed were plaguing him again. "How does a person ignore his thoughts and feelings?"

John sighed. "I don't know. Besides I have something else that's on my mind. It's about an experience I had on the mountain."

Eric came to attention. "I've been wondering about what happened after you left here that first morning."

"Yes, it's quite the story."

"What story is that?" Ned asked as he came into the kitchen. He stopped and stared at John. "And why are you drinking coffee, Dad? I don't think a stimulant is what's best for you."

Eric started laughing and so did John.

"So this is what I get for caring?" Ned asked.

John sobered immediately. "No, of course not. You're just a little too protective at times, but I appreciate your concern."

Ned came over and gave John a quick onceover. "Thankfully, you do look much better."

"And how about your bruised body, Ned? I just found out you were in an accident."

Ned gave Eric an annoyed look. "Thanks for sharing, Eric."

John stood up and reached out for Ned's shoulder. "Ned, I want us to always share something like that. Maybe that idea didn't come across when you were a kid, but I want to get it right from now on."

"I wanted to call when it happened, but—" Ned hesitated. "Maybe I didn't want you to know how scared I got. It's like I couldn't depend on anything."

"You can depend on me," John said. "Because I know what it's like to be scared. I've lived with the feeling my whole life."

Ned blinked back. "I don't understand. You always had it together. Nothing that happened seemed to shake you."

John grabbed for the table and slumped back down in his seat. "That's what I hoped you'd think, but underneath, it was a struggle. I had to hide what I was feeling, plain and simple." He stared down at the floor. "So now you know. Your father isn't the tough guy he pretended to be."

Ned didn't say anything, but stared down at the floor too. Finally, he looked at Eric and then back at John. "Eric said we're a lot alike and I didn't think so. I said you were the better man. But maybe he's right about us."

John frowned. "I'm sorry if I've let you down."

Ned put a hand on the table and leaned in. "I'm not disappointed. I'm relieved. It's been so hard trying to be the 'perfect' guy I thought you were. Now maybe I can just be me."

John looked up and smiled. "That's all I ever wanted for you."

Ned smiled too. "Good, now that that's settled, are you ready to go back to bed for a while longer? It's just after six in the morning."

"Can I just finish my coffee?"

Ned shrugged and went over to the counter. "Fine, let's have a cup together, and you can include me in that story you were going to tell Eric."

* * *

John looked at his audience. Both Ned and Eric were waiting for him to talk about what happened. They wanted to know how he ended up burned and hurting in a bed with Ned watching over him. Going back to the beginning was difficult. "Ned, I just told you how scared I've been in my life. One of the scariest moments wasn't having my father beat me and leave me crying in a corner—"

Ned jerked up. "Your father beat you?"

John held up a hand. "That's something we can talk about later. For now, I want to go on with my story."

Ned sucked in a breath. "Sorry."

"Being beaten by my dad wasn't nearly as bad as thinking I'd failed you. The first instance comes from an outside force, but the fear that we haven't done better ourselves is what tears a person up inside. And that's how I felt when I left you that morning. I came here thinking there had been a mistake, that the call I received from you had to be something we could talk about. But after I learned how you felt, I didn't know what to do next. Anyway, I decided to drive up the mountain and give myself time to deal with the horror of what I was facing. I'd lost my son, but not to some disaster. You hadn't been hit by lightning. No, I'd lost my son because I wasn't the parent I should have been."

"Dad, I'm so sorry," Ned whispered.

"Don't be sorry. I needed to hear what you felt. It stirred up what I hadn't faced in myself. I was so proud of you, and I was proud of myself for being a good father. I raised a beautiful boy. Yet,

290

underneath, I'd never come to grips with my past. I was still trying to prove I was better than my own father."

"What happened next?" Eric asked.

John smiled, remembering the first time he saw the old man outside his car. "I was so tired that morning. I pulled over a couple of miles out of town. I parked on a side road and fell asleep. It was almost night when someone tapped on my window. An old man found me and made it clear he wanted me to follow him. He lived way back in the woods, in an old shack. He invited me in, fed me, and insisted I stay the night. He never said a word, but he had the kindest eyes I've ever seen. The next morning, I woke up and saw him on his bed. He was dying." John paused and looked down at his bandaged hands. He remembered how hard he tried to revive the old man. "I couldn't save him."

Eric nodded. "I know that feeling. My father knew it when he traveled these hills trying to help and couldn't."

Ned spoke up. "You said he was old. Maybe it was just his time."

"Maybe," John said.

"So where did the fire come in?" Eric asked.

"After the old man died, I tried to get back to my car to report what happened. I was in the woods, not thinking very clearly, when I smelled smoke. I looked back and saw that the shack was burning. I ran back and tried to get the old man's body out." John paused again, wishing he'd been stronger. "But I couldn't do it. After that I tried to keep the woods from burning. At least I managed that. When I had the strength, I searched for my car and found it, but it wouldn't start. So I started walking. And here I am."

"I'm grateful that someone found you," Ned said.

John nodded. "Another kind person, just like the old man." He looked at Ned and Eric. "We need to retrieve the old man's body or what's left of it. He needs a proper burial."

Eric frowned. "John, about that old man, you said he never spoke."

"Not a syllable."

"Right," Eric said. "Did he have white hair, blue eyes and a long scar on his right cheek?"

John returned a questioning look. "Yes, did you know him?"

Eric shook his head. "No, I didn't, but a lot of the folks around here have talked about him."

"Why is that?" John asked.

Eric sat back and sighed. "He's been dead for fifty years, but he shows up every now and then when someone wanders into the woods around the old cabin where he lived."

John stood up, frowning. "That can't be right. It had to be someone else. The man I was with—" He rubbed his forehead, trying to get his mind working. It was blanking out. "What's happening? Am I going crazy too?"

Ned was on his feet too, taking John's arm. "Dad, calm down."

John felt his chest heaving, and his legs wanted to buckle. He couldn't think or help himself. Instead, he had flashes of being in the burning shack, fighting the fire, fighting for his life. He wasn't able to breathe.

The flashes turned into a vivid vision. The old man appeared in the midst of the smoke and flames, smiling at him. His father was there too, standing over him with a strap in his hand. "I love you, John. No matter what, I love you."

In that moment, he became a child again, trembling in his father's arms, not knowing what to believe.

"Dad, we'll get through this," someone said.

When he looked up, he saw Ned. Ned was still holding onto him, trying to keep him on his feet.

Fifty-Two

MATTHEW WONDERED HOW Eric had convinced him to tramp around in the woods. His day had started out perfectly fine. He'd been enjoying time with Lea and Jacob. Jacob was excited about some of Eric's old toys that Margaret brought over, and Matthew and Lea were happy too. They cuddled on the sofa, watching Jacob play with some wooden blocks. For the time being, the little boy was safe in their care.

Around ten, Eric called and asked for Matthew's help. He shouldn't have agreed to Eric's proposal. He was willing to assist with the clinic, but this was a different matter. He was out in the middle of nowhere, trudging through the woods, and they weren't the nice kind of woods one thought of when they imagined a pristine forest. The undergrowth was thick, with fallen trees and branches everywhere.

Matthew didn't know how long he'd been following Eric through the tangle, only that Eric claimed to know where he was going. Matthew was starting to doubt it. "How much further do we have to go? And tell me again, why do we have to find this cabin John supposedly burned down."

Eric was a few yards ahead and glanced back at him. "It's important. John thinks he's losing it. We have to determine how much of his story is true."

"Maybe John is crazy. He thinks he had dinner with a ghost."

"We found his car," Eric said. "At least that much of his story is factual."

Matthew tripped on some decaying wood, swore softly and kept going. "I can understand why he looked like he did. A person could break a leg traipsing through these woods."

"That wouldn't account for his burns."

"So why do you think you know where this old man's cabin is?"

Eric got up on the stump of a tree that had been cut down and scanned the area. "As a boy, I explored whenever I could. I remember going into that cabin a number of times. Then I heard the stories about a ghost hanging around the place and got scared." He looked at Matthew and waved him forward. "Come on, I think I see the clearing where the cabin was."

A small branch sprung back and caught Matthew's cheek. He squinted and rubbed at his smarting face. "Why did I have to come along? Couldn't you have taken Ned?"

"Ned won't budge from his father's side. He told me he thought Elkville was cursed. Teresa and I reassured him that he was overreacting, but then John had a bad setback. Now, Ned's all spooked again."

"John Finney and his son both flip out too easily."

"Maybe so. That's why you're here, Matthew. You can help me find out what's really going on with John's story."

Matthew stopped and scowled. "Hey Eric, did you just say that Ned thinks Elkville's cursed? I haven't thought about that word since we were at the Ferguson's."

Eric turned and looked back. "Cursed is probably too strong a word. Ned's just convinced he has to get his father out of Elkville. But he's not thinking rationally." Eric started walking again. "Hey, good news, we're almost there."

Matthew forced his way through more tangles and thick brush, not daring to have his eyes forward for fear of losing his footing. He had to watch every step he took. When he got through to an area that was easier going, he finally looked up. A charred piece of ground with burned timber and ash lay straight ahead.

"This is it," Eric announced. "This is where the old shack stood."

Matthew caught up with him. "Hell of a burn. It's a good thing the fire didn't spread."

Eric waved him forward. "Let's see if we find the remains of an old man's body."

Matthew pulled back. "No way am I going to walk around in all that ash. I'll ruin my shoes. They're almost new, and they weren't cheap."

"Fine, I'm wearing an old pair," Eric said.

Matthew felt a chill and hunched his shoulders. "Is the wind getting colder?"

Eric stared back. "What wind? There's not a leaf stirring. Now, wait here, and I'll check out what's left of this place."

Matthew watched as Eric walked around what used to be a fireplace wall. When he stooped down and picked up something, Matthew was curious. "What did you find?"

"It's a bowl, but it's chipped."

"Keep moving. You're not looking for chipped dishes," Matthew said. He wanted to be done with the whole idea of old men in shacks and most of all, ghosts.

He leaned over to tighten a shoelace when he felt another chill. He straightened up and scanned his surroundings. A short distance from where he stood, he saw someone headed in the opposite direction. "Hey you! Come back."

The person turned for a brief moment, eyed Matthew with watery, blue eyes and then kept going.

"Eric!" Matthew shouted.

Eric was checking out the coil remains of a mattress. "What is it?"

Matthew pointed just as the man he'd seen was lost in a thicket of trees. "There was someone here."

Eric looked his way. "I didn't see anyone."

Matthew walked into the surrounding woods, moving as quickly as possible, hoping to get a glimpse of the person he'd seen. He was disappointed. If there had been someone around, the heavily treed area hid them from sight. He looked back to Eric. "I called to him, but he wouldn't stop."

Eric stepped out of what had once been a doorway. "Maybe he was hard of hearing or just didn't want to talk." He walked over and waited for Matthew to return to the cleared area. "I'm not a fire expert, but I think this place burned recently."

Matthew joined him. "Did you find anything interesting?"

Eric stared at the dish he was holding. "Nothing that would prove John's story about an old man dying. But I'll take this bowl back. Maybe John will recognize it."

"John Finney's in an agitated state. Maybe when he was out here, he stayed in the cabin, hallucinated and accidentally set it on fire."

"Who knows? So tell me about that person you saw, what did he look like?"

"I only got a brief look, but I'm sure he was old, and he had blue eyes."

"Anything else?" Eric asked.

"White hair. He had white hair."

Eric laughed. "Oh my, Matthew, you just described the ghost that John talked about."

Matthew felt another chill. "I don't want to hear about ghosts."

Eric turned and started walking away from the clearing. "Okay, but I'm telling you that John is no more crazy than you are. So go easy on him if you talk to him about what he saw."

Matthew grumbled to himself as he followed Eric. He'd only gone a couple of yards when he felt someone tap his shoulder. He turned, but there was no one there. What he did see was the actual shack where the ruins had been. In the next moment, it faded from sight. He didn't say anything to Eric. All the talk about ghosts had him seeing things. He had to ignore it all and keep walking.

* * *

Teresa was the person in charge of the clinic while Ned was keeping his father company. Eric and Matthew were on a mission to check out the woods and John's story. The clinic bell dinged, and she looked up as Margaret let herself into the waiting room. She hurried over and gave Margaret a hug. "What a nice surprise."

Margaret smiled and hugged her back. "Thank you, Teresa. You always brighten my day."

"Did you walk all the way over?"

"No, Paul said I could use his truck while he's away."

"It's a nice truck. I've seen it parked in his driveway."

"Very nice," Margaret said. "When my husband was alive, we only had the one car. I drove it to the store and places like that. It was pretty old when he passed. Anyway, I gave it away to a young man who didn't have much and needed transportation. Paul's truck is quite the improvement."

Teresa pointed to the basket. "I see you brought something with you."

"I figured a picnic style lunch might be nice." Margaret leaned in close and lowered her voice to a whisper. "How are the two Finneys doing?"

Teresa whispered back. "Not so good. John is very upset, and Ned isn't taking it well."

"I never found out the latest. Why is John upset? I thought he and Ned were speaking again."

Teresa took Margaret's arm, led her into the waiting area and closed the door. "John claims he parked a couple of miles out of town the morning Ned and he parted company. He was having a very hard time. An old man came out of the woods and invited John to stay with him in this old shack. Unfortunately, the man died the next day, just before his shack burned down."

"An old man came out of the woods?"

"Yes, he had white hair and blue eyes. But Eric says that guy died years ago. Anyway, when John heard that, he started to question his sanity. Eric and Matthew are trying to check out his story."

Margaret's face lost its usual pleasant expression. She put the basket down on a side table and took a seat in one of the chairs.

Teresa quickly sat down next to her. "What is it? You look upset."

"I'm sure that Eric's told you about how guarded his father could be."

"Yes, he did. He was sorry that you were burdened with keeping his secrets."

Margaret put her clasped hands in her lap. "My Ricky meant well, but—"

Teresa smiled. "I think Eric was relieved when the two of you could finally talk about it all."

Margaret looked down and shook her head. "I haven't told Eric everything."

"There's more?"

Margaret nodded. "Yes, there is. When Eric gets back, I need to talk to him, and I want John Finney to hear what I have to say." She looked up. "And you too, Teresa. From now on, I want everything out in the open so we can discuss things as a family."

Teresa grinned. "I love that."

Margaret stood up and grabbed the basket. "Listen, I have to run back to the house. I forgot something. See you in a bit."

Fifty-Three

"DAD, PLEASE TALK to me," Ned said. His father, John, was sitting at the kitchen table, avoiding any conversation. John had told Ned he couldn't tolerate staying in bed any longer. But once he moved locations, he'd gone back to clamming up.

Ned offered a teasing smile. "How about a cup of coffee?"

John shook his head. "No, thank you."

"Juice? Water?"

"No, I'm fine."

"Well, I'm not fine," Ned protested. "I have a million questions and since you're well enough to be up and about, maybe you could answer a few."

John let out a sigh. "Ask away."

"I don't know anything about your childhood. You never shared a thing with me. Why not?"

John's brows narrowed. "You don't share the things I went through with your children, Ned."

"I'm twenty-nine. I think I'm old enough to hear whatever."

"I don't know how to talk about it, but I'll try."

"Tell me about your mother."

"She died when I was born. Different relatives took me in."

Ned tried to imagine what it was like to go from one home to another, never having any stability in one's life.

John continued. "As I got older my father usually had me on weekends. When I was old enough, I stayed with him full time."

Ned cleared his throat. "You said something about your father beating you."

"He was an alcoholic. When he was sober, he was great, but when he drank—"

"I wish I'd known all this sooner."

"Why?"

298

"Because it's a way of you letting me into your life."

"Hearing a bunch of crap?"

"Yes, because I know where you're coming from. Up until now, I've been living in this make believe world where you pretended everything was perfect. But I guess that's the way it is with most people. I talked to Paul Glass—"

"The psychiatrist you told me about?"

"Yes, that's the guy."

"You said he was very helpful."

"At first, until he decided otherwise. When I called him on his actions, like telling me one thing and doing another, he had a heart attack."

"My goodness, Ned. That must have been rough."

"I felt really bad afterwards. I hadn't wanted to hurt anyone. All I wanted was the truth."

John let out a contemptuous chuckle. "The truth isn't an easy thing to pin down. For instance, the truth was that my father beat me. The truth was that he also told me how much he loved me. How does a kid deal with that?"

"What did you do?"

"Nothing. I grew up and got the hell out of my father's house." John looked up and stared at Ned. "You said I didn't want you. And it was true. When I found out Judy was pregnant, I thought my world was ending. I didn't know anything about raising a child. What if I turned out to be like my father? That was such a horrible thought, I didn't know if I could go on. And Judy was probably worse than me. She came from an abusive home, too. After you were born, she hid in her room trying to escape her past and not knowing how to deal with her present. It was a mess. Finally, she left."

Ned huffed out his disappointment. "Eric said I was probably an unexpected pregnancy. Thanks for confirming it."

John sat up straighter and glared back. "Just stop right there, Ned. I thought you said you wanted the truth."

"I do, but—"

"Well, here it is. You weren't a planned child. You came along when I wasn't ready to be a father. But you've turned out to be everything and more than I could have wanted in a son. You're a son that anyone would be proud to have. And this crap about me doing what I did just to be responsible is ridiculous. Sure that was part of it, but I did what I did because I loved you. You were this beautiful little boy that made all the struggle worthwhile."

Ned raised his eyes to meet John's. "Really? You really felt that way?"

"Ned, I feel the same about you now. If anything happened to you—"

"Or you, Dad! You've always been my hero."

John sat back. "I never think of myself that way."

"I wish you'd change your mind."

"My mind? After that episode in the shack, my mind is spinning. You might be looking at a crazy person."

"No, I refuse to believe that."

"So you think my story has some validity?"

Ned shrugged. "I know you experienced something, and I don't believe for a moment that you're crazy. So it's a mystery."

"A mystery that's bugging the heck out of me. Anyway, I appreciate that you wanted to talk about my past. I do feel better. Maybe I will have that cup of coffee you mentioned."

Ned got to his feet and went to the counter. "Coming right up, and maybe you can have a glass of water on the side."

John stared at Ned with an appraising eye and smiled. "It's a deal."

* * *

The ride back to the clinic with Matthew was a little too quiet. Every time Eric looked at his passenger, the man seemed preoccupied. "Are you alright, Matthew?"

"I'm just keeping my thoughts straight after visiting your childhood adventure land. I had a very different kind of childhood. While you were exploring the woods and being scared by ghost stories, I was visiting a library, educating my mind."

"Nature can be more soothing than a library if you give it a chance. Those woods we just visited might be a little much, but I often found other areas that were very meditative."

"I'll have to take your word on that."

The remainder of the ride to town was quiet. Eric spent the time reminiscing. No matter how Matthew felt, he was happy that he hadn't spent his time in a library as a child. His best memories were about being in the outdoors, experiencing the solace of open skies, fresh air and the shade of trees in summer.

Once they arrived back at the clinic, he noticed Paul's truck in the parking lot. "Looks like my mom is here," he said.

Matthew unfastened his seatbelt. "I bet she likes driving that fancy truck of Paul's."

"Let's see if she's brought any goodies over."

Matthew patted his mid-section. "I've had enough of her goodies. I'm putting on weight."

Eric opened his door and started to get out. "If she has brought us something delicious, does that mean you don't want any?"

Matthew opened his door and scowled. "I have to draw the line somewhere. I might as well start now. Besides, I'll only stay long enough to talk with John Finney. After that, I'll get back to Lea and Jacob."

Eric closed the car door. "Let's be careful when we talk with John."

"You're right. The Finneys take the cake when it comes to emotional meltdowns."

"We all have buttons that can trigger our feelings."

"You have a point," Matthew said. "You're proof of that."

"One time," Eric said forcefully. "I lost it once at the Ferguson's."

Matthew paused. "Wait a second. What about the time you visited your dad's grave and went off to the mountain? You wrecked your car and nearly froze to death."

Eric ignored Matthew's remark and headed for the clinic. He was sure the surgeon had experienced something scary in the woods. Teasing someone else probably helped to keep him from thinking about his fears.

Once they were inside the building, Teresa was quick to greet them. "Guess what, Eric! Your mom has made a picnic lunch for everyone. She brought over fried chicken, potato salad, fresh rolls and a peach cobbler for dessert." She looked at Matthew. "You're invited too. I called Lea and asked if she wanted to come, but she said she and Jacob had an early lunch because Jacob couldn't wait. But she said you should stay and enjoy yourself."

Eric smiled. "Matthew can't. He's trying to diet, so—"

Matthew sucked in his gut. "Never mind, Eric. I'll start tomorrow. I'm starving after hiking for miles in that hellish place you dragged me through."

"Miles?" Eric objected. "I don't think so."

Teresa hugged Matthew's arm and gave it a squeeze. "Sounds like a tasty lunch will do you good."

"Thanks, Teresa," Matthew grumbled. "No matter what your husband says, that woods was designed by the devil himself."

Eric ignored him. "Where are we going to eat?" he asked. "The kitchen table only seats four."

"Margaret thought of that," Teresa said. "She brought along a card table we can use for an extension. She's thought of everything."

Eric's eyes lit up. "That's my mom," he said proudly.

Fifty-Four

AFTER LUNCH, MARGARET sat drinking her iced tea and smiling. Once again, she'd provided a meal that everyone enjoyed. The two Finneys, Teresa and Eric, and Matthew were all looking very satisfied.

John Finney lifted his glass in a toast. "To Margaret, I've never tasted her cooking before, and I didn't know what I was missing. Now I acknowledge her as a true genius in the kitchen."

Margaret blushed as everyone lifted their glasses and nodded their agreement. "Thank you, John. With that kind of compliment, you have a standing invitation to share whatever I make in the future."

Ned nudged his father. "Good going, Dad. Now, I'm counting on you to take me along if you attend one of Margaret's feasts."

John raised his chin. "Perhaps I will if you behave yourself."

Everyone laughed and Margaret used the moment of levity to breach a touchy subject. When she gingerly tapped her glass with a spoon, everyone looked her way. "Excuse me, but I'd like to share something with all of you now." She looked at Eric. "Sorry, my dear boy, but I probably should have talked to you about this subject some time ago, but it didn't seem necessary until now."

"What's this about?" Eric asked.

Margaret looked at John Finney. "John, I know you recently had an experience that made you wonder."

John lost his smile and nodded. "You're certainly right about that."

"Well, I might have a story that makes you feel better. It's about Eric's dad. He had an experience too."

Matthew had been blissfully leaned back in his chair, but he sat up and targeted Margaret with intense eyes. "You're not going to talk about a ghost, are you?"

"I'm going to tell everyone about a person who helped my Ricky. It happened a long time ago, when Eric was still a baby."

"Yes," Matthew said, "but does it have something to do with an apparition?"

Teresa had been sitting quietly, holding Eric's hand, but she looked at Matthew with pleading eyes. "Please, Matthew," she said, "can you ask your questions after Mom finishes. I'm so interested in Eric's family history."

Matthew sat back and crossed his arms. "Sorry, Margaret, please proceed."

Margaret smiled at Matthew and Teresa. "As I was saying, Eric's father was out in a terrible snowstorm, and his car broke down a couple of miles out of town. Now, my Ricky was a stubborn man, and he was determined to get himself, and our car back home. So he started pushing it and trying to steer at the same time. Needless to say, it wasn't easy. The roads were slippery. Still, he was proud of himself. He told me he did quite well going downhill. It was the dips and rise in the road that were the problem. Just when he was getting too tired to keep going, a man came out of nowhere and offered to help him. Ricky was very grateful, but the stranger was old, and Ricky didn't think the man would be much help. He was wrong. The old man did such a good job pushing, they got the car back to Elkville. Then the old man disappeared."

"Did Dad find out who he was?" Eric asked.

"He tried to ask around," Margaret said. "In fact, he was quite adamant about getting some information at the general store. That's when all the old timers who hung out there started laughing at him. They insisted he'd seen a person by the name of Callum. The problem was that Callum had died years before. Ricky was accused of asking about a ghost. Ricky came home incensed. He was so angry, that he forbade me to ever talk about the incident again."

John clasped his hands on the table. "Do you think the man your husband saw might have been the man I saw?"

"Ricky said the man had a long, distinctive scar on his cheek," Margaret said. "But there's more to the story. Later, when Ricky got his medical bag out of the car, he found something inside. It was an old cracked, china cup. Of course, Ricky wanted nothing to do with it and told me to throw it out. But I couldn't. I hid it way back in the top of one of the cupboards."

John shook his head. "Your husband made house calls. Maybe one of his patients put it there."

"Perhaps, you're right," Margaret said. "But I brought it along to show it to everyone." She looked at Eric. "It's in the picnic hamper, Eric. Would you get it for me?"

"Sure." Eric looked at Matthew. "While I'm getting it, Matthew can get the piece of china I found at the cabin."

Matthew stood up reluctantly and started for the hall. "If you insist."

Eric immediately went to the picnic hamper and retrieved a wrapped object. He held it out to Margaret. "Is this what you want?"

Margaret took the wrapped piece and held it close. "I'm still grateful to that kind, old man who helped my Ricky get home. Goodness knows what might have happened if he hadn't come along. But before I unwrap the cup, let's wait for Matthew."

Matthew came in a minute later. "Here you go, Eric, one chipped bowl."

John let out a gasp. "Good lord, that's the bowl the old man used for the soup he gave me."

Matthew grunted. "How can you tell?"

"Look at the style and pattern," John said. "I'd never seen anything like it before."

Margaret bit her lip. "Oh, John, I can't believe it," she said as tears ran down her cheeks.

"What is it, Mom? Why are you crying?" Eric asked.

Margaret unwrapped what she'd been holding. She held it up so that everyone could see it.

Eric grabbed the cup and held it next to the bowl. "They're part of the same set."

"Eric, you never told me what you found when you checked out my story," John said.

"I found your car and the shack. I found the dish when I was walking around in the remains," Eric said. "However, there was no body."

"I see," John said. "Thanks anyway, Eric."

Matthew came over and examined both pieces carefully and handed them back to Eric. "Whatever, I need to get back home."

"But Matthew, didn't you say you saw an old man in the woods?" Eric asked.

Teresa's eyes widened. "You saw someone?"

Matthew moaned as he wandered back to his seat and sat down. "This is exactly why I never wanted to come back to Elkville. It's always something with this place."

The entrance bell rang out as Matthew was complaining. A cry of distress followed. "Help me!"

"That's Mary," Matthew said as he jumped up and ran to the front of the clinic. Eric, Teresa and Ned followed him.

* * *

Matthew's heart sunk when he saw Mary. She was standing in the treatment room with blood all over her hands and clothes. He quickly ran over to where she stood. "Are you hurt?"

"It's Pa!" she cried.

Eric was already running past them to the outer door. Matthew gave Mary an order to stay put and followed Eric outside. Ned was close behind them. Mary's truck was half parked on the sidewalk with the driver's side door open. The cab was empty. Everyone ran to the back of the truck. Mary's father was sprawled out on the bed with his wife lying over him. Blood was pooled around the couple. Eric quickly put the tailgate down, and Matthew and Ned were able to jump up and onto the truck bed.

After that, Matthew, Eric and Ned worked as a team and were able to stabilize the injured man's condition. Fortunately, his wife had put enough pressure on his wound to keep him from bleeding to death. However, her help had cost her the little energy the very sick woman had to keep going. She was in bad shape herself. Once, both people were able to be moved, Ned and Eric had decided it best to take the couple to a hospital in Blacksburg.

Matthew was left behind to try to help Mary. A victim of the trauma she'd been privy to, she wasn't doing well. At first, Margaret and Teresa were able to tend to the young woman. Mary didn't say a word. She allowed them to help her wash up and change into one of the extra tops that Teresa kept at the clinic. Afterwards, she retreated into herself completely. Backed off into the same corner that Jacob had used to hide himself, she shook more violently when either Margaret or Teresa approached.

Looking at her, Matthew could see Mary's resemblance to Jacob. But in Mary's case, he knew that a cookie wasn't going to help. And he did want to do something to reach her. Maybe it was because he'd gotten to know Mary a little and sensed her integrity. Maybe it was because she'd looked out for her brother and had taken steps to protect him. No matter, Matthew felt he needed to be there for her.

With Teresa and Margaret stationed on the other side of the room, Matthew walked over to where Mary stood, but he kept some distance between them. "Mary, we're taking care of your parents. They're both going to get the help they need."

Mary took in a quick, ragged breath but didn't look at him.

Matthew had a sudden idea, sort of an alternate "cookie" idea. "Mary, would you like to come home with me? Jacob and Lea are there. You can stay with us until you feel better."

Mary continued to stare at the floor for a long moment. Finally, barely looking up, she ran to Matthew and threw herself in his arms.

"Shouldn't have run off!" she cried.

Matthew didn't know what to do, so he did the only thing he could. He held her like he'd held Jacob. She was frail and shaking so hard that her teeth chattered. "It's going to be okay, Mary."

"No," Mary sobbed. "I shouldn't have run. Should've stayed put."

"Stayed where?"

Mary pulled away and clasped her arms around herself. "With Ma! But my pa tried to, to—"

Matthew instantly understood what Mary had gone through. "You mean your father tried—"

Mary nodded. "I run from the cabin and hid, but then I heard Pa scream. He been drinkin' all morning and must have gone after Ma." Mary swallowed hard and swiped at her tears. "Ma had her knife ready."

Matthew came over and held Mary again. "It's not your fault, Mary. You did your best."

When Mary calmed down a little, Matthew waved Margaret over. "Margaret, would you call Lea and tell her we're going to have another guest staying with us."

Mary looked up at him with fresh tears. "I promise I won't be no bother." She hesitated again. "Me brothers and sisters. I have to go back home."

Matthew frowned. "How many are you talking about?"

"Four still left with Ma and Pa," Mary said.

Margaret hurried over and took a tissue out of her pocket. She patted down Mary's wet cheeks. "Mary, if they need a place, they can stay with me."

Teresa rushed over. "I'll help, too."

Mary backed out of Matthew's arms, looked down and nodded. "I can't stop bawlin'."

Margaret put her arm around Mary's shoulders. "Come on, dear girl, let's go to Matthew's house. We'll sort it out there. Then, we'll get your family settled too."

* * *

John walked into the treatment area as Teresa was saying goodbye to Mary, Margaret and Matthew. "Quite a lot going on. I didn't want to be in the way, but I couldn't help but watch what was happening. That man with the stab wound was very lucky to have all of you there for him."

"It's surprising how quickly today went from a pleasant lunch to a life and death situation." Teresa paused. "How are you doing, John?"

"I'm feeling better physically, and hearing Margaret's story about her husband and seeing the china helped to ease my mind a little."

"No matter what, you saved the woods. Eric said there could have been quite a fire if you hadn't put out the sparks from the burning shack."

John leaned heavily on a counter. "Yes, but I might be the one responsible for the shack burning in the first place."

Teresa gestured him towards the hall. "You're tired. Come and lay down. We can talk while you're resting."

Once John was in bed, he realized Teresa was right. He'd been up since early morning, and his body was feeling worn again. "Teresa, I'm worried about Ned. How is he going to run this place on his own once you and Eric leave?"

Teresa smiled. "We've promised to stay as long as necessary. Plus, Raymond Ferguson said he'd find help for Ned."

"I watched my son with that injured man, how calm and competent he can be. That's the Ned I always knew before all the turmoil started."

"If you don't mind me asking, how are you two doing now?"

"It's strange, but maybe Ned's anger and outrage were what was needed. His behavior got me out here, and we've started talking about all the stuff I tried not to share. I don't have to pretend I'm a super dad anymore. I can come clean with Ned, faults and all."

Fifty-Five

WITH THE MOUNTAIN road winding upwards, Eric was happy to be returning to Elkville. He missed Teresa. They'd grown even closer after spending almost all their time together recently. After a long day, he was looking forward to a relaxing evening. He glanced over at Ned. The young doctor was at the wheel as they returned from Blacksburg. "Are you sure you don't want me to drive, Ned? You look tired"

Ned chuckled and shook his head. "Now why would you ask me something like that when you know I'm the better driver under the circumstances?"

"Look who's very full of himself?" Eric said.

"Sorry, but it's true. You've had a couple of close calls, remember?"

"Under extreme circumstances," Eric said. "But I've been driving these roads since I was old enough to reach the pedals and see over the steering wheel."

"Is that so?"

"When my father was exhausted, he trusted me to get us to the next call while he dozed."

"Your father sounds like he could make some reckless decisions. First, he's taking a child along, and then he's using them as a chauffeur."

"Are you deliberately trying to aggravate me?" Eric asked.

"I'm just expressing my feelings like you and Teresa suggested."

"That doesn't mean you go around criticizing people and situations that you know nothing about."

"Don't get all upset. I'm being honest, but I guess you don't want to discuss the truth. Neither did Paul Glass. Talking to him was a total disaster. So I suppose I'll have to keep my thoughts to myself."

"I'd advise you to try," Eric said.

310

"I think you're angry at me."

"Not angry, just tired of your crap."

"My crap?" Ned objected.

Eric stared at Ned with waning patience. "You're not that much younger than I am, but I swear, sometimes I don't think you have a clue about how to conduct yourself."

"I knew exactly how to conduct myself until I ran into the likes of you and Matthew."

"And how was that?"

"I kept everything to myself. That way people never had to hear anything they didn't want to hear. But you and Matthew made it clear that a person could say whatever, and it was fine."

Eric remained quiet. He felt as tired as Ned looked. Getting Mary's father and mother to Blacksburg had taken constant monitoring on his part. It was especially difficult when the father had started to regain consciousness and began fighting Eric's efforts. Then there was the mother. Besides being sick, she was in a panic-stricken state, and he had to constantly reassure her. While Ned was driving, he'd been holding down the fort in the back of an old borrowed van. It was a less than ideal way of transporting a patient, but there weren't any other options at the moment. It was an issue that Raymond Ferguson needed to address.

"Hey, are you okay?" Ned asked.

"Yes," Eric grumbled.

"Then tell me why you made that wisecrack about my conduct."

"Let it go, Ned. Like you said, Matthew and I are the problem, not you."

"You're being very sarcastic," Ned complained.

When Eric didn't answer, Ned seemed determined to engage in conversation. "By the way, you did a decent job with those two we had to get to Blacksburg."

Eric was almost tempted to comment on Ned's reference to Mary's mother and father as "those two." Although Ned couldn't have been more capable when it came to their medical needs, he didn't seem to relate to his patients on a deeper level of caring. Still, it wasn't Eric's job to judge the man so he kept his mouth shut.

"Do you know you're scowling?" Ned asked.

Obviously, Eric's thoughts about Ned were coming across with his body language. "Can we stop talking about me? Just drive."

Ned wasn't content to let Eric's comments go unanswered. When they got to a pullover in the road, Ned did just that, he pulled the van over.

Eric sat up and looked around. "What's going on?"

"You don't like me, do you?" Ned asked in a sullen tone.

"You stopped the van to ask me that?"

"Yes."

"What difference does it make, Ned? You love yourself enough for both of us."

"That's unfair. You don't know me!"

Eric put his seat back, shut his eyes and refused to reply.

Ned started the van and got it back on the road. "I'm sorry, Eric. I mean it. After what happened with my dad, I realize I don't know much about interacting on a personal level. I'd like you to help me figure things out."

Eric put the seat up and stared back. "You think you're ready to hear what I have to say?"

* * *

Ned gripped the steering wheel a little tighter. Eric had asked him a question. Did Ned actually want to know what Eric thought? He'd recently begun to interact in a whole new way. He said what he thought. Unfortunately, he'd been dismayed with the results most of the time.

There had been some positives. His father had come clean about his background. That was good, but Ned could tell Eric's thoughts might be about Ned's character. His father told him how great he was. Was his dad right? Ned's recent "tell it like it is" had nearly destroyed his father. The usually, rock-steady man floundered. Now, he was physically hurting and even seeing ghosts.

Ned gathered up his courage and glanced at Eric. He had to find out what the man thought. "I'm ready," he said.

When Eric spoke, his voice was soft and didn't have the edge like it had earlier in their conversation. "Let's get something straight about what I think. You're not at fault, Ned. You were brought up a certain way and your personality was created around what you believed. The problem I see is that you became so concerned about yourself that other people's feelings weren't acknowledged."

Ned stiffened. "From what I've observed, everyone is primarily concerned with their own interests."

"That's exactly right. Most people are. But if you want more from your life than satisfying your ego, you have to go beyond that kind of system. Being compassionate and able to relate to what others are going through makes you a much more caring human being."

"But what's the point?"

"Are you asking what you get out of it?"

"Yes, I guess I am."

"Perhaps you'll get that relationship you talked about."

Ned grimaced. "How do I become the compassionate, caring person you're describing?"

"You start by practicing on yourself."

"I thought you said I'm already in love with myself."

"From an ego standpoint, you are basically selfish. We all are. But I'm talking about loving yourself like you did little Jacob when you held him. He didn't have to be a successful doctor for you to care about him, did he?"

Ned thought about holding the little boy. He only wanted the best for the child, and he'd do whatever he could to make that happen. "Jacob was a surprise. I never expected to feel the way I did."

"When you can embrace the little kid inside of you the same way, it changes how you see others. That's when understanding and wisdom kick in."

"So, Eric, do you like the kid inside of you?"

Eric laughed. "I'm working on it."

"So it's no easy fix."

"I'm afraid not."

"I'm concerned about my dad. He's convinced he saw a person at that shack. I know Margaret came up with the story of a ghost, but the whole thing is still iffy. What if my father is mentally unbalanced?"

Before Eric answered, a deer jumped out of the brush and ran across the road, directly in the path of the van. Ned did a sharp turn of the wheel to avoid it. Time slowed as the van headed towards the shoulder. He was sure he wasn't going to be able to correct in time, but by some miracle, he avoided crashing down the deep embankment.

When he stopped the vehicle, his heart was pounding and his body was shaking. "Damn, that was close!"

Eric had his hand braced against the dash. "It was," he gasped.

After they were both able to breathe a little easier, Ned looked at Eric. "I know vehicles and what to expect when I perform certain actions. In this case, I don't know how I managed to stay on the road."

Eric shrugged. "Some things you just can't explain."

"What are you trying to tell me? Are you saying that you believe that story about the old man?"

"I've witnessed a lot of strange stuff," Eric said. "None of it has a rational explanation, but I've learned to have an open mind."

Fifty-Six

NED WAS PRESSED into babysitting duty. On the day after his trip to a Blacksburg hospital with Jacob's injured and sick parents, he was going to watch Jacob. Taking care of a child wasn't something he felt comfortable with, but what could he do? Mary had retrieved her four siblings from their home in the mountains. Now they were all staying in Elkville, and everyone was helping out.

Paul had offered his house as a place of shelter for the group. When Margaret told the psychiatrist about the situation, he insisted that he wanted to do whatever he could. It seemed like a better solution than the group bunking out at Margaret's. Paul's newly remodeled house had bigger bedrooms, a smart kitchen and plenty of food in the cupboards.

Eric and Teresa, along with Margaret, had assumed child care at Paul's house. They were caring for Mary's brother and three sisters. The children ranged in ages from eight to thirteen years. Eric was trying to cope with the oldest, a boy named Brody. The teenager had a standoffish attitude, but he could get aggressive if he didn't want to cooperate. His sisters, Josie, Lucy and Sadie were very shy, and Teresa and Margaret were working with them.

Mary, Lea and Matthew had to drive to Blacksburg. They wanted to get clothes for all the children, along with some other much needed supplies. They also wanted to stop at the hospital to check on Mary's parents. They wanted to visit Mary's aunt too. Mary needed to explain the family situation to her and see if her aunt had any ideas about what to do.

However, Lea and Matthew didn't want to take Jacob along since he might be overwhelmed with the city and extensive shopping. Since Jacob didn't get along well with his siblings, Ned was asked to care for him. If anyone came into the clinic, his dad could be his assistant. His burns were healing nicely, and he was doing very well.

It seemed like a straight-forward plan. And if Ned really thought about it, he was relieved that he didn't have Teresa and Eric's job, dealing with four, wary children. But he knew little Jacob, and the child liked Ned. How hard could it be to entertain him?

Everything was going well when Matthew brought Jacob to the clinic. The little boy walked into the waiting area, holding Matthew's hand. He seemed quite pleased with himself when Ned crouched down and told him how handsome he looked. The trouble started when Matthew delivered his news. He told Jacob that he was to stay with Ned. The announcement didn't go over well. Matthew's parting words to Ned, "Just hang in there," were lost to Jacob's screams of alarm. Ned had to hold him back when he tried to bolt out the door in pursuit of Matthew.

Ned hoped that the little boy would calm down once Matthew's vehicle disappeared out of the parking lot. The opposite happened. Jacob started running around the clinic, crying out in panic. His movements were haphazard as if he didn't know which way to go. Ned pursued the child, trying to use words of comfort to slow him down.

Jacob paid him no attention. As his panic escalated, his eyes overflowed with tears, and he continued dashing about the area. Not watching where he was going, he ran into a cabinet and bounced off. He fell to the floor and shrieked out in pain.

Ned was used to the chaos that could occur in the ER, but this was different. Matthew Howell trusted Ned to keep Jacob safe. But two minutes after Matthew left, the child was sitting in a heap of tears.

"Dad!" Ned yelled out for his father who had excused himself to take a nap. "Dad, get in here!"

John came running in with earbuds still attached. "I was listening to music," he explained. "What happened?"

Ned crouched down next to Jacob and scooped him up off the floor. The boy was still crying, but in a dazed sort of way. "He went ballistic as soon as Matthew left. Then he ran into a cabinet."

John hurried over. "Oh my, he has quite a bump. I'll get some ice."

Ned did his best to remember what Eric had said about soothing a child, but his mind blanked. When he tried to get a better look at Jacob's forehead, Jacob didn't make it easy. He had his head half buried in Ned's shoulder. With Jacob's tears wetting Ned's shirt, Ned could only hope the boy hadn't seriously injured himself.

John came running back in with a bag of frozen vegetables. "Give him to me, and you can put these peas on that bump," he instructed.

Ned did as he was told, relieved that his father had some experience with raising a child, namely him. Once he'd transferred his burden to his father's arms, Ned watched the ease with which his father handled Jacob. Gently swaying from side to side, the older man began to sing a children's tune. Ned vaguely remembered hearing it before. It seemed to help Jacob settle a little. Ned was able to apply the frozen peas to Jacob's forehead and questioned his father. "I didn't know you could sing."

John's face brightened with a sheepish grin. "I haven't since you were in diapers. But it felt like the right thing to do. By the way, did you ever get your watch back?"

Ned nodded. "Finally, yes."

"Go get it, son. Jacob needs something to distract him while you make sure he's alright."

"Are you sure? Matthew left some toys for him. Wouldn't one of those be better?"

"Nice idea, but Jacob needs something more than a toy. You better get your watch."

Ned started for his bedroom. When he found out he was babysitting Jacob, he'd deliberately not worn the timepiece. Why tempt the child when it was clear how much Jacob coveted it. Matthew told him that it took a real fight to get Jacob to relinquish his prize. But Ned had no choice but to give it to the child again.

After Ned had a chance to examine Jacob thoroughly, he felt better. With the little boy basically intact and showing no signs of real damage, Ned could breathe easier. He sat in his office chair going over paperwork with Jacob on his lap. On a positive note, Jacob wasn't panicked over Matthew leaving anymore. He had Ned's watch to occupy him.

John came in to check on them. "How's everything going?"

Ned shrugged. "I'm just hoping that Matthew doesn't have a problem when he sees Jacob's head. I had the kid for two minutes, and he practically knocked himself out."

"That's children, Ned. Anyway, since you don't need me, I'll go take that nap."

"Dad, I might need you to take Jacob if someone comes into the clinic."

"You've got it, son. I'll be just a few feet away."

Ned watched his father leave and let out a heavy exhale. He pondered his morning so far and came up with a conclusion. Babysitters were definitely an underpaid and unappreciated group of people. He'd remember that if he ever had children of his own.

As the hours passed, Ned's father never got the nap he wanted. A number of people came into the clinic, and Ned had to ask his father to care for Jacob. When he had a chance to look in on them, John was sitting in a chair, holding Jacob, and reading him a book that Matthew brought along. Again, Ned had vague memories. He didn't only remember being sung a nursery song, he had also been read to. It made him wonder why he'd forgotten so many good times with his dad. Then it hit him. He'd had so many good times that he'd taken them for granted.

When it was lunchtime, Ned closed the clinic and made some sandwiches. After he announced that their food was ready, John and Jacob came into the kitchen together. Jacob was hanging on to John's hand. "So what have you two been up to?" Ned asked.

John looked at Jacob instead of answering. "Tell Ned what we've been doing, Jacob."

Jacob looked down shyly, then spoke up. "Bidding bocks."

"Yes," John said. "We've been building with blocks."

Jacob approached Ned and tugged on his pants leg. With misty eyes and a trembling lip, he suddenly turned sober.

Ned crouched down. "What is it, Jacob?"

"Want Pa," Jacob cried out in a demanding tone.

"Sorry, but Matthew won't be back until later."

Jacob backed up and repeated his request in a high-pitched wail. "Want Pa!"

When Ned shook his head, Jacob turned and ran for the clinic entrance.

Ned and John caught up with the little boy as he was trying to open the entrance door. Ned looked at his father. "I thought he might have forgotten about Matthew."

John shrugged. "No, I'm afraid not, but maybe lunch will cheer him up."

Jacob kept tugging at the door knob. "Want Pa!"

318

Ned picked Jacob up and tried to explain things to him. "You'll see Matthew later, but for now, you have to stay here with us."

Jacob let Ned know it was the wrong answer. He struggled in Ned's arms. After a moment, he got frustrated and started to wail out his unhappiness.

Ned looked at his father. "What should I do?"

"He looks tired, and when kids get tired, they can be cranky," John said. "Maybe that's why he thought of Matthew. Matthew is his security person."

"Where's that watch, Dad? Maybe it will help?"

"I don't know. Jacob had it, but I don't remember seeing it for a while. He must have put it down somewhere. Or—"

"Or what?"

John crossed his arms. "Or he might have hid it when I left the room to use the facilities. He's a very smart boy, just like someone else I know."

Ned had to ignore the idea that his watch was missing. He had more pressing problems. Jacob was crying harder and struggling again. He didn't dare set the boy down. Jacob didn't need a second bump on the head. "Dad, think of something else we can give him!"

"I don't know what to tell you, Ned. I can't think of anything. All I can say is that it might be a long afternoon."

Jacob's helpless cries were starting to cause Ned's fears to escalate. He'd worked so hard to be a take-charge doctor, but he didn't know how to ease Jacob's misery. He looked at his father again. "You take him, and I'll find something to make him stop crying."

"Okay, but Ned, it's going to be alright. This is just what children do sometimes. They get upset and cry."

"Did I cry like Jacob?"

"Of course."

Ned started his search for something to calm Jacob, all the while thinking about what his dad had faced as he tried to take care of a baby and wife. With Jacob's loud crying filling the clinic with sounds of woe, his father was starting to look like more of a hero than ever.

Fifty-Seven

BY THE TIME Matthew got back to Elkville, he'd had quite the day. It had been one he'd long remember no matter how much he wanted to forget it.

Mary and Lea hit it off beautifully, and Mary, the shy, introverted young woman turned out to have more to say than Matthew thought possible. Mary didn't talk to Matthew directly. The conversation was between his wife and Mary. His job was to drive the vehicle they were in and listen to their exchange.

Lea seemed to have endless questions, and Mary had endless answers. By the time they completed the trip to Blacksburg, Matthew knew everything about Mary's family. He'd been privy to the story of how her parents met and married, how the father started drinking and the mother became more bitter with the birth of each child. The lives of all twelve children had been laid out. The vivid details that Mary included made Matthew wonder how any of the children survived some of the harsh conditions they'd lived through.

In one way, it was fascinating that Mary could be such a databank of information. Matthew ended up knowing more about her family history than he knew about his own.

Once they arrived in Blacksburg, they visited Mary's aunt. She was well schooled in conversation too. When Matthew, Lea and Mary showed up at her door, she'd been delighted. She seated them in her living room and insisted that Mary bring her up to date on all that was happening. Comments were passed back and forth as time dragged on and on. Matthew had nodded off several times, but Lea kept waking him up and giving him that "don't be rude" look.

After the visit to Mary's aunt, they stopped at the hospital to see Mary's parents. Mary's father didn't want to see them, but Mary's mother allowed a short visit. After meeting with Lea and Matthew briefly, she made it clear that she wanted to talk to Mary alone. Matthew had no objections. He was knee deep in information overload and was content to wait in the visitor area with Lea.

Lunch helped a little, but after a quick bite, the shopping began. Lea couldn't have been more enthusiastic about purchasing whatever was deemed necessary for Mary and her family. Mary was extremely appreciative, which was very nice, but Matthew didn't know how he managed to carry all the bags from one store to the other. If he thought tramping through the woods was bad, the endless journey through a good-size mall was worse. At some point, he allowed his mind to go numb. It was a mercy move that helped him to hang in there when he was tempted to give up his will to live.

The conversation between Mary and Lea on the return trip was a recap of the day. Their visit to the hospital to check on Mary's parents was one of the first topics they went over. Happily, it was agreed that the parents were getting the care they needed. But neither of them was in good shape, and Mary was worried about their future. Lea listened to Mary's concern and encouraged Mary to give herself a break and indulge in a little self-care while her parents were away. It seemed to work. Mary perked up a bit.

When that subject had been sufficiently aired, more cheerful ones were brought up. Bits and pieces about the family were rehashed. Mary's aunt and Mary's stay with her was a cause for banter, as was the mall outing and what had been purchased and where.

When they arrived in Elkville, Matthew realized that he'd hardly thought about the drive through the mountains. With all its ups and downs, winding roads and scary drop-offs, the trip had once felt almost traumatic, but with Lea and Mary's constant conversation never letting up for more than a few seconds, Matthew's mind had switched to autopilot. He pulled up in front of Paul's house, turned off the car engine and was shocked to know he'd driven home at all.

He sat in the driver seat after Lea and Mary got out. He hoped to remain there until he regained some sense of himself, but it wasn't to be. Lea's smiling face on the other side of the window and the little tapping sound she made on the glass told him he had to unload the car.

He accomplished the task and was about to go home and take a hot shower when Lea reminded him of one small detail he'd forgotten. He had to pick up Jacob at the clinic.

Instead of feeling even more exhausted by his next errand, Matthew brightened a little. He almost managed to smile when he thought about seeing the child again. He'd tried his best to keep some emotional distance, and he constantly reminded himself that he wasn't Jacob's father. But it was impossible not to think of him as an important part of his life.

By the time he got to the clinic, the day's events were slipping away. He was even looking forward to the evening ahead, one that he'd spend with Lea and Jacob. When he entered the clinic, he didn't see anyone. Everything was quiet. He quickly walked to the back and checked the kitchen. That's when he heard Ned's voice and headed to Ned's room. When he got there and looked in, he smiled. Ned and John were sitting on the floor with Jacob standing in front of them. He had his back to Matthew.

Matthew didn't want to frighten the child, so he called to him in a quiet voice. "Jacob?"

Jacob turned around and instantly shouted out one word. "Pa!"

In the next instant, Jacob was running towards him with arms outstretched. "Pa!"

Matthew smiled and picked him up. "How's my young man?"

Jacob hugged him tight, but his show of affection didn't last long. Jacob pulled back and shouted out his news. "Techsope!"

Matthew quickly noticed that Jacob had a stethoscope around his neck. "So how did you get this?"

Ned and John were on their feet and coming over to where Matthew was standing.

"Good to see you back, Matthew," Ned said.

Jacob squirmed in Matthew's arms. It was his way of indicating he wanted to be put down. Once he was on his own two feet, he looked up at Matthew and started to pull on his pant leg.

"He wants you to sit down, Matthew," John said with a grin.

"On the floor?" Matthew complained, but when Jacob continued to yank on his pant leg, he reluctantly settled down on the carpet. When he looked up, he was eye to eye with Jacob, a very serious Jacob.

Matthew felt the weariness of the day returning. "What now?" he asked.

Jacob wasn't fazed by Matthew's lack of enthusiasm. Taking on the role of a physician, he put the stethoscope's earpieces in his ears and pulled on Matthew's shirt.

"He gets quite insistent if you don't do as he wants," Ned said.

Matthew scowled. "What's that?"

"He wants to listen to your heart," John said.

Matthew was surprised by the idea, but he unbuttoned his shirt and allowed Jacob to proceed. He even started to worry a little when Jacob moved the scope around with a grimace on his face.

Finally, Jacob removed the earpieces and delivered his report. "Too fass, Pa."

Ned and John both started laughing.

Matthew looked up with a frown. "What's going on here?"

"Looks like we have a future doctor in our midst," Ned explained.

Matthew couldn't help but smile too. If Ned was right, he was quite sure Jacob would take his craft seriously. His smile slipped away when he noticed Jacob's forehead. He ran a finger over the injured area. "How did he get this bump?" he demanded.

Jacob pushed Matthew's hand away and backed up. "I fine," he announced. "I 'ungry."

Matthew got to his feet, picked Jacob up and shook his head. "I guess it's time to go home and feed you."

Ned walked Matthew to the door. "I wouldn't try to take that stethoscope away from him. Once I gave it to him, he liked it even more than my watch." Ned paused and sighed. "I hope I find it one of these days."

"What happened to your watch?" Matthew asked.

"Dad and I think Jacob stashed it someplace, but the kid's good. We both looked for it, but we never found it."

"Sounds like you had quite a day."

Ned crossed his arms. "I had to follow your advice."

"What advice?"

"I nearly panicked a couple of times, but in the end, with Dad's help and Jacob's cooperation, I hung in there."

Fifty-Eight

A MEETING OF sorts took place at breakfast the day after Lea and Matthew came back from Blacksburg. The Howells hosted the meal. The attendees included the Lloyds, Eric, Teresa and Margaret, along with the Finneys, Ned and John.

Lea looked at her guests and then at Matthew who sat to her right. Jacob sat in a new booster seat on her other side. "I hope everyone got enough to eat," she said with a smile.

There were contented comments all around, and Matthew spoke up. "We wanted to get everyone together to talk about how to go forward from here." He looked at Ned. "How are you doing, Ned? Are you planning to stay or go?"

Ned leaned back in his chair. "I'm going to stay."

His father, John, patted Ned's back. "I have every confidence in you, son. And hopefully, Raymond Ferguson will find someone to help you out before too long."

Matthew looked at Teresa and Eric. "Have you two figured out what you want to do?"

Eric glanced at Teresa and back at Matthew. "We might be able to help Raymond out."

"You hate this place, Eric, why would you stay?" Matthew asked.

Eric shrugged. "I was discouraged with how little things have changed in the area. But yesterday, spending time with Mary's brother and sisters, I feel more hopeful."

Teresa squeezed Eric's hand. "We were up half the night, talking about the possibilities."

Eric continued. "More than a clinic is needed. We came to the conclusion that Lea and Mom's idea was on track. If things in the area are going to move forward, an outreach program is also needed."

Margaret took Eric's other hand. "What are you saying, Eric?"

324

"I'll let Teresa explain," Eric said.

Teresa looked around at everyone. "First of all, Eric and I love working together. And we could do more of that in Baltimore, but it wouldn't be the same as being here."

Lea sat up and stared back. "So you really are staying in Elkville?"

Teresa blushed. "We haven't figured out how the financial end of things would work with the outreach program, but—"

"My dad was already willing to fund it," Lea said. "I'm sure he'd be willing to consider any ideas you have."

"Really?" Teresa asked. "We could spend time working in the clinic and also work with the children. An outreach program could give kids a chance to explore new ideas and change the way they see the world."

"You're right," Margaret said. "Little Jacob is a perfect example. When I think about how different he is now, well—"

Ned smiled. "I was surprised at how bright and quick to learn little Jacob is."

John nudged Ned's arm. "Give him a few years, and he'll be working alongside you, Ned."

"I wouldn't doubt it," Ned said. "Jacob is one determined little boy. I think he'll be great at whatever he wants to do."

Hearing his name mentioned a number of times, Jacob looked up from some colorful, plastic letters he insisted on bringing to the table. Lea had found them in a toy store. He held up one of them. "B."

Lea leaned over and kissed his cheek. "That's excellent, Jacob."

Jacob smiled and repeated the letter.

"Very good, young man," Matthew said proudly. "We bought him other toys to play with, but he decided he likes the letters."

Margaret looked at Lea, then Matthew. "Do you know what you're going to do about—" She paused and looked at Jacob. "About the boy's future?"

"No, we don't," Lea replied. She looked at Matthew. "Matthew, I want to stay here for a while, at least until something is settled with Jacob. But I know you have to get back to Chicago. You have responsibilities there."

Matthew's face took on a serious expression. "I've been talking to Ralph. He can't run the practice on his own. Until a better solution is found, you're right, I'll have to go back. I'm sorry."

Margaret frowned. "When will you be leaving?"

"If I can get a flight, I better leave tomorrow."

Lea bit her lip as a tear slipped down her cheek. "I'll miss you."

Jacob noticed her unhappiness and immediately reached out to her. "Ma!"

It was the first time the little boy had ever referred to Lea in that way. She quickly picked him up and held him close. "I'm not your mother, Jacob, but I'd give anything if I could be."

* * *

Once breakfast was over and everyone left, Lea stared out the kitchen window noting the changes that were taking place. The big tree that stood in the yard was getting its new leaves. Their vibrant, spring green color reminded her of her first spring in Baltimore. It was the spring when she met Margaret and Eric, and they took her home to live with them.

Everything about life was a challenge at first. Her memories were gone, but her anger and impatience remained. But no matter her mood, Margaret and Eric were always there for her. If it hadn't been for them, she might not have ever made the journey back to herself. She would have never been ready for a happy relationship with Matthew.

In the past months, with her old personality taking over, she'd squandered so much of her time with the man she loved. Now, he was going back to Chicago. There would probably be weeks between visits. The thought made her cry every time she thought about not having him close. But she worried that her tears weren't helping Matthew. He wasn't leaving because he wanted to. He was leaving because his obligations had to be honored.

When they discussed the situation, there didn't seem to be any immediate solution. They both cared deeply about Jacob. They both would happily care for the child as if he were their own. But his fate wasn't in their hands. Mary said her mother claimed she was too sick to consider any type of long-term arrangement.

Lea turned away from the window and walked into the living room. She only had one more day with Matthew, and she wanted to spend every moment she could with him. She smiled when she saw him on the couch, reading. Jacob, the sweet little boy who called her his ma, was putting together some small, plastic building blocks. He seemed to like them more than Eric's old wooden ones.

Lea sat down next to Matthew and snuggled close. "I get the idea that Jacob is a forward looking type of child, not one to get stuck in the past."

Matthew put his book aside. "I had to be quite firm when he tried to take charge of my phone. He was fascinated by the icons and the idea of swiping."

"He's changed so quickly. He was so afraid at first. Now, he's quite bold and full of curiosity."

Matthew laughed. "I think he gave Ned Finney a day to remember."

"But one thing hasn't changed, Matthew, the way he thinks of you. He's going to really miss you, and so am I."

"We can only hope that his parents consider letting us take care of him, that we can take him back home someday."

The word, home, struck a deep chord in Lea. And yet, she didn't know where home was. "We were both born and raised in Chicago, but when I think about these last weeks with you and Jacob, this feels more like home."

"But don't you think that once we buy a house in the suburbs and start raising a family, you'll feel the same way about Chicago again?"

"I guess you're right. It's being together that's important. I almost let that fact slip through my fingers these past months. Now, I don't care where I am as long as we're together."

Matthew pulled back and stared at her. "Do you mean that, Lea?"

Lea saw the fear in his eyes and realized he was still worried about how she felt. She put her hand on his chest. "Matthew, listen to me. I might have had a crazy, emotional setback, but I love you. Wherever you are, that's where I want to be. It's the reason Elkville feels like home. It's because we've been here together, sharing our days and nights, not being separated by anything."

Jacob came over and climbed up onto the sofa. With a hand on Matthew's shoulder and balancing on his knees, he pointed to Lea and then to Matthew. "Ma . . . Pa."

Lea felt her eyes getting misty, but she forced herself not to cry. "Matthew, what are we going to do? He doesn't understand any of this. If we have to give him back, what's going to happen to him?"

Fifty-Nine

MATTHEW WOKE UP around seven, showered, got dressed and went downstairs. Lea was already up. She'd packed him a lunch for his trip. They had a few quiet moments in the kitchen before he left. "Lea, are you sure I should say goodbye to Jacob before I leave? I hate that you'll have to deal with another tantrum."

"Don't worry about me," Lea insisted. "It would be worse if you left without letting him know what was happening. By the way, Mary suggested that I take Jacob over to Paul's house this morning. She thought it would be nice if he got together with the other children."

"I thought he didn't get along with them."

"I know, but they are his family. Besides, it might distract him from thinking about you being gone."

"I guess," Matthew said as he kissed her. "I'll call you once I reach Blacksburg."

"I love you," Lea whispered.

"I love you too," he said. "And somehow we're going to work this thing out, okay?"

Lea nodded. "You better keep moving. Eric will be here soon to drive you to Blacksburg."

"It was nice of him to offer."

"That's just how he is."

Matthew smiled. "Yes, I'd say if you had to get hit by someone's car, Eric was the man you'd want driving it."

Lea smiled too. "I put an extra sandwich in for him. Don't forget to give it to him."

"I'll remember," Matthew said as he started out of the room. He climbed the stairs quickly, wanting to get his goodbye to Jacob over before his emotions were too engaged. But when he saw the little boy, curled up on his makeshift bed, he hesitated. He couldn't stop thinking

328

about Lea's question. If they had to give Jacob back to his mother and father, what would become of him?

He crouched down and shook Jacob's shoulder. "Jacob, wake up," he whispered.

Jacob came awake with a start and stared up at him for a long time. After he seemed to recognize Matthew, the little boy smiled and reached out for him. Matthew hesitated. If he picked up Jacob, it would be so hard to get Jacob to let go of him. Finally, he picked him up anyway and held him close. "I have to leave, but I'll be back."

As soon as Matthew delivered his message, he waited for the inevitable screaming fit and Jacob clinging to him hysterically. When it didn't happen, he wondered why? He laid Jacob back on his bed and covered him. Jacob's reaction didn't make sense. Why wasn't the child having a fit?

Jacob looked up at him. There were tears running down his face, but they were silent tears. Jacob held up a hand and waved. "Bye, Pa," he whispered back.

Matthew felt a chill take hold, but he couldn't think about it. He had to leave.

* * *

Eric pulled away from the Howell residence and gave his passenger, Matthew, an anxious glance. The man gave off a very heavy vibe. "What's wrong?"

Matthew shot back a look that told Eric to keep his questions to himself. However, he did offer a few words of explanation. "Leaving Jacob is getting harder."

"He's a great kid."

Matthew grimaced. "A great kid with a very uncertain future."

Eric decided to change the subject to one that Matthew found less difficult. "You mentioned your partner, Ralph, yesterday. From what you've said before, he seems like a nice guy."

"He's been a good friend. Now he plans on getting married."

"Have you met the woman he's marrying?"

"Nicky is great. They make a fine couple, but I'm beginning to worry about Ralph."

Eric thought about the role of a surgeon. "Are his skills slipping?"

329

"No, that's not the problem. It's this crazy idea he has for his retirement."

"Retirement? How's that going to affect you?"

"I'll have to wait and see."

"So don't leave me hanging, Matthew, tell me about Ralph's crazy idea."

"If Ned Finney wants to leave in a year, Ralph and Nicky might be willing to run the clinic."

Eric laughed. "My lord, before you know it, Elkville's clinic could have a medical staff that includes a top-notch surgeon."

"And a great RN. Nicky is the best in the business. But Ralph's still in the thinking stage. Who knows what he and Nicky will end up doing. I'm just surprised that they'd consider Elkville."

"Look at Teresa and me. We're going to give it a year."

Matthew gave him a teasing scowl. "Yes, but I already knew you were a little nuts."

"Maybe, but I enjoy working with Teresa. In Baltimore, we have time for a quick hello in the morning. When evening comes around, we're both tired. After a meal and a few minutes to relax, we end up going to bed without ever having a decent conversation."

"But your work is meaningful, right?"

"Yes, but why can't it be the same here?"

Matthew adjusted his seat to a reclining position. "I don't know. I think I need a few more winks. By the way, thanks for driving me to Blacksburg. I appreciate it."

"You're welcome," Eric said as he turned on the radio. "I hope you don't mind a little music. Teresa said it makes the drive a lot more pleasant."

"Whatever," Matthew said as he closed his eyes.

Eric began to relax as he listened to some old pop tunes. He agreed with Teresa, music helped make the miles slip by more quickly. But when he looked at Matthew, he wasn't so sure about his passenger's state. The man had dozed off, but he was still frowning.

The first hour of the trip was uneventful. Eric had enjoyed the way the mountains were greening and the simple joy of driving on a pleasant day. When Matthew woke up, Eric turned off the music. "Feel better?" he asked.

"I must have been tired," Matthew said as he put his seat up. He stared out the side window. "Do you know I'm actually starting to feel I know this road?"

"When you've driven it as many times as I have, the twists and turns are all familiar."

"Still, when I think of Elkville, it's like we're descending from some foreign land whose inhabitants never quite made it into the real world."

"People are people, Matthew. Look at Jacob. It only took a short time for him to pretty much acclimate to that real world you're talking about."

Matthew smiled. "He's something, isn't he?"

"Jacob and his siblings have the potential to leave behind a lot of ignorance. It's the reason that Teresa and I want to stay in Elkville. If we can introduce a more updated world to the children, eventually the cycle of poverty could be broken."

"It's a worthwhile endeavor, I'll give you that. So do you think Jacob's sisters and brother can progress as quickly as Jacob?"

"The girls show definite promise. The older brother, Brodey, is a different matter. He's suffered a lot of abuse, but unlike his sisters, who are shy and withdrawn, he's following in his parents footsteps."

"How so?"

"There's a lot of anger there, even rage. You can see it in his eyes. Jacob's father might not have been the only one who abused Jacob."

Matthew grabbed for the dash. "Oh hell, Eric, stop the car! We have to turn around."

"Why? What is it?"

"Just turn around," Matthew bellowed.

Eric pulled over as soon as he could and did as Matthew demanded. As they headed back towards Elkville, he checked his passenger. Matthew's face had lost most of its color and his breathing looked shallow. "Talk to me. What's going on?"

"You know that horrible premonition I had a while back."

"Of course I remember."

"I just had another one."

"Tell me what you're feeling."

Matthew rubbed his forehead. "It's probably just my fears acting up. It's probably nothing."

"Then why are we driving back to Elkville. You have a plane to catch."

"Never mind the plane."

"What aren't you telling me?" Eric asked.

"I know you had that feeling about Teresa and how she might be in danger, but have any of those kinds of feelings actually come true?"

Eric's eyes turned wistful. "Once, my grandmother seemed like a healthy woman, but before she had a fatal stroke, I knew she was on her way out. Some might think I have a gift, but it never felt like that."

"I just pray that I don't have that kind of gift."

* * *

Lea walked a moody Jacob to Paul's house. His sister, Mary, had invited her to bring the little boy over. Mary wanted him to know that he could be with his family again. Jacob balked at the idea, but Lea finally convinced him to go.

When Lea arrived and was invited in, she could see that Mary was proud of how Jacob's sisters looked. They'd had proper showers and were dressed in new, clean clothes. They were less timid than Lea had expected. With Margaret and Teresa's help, they were quickly learning that they were safe in their new environment.

Jacob was the one who was still very wary. He wanted to stand behind Lea. Mary smiled and told him that he didn't need to be afraid. Jacob listened, but he resisted Mary's touch. Lea was pleased that at least he wasn't crying.

Jacob's sisters, Josie, Lucy and Sadie, seemed anxious to explore this very different version of their brother. Jacob looked away when they crowded around him, giggling and touching his new blue t-shirt with its happy, smiling dinosaur on the front.

After a few minutes, Jacob began to relax a little. He stayed close to Lea, but he watched his sisters with interest. They had started playing a game that Mary had picked out for them.

When things seemed to be going well, Mary invited Lea to come into the kitchen while she got together some cookies and drinks for the children. Jacob trailed behind them, but after a while he went back into the living room to watch his sisters. Mary seemed very happy to see him getting more comfortable.

"Let them be," Mary advised Lea. "It's good for Jacob to spend time with his sisters."

Since Jacob seemed alright with the idea, Lea agreed with Mary. The little boy would find out that his family included friendly members, not just a father who didn't have his best in mind.

Jacob's panicked scream cut in on Lea's thoughts. She ran from the kitchen and into the living room, only to see Jacob being dragged from the house by an older boy.

Mary ran past Lea. She was yelling. "Brodey! What are you playin' at?"

Brodey paid her no attention. He had a firm grasp on Jacob's arm as he stomped down the sidewalk and kept going. Jacob was screaming and trying to resist, but he was no match for his older brother.

Brodey finally stopped in the middle of the street and gave Jacob a hard shaking. "Ya think ya better than the rest of us? Well, ya not. Ya goin' back where ya belong!"

Lea ran to catch up with the teenager. Mary stayed on the porch trying to calm her little sisters as they clung to her for support. Lea stopped a couple of yards from where Brodey stood. "Please, let Jacob go," she begged. "He's just a little boy!"

"Ma!" Jacob cried out as he struggled to free himself.

Jacob's plea seemed to infuriate Brodey. He took his free hand and slapped Jacob across his face, bloodying his nose. "She ain't ya ma! Ya hear me?" he said, still holding Jacob's arm and shaking him again.

Lea felt helpless to do anything. She didn't want to antagonize Brodey further for fear of what he might do to Jacob. As she stood trembling in the street, a car pulled up alongside her. Eric and Matthew got out.

"Stay back, Lea!" Matthew ordered as he and Eric placed themselves in front of her.

Jacob made another attempt to get away. With blood running down his face, he reached out to Matthew. "Pa!"

Brodey immediately retrieved a knife he had in his boot. "Git back!" he hissed. "I'm nota 'fraid to cut ya."

Jacob looked at Matthew with narrowed eyes and back at the knife. In the next moment, he tried to grab the knife from his brother. Brodey retaliated by kicking him so hard in the ribs that Jacob was hurled to the ground.

Matthew and Eric both rushed forward at the same time. As they did, Brodey turned tail and sprinted down the street.

Jacob lay gasping when Matthew got to him. "Jacob, I'm here! Jacob, stay with me."

Jacob's eyes were barely open as he tried to breathe, but he reached out for Matthew's hand.

Lea ran up and knelt down next to Jacob. He looked so small and broken. "Matthew, you have to do something for our Jacob!" she cried.

Eric pulled her back. "Lea, please, we'll take care of Jacob, but you have to calm down,"

Lea swallowed hard and nodded.

Margaret came hurrying down the street. Earlier, she'd told Lea that she was going out for a walk. "What happened?" she called out.

Lea rushed into her arms and started crying. She tried to answer Margaret's question, but the violence she'd witnessed and seeing Jacob so cruelly treated had her entire body shaking.

Sixty

JOHN FINNEY FELT like he was in some horrible nightmare. First, he'd thought he'd lost his son. Then he'd had a crazy experience with an old man who'd died fifty years before. He questioned his sanity afterwards.

He was just starting to think things were coming together in a good way when an innocent, little child was brutalized. Jacob, a beautiful boy who won over John's heart just days before, lay in one of the clinic beds with injured ribs that made every breath a painful struggle.

Everyone around him was suffering too. Matthew, Lea, Eric, Teresa, Margaret and Ned were all devastated by what had happened. The blessing in all the horror was that Eric and Matthew returned when they did. If they hadn't, Jacob's brother might have stabbed him or someone else before it was all over.

With the history of violence that the teenager had lived through in his thirteen years, he might have followed in his parents' footsteps. He might have used a knife to take care of a perceived problem. From what Mary said, Brodey resented the assistance Jacob and his sisters received. With his parents gone, he assumed the role of head of household and was determined to restore the family's original presence in their mountain cabin. He was going to take Jacob back home whether the child wanted to go or not. And violence was the tool he'd been taught to use when his plans were met with resistance.

Presently, Brodey was hiding out in the mountains. Mary had gone to look for him, but she'd been unsuccessful in finding him.

* * *

Matthew sat by Jacob's bedside watching. The little boy was drifting in and out of a troubled sleep. But as he kept his vigil over the child, it was Lea's voice that filled Matthew's thoughts.

"Matthew, you have to do something for our Jacob!"

Lea had practically screamed out the words while Jacob lay in a heap on the ground. Now, he couldn't stop thinking about how adamant she was. Did she doubt his commitment to the child?

Matthew knew he'd done everything in his power to ensure that Jacob was getting the best medical care he could provide. How could Lea possibly think he wasn't going to be there for him? Where else would he be? When the answer came to him, it slipped out in a hoarse whisper. "I was on my way back to Chicago."

He thought about his trip and napping in the car as Eric drove him to Blacksburg. He had a plane to catch. He had responsibilities to take care of. He had a practice that demanded he do his job.

But what would have happened if some terrible urging hadn't told him to go back to Elkville? What if he'd slept a few minutes longer? Who would have been there for the people he cared about? Would Lea have been able to rescue Jacob when his brother, Brodey, was threatening people with a knife? What if he'd used it on Lea? What if he'd used it on Jacob?

The ideas twisted and turned in Matthew's gut as he remained at Jacob's bedside. Occasionally, the little boy would wake up and stare at Matthew. Sometimes he'd reach out a hand. Sometimes he seemed too weak to move and pleaded with his eyes. The message was clear. "Pa, don't leave me!"

And yet, that morning when Matthew was telling Jacob goodbye, Jacob had stared at him with a different look. Jacob didn't scream or have a fit. He seemed to have come to a conclusion, that Matthew would always be leaving him. Jacob was learning that he couldn't change that fact, no matter how hard he insisted on Matthew being there for him.

Maybe Lea had felt the say way. After they were married, everything was wonderful. Matthew had cut back on his work. They had more time together. They could take leisurely walks and have long conversations. They had time to express their love in the bedroom.

Slowly, things changed. Matthew told himself that Lea was the first to interrupt their way of life, but he didn't know if it was true. He remembered talking to her, telling her that his partner, Ralph, needed more help. He wanted Matthew to take care of more of the case load. Lea had sat and listened to him and nodded. Like Jacob, she was resigned to what was coming. Matthew would get so busy that he'd be too tired for walks or lengthy conversations.

Lea got busy too. She was enrolled in classes and started getting interested in her father's business. Soon she was putting in more hours with her activities than Matthew.

Going over how their marriage and relationship slowly dissolved, Matthew could understand why Lea's old personality got a foothold. It was suited for the life they had, a life that had little intimacy or room for matters of the heart.

The more Matthew reflected on their past, the more he saw their future spread out in front of him. He'd go back to his life as a busy surgeon, and there would be little time left for a relationship or family.

Is that what he really wanted? Was he more comfortable being his own man to the extent that he pushed Lea away? He thought about his talk with Eric on Margaret's front porch and how he'd railed against being more sensitive and feeling things he didn't want to feel. He'd been so upset, he'd had to take to his bed with his head pounding.

As the questions kept coming, and he explored more of his life, he felt like he was sinking into a place where there were no solutions. He'd always believed that people could combat that thing called depression. They simply needed to stop thinking their crappy thoughts. But in his case, it felt more complicated.

His entire life was coming into question, filling up file after file with events that shaped who he was. How could he sort it all out? Where was that light at the end of the tunnel that people talked about? All he could see was how he screwed up with Lea and with Jacob. He tried to justify his actions, but he couldn't lie to himself. Being truthful was a necessary component in his life, no matter what it demanded of him.

Sixty-One

LEA SAT ON the living room sofa, close to Jacob. After some time recuperating at the clinic, he was well enough to come home. He lay propped up on the sofa, sucking his thumb. Margaret had come over to see how he was doing. She sat next to Lea.

"How are you coping with all this?" Margaret asked.

Lea paused. "I kept trying to feel optimistic, but look at our boy, Mom. I know he's still physically hurting, but there's more to it. He's lost interest in the things he liked before, like his toys and books."

"He's had quite a shock. Getting dragged out of Paul's house by his brother had to really scare him."

"Thank goodness Mary finally found Brodey and got him to agree to go to Blacksburg."

"Another brother is going to take him in?"

"Yes, Mary thinks their older brother, Dale, will give Brodey the stability and structure he needs to straighten out."

"Where's Matthew?" Margaret asked.

"He's taking all of this very hard. Since Jacob came home, Matthew checks on him, but then he retreats to our room." Lea took out a tissue and swiped at her eyes. "I'm worried about him."

"Ma?" Jacob called out.

Lea quickly reached out to the little boy and held his hand. He seemed to be watching everything she did. "I'm alright, honey," she said with a forced smile. "Everything's okay."

Jacob stared back with a frown and started sucking his thumb again.

"Sometimes when children are part of something traumatic, they're extra sensitive to what's happening around them," Margaret explained. She retrieved a cup from the coffee table and offered it to the little boy. "How about some juice, Jacob?"

338

Jacob turned his head away, letting Margaret know he wasn't interested.

Margaret put the juice back and sat down next to Lea again. "Lea, you have to be the strong one now, with Jacob and Matthew," she said.

"I think Matthew blames himself for not being here for Jacob and me. I've tried to talk to him, but he doesn't seem to hear what I'm trying to tell him."

"This whole thing's been a shock for everyone. Eric feels like he should have been more alert to the situation too."

"He barely knew Brodey."

"Eric and Matthew set a very high bar for themselves. So it's up to you to hang in there while Matthew works things out, and Jacob regains his confidence."

Lea smiled at Margaret. "It's strange, isn't it? I used to think I was the one who had all the problems."

"Everyone has problems. And you should be very happy with how you've coped with yours. In fact, I think you're doing a lot better than I am."

"What's going on?"

"I'm still confused about what to do with my life. Eric suggested I go to Chicago, but maybe I should stay here and help with the outreach program."

"You've already done enough here. Let Teresa and Eric take care of the program. Go to Chicago."

"But I feel guilty leaving."

"Now you know why Eric sets the bar so high. You and his dad are both perfect examples of people who try to save the world. But if you take care of your own needs, that would be a good example for Eric."

"Thank you, Lea." Margaret stood up and glanced at the clock on a side table. "Well, I have to get back home. Paul said he was going to call me at about this time. I'll see how he's doing."

Lea stood up too. "Give him my best," she said as she hugged Margaret.

"Ma, tirsty," Jacob whined.

Lea let go of Margaret and smiled. "My goodness, he's starting to talk again."

"Yes, but I don't think it's because he needs a drink."

"You're right. You just tried to give him some juice."

Margaret smiled. "I have an idea. Hug me again."

"Sure," Lea said as she smiled and embraced Margaret.

"Ma!" Jacob whined in a louder voice.

Margaret laughed this time. "You know I think he's a little jealous."

"Is that good?" Lea asked with concern.

"I think so. It means he's coming out of his shell."

"Ma!" Jacob called a third time and pointed to the cup on the coffee table.

Lea quickly picked it up and tried to hand it to him. "Here you go, pumpkin."

Instead of taking the cup, Jacob stuck out a lip.

Lea looked at Margaret again. "Am I doing something wrong?"

"No, it's probably that Jacob had a lot of people caring for him at the clinic. So he might need a little, extra babying for a while."

"I don't have a problem with that," Lea said as she held the cup to Jacob's mouth. He took a little sip and paused. After a second sip, he pushed the cup away. "Tanks," he said with eyes that were a little brighter.

Lea kissed Jacob's forehead and looked up at Margaret. "You're right. I think he's coming back to us. Now, if we can get Matthew to do the same thing, we can be a family again."

"Yes, but be patient. Matthew might take a little longer."

* * *

Ned watched his father packing his suitcase, but he wasn't happy about it. John was returning to Utah. "Dad, are you sure you're up to going back to work? You must have enough sick leave to stay here for a while longer."

John put a shirt down and looked back. "Ned, if I stay here any longer, it's going to be even harder for me to leave."

Ned swallowed the lump that was stuck in his throat. "I feel like we're just getting to know each other."

John sat down on his bed. "I agree. And I'm grateful that you've helped me to understand myself a lot better."

"So stay for a couple more weeks. We'll do some camping like we used to do."

John's brows narrowed. "Do you mean that? Do you really want me around? I've always felt like you liked being on your own."

Ned pulled a chair over. "I've felt the same way about you. I thought you were happy to be rid of me when I went off to school."

John laughed. "I guess we still have a lot to learn about each other."

"Dad?"

"Yes?"

"Stay for a couple of weeks."

John studied his clasped hands. Finally, he looked up and smiled. "I'd like that."

"Good, we can do some hiking and see what these mountains are all about."

"I'd like to think we'll have a much better experience than I had on my own." John paused. "Ned, on another topic, I've been thinking about Matthew Howell."

Ned chuckled. "As an intern, I saw a lot of guys like him. They're no nonsense types. I guess I thought I needed to be like that too."

"Why?"

"When you're taking care of someone who's got a real medical problem, you can't get emotionally involved."

"I understand that," John said. "When I'm training people to handle a crisis, I try to instill a similar attitude. However, look at Eric or Teresa. They're both one hundred percent professional if need be, but they're not afraid to help people afterwards when they're having a difficult time emotionally."

Ned shook his head. "I guess I was lucky that they were there for me after my accident. If Matthew Howell had been in charge, he'd have probably told me to suck it up when I was limping around."

"You might have Matthew all wrong. That's why I'm asking you what you think about him."

Ned smiled. "Jacob sure loves him."

"Kids seem to sense when they can trust someone. But from what I've observed, Matthew's having a very hard time after what happened to the boy."

"I know he refused to leave Jacob's bedside."

"It's more than that. Didn't you notice his hands?"

"What about them?"

"It's very subtle, but they're not rock steady like a surgeon needs them to be."

Ned stared back with concern. He respected Matthew Howell and didn't want to see the excellent surgeon fail. "That could be a big problem. I'll talk to Eric about it. He and Matthew are good friends."

"Maybe that's what Matthew needs right now, someone to talk to."

* * *

Eric stepped outside the clinic to get some air and clear his head. When Ned informed him of Matthew's condition, Eric wasn't sure about how to go forward. He forced a smile when he saw that Teresa had followed him outside. "It's a pleasant day," he said in a soft voice, trying to hide the fact that he wasn't feeling very good about his task.

"Is something bothering you, Eric?" she asked.

Eric noted the expression of concern on Teresa's face. "You're very tuned in."

"So talk to me. Tell me why you have that look in your eyes."

"A look?" Eric asked.

"Yes, Jacob's eyes can have the same uneasiness."

"Ned suggested I talk to Matthew, but he can be very set in his ways—"

"Like your dad when you tried to talk to him or your mother?"

Eric could feel his anger coming to the surface. "I feel like I'm always trying to convince people of something, and I'm tired of being resented because of it."

Teresa laughed. "I guess that's just part of sometimes being a lot wiser than other people. People like holding on to what they believe, and you challenge them."

"I don't mean to."

"But you care, my sweet husband. And I don't think you can help yourself. But there is something that you might think about."

Eric gave her a sidelong glance. "Please, go on."

"When Matthew was here with Jacob, he looked like he was the one who got slammed to the ground."

"That's understandable. He loves that child."

"Don't say that to him."

342

Eric turned and looked at the mountains. "You're right. The guy doesn't seem comfortable with the idea at times."

Teresa let out a heavy sigh. "Love can be a bastard."

"Teresa, I've never heard you talk like that."

"Sorry, it just came out."

Eric turned and took her hands. "Has loving me felt like that?"

"Yes, when you shut me out, it did. I loved you so much, and I knew you loved me, but at times—"

"Go on," Eric urged.

"You were so far away, living in your own world. And I didn't know how to reach you."

"But I'm here now. And if I go off again, throw a glass of ice water in my face."

Teresa laughed. "I might just do that."

"I can't change the past," Eric said as he squeezed her hands. "But I promise that I'll always try my best not to repeat it."

"And I promise that no matter what, I'll always try to bring you back from wherever you've gone. But for now, you have to try to do that for Matthew."

"Alright," Eric agreed, "but that doesn't mean I have to like it."

Sixty-Two

Eric knocked on the door and waited on the porch of the Howell residence. He was quickly greeted by very cordial Lea who invited him into the living room.

"I'm so happy that you're here, Eric," Lea said.

Eric kissed her cheek and tried to look relaxed in spite of the fact he was dreading talking to Matthew. Teresa's pep talk helped a little, but he was tired of fighting Matthew's temper and attitude. "I thought I'd check and see how you guys are doing."

"Come say hello to Jacob," Lea said as she walked over to the sofa.

Eric smiled at the little boy. "Jacob, I like your shirt and the rocket ship that's on it."

Jacob looked down at himself and frowned. "Tanks."

Eric reached into his pocket and crouched down next to Jacob. "I have something for you."

Jacob became more alert and blinked back.

"When I was a little boy, I liked dinosaurs." Eric said. "When I saw your dinosaur shirt the other day, I thought about one of my favorite toys. Maybe you'll like it too."

Jacob's brown eyes widened with curiosity.

Eric held out a tiny, plastic Tyrannosaurus Rex.

Jacob stared at it for a long moment with creased brows. Slowly, he reached out and took it out of Eric's open palm. Examining it carefully, he fingered the toy's miniature teeth. "Dinsore," he said, still looking very stern.

"Yes, when they were born, these dinosaurs were very little creatures, but when they grew up, they became very strong. And when you grow up, you're going to be very strong too."

Jacob held his new toy close and almost smiled. "Tank ya."

Lea patted Eric's shoulder. "I think that toy meant a lot to you, Eric. Thank you for giving it to Jacob."

Eric stood up. "I used to pretend I was a Rex. It helped when I was having a hard time with my father."

"I wish you could give Matthew something to make him feel better," Lea said.

"Would you like me to talk to him?"

"Yes, but I'm sure it won't be easy. He's shut himself off in our bedroom most of the time."

"I see," Eric said as he headed for the stairs. He had to steel himself for the accusations Matthew usually put forth when he was on a rampage of self-pity. But it wasn't fair for the man to claim Eric was guilty of some crime just because Matthew was getting more sensitive. As he made his way to the upper floor, he made a bold decision. He had to take a stand with Matthew. He paused at the master bedroom door, took a steadying breath and knocked.

"Come in," Matthew said.

Eric opened the door and saw Matthew sitting at a desk that sat in a corner of the room. "Hello," Eric said.

Matthew turned around, smiled, and stood up. "Nice to see you, Eric. What can I do for you?"

Eric looked around, feeling like he'd entered an alternate version of reality. It was the only thing that could account for a smiling Matthew Howell.

* * *

Matthew had spent the last couple of days trying to get to the bottom of that thing called his life. He was already in a bad mood when the doorbell rang. The sound of Eric's voice in the foyer triggered an immediate bout of resentment. Eric seemed to think his mission involved being there for the lame and hurting, especially when it came to his friends. And he considered Matthew a friend.

The thought of Eric thinking he could doctor Matthew's pain and make it better was infuriating. How dare the man think he could help with a situation that had Matthew stopped dead in his tracks? On the other hand, there was a part of him that refused to let Eric know just how far he'd traveled into the waters of despair.

Even if his emotions were in shreds, even if he felt like his career was over and he had no future, he was determined not to play the victim in front of Eric. He still had a little pride left. He had to pull himself together. Every precious bit of willpower that still remained had to be harnessed if he was going to present Eric with the confident Matthew Howell he once knew himself to be. It was the one small gift he could still give himself.

His efforts were rewarded as soon as Eric peeked inside the door. The surprised look on the guy's face was priceless and almost worth the tremendous discipline it took for Matthew to smile. After a couple of days of trudging through the sludge that made up the foundation of his life, he was surprised that his facial muscles were capable of such a feat.

His greeting, "Nice to see you," didn't come out easily either. Matthew had to focus every bit of self-control in order to pronounce each syllable. His voice almost broke in the process. He'd been on a hunger strike and refused even water. It was stupid on the one hand and yet satisfying when he felt his body weakening. He was tired of always having to be the strong Matthew Howell, the hardened warrior everyone seemed to think he was. The mantle demanded too much. He wasn't only supposed to be there for Lea and Jacob, he was supposed to be there for the endless patients lined up to demand his services. Maybe his partner, Ralph, was right about the idea of retirement.

For the time being, he had to put on an act for his visitor. "Tell me what's going on, Eric," he said, gesturing the man into the room.

Eric came forward slowly, staring intently. "Going on? Not much. It's been pretty quiet at the clinic."

His baffled look made Matthew smile again. Instead of resentment, he was starting to enjoy watching Eric's obvious confusion. "Just another lazy day in Elkville, right?"

Eric's look of concern suddenly turned into a relieved smile. "You know, Matthew, I have to confess something."

Matthew crossed his arms, but he kept his tone upbeat. "What's that?"

"I came over here thinking that I didn't want to have this conversation."

"Why? What's the problem?"

Eric shrugged. "In the past, you've seemed to think I was at the root of your problems. It's such a relief to know you're doing okay."

"Of course I'm okay."

"Excellent," Eric said as he started to back up. "But I don't want to intrude, so I'll let you continue doing what you were doing and get back to the clinic."

"You don't want to stay and chat?"

"No, I'll be on my way," Eric said as he gave Matthew a final wave and turned to the door. "Teresa will probably want to take a walk later with the weather being so nice."

Matthew should have been pleased with himself. His plan had worked. His pain had been masked, and Eric was leaving. But instead of feeling satisfied, he found Eric's cavalier attitude unbelievable. In fact, the man's lack of sensitivity to Matthew's plight unleashed all the anger he'd been holding in. It was everything he could do to keep his voice steady when he spoke up. "Before you go, let me ask you something."

Eric was about to open the door and turned around. "Yes?"

"Do your patients actually pay you?"

"Yes, they do."

"Don't they realize that you're a complete idiot when it comes to diagnosing a situation?"

"Actually, they seem very happy. I rarely have a complaint."

"How nice for you."

"What are you going on about?" Eric asked. "Why are you suddenly concerned about my patients?"

"I'm just thanking my good fortune that I'm not one of them."

Eric arched his brows. "Sorry, friend, but you're not making any sense."

Matthew came forward and thrust his trembling hands out in Eric's direction. "Are you blind? Didn't you notice what's happened to me?"

Eric's voice took on a quiet but direct tone. "What do you want from me now? Am I supposed to think that I'm responsible for wrecking your surgical career, too?"

"Did I say that?"

"Matthew, since I helped you, you've held me responsible for something I never meant to happen. You've accused me of essentially cursing you. Well, I promise that I'm not infringing on your precious rights ever again."

"That's a great attitude! Is that how you'd handle a person who got hit by a truck? You'd tell them you didn't want to infringe on their rights when they were bleeding out?"

Eric scowled back and his voice took on more volume. "I can't help where I'm not wanted."

"How about having a little compassion? Is that too much to ask?"

Eric averted his eyes. "Of course not, but I will not bear the brunt of your anger either."

"Isn't that convenient? You've decided to become all smug and defiant in the middle of my breakdown."

"Is that what you feel is happening to you?"

"I'm losing everything, and I don't know how to do anything about it!"

Eric held out his hands to Matthew. They were trembling too. "What about my problems? Look at what happens to me when you start yelling? Did you ever consider what I'm going through?"

Matthew turned away. "What are you talking about? You're the golden boy. Lea says you're a healing angel. How could you possibly have any real problems?"

Eric grabbed Matthew's arm and turned him back around. "Oh no you don't! I will not be dismissed by you!"

"Just leave, Eric. Obviously we have nothing to say to each other."

"Right, you have to concentrate on poor Matthew. You don't have room for anyone else's emotional troubles."

"What about you? So your father made your life difficult, well join the club."

"Forget my father. Let's get back to that 'golden boy' crap and examine what that means. When I put my hands on your hurting brow that time at the Ferguson's, I didn't have any control over how you'd be affected. I just had this overwhelming feeling that you were suffering, and I could do something about it. So I did. And I've been paying for it ever since. As for my healing abilities, who wants them? In the past, I would have probably been burned at the stake for possessing such abilities. As for current times, while you're being this big-shot surgeon who's totally respected, I'm a guy who's trying to hide my abilities so I don't get laughed out of the medical profession."

"Fine, so we're both screwed," Matthew said as he sat down on the bed.

Eric waved off his remark. "That's ridiculous. If you start taking care of yourself, your hands will be fine, and you can go back to your job."

"I don't think so. I've been looking at how I've conducted my life, and I'm not very proud of my track record. Even after we were married, I let my career get in the way of my relationship with Lea. I think it explains why she had that recent episode and ran off. As for Jacob, even if we were able to adopt him, I'd probably fail him too."

"Can I ask you something? A while back, Teresa, Ned and I were discussing why we became doctors. It was expected of me, but why did you choose what you do?"

"I sure as heck wasn't going to be a lawyer like my father."

"So it was your way of getting back at him?"

Matthew thought about the fights he'd had with his father and how insistent his father was that he'd take up the law. "I wasn't going to be bullied into a future I detested."

"So the answer is yes, but at least you're great at what you do. And you seem to like how capable you are. That's a plus."

"But what's it doing to my life with Lea?"

"Matthew, tell Ralph to add another partner as soon as he finds someone. It'll lighten your work load, and you can spend more time away from the job."

"That's an option, but I don't know if I'm ready to return to Chicago yet. So much has been stirred up these last few days. I think I need time to know what I really want."

Eric hesitated. "You can't figure out your whole life all at once. So take the pressure off. And no matter what, I am a friend. Please remember that."

Matthew could hear the sincerity in Eric's voice and looked up. "Is that your way of saying you're sorry for acting like a jerk?"

"A jerk?" Eric asked, but when he saw Matthew's teasing smile, he relaxed a little. "I'm sorry if I appeared that way, but I'm tired of fighting with you."

"You're right," Matthew said. "So I'll try to stop making you feel you're at fault, even if you are at times."

Eric laughed. "I guess that's the best offer I'm going to get out of you, so I'll take it."

There was a knock on the door, and Lea looked in. She was holding Jacob. "Somebody was asking for you, Matthew," she announced.

Jacob looked at Matthew with a frown. "Pa?"

Matthew got up and went over to where Lea was standing. "How's my young man?"

Jacob reached out to him. "I 'ungry."

"What?" Lea laughed. "I just asked him if he wanted to eat, and he refused."

Matthew carefully took the little boy from Lea. He was sure Jacob's ribs were still recovering, and he was surprised and grateful for the boy's pain tolerance. "If he's hungry, I guess that means that I need to fix him something."

Eric came over and ruffled Jacob's hair. "I think your 'pa' needs to eat too, right Matthew?"

Matthew gave Eric a quick look of appreciation. The guy couldn't help himself. He was caring to the core. "If you say so, Doctor Lloyd, maybe I will. And how about you? Would you like something?"

Eric patted his stomach. "I guess I could have a bite to eat, Doctor Howell, on one condition."

"What's that?"

"I need some coffee, too. Ned is getting worse. I find water bottles appearing on side tables when I'm reading, and he's keeping a close eye on the coffee pot."

Matthew couldn't imagine working at the clinic and rubbing elbows with Ned Finney every day. He smiled as he carried Jacob to the stairs. "I hear your pain, Eric. I'll put on a fresh pot."

Sixty-Three

PAUL LOOKED AROUND the living room of the house he'd rented in Chicago. He was starting to adjust to the place and think of it as his home, at least for the time being. It had come partially furnished, so he had what he needed as far as the basic necessities. The couch he sat on was fairly comfortable. He leaned back as he held his phone to his ear and talked to Margaret. "My goodness, from what you've told me, there's been a lot happening since I left Elkville."

"I agree, Paul," Margaret replied. "I couldn't believe it when Eric announced that he and Teresa would be taking off a year to spend it here. For the time being, they've gone back to Baltimore to make arrangements with their practices."

Paul nodded. "When they return, they could make a real difference with that outreach program."

"My Ricky would be so proud of them." Margaret said quietly. "The dear man always wanted something better for the people in the area."

"I'm sure that both of you inspired Eric to feel the same way."

"Perhaps, but that's enough about my news, tell me about what you've been doing."

Paul smiled. "I've been enjoying my volunteer work at the hospital. It's not like I'm there in the role of a psychiatrist, so there's no pressure. At the same time, I think I've helped a number of people who wanted to talk to someone."

"Sounds like just what you needed," Margaret said in a firm, affirmative voice.

"I miss Duke," Paul said. "How's he doing? I hope he hasn't been too much trouble."

"He's been a very good dog. In fact, I've grown quite fond of him. He follows me wherever I go in the house, so I had to make him a couple of extra beds to use in different rooms. I'm going to miss him when you come back and pick him up."

"I plan to do that very soon. I'll get Duke and my clothes and drive my truck back to Chicago. What about you? Do you know what you'd like to do next?"

Margaret's sigh was audible. "I don't want to make a mistake and do something I'll regret, but—"

"Margaret, please, go on."

"I think I might move to Chicago. Teresa and Eric want me to rent a place there."

"You know you can always stay here."

Margaret paused. "If I do that, I want to sublet part of the house."

Paul knew what Margaret was saying. She didn't want him paying her way. She needed a sense of independence. "That's probably a very good idea. As I told you, this house has a separate apartment that would give you the privacy you want."

Margaret paused again. When she spoke, her voice had a bit of excitement in it. "Then I think I'll try it for a month or two if that's alright with you."

Margaret couldn't see him, but Paul's smile broadened into a grin. "That would be wonderful. We'd be neighbors again."

"Yes, and maybe we can return to Chicago together. I can help with the driving."

"I'd like that, Margaret. I'd like that very much."

Sixty-Four

LEA FELT LIKE she could breathe a little easier. Jacob was recovering nicely and even playing with his toys. He was particularly partial to the little T-Rex that Eric gave him. He always kept it in his pocket. Matthew was slowly recovering too. They'd been talking about how to go forward. Even though nothing was settled, he wanted her to voice her wants and desires.

Matthew's questions had her asking herself how much time she wanted to devote to hearth and home and how much to projects like the clinic. She'd told Ned she wasn't interested but observing Teresa and Eric had her wondering if she wouldn't want to contribute too. In the meantime, she'd settle for quiet days in Elkville. However, she missed Teresa and Eric. They had to take care of lots of loose ends in Baltimore. She hoped they wouldn't be gone too long.

Thankfully, Margaret was still in Elkville. As they sat in the kitchen having morning tea, Lea felt a bout of sadness welling up. "I'm going to miss you so much, Mom," she said. She wanted what was best for Margaret so she was trying to keep her emotions under control and her voice steady. "In spite of that, I'm so glad you're going to Chicago."

Margaret gave her a look of concern. "But Lea, you're going back to Chicago soon, too, aren't you?"

Lea shook her head and glanced at Jacob. The little boy was sitting on the floor nearby, playing with his plastic letters. Matthew had been teaching him how to put letters together. Jacob seemed very interested. "Until something is settled with Jacob, I'm staying here."

"What about Matthew? You want to be with him, don't you?"

Lea grabbed her mug, grasping the handle, wishing she could hold on to Matthew just as tightly. "I want to be with him more than anything, but he understands where I'm coming from. In fact, he's not ready to go back yet either."

"But I thought his partner needs him," Margaret said.

"Ralph's been very understanding, especially after what happened to Jacob. I also found out that he wants to retire before too long."

"Is Matthew upset about that?"

"Probably, he didn't tell me about Ralph leaving until recently. I think it was too painful a subject. From what I know, Ralph's been kind of a father figure for him."

Margaret smiled. "I can see that. When you and I had dinner with Ralph and Nicky that time in Chicago, the two of them were like a couple of doting parents."

Lea laughed. "Yes, and Matthew acted like he was annoyed with their concern, but I know Matthew. On some level, he needed their support. When I ran off and lost my memories, he fell apart. He wouldn't want me saying it like that, but I think it's the truth."

"So what's Matthew going to do if Ralph leaves the practice? I'm sure it's too much for one person."

"For the time being, Ralph thinks he's found a couple of people who are candidates for taking his place. If one of them comes on board, it'll take the pressure off of Ralph and Matthew."

Jacob came over to show them what he'd been doing. "Ma!"

"Yes, sweetie, what is it?" Lea asked.

Jacob shook his head and thrust out two letters. "Ma!"

Lea saw that he'd used the letters to make the word, ma. She smiled broadly. "You're such a bright little boy, Jacob. You're learning to spell."

Jacob frowned and looked around. "Pa?"

"He'll be back soon. He's helping Doctor Ned."

Jacob stuck out a lip and went back to his letters.

Margaret sat up more attentively. "Matthew's at the clinic?"

Lea grinned. "Ned and John went for an overnight camping trip, and Matthew agreed to help out until they return later this morning."

"So he's all alone there?"

"Yes, but Ned told Matthew that things are still quiet for the most part. He didn't think Matthew would have much to do."

"Oh my, I hope for Matthew's sake that there aren't many patients to tend to."

"Hopefully, Ned and John will be back before anyone shows up."

* * *

Matthew stood at the filing cabinet, dropping another file into the mostly empty drawer. He couldn't believe that it was only ten in the morning. He'd already seen an endless number of patients. As he was about to close the drawer, he heard the clinic door chime again. "You have got to be kidding," he muttered. "I thought this place was supposed to be quiet."

At least people weren't just walking into the clinic treatment area. He'd corrected that problem. He'd made a large sign and taped it to the inner door. He'd printed out the words, "DO NOT ENTER! REMAIN SEATED IN THE WAITING AREA!" He'd even drawn a "No admittance" symbol in case people had trouble reading.

When he looked up and saw the door opening anyway, he was about to object, but it was Ned and John returning. "Good, you're back," he huffed out.

"Is something wrong?" Ned asked.

"You lied. That's what's wrong. It's been non-stop traffic all morning."

Ned came striding over. "It's usually quiet."

Matthew slammed the filing drawer closed. "Not anymore, Doctor Finney. Business is booming."

"Do you know why people are showing up?" John asked.

"Word got around," Matthew said as he headed for the kitchen. His head was pounding, and he needed caffeine. "It seems this clinic is now the main source of medical care for a number of neighboring towns or hamlets or whatever you call the forsaken settlements in the area."

Ned was close on his heels. "Margaret said that would happen, but I'm still surprised."

Matthew walked over to the counter, saw the empty coffee pot, and glared back at Ned. "I didn't even have time to brew a pot of coffee when I got here at seven. People were waiting in the parking lot."

"At least you had time to make that sign," Ned said with a teasing smile.

"I don't want to talk about it," Matthew complained as he rubbed his temples. "I have a headache, so go make yourself presentable so you can take over."

John motioned to Ned. "Take a shower, son, and I'll help Matthew get some coffee brewing."

Matthew gave John a nod. "Thanks."

After Ned left the kitchen, John took over coffee duty. "Sit down, Matthew, and relax," he suggested. "Sounds like you had a tough morning."

Matthew took a seat at the table. "At one point, a whole family rushed in and surrounded me. Every one of them had a complaint, from the grandfather with arthritis to the ten year old with a bad rash. They were all talking at the same time. I finally managed to get some order going, but it wasn't easy."

"That sounds like an accomplishment," John said as he grabbed some frozen corn from the freezer and handed it to Matthew.

"I'd put it up there with attempting to juggle feral cats."

John laughed. "Thank you for taking over for Ned. It was great having some time in the mountains with him."

When the clinic door chimed again, Matthew moaned, but John held up a hand. "I'll go and take care of whoever it is," he said. "They can wait until Ned's ready to see people."

Matthew put the bag of corn over his forehead and closed his eyes. He inhaled deeply, enjoying the aroma of fresh coffee brewing. A few moments later, John was back.

"Matthew, there's a man here who has some questions about the clinic. Could you talk to him?"

Matthew stood up and threw the bag of corn on the table. "Of course, I've had two minutes to rest. That's enough for anyone with a blinding headache."

"Sorry," John said as he led Matthew to the front of the clinic.

A tall man stuck out his hand to greet him. "Hello, I'm Jesse Archer."

Matthew shook the man's hand. "Matthew Howell."

John extended a hand too. "I'm John Finney, but you'll have to excuse me." He looked at Matthew. "I'll tell Ned he has a visitor."

Jesse looked at Matthew. "I stopped in to see this new clinic I've been hearing about."

Matthew did a sweeping gesture with his hand. "Well, here it is, Elkville's new medical facility."

Jesse looked around. "Are you the doc in charge?"

"No, I'm just helping out Doctor Finney. He'll be available very soon if you want to talk to him."

Jesse frowned. "I wish this place was around a couple of years ago. My uncle's appendix went out on him before he made it to Blacksburg. He died a short time later."

"I'm very sorry to hear that," Matthew said. "But we probably wouldn't have been able to help your uncle even if we were up and running. We're not set up for surgery."

Jesse wandered over to a corner of the room that had two chairs and a small table between them. He sat down and shook his head. "I moved away from these hills when I was a teenager. Lived in Blacksburg long enough to marry and raise a family there."

Matthew took a seat next to Jesse. "But you don't live there anymore?"

"My wife passed, and my kids moved off to raise their own families. I decided to come back to this area and see to my parents. They're getting pretty old, but they won't move to Blacksburg." He smiled. "Good thing I like living in these hills too, and it's done well enough since I'm the only mechanic that's close."

Matthew didn't know what else to say and stood up. "Can I get you a cup of coffee while you're waiting for Doctor Finney?"

Jesse smiled. "That's very kind of you, but I'm not here to be imposing. I'm just fretting a bit. After losing Uncle Leland, I'm wondering what would happen if one of my parents had an emergency. Blacksburg's a long ways off. I sure wouldn't want to lose one of them too."

Matthew felt his chest tighten when he thought about Jacob. What if Brodey had stabbed him? What if he needed emergency surgery?

Ned came walking into the room, and Jesse stood up. Matthew made the introductions and excused himself and returned to the kitchen.

John was pouring some coffee into a mug. He brought it over to Matthew. "Jesse seems like a nice guy."

"Yes, he does," Matthew said. He sipped his coffee, but he couldn't stop thinking about Jesse's concerns. The clinic was a first step in bringing medical care to the area. But Jesse had a point. If there was a serious emergency, the clinic wasn't going to help very much.

Matthew was halfway through his coffee when Ned came back into the kitchen. He looked at Matthew with a frown.

"What is it?" Matthew asked.

Ned glanced at his father and back at Matthew. "I want to apologize."

"For what?" Matthew asked.

"My father taught me manners, but sometimes I forget them. I just looked at the long list of patients you took care of today, and I realized I hadn't even thanked you. So I want to let you know how much I appreciate your assistance, not just for today, but for every time you were here when needed."

Matthew nodded. He was forced to be polite since Ned was being so sincere. "I'm glad I could help."

Ned walked over to the counter, picked up the coffee pot and brought it over to the table. Without asking, he refilled Matthew's mug.

Matthew scowled back. "What's happening here? Is Ned Finney actually taking care of my caffeine needs?"

Ned laughed. "I have a great idea, Matthew."

Matthew couldn't help but notice how bright Ned's blue eyes became. He was almost afraid to ask his next question. He raised his mug to his lips to take a sip. "What idea?"

"My dad says there's nothing like a fresh cup of coffee in the great outdoors. How about if you come along with us on a camping trip to the mountains?"

Matthew was about to swallow his coffee when Ned suggested something horrifying. To be stuck on the side of a primitive mountain, trekking through the wilderness with Ned Finney was so awful that he swallowed wrong and started choking. When he finally came up for air, Ned was looking at him with concern.

"I'll take that as a 'no'," Ned said. He came over and patted Matthew's back. "But just remember, if you ever change your mind, the offer stands."

Sixty-Five

MATTHEW LOOKED OUT the kitchen window at Lea and Jacob. They were in the back yard, planting flowers in a little garden. Matthew had never been involved with anything garden related before with one exception. He remembered his grandfather raising vegetables.

When Lea asked him to prepare a piece of ground, he wasn't sure what to do. But Lea looked up at him with such a happy, expectant face that he didn't want to disappoint her. He discovered his task to be quite straightforward after she explained what was needed. Using a shovel borrowed from Margaret, he turned over some weedy areas to expose the soil, broke up the clumps of dirt, and raked it out. It was as simple as that. Now, Lea was showing Jacob how to plant seeds.

It was a peaceful scene that helped to further sooth Matthew's mind. Eric had been wise in pointing out that Matthew couldn't dissect his entire life all at once. His advice was helpful. For the time being, he had to do his best to calm himself and be there for Lea and Jacob. His steadier hands were an indication that he was on the right track. He stared at them and noted the blisters he'd gotten during his gardening task. From now on he'd have to make sure to wear gloves.

As soon as he had the thought, he realized that if he went back to Chicago, the only gloves he'd need were the surgical kind. He turned from the window and decided not to think about it. He'd get another headache, and his body would be stressed again. But even giving himself a break was stressful. Was he morphing into some kind of weakling instead of ploughing through life no matter what?

He walked into the living room and grabbed some literature he'd brought back from Chicago. The doorbell rang as he was about to sit down. He threw down the papers, went to the foyer and opened the door. Mary was standing on the porch, nervously tugging at her sweater. He waved her inside. "Nice to see you, Mary."

Mary smiled shyly, stepped in and nodded. "Can I talk to you and Lea?"

Matthew took in a hasty breath. "Is this about Jacob?"

Mary nodded again.

* * *

Lea sat on the couch with Matthew. Jacob sat between them. As soon as the little boy saw their visitor, he avoided making eye contact with Mary. With eyes averted, he focused on the T-Rex toy he was clutching.

Mary sat across from them and stared at Jacob for a long moment and bit her lip. "Our pa's gone," she said softly.

Matthew sat up. "What do you mean?"

Mary wiped a tear away and shook her head. "Crossed over. Police found him after he run off from the hospital."

"You said his wound was infected, and he was very ill," Lea said. "Why would he leave the hospital?"

Mary sucked in a breath and sat up straighter. "He needed to come home, to the hills he loved," Mary said as she began to cry.

Lea got up and hurried over to her. "I'm so sorry, Mary."

"He weren't such a good one, but he was my pa."

Jacob stopped playing and stared at Mary.

Mary started to sob when their eyes met. "Poor thing, your pa's dead."

Jacob stuck out his lip, climbed into Matthew's lap and started sucking his thumb.

Matthew cradled Jacob protectively. "I'm sorry too, Mary. What can we do to help?"

"Ma's too sick to go back to the cabin. When she's well enough, she goin' stay with Auntie. I'll take the four girls with me and help 'em out. I might even get my job back if I'm lucky."

Lea stood up and held herself anxiously. "What about Jacob?"

Mary started tugging at her sweater again. "Ma's got 'er hands full. She said you can have 'em if you want 'em."

Lea smiled. "Of course we want him, Mary."

Mary nodded. "I told Ma how sweet you are on 'em, how good you been." She hesitated. "She don't want to give 'em up, but she knows she can't do for 'em like you can."

"We'll take care of him like he's our own child," Lea said.

"Ma's willin' to sign papers to make it legal. So you sure you want that?"

Lea looked back at Matthew. "Matthew?"

Matthew hugged Jacob closer. "Yes, we're sure."

Mary stood up and approached the couch. She reached out and stroked Jacob's cheek. "You be a good 'em, Jacob. Make our ma proud."

After Mary left, Lea and Matthew stood in the foyer. Lea looked at Matthew who was still holding Jacob. She was almost afraid to breathe too deeply for fear she was dreaming. "Matthew, we're really a family!" she announced in a breathless voice.

"Did you hear that, my young man?" Matthew said with a smile.

Jacob frowned, not sure about what was going on. Like he'd done so many times before, he pointed to Lea and then to Matthew. "Ma! Pa!"

Matthew put his arm around Lea and pulled her close. "Yes, Jacob, from now on, we're your mom and dad."

"Forever and ever," Lea added.

Sixty-Six

LEA'S SUITCASE WAS on the bed. She was packing. She and Matthew would be returning to Chicago the next day, and they'd be taking their little boy with them.

Jacob stood by the side of the bed watching her. When she put his clothes in the suitcase, Jacob moved closer and looked up at her. For the past couple of days, both she and Matthew had been trying to explain their plans to Jacob. "You and me and Pa are all going on a trip together, Jacob. You're going to ride in an airplane. What do you think about that?"

Jacob put his hand in his pocket, took out his T-Rex toy and held it out for Lea to examine. Lea smiled. "Yes, Jacob, we're all going together, and you can bring your T-Rex."

Matthew came walking into the bedroom, carrying a mug. "I thought you might want some tea, Lea," he said as he put the cup down on the dresser.

Jacob ran over to Matthew. He reached up, wanting Matthew to hold him. Matthew picked him up and smiled. "It's okay, young man, you're going with me and your ma this time."

Jacob leaned into Matthew's shoulder still holding on to his toy.

Matthew walked over to the bed and looked at Lea. "Guess what? Ned called."

"Does he need you at the clinic?"

"No, but he was excited. It seems he finally found his watch."

Lea frowned. "I forgot all about it. Where was it?"

"It was in with some clothes in his dresser."

"Goodness, that would probably be one of the first places I would have looked."

362

"I guess you and Jacob think alike. When you were having a hard time at your parents' house, Paul Glass found your diary in with your socks."

"That seems like a lifetime ago," Lea said. She put a hand on her stomach and sucked in a breath.

"What's wrong? Aren't you feeling well?" Matthew asked with a frown.

Jacob seemed to notice Matthew's concern and looked up at Lea. "Ma?"

Lea smiled. "You talk about me and Jacob. Look at the two of you, both staring at me with the same look on your face."

Matthew scowled. "I can't help it. I just want all of us to be okay. Is that too much to ask?"

"But we are okay. We're more than okay."

Matthew blinked back. "What do you mean?"

"Remember how I ordered some pregnancy tests for the clinic?"

"Yes, it's nice that you're still trying to help out."

"I used one of those kits this morning."

Matthew stepped back, holding Jacob a little closer. "You did?"

Jacob reached out to Lea with both arms. "Ma?"

Lea took him and kissed his cheek. "Jacob you're not going to be an only child," she said with a smile. "You're going to have a little sister or brother."

"Are you sure?" Matthew asked.

"According to the results, I am. But are you happy about it, Matthew? I know you probably weren't expecting—"

Matthew's face relaxed into a smile as he gathered Lea and Jacob into an embrace. "Of course I'm happy."

A tingle of excitement and joy made Lea smile even broader. She was going to be a mother to their little boy and to a new baby. Finally, she pulled back and looked up at Matthew. "I've been thinking of all the things we'll need to do when we get back to Chicago. We'll have to find a house, set up a nursery, and—"

"Lea, don't start doing too much," Matthew ordered. "Promise me that you'll be careful and—"

Lea heard the strain in his voice. "Matthew, please—"

Matthew's frown deepened. "What is it? Do you need me to get you something?"

Lea handed him Jacob and stepped back. "I need you to stop worrying. You've done way too much of it since we've been in Elkville. Let's start a whole new chapter with no more excessive stress."

Matthew hesitated, but he finally smiled again. "Right."

Lea giggled. "I've been reading up on angels, and do you know what I found?"

"Angels, why would you be reading about angels?"

"Because I think I'm married to one who's still learning the ropes."

"Me? An angel? Please, Lea, that's not the way I see myself."

"I didn't say you had to believe it, did I?"

"No, you didn't, but—" Matthew paused. "So what did you find out about these, these beings called angels?"

"They're unconditionally loving, and they don't spend time worrying."

"Well, that proves I'm not one of them. After all the crazy stuff that's gone on, worry has become part of my life."

Lea grinned back. "Maybe, but the traces are there, so I'm calling you my angel-in-training. And little Jacob is our tiny angel."

Matthew let out a heavy sigh. "I guess I can live with that."

"I'm excited. My other angel, Eric, and his sweet Teresa are finally back in Elkville. It's going to be fun having them over for dinner tonight."

"Yes, it's seemed strange not having them around."

Lea bit her lip and sniffled. "I'm going to miss everyone."

Matthew put Jacob down and held her close. "I don't know what to tell you, but I'm sorry that you're feeling sad."

Jacob tugged on Lea's shirt. "Ma?"

Lea pulled away and swiped her eyes. "It's okay, sweetie. Ma's fine."

Jacob stared back for a long moment, but he finally went over to some toys he'd been playing with earlier and sat down on the rug.

Lea glanced at Matthew and lowered her voice. "My goodness, I don't dare act weepy with our little angel around. He's watching me constantly."

"I guess I'll have to be careful too."

"About what?" Lea asked.

"You said I tend to pout. I don't see it that way, but I guess Jacob might."

Lea had to smile. "He's going to keep us both straight."

"Whether we like it or not," Matthew said. "On the plus side, he's gotten use to sleeping in his own room."

Lea laughed. "I guess that means we'll have to do all our crying and pouting when he goes to bed."

Jacob got up from where he was playing and ran back to Matthew. He tugged on his pant leg. "Pa, I tirsty."

Matthew dutifully took Jacob's hand. "He'll also keep us well exercised going up and down the stairs trying to keep him fed and sufficiently hydrated."

As Lea watched Matthew and Jacob leave the bedroom, she thought about how she'd described Jacob as a little angel. The description fit. Her little boy constantly kept an eye on her moods. She wouldn't be able to slip into her old personality without him letting her know what was happening. It gave her a warm feeling that outweighed her previous sadness. She was moving back to Chicago, and her two angels were going with her.

Thank you for taking the time to read Traces of Angels, the second book of my series, OPEN WIDE MY HEART. If you enjoyed my story, please consider telling your friends. Word of mouth is an author's best friend and much appreciated.

Warmest wishes, S. S. Bazinet

For more information about my books or to find out what's new, please visit my website, SSBazinet.com.

www.ingramcontent.com/pod-product-compliance
Lightning Source LLC
Chambersburg PA
CBHW071211250626
47159CB00001B/280